A TRILOGY
Three Homes for the Heart
Book 3

The Gazebo

By

Dorothy Minchin-Comm

Order this book online at www.trafford.com
or email orders@trafford.com

Most Trafford titles are also available at major online book retailers.

Printed in the United States of America.

ISBN: 978-1-4669-7003-8 (sc)
ISBN: 978-1-4669-7004-5 (hc)
ISBN: 978-1-4669-7005-2 (e)

Trafford rev. 11/21/2012

www.trafford.com

North America & international
toll-free: 1 888 232 4444 (USA & Canada)
phone: 250 383 6864 ♦ fax: 812 355 4082

Dedication

Within the vast expanses of Eternity

we are each given a small portion of Time.

This book is dedicated to my dear family, friends, and colleagues

who have shared this little window of life with me.

I am forever grateful that we all arrived in the right places

at the right times.

Thus we bacame travel-companions on the Journey.

Table of Contents

Introduction

"Somewhere between the bookends of life ... "

I debated about building this third house. Although the possibility lurked in the back of my mind for a very long time, I knew that the structure would have to be stronger than anything that had gone before. More enduring, more fully furnished. It *ought* to be the most secure and inviting home of all. Indeed, it opens up with our living at the prime of our careers. Riding the crest of the wave.

Then we get old. One morning we look in the mirror, and there it is. This discovery is not for the faint-hearted. The consolation, however, is that by this time we have worked out most of the agenda we set for ourselves. Soon we want to sit in the Gazebo, relax, and watch the world go by. The world is welcome to look in on us, for we have nothing to hide. In fact, by now we may even have something useful to share with passersby.

Because old age is for remembering, a chorus of voices surrounds us, telling us how to relate to the past. Some say: "If you look only on the past and present, you'll miss the future. Remember," they pontificate, "that change is the law of life."

Others say, "Never try to re-enter the past. You will surely be disappointed. Besides, it no longer exists." They are fatalistic about the future. Having migrated from their homelands under duress, many of them have no desire to remember anything about the Old Country. They tried to make a new start, *new* in every way.

Yet others look back with acceptance—even contentment. "You are always at home in your past. In fact, going there enables you to live doubly." This book, therefore, unabashedly preserves the Past. Mine. It goes out to what is essentially a Now Generation.

Born the week of the stock-market crash in 1929, I became a poster child for the Great Depression. I was eight years old when Hitler marched on Austria and World War II began. I am but a small footnote to history, a very ordinary person.

At the end of a long life, however, one faces the difficult task of wanting to "know oneself." The record of the journey has sometimes been trivial (even frivilous). Also, it contains a little of the profound. Perhaps even an occasional trace of the imperishable.

We are allowed, however, to make our Journey just once. Because I have never been old before, I was surprised by an urgent, innate sense of need to share my road map with fellow travelers. I believe that this is the point when we are all ready to explore the depths of love as well as the outer limits of life itself.

Therefore, my Gazebo stands open. Drop in for a visit.

Dorothy Minchin-Comm, PhD
Professor of English (Retired, Professor Emerita)
La Sierra University
Riverside, California
2012

By the same author ...

BOOKS

1. Yesterday's Tears (1968)
2. To Persia with Love (1980)
3. A Modern Mosaic: The Story of Arts (1981)
4. His Compassions Fail Not (1982)
5. Encore (1988)
6. Gates of Promise (1989)
7. A Desire Completed (1991)
8. Curtain Call (1999)
9. Glimpses of God (1999)
10. The Winter of Their Discontent (2004)
11. Health to the People (2006, with P. William Dysinger)
12. The Book of Minchin (2006)
13. The Celt and the Christ (2008, with Hyveth Williams)
14. An Ordered Life (2011)
15. The Paper House (1990, 2012)
16. The Bamboo House (2012)
17. The Gazebo (2012)
18. The Trials of Patience Dunn (2012, in progress)
19. A Song for David (2012, in progress)
20-24. My World: A Personal View [Travel journals, 4 volumes]
    I. The Far East Revisited: A Term of Service (1970-1974)
   II. Return to Service in the Far East (1974-1978)
  III. Home Base: Southern California (1978-1988)
  IV. Retirement and Other Adventures (1989-2010)

ACADEMIC RESEARCH AND BOOK-LENGTH SYLLABI

1. The Changing Concepts of the West Indian Plantocracy in English Poetry and Drama, 1740-1850. [Doctoral dissertation, 1971]
2. The Bible and the Arts (1974, 2001)
3-4. Studies in the Humanities (1977, 1979). [2 volumes]
5. Discovering Ourselves Through the Arts (1981)
6. Christianity in India. [Monograph, 1992, 1995, 1996]
7. Archdeacon Thomas Parnell. [Monograph, 1992, 1995, 1996]

OTHER

Miscellaneous articles, news stories, biographical sketches, multi-media scripts, and editing assignments.

CHAPTER 1

A Different Kind of Poem

As vacation time arrived in mid-1973, I conceived an extensive circle tour of the Far East. I intended to make use of every hour of the twenty-one days we had been granted. With furlough coming up the following year, this would be the last time we might undertake such a journey for all of the family, together.

My plan included some personal details, I was aching to see my own hometown again, Singapore. Although it wasn't far away, it had, so far, remained inaccessible to me. Another part of the trip into the past would include tracking pioneer missions in Borneo.

Of course, it could not be a simple matter of buying the tickets and getting on a plane. Under martial law, we labored for days to get the court clearances that would allow us to leave the Philippines. In one day alone we went to three courts in three different sections of Manila. We stood in line for hours in 100-degree temperatures and encountered several quite obtuse civil servants. All of us were fingerprinted purple—virtually through the epidermis, clean to the bone. (No one ever offered us any way to remove the indelible purple ink from our fingers.) I think Mum held the record with fifty-two fingerprints in one day.

Contrary to expectations, we finally achieved our clearances and were able to escape.

Silk-clad Thai stewardesses greeted us with orchids as we boarded the DC 8, named "Srichulalak," and took off to Bangkok. Our cousins Ben and Lynette Youngberg and their three children met us at our destination.

In the following days, of course, we did the tours of the *wats* (temples) where we strolled among *stupas,* encrusted with semi-precious stones, glass, and gold leaf. They looked like giant layered wedding cakes, gone wild in bril-

liant Technicolor. The roof-lines
bristled with spirit-defying pinna-
cles, while countless grotesque
devas (temple guardians) graced
the walls and doorways. In a
water taxi we explored the *klong*
(canals), where people slept, ate,
bathed, and marketed in one
seething mass of human life.

Out on the streets we
watched the Buddha-makers
plying their trade. I bought an
eight-inch image for about
$3.00. One has to bargain
briskly for the god in order not
to be cheated. The haggling went
on in the light of the black-
smiths' fires. Also available were
antique images, plus assorted
heads, arms and legs (broken off
from the *wats* out in the
provinces). For either worship or
souvenirs. It didn't matter which.

Almost ten feet tall and weighing 5½ tons, the
solid Golden Buddha in Wat Traimit Temple,
Bangkok, is the largest gold statue in the world
and is often overlooked by tourists. The pure gold
reflects a transparent, dazzling "inner" light.

In one gateway a woman sat with a bamboo cage crammed full of
sparrows, a chaotic flurry of feathers and chirps. One might buy some of the
birds and then release them to freedom, thereby earning merit with the gods.
(A resourceful idea for people who've run short on good deeds to do.)

Across the street, the Sunday Market was in full swing. Once a week, for
about twenty-four hours, the central park erupted into a full-blast marketplace.
The fruit stalls bulged with bananas, durians, rambutans, giant-size pineapples,
along with dried fish and various other nameless edibles. The smells of things
crackling in a hundred frying pans or charcoal pots permeated the air.

Cages of birds, snakes, and animals, plus tanks of fish and miles of fine fabric cluttered the alleyways. All kinds of impresarios offered entertainment. Like the men who dragged an unwilling mongoose into deadly combat with a cobra. Quack medicine men called from their stalls promising to cure old age. All the while, the trinket dealers proclaimed their wares in full voice.

In Timland, we found a community of monkeys presiding over the spirit houses there. One jumped into Mum's arms and ate the orchid pinned to her dress. When she tried to break off the sudden friendship, he nipped her arm. A bad bruise, but it didn't draw blood.

The housing of missionaries can vary enormously from one country to another. When we reached the lovely city of Penang, we found our long-time Canadian friends, Ed and Ethel Heisler, living in an amazing house. By comparison, the best mission house in Manila looked no better than a gatekeeper's lodge.

In Penang the broad *jalan* (streets) were lined with ancient trees that only partially hid the huge colonial and Chinese mansions that were set

A part of the Floating Market drifts along a *klong* (canal) in Bangkok.

Dr. Ben Youngberg, off-duty from his work at Bangkok Adventist Hospital, sits with one of his rare wild cats. Since boyhood he has enjoyed taxidermy.

back in spacious lawns and gardens. Heislers' house was a wide-open, airy place with green tile floors, pillars at the front, four bathrooms, five bedrooms, and a central living area large enough to serve as a concert hall. When the Penang Hospital bought it, the house was a rundown Chinese heirloom, a veritable cockroach nest. Now, in this exotic, almost-on-the-beach setting, it struck us as a remarkably pleasant home for the hospital administrator and his nursing supervisor wife.

Ethel set out a cosmopolitan supper, reminiscent of the international living they and we have enjoyed over the past many years, beginning back in Inter-America. We ate pizza (American/Italian) and roasted breadfruit (Jamaican) with a fruit salad (universally tropical) served in a Jamaican wooden bowl. The table was set with an embroidered tablecloth (Nicaraguan) and wooden dishes (Filipino)

Penang also had its quota of temples and pagodas. What gave our crowd the most uniform pleasure, however, was the salt-water, Olympic-size pool at the Swimming Club. One night we and the six kids (our two and the Heisler four) swam in a warm downpour of rain at 9 p.m.

For the next nine days our journey morphed into a road-trip. We rented a fire-engine red Toyota Corona Mark II. Almost new and with air-conditioning, we could hardly remember the boney old Bedford van we had to live with back in Manila. Even I almost got emotional about this unexpected kind of comfort!

Left. As durian goes, the best is said to come from Thailand. Right. Leona Minchin and her niece, Lynette Youngberg, bring it home to eat. Young Jerry Youngberg appears undecided. He would, perhaps, like to distance himself from the odiferous food as other family members have done before him.

On Wednesday afternoon our two-car convoy headed south into Malaysia and on to the Cameron Highlands. The narrow Malaysian roadways took us through shady rubber plantations punctuated by tall, slim coconut palms. In the lowering light, the rubber trees leaned toward one another, making long Gothic arches stretching back almost to infinity. After dark we accomplished the thirty-seven mile ascent up to Tanah Rata in a downpour of rain. (Someone has estimated twenty-four curves per mile on that stretch of road.)

Friday morning we came down out of the mountain retreat and headed on south. Here we saw much less dead-end poverty than appears in the rural Philippines. Moreover, scenery in the lowlands remained glorious. One *kampong* (village) had as a backdrop a screen of bougainvillea, spread like a net among the tall trees. At least seventy-five feet high, the bushes were laced through with lavender and blue morning glories in full bloom. Banks of tree ferns, knee-deep in tangled dark green vines, sparkled like diamonds in the morning dew, while the mists rolled themselves up out of the deep blue valleys.

A stop at a tea plantation almost stripped some of us naked. The waist-high tea bushes had branches strong as oak. Planted close together, they clutched at us like a steel trap. We entertained the tea-pickers as we tried to take pictures without literally having our clothes ripped off.

At Batu Caves, eight miles north of Kuala Lumpur (the capital of

Malaysia) we dragged our reluctant, hungry kids up 275 steps to the Hindu temple at the top. Shadowy and imposing, the caves were lighted only by ragged holes high in the ceiling. One little shrine to Hanuman (the monkey god) featured a skeleton of a monkey dressed in red robes and loaded with flower garlands.

Once more at the bottom of the steps, we bought hot *mee goring* (noodles) from a hawker. The kids, however, were put off by the unconventional source of lunch. So we had to bend the rules and let them fill up on Eskimo pies and popsicles (from another vendor).

Walt and Dorothy take an elephant ride in Timland.

We spent the weekend at the Methodist Camp in Port Dickson. Flower gardens and bird songs made it an idyllic retreat. The kids, however, swam all day and acquired blazing sunburns. Larry cried out in pain if you even looked at him. At low tide we watched millions of slate-blue crabs with pink legs. They traveled in platoons so that the entire beach appeared to be on the move.

Our detour to historic (14th-century) Malacca brought us in to a relatively unknown part of Malaysia. Ed had reserved a bungalow for us at Tanjong Kling, advertised as a government rest house. As it turned out "Banglo Kerjaan" was an enormous two-story house surrounded by verandahs, standing 100 feet above the beach and enclosed in a dense grove of trees. A relic from Victorian colonialism, the mansion had six bedrooms, each with a 12' x12' bathroom. They were furnished with massive teak wardrobes, and acres of mosquito netting draped from the twenty-foot ceilings. Two VWs could have passed in the central hallway without incident.

In this titanic setting, people looked hardly bigger than termites coming out of the woodwork. The dining room table could have seated an entire del-

Left. Overseas housing can vary amazingly, even in urban settings. In Penang Ed and Ethel Heisler lived in a renovated Chinese mansion (five bedrooms) on the hospital grounds. Right. Back in Manila Walt and Dorothy Comm had a small three-bedroom "cottage." No matter! We remained best of friends!

egation at the United Nations. When we set out supper, those at one end of the table needed field glasses to identify those at the other end. Spooked by these surroundings, the four girls packed themselves into just two beds,

Left. Entrance to the temple within Batu Caves. Right. Inside is a panorama of the Hindu legend of Lord Muruga. He was so powerful that his mother could not bear him as a single child, so he had to arrive in six phases.

hugging one another for safety.

The next night gave us a 180-degree turn-around. At Kota Tinggi Falls in Johore Bahru, our chalets clung to the mountainside and were designed to look part of the jungle itself. Since they were small, designed for four occupants only, we did a lot of floor-sleeping.

Sadly, the rainforest resort had already started to be over-commercialized. Still, one friendly, familiar feature remained from my childhood. A tremendous rainstorm hit us while we were eating supper together in Heislers' chalet. Its violence and the hazards of the long flights of slippery steps to and from each chalet made it easy to persuade Mum to stay and sleep right where she was. No swimming in the cool pools that I remembered under the waterfalls. Not that night.

The storm was a spectacular show. Transfixed we watched the swollen falls crash down the mountain. The black jungle dripped and groaned all around us. No terror scene created on a movie set could match this personal demonstration of the Creator's power. Every explosion of thunder was followed by a great crack of lightning that lit up the whole gorge like the electronic flash of a cosmic camera. On what a scale you could take pictures with that equipment! Eventually, the storm

Left. When Ed Heisler booked us a night's lodging at Tanjong Kling Rest house, it was described as a "bungalow." Below left. The gigantic proportions of the house truly intimidated us. We overlooked the historic Straits of Malacca. Below. Dorothy, Lorna and Larry stared at one another across the huge bedroom, under a vast mosquito net suspended from a twenty-foot ceiling.

The children in front of the guest house in Cameron Highlands. (L-R). Larry Comm, Beth Heisler, Bruce Heisler (standing), Lorna Comm, Barbara Heisler, Beverley Heisler.

subsided, but the falls roared on.

The next morning we continued on to Singapore. As we drove over the causeway, unchanged in thirty-seven years, my homing instincts escalated by the mile. This would be the highlight of the whole journey for me.

Officially we lodged in the three-bedroom apartment at 800 Thomson Road. Don and Doris Roth attended to our every desire, either real or imagined. Those four Singapore days evolved into an indescribable mix of past and present, joy and sorrow

Of course, we went over all of the public parts of Singapore and its evolution into an ultra-modern city. At noon on Friday, our little red Toyota went back to the rental agency. Before we gave it up, however, we visited the old harbor area and the government buildings dating from colonial days. In a way, the new, progressive parts of Singapore are not very interesting. As Choo Yeow Fong (an old friend from Malayan Seminary days) said, "I have no more pleasure driving here now. Not only is the traffic so heavy, but the big buildings also make it look like any other city anywhere. It's beginning to lack character."

Knowing that we had to return to the Philippines, to our moody Bedford van, and to Manila traffic, we had to agree with him. We could understand that disciplined traffic, of itself, might be a little boring when one has become accustomed to all of those other kinds of exhilaration on the road.

Then we had other things to see. We visited the room in Youngberg Hospital where my Dad lived his last days, just four-and-a-half years ago. Of course, I had to go through our house at the top of the little hill, 10 Woodleigh

Close. All the while, dear friends, old and new, were entertaining us for almost every meal.

One day, I spent a couple hours by myself on the compound of Southeast Asia Union College. I stopped by my Dad's old office and the two classrooms where I had sat from Grades 1 to 5. I also looked in many other odd places connected with strange little private memories. Things that I would have been hard pressed to explain to anyone else.

After Sabbath at Balestier Road Church, we went out to the Chinese Protestant Cemetery in Jurong where Dad lies. Don Roth helped us

The rubber plantations of central Malaysia.

get flowers. Lavender chrysanthemums and orchids for our family. A smaller basket of yellow and white mums for Albert Markey. (A dear man whom I'd never met—a classmate of Dad's at Darling Range School, Western Australia.) He wrote and asked me to place flowers for him. So we set his basket on the white slab in front of the black marble headstone and took a picture to send him.

Finally, Roths planned a lovely open-house evening for us. *Popia,* a Singapore specialty was the chief menu item. Very literally I hadn't tasted it since childhood. Into a thin "rice skin" are rolled: shredded boiled eggs, cucumbers, noodles, crushed peanuts, lettuce and other things too mysterious to be named. The roll is then stuck shut with a thick brown, sweet sauce. I can't begin to describe the flavor. Knowing how many, many hours it takes to prepare, I felt that this gesture from our friends elevated our last meal in Singapore almost to a communion experience.

The next day our commercial flight set us down in Kuching, Sarawak, the land of the White Rajahs. Our mission here was also very personal. I

In Singapore Leona stood once again at the grave of her husband, Gerald H. Minchin.

intended to follow the mission trails of the Gus Youngbergs who first came to the Far East in 1919. Armed with my Nikon camera and a cassette recorder I prepared to make as perfect a record as possible to send home to Aunt Norma Youngberg (my mother's older sister).

We were met by Hugh Johnson, the jungle pilot. I couldn't believe the sophistication of his communication network there in the Borneo jungle. In Manila we can't even have telephones in our houses. Hugh had eleven amateur radio stations set up and sixteen jungle airstrips for his four-seat Cessna. The little plane was named *Malaikat* ("Angel"). On the other side of its nose we read "Messenger."

We visited two schools that had been on my Dad's inspection list, back in 1936. Sunnyhill School was just outside of Kuching. Ayer Manis ("Sweet Water") School for 200 students was managed by Clarence and Alice Goertzen (friends and co-workers from our Newfoundland days). Only a couple of the original thatch buildings remained (from 1932).

Here we had another cemetery pilgrimage to make. One of 2,500 prisoners, Gus Youngberg had died in the Japanese concentration camp at Batu Lintang in Kuching. In preparation for our visit Bonnie Johnson had scoured the moss and mold off of his headstone until it was almost white. Mum and I planted a living fuchsia bush on his grave.

Now we followed the pioneer trail in earnest. Alice Goertzen joined us, and we took a domestic flight to Bintulu in Northern Sarawak. It was very domestic with cages of baby chicks in full chorus at the back of the cabin. We made one stop in Sibu in order to take some roosters aboard. At this point the passengers were far outnumbered by the poultry. When we landed, Hugh

Johnson and *Malaikat* waited for us on the runway.

Hugh made two trips to transport us all to Bukit Nyala ("Hill of the Light") up the Tatau River. The Youngbergs had built this mission outpost among the Ibans (Sea Dyaks) in 1930.[1]

We stored most of our baggage in the control tower and carried little more than a handbag apiece up river. Walt, Alice and the kids went first. We watched *Malaikat* leap into the white afternoon sunlight after a spurt of less than 350 feet. It waggled a wing tip at us and disappeared out over the jungle. Turasi Sinaga remained with Mum and me. She and her husband Elam had worked among the Ibans on the river for twenty more years after the Youngbergs moved to Singapore. As we waited for *Malaikat's* return, we realized that Turasi seemed to know every other person in Bintulu Town.

Our turn came, and we made the fifteen-minute trip to Bukit at a groundspeed of 180 mph. Over the rainforest, the snaky, brown Tatau River curled among the hairy mountain peaks. The grassy landing strip was just 500 yards long. "It has a perpetual soft spot in the middle," Hugh apologized. "It's one of the Mission's poorest airstrips."

The golden green trees leaned over us as we climbed the 185 steps to the house. This dense jungle on three sides and steep hill in front was the protection for which Gus Youngberg had consciously planned. Unfriendly visitors could approach the house only from the front. They would be visible every step of the way up the hill.

Though a little shabby now, the house at Bukit was still quite handsome. Uncle Gus built it of very hard billion wood and skirted it

In Singapore's Botanical Gardens Dorothy found her very own tree—the one she used to climb when she was a kid. The branches were conveniently arranged, a place to sit and eat picnic sandwiches.

with verandahs. Between the house and the old kitchen two enormous wooden, ironbound tubs caught rainwater. A bathroom area was curtained

Making *popia* is labor-intensive. Left. First the wrappers. Right. Then assorted ingredients, all sealed in with a thick brown sauce.

off on one side. Beside a small wooden tub, bathers sat on a cracker tin and sloshed water over themselves. All of us slept on the floor.

Next day we took a three-and-a-half hour river trip upstream on the motor launch. We disembarked at several landings, jumping on loosely tied logs and then stumbling ashore. We climbed slim ladders up to the longhouses. The clean living quarters occupied by Adventist Christians stood in stark contrast to those of the betel-nut-chewing tribes-people. Pigs and chickens roamed freely down below, scavenging everything that fell through the cracks in the bamboo floor above.

Today, only occasionally, do the Ibans take heads. Behind them, however, lie generations of accomplished headhunting. On our river trip, one man, at my request, showed us a basket of three heads "My grandfather take," he told me, with a toothless grin. Hardly! They smelled depressingly fresh. Nowadays, however, few heads can be found because the tourists have taken them all.

Hugh tended to the same medical needs as those that Gus Youngberg used to treat decades ago: Stomach aches, ringworm, worms, goiter and—above all—bad teeth. Hugh pulled a lot of teeth to the cheers of full and enthusiastic audiences.

After one more night sleeping on the billion-wood floor, we returned to Bintulu on the mission launch. The sights we saw and the hours we spent closely paralleled the way Gus and Norma Youngberg had traveled forty-three years earlier.

En route to Sabah (formerly British North Borneo), our commercial plane stopped in Brunei, a tiny, fiercely independent nation. It and its sultan can afford to do whatever they wish because the land has enormously rich oil resources.

The sprightly little *Malaikat* ("angel") plane landed at Bukit Nyala.

Charles and Connie Gaban—recently our students at Philippine Union College— greeted us in Kota Kinabalu (Jesselton in colonial days) When we arrived at the Tamparuli guest house, Larry took one look at the beds prepared for us and flung himself down on one of them: "Isn't a soft bed good!" It's all right for him to endure a little hardness. After two nights on the billion-wood floor, however, we were all glad to see the beds—though we tried not to flaunt our joy too loudly.

It was from this now prosperous school in Tamparuli that the Japanese soldiers arrested Gus Youngberg and took him as a prisoner-of-war to Kuching.

For me, seeing the old mission settlement on Signal Hill and reliving

Left. The long flight of steps up to the house at Bukit Nyala puzzled many a weary visitor. They were a safety device to protect from the headhunters along the Tatau River. Right. The house was enclosed by dense forest on three sides and could be approached only from the river.

Dyak longhouses. Above. An old man and his wife displayed their basket of heads. Above right. A woman rolled up her wad of betel-nut. Right. Curious spectators on the longhouse verandah watched Hugh Johnson extract teeth.

childhood memories climaxed in attending the Malangang Church up the Tuaran River. We walked through coconut groves and rice paddies to a delightful jungle church. Only a shed, but it was full. Women in dainty *bajus* and bright *sarongs* and men in immaculate white shirts, all greeted us with *Selamat Pagi* ("Good morning").

Directly in front of the church was a mud-hole containing three *carabaos* tranquilly soaking their hides. 'Twas an unmercifully hot day.

Eager to give Auntie Norma every possible image to help her recall her Borneo years, I climbed through a barbed wire fence to photograph these somewhat inactive "church members." I stared at the huge black beasts and wondered. "What shall I do if they chase me?" I asked Larry.

Left. The view of Tatau River from the "Hill of the Light." Right. The present mission launch on the river, the *R. F. Cornell.*

He looked at me with his usual slow, philosophical grin, "Well, you can do pretty many things if something is chasing you." The *carabaos,* however, just looked at me and went on chewing their cuds.

Our last night in Borneo, our friends took us back to the old mission house on Signal Hill where they had prepared a *makan besar* ("big feast"). A staggering layout of food, all distinctively native to Borneo! I had my tape recorder ready and everyone, in close harmony, sang "Come and Go With Me to My Father's House." This would be part of my gift for Auntie Norma.

Although Sabah and the Philippine Islands are within sight of one another, at the time the two countries were not on speaking terms. Therefore, we had to fly home by way of Hong Kong. That detour gave us a long, sustained view of Mt. Kinabalu with a lesser mountain, *Anak* ("child") Kinabalu on its knees.

The trip truly qualified as a once-in-a-lifetime happening. From one viewpoint, travel money had been well spent. That is, it was good for Walt and the kids to share that part of my world.

At the next level, I had given myself a grand re-entry into my childhood. William Wordsworth spoke of "emotion recollected in tranquility" as being the essence of the poetry. The Circle Tour had become a kind of epic poem that was all mine.

Still, there was one more step. Back in California my seventy-seven-year-old-Auntie Norma had been long been detached from her Singapore and Borneo life. Both the time and place were too remote for her ever to expect

Left. The grave of G. B. Youngberg. Right. Norma Rhoads-Youngberg. The first mistress of Bukit Nyala and a dreamer of dreams. Also a writer of stories.

any kind of re-connection. Now I would prepare a photo album with detailed commentary, tuck the cassette tape in the back cover, and mail it to her.

Only after she received the gift, did I realize that I must have exceeded even Wordsworth's vision. "I am allowing myself just two pages a day," she wrote. "It is so precious. I must just linger over every picture, every moment."

She, not I, was the one who wrote fine poetry. This time, however, maybe I had created a kind of poem worthy of Wordsworth's standard. According to Norma Youngberg, I might have even gone a little beyond it.

So we returned to Manila. Back to classes and to paying our debts. Our next big thing would be our furlough year and a trip to Australia in 1974. Might that be a kind of poem too? Just the thought made me catch my breath in anticipation!

Notes

1   For the story of Gus and Norma Youngberg's pioneering mission among the headhunters on Tatau River, see Norma Youngberg and Gerald Minchin, *Under Sealed Orders: The Story of Gus Youngberg* (Mountain View, CA: Pacific Press Pub. Assn., 1970).

CHAPTER 2

A Digression on Hair

Walt always had a substantial bond with his older sister, Esther. Although she never had the opportunity for the education that would have made her an excellent teacher, she was the one member of the Comm family who gave him encouragement— financial and otherwise—to get through college. Being deferred to farm work during World War II, it took him seven years to achieve the goal. She, nonetheless, cheered him all the way through.

We returned the favor when Gwen, Esther's eldest child had lived with us and helped with our two three-year-olds. We all attended Andrews University, Michigan—Gwen as an underclassman and we two as graduate students. Likewise, in 1971, Esther sent her youngest, Brian, to live with us in the Philippines for the school year. He made one more lively addition to the little American school on campus and was a (slightly) older brother to Larry and Lorna.

Just before Christmas that year Brian participated with all the other kids in the "Great Lice Hunt." All of us parents were shocked and repulsed by the news that every youngster in the school had head-lice. They had been brought in by a South Sea Island family. They wanted, naturally, to take advantage of the American school program instead of the local elementary school that proceeded in Tagalog, the main Filipino dialect.

The teacher, Mrs. Bo Morton, broke the mournful news to us parents. Our "Chief Officer," Gordon Bullock, got the hospital pharmacy to mix up some powerful powder for us. "No child will be allowed back in school," he wrote, "until this problem has been scratched." That meant that we had only Christmas vacation time to de-louse our kids.

We and the Gulley family planned to take our aggregate of seven kids up to the mountain resort of Baguio. Before we left, however, we gave our boys butch haircuts. Then our house-girls, Beth and Zeny went over Larry and Brian to pick out the remaining unhatched nits and apply the DDT powder we had been given.

Of course we could have used Bobo. A little jungle monkey, she had been given to Larry when we first arrived in the Philippines. Walt built a covered cage around a tree in the back yard to contain her antics. She watched us intently through the dining room window and tried to grab the dogs' plumy tails whenever they passed by. Since the problem of head lice is rather prevalent in the *barrios,* people would rent out the services of their monkeys for a tidy price. Our Bobo would have served us for nothing. We wanted to preserve at least some of the boys' dignity, however, and left the job to Beth and Zeny.

Meanwhile, Dottie Edwards (the college president's wife) actually became contaminated from her daughter's hairbrush. Words cannot describe her trauma. Leona, and I kept imagining that our scalps were itchy too. Did we

Although Bobo was given to Larry, the whole family loved the little jungle monkey. Even the dogs reached a kind of understanding with her.

have bugs too? (Fortunately not, as things turned out.) We decided, however, to give our three girls, Lorna, Sharon, and Sonya, permanents while we were in Baguio. Surely no living creatures could live through a dousing of those strong chemicals. This, in addition to the other treatments we'd already used. By all means, our kids would return to school in January clean!

We arrived for our appointments at the beauty salon in Baguio to find an American tourist demanding immediate attention. In the manner of too many "Ugly Americans" traveling abroad, she thought that if she shouted the "natives" would serve her more promptly. The Filipina girls graciously kept working, neither breaking step nor acknowledging the tirade.

Leona drew one of the hairdressers aside. "Our children have had a problem with lice." she whispered. "You don't want to use their combs and brushes on other customers."

Then we sat down to watch the beautification and "elimination" process evolve. The arrogant American had been thoroughly insulted. Why did she have to wait in line behind three youngsters who could have cared less about having curly hair. Finally, she flounced into an available chair. The hairdresser picked up the un-sterilized combs and brushes she'd used on our girls.

Leona and I smiled at each other silently, exchanging the same unspoken thought. "She's probably going to go out of here with more than she brought in." Never confront a person in a foreign country and think for one moment that you will have won a victory. Sometimes rudeness neatly carries its own punishment.

Then again, we had still other kinds of hair crises.

As the school year approached its end in 1972, Esther decided to come to the Philippines for Brian's graduation from Grade 8. My mother was in Los Angeles so they could travel out together. In order to get the China Airlines discount that we employees in the Far Eastern Division received, Esther had to fly from Alberta, Canada, to Los Angeles. There Eileen would see them onto the plane and away.

On the Manila end, I served as travel agent, negotiator of visas, and purchaser of tickets. I also solicited the hospitality of friends in Japan, Taipei, and Hong Kong in her behalf. Although this took many weeks, I felt that I had anticipated every possible

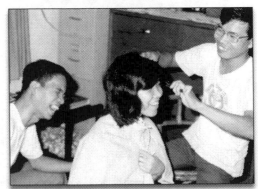

To a great extent hair styling was do-it-yourself at home affair. In fact, the campus barbershop was a happy and profitable place. Abel Laureles cut Beth's hair while a friend waited his turn.

After spending the school year in the Philippines, Brian was there to greet his mother, Esther Robertson, at Manila Airport when she arrived with Leona Minchin. Right. He had a flower for her on the occasion of his Grade 8 graduation.

complication. We all settled back to watch the unfolding of Esther's "adventure of a lifetime."

As it turned out, I had not foreseen one eventuality, but that still lay ahead in the future. In due course, Esther and Mum arrived. Our little campus house overflowed with family—not a common occurrence for those in overseas mission service.

Brian was a member of a class of just three seniors. Still, Bo Morton arranged a fine ceremony out on the lawn in front of the school, complete with sermon, flowers, tributes and refreshments. Those kids out there under the palm trees probably can look back on that humble little evening party with pleasant memories. Indeed, with as much nostalgia as anyone who undergoes that same rite of passage in America—with all the noise and expense involved. (Might we find a lesson in here somewhere?)

We spent the next month showing Esther around Luzon—from top to bottom. She bought gifts for the family at home and had three elegant dresses made from the embroidered *ramie* fabric for which the Philippines is so justly famous.

Then came the time for her and Brian to fly back to Los Angeles where her other son, Les, and nephew Roger would meet their plane.

One day Esther and I shopped in the Greenhills Market. I saw Esther lingering over a display of cosmetics. "I need to color my hair before I go home," she mused. "What kind would you buy? I just want to cover the gray and keep my regular color."

The display was attractive. After all, this was Greenhills Supermarket. Supposedly the merchandise would be safer than something out of an open market stall. Still, I advised caution. "Most people here just want their hair black. I wouldn't use any of these." I scanned the range of strange labels displaying Japanese and Chinese characters. "Not unless I found a brand-name that I recognized."

With that, I moved on toward the checkout counter, not realizing that Esther still lagged behind.

The day of Esther and Brian's departure came. The bags stood packed and ready at the front door, plus a couple of boxes of *pasalubong* "traveler's gifts." We laid out her prettiest new dress and set the table for lunch. "I'll just take a shower," she said.

"OK. But remember it takes a full hour-and-a-half to drive across Manila to the airport at this time of day."

Some forty minutes passed while we waited lunch. "Esther." I tapped

Left. "Unimart" was Manila's first modern super market. It compared favorably with any other such retailer in the world—except in the matter of hair dye. Below left. In contrast, there were always the open-air markets. Below right. The rather gory meat stall for some. Right. The sellers of *tokwa* (bean curd) for vegetarians.

urgently on the bathroom door. "Please come. Time's running out."

"Yes, I'll be there."

Another twenty minutes. "Esther. We've got to leave."

"Yes, yes," a muffled voice replied.

Having nothing better to do, the four boys stared one another down over the supper table. L-R: Brian Robertson, James Gulley (not yet quite certain of the rules), Larry Comm (back to camera), and John Gulley.

More time passed, and we began to fear foul play there in the bathroom. I now pounded on the door with great purpose. "You're going to miss your plane, Esther. We have to leave."

A great groan accompanied the opening of the bathroom door. There stood my usually-in-charge sister-in-law in her bathrobe, her damp hair a brilliant shade of hot pink! "What am I going to do?" she wailed.

The family gazed, speechless with wonder. I was so taken aback that the perfectly justifiable retort of "I told you so" never even came to my mind.

Out in the garage, we found a wide-brimmed straw hat such as the rice-planters used. To be sure, it was not the right accessory for the embroidered dress, but how many options did we have?

Once on the road, Walt made a heroic charge through the people, bicycles, *calesas,* hand-carts and jeepneys, getting us to the airport in the nick of time. (Manila traffic, I repeat, is like nothing else in the whole world.)

"Well, at least, I ought to be able to get it fixed in Hong Kong." Esther and Brian hugged us and turned toward the departure gate. "I just can't let Les and Roger see me like this." What a distressing end to the Philippine experience for both of them! The straw hat covered Esther so completely that you would have been hard-pressed to know that she even had a face, let alone hair.

From the observation deck we watched Esther and Brian cross the tarmac to their plane. In moments, Air Canada was airborne and winging across Manila Bay and Corregidor Island, nose to the north.

The one-hour flight set Esther and Brian down in Hong Kong before we could even scrabble our way through the traffic and reach home.

The pink-hair crisis weighed heavily on everyone's mind. Much later, we learned the rest of the story. It may now, however, enter the record as an authentic piece of family folklore.

Esther wriggled a little further up into her hat and walked boldly through Hong Kong Immigration and Customs and out through the exit marked "Nothing to Declare." She would, of course, have liked to declare something, but it would have been nothing of interest to the Chinese officers!

Back home in British Columbia, Canada, Esther (left) provided a picnic at Lake Okanagan—as always busy with food service chores. One of her guests, Mary Stellmaker from Australia, stood by.

We had booked our Canadians into the Grand Hotel in mid-town Hong Kong for the night. That was the convenient stopover we always used on our transits through the city. Immediately, Esther went out to find hair color. Counting herself very lucky to discover a U.S. brand name that she recognized, she returned to the hotel clutching her purchase.

All might have been well, except....

In the Orient, bathrooms tend to be constructed wholly of hard-surface tiles. No carpets, decorations or spacious counter-tops. Nothing to be aware of when you hose down the whole room for cleaning. (Moreover, these bathrooms provide the most amazing acoustics for those opera buffs who wish to sing in the shower.)

Into this pristine space, Esther went to deal with her problem. Opening the bottle of dye, she set it on the back of the sink. Then she went to work dabbing brown into the fuzzy pink nest on top of her head. She smiled to herself. "When Les and Roger meet me in Los Angeles, they'll never know what happened."

She knew well enough that those two lively lads would spare her nothing if they saw the pink hair. She would have had to protect herself with the straw hat as a shield around the clock, and even that could never have saved her from their persecution.

Then suddenly, it happened. In a single reckless movement, she knocked the bottle of hair color onto the floor. The glass shattered into a hundred pieces. A great howl of pain reverberated around the walls.

Out of bed in a single leap, Brian stood at the door, appalled. Irregular spots of brown now spread randomly over the field of pink. With unusual teenage empathy, Brian could only gasp, "But Mo-o-o-om!"

The case had to be closed for that night. You couldn't go out and buy another bottle of hair dye after midnight. Not even in Hong Kong.

Esther lay sleepless on her bed, watching the neon lights from the street dance on the ceiling. She tried to plan the next day. "We'll have to stop in Honolulu after all," she mused. "I will not arrive in California looking like this. Absolutely not."

In the morning the ill-fated travelers took a taxi to the airport. Esther again set the straw-hat firmly in place. Probably not a soul in Hong Kong realized the extent of her frustration.

Flights from the Far East customarily arrive in Honolulu at about 3 a.m.. Esther eyed her fellow travelers with distaste. Why did they have to be here? Why couldn't they be off sleeping somewhere? She and Brian boarded the shuttle bus as unobtrusively as possible, rice-planter's hat and all. They would simply have to batten down until complete repairs could be made.

That night in the hotel helped put things in perspective. Obviously she had now passed far beyond what any home remedy could do for her. The next morning, she spotted the nearest beauty salon and watched from a distance until she saw the doors open.

Once inside, she removed the rice-planter's hat. A sigh of surprise and sympathy rose from the girls around her. Unlike her usual frugal self, Esther didn't even ask what the repairs would cost. She needed help and needed it now. Price could be of no consideration whatsoever.

She spent the rest of the day in the salon. Hours passed—with bleaching, coloring, and applying oil to the frizzled, damaged hair.

Happily, she looked quite normal when she stepped off the plane in California the next day. Brian apparently chose to honor his promise not to speak of the matter to anyone. As far as we know, Les and Roger never knew the difference. They could easily attribute her exhaustion and nervousness to the long, trans-Pacific flight itself.

I've always wondered what Esther did with that hat. She never returned it to us, and I never saw it in her house. Such an emblem of heroic suffering, one might argue, should have been preserved as a family heirloom. Indeed, for generations to come, it could have spoken to the virtue of wise choices and pain of impulse buying.

CHAPTER 3

Study Leave, Again

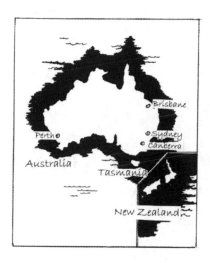

Most normal people, when they have earned "home leave," spend their time visiting friends and vacationing. On the other hand, Walt and I repeatedly invested our furlough time in high-intensity stretches of graduate study. This time Walt would do his DMin (Doctor of Ministry) degree at Andrews University in Michigan. Hopefully, within one year he would reach the "only-dissertation-left-to-complete stage." I would teach two classes in Andrews' English Department and otherwise hold the family together.

On Thursday evening, May 16, 1974, a graduation ceremony was prepared at our little elementary school. Larry, Lorna, Sharon (Gulley), and Julie (Gouge) had finished Grade 8. All of the parents turned out to celebrate what everyone hoped would be not only an emotional but also an intellectual milepost for the kids.

Our furlough time had arrived, and the usual pre-travel panic had set in. We would be away for a year. During that time the general framework of our campus home would remain. The house would be occupied by whoever came by and needed a place to stay. We packed crates of personal possessions to store in the garage and sold some stuff. Beth and Lolita, our ever-loyal Philippine daughters, would stay on with the house and take care of the three dogs.

In early July Walt's brother Harvey and his wife Helen (from Alberta, Canada) and his sister Mary (from Washington State) arrived. By that time we were embroiled in closing down our classes and computing grades. To be sure, our relatives saw how we lived life on a mission compound, but they saw it with dial turned up to maximum speed. We did as much sightseeing and visiting the markets as was humanly possible. We even stretched one single weekend to include Baguio, Subic Bay and Hundred Islands.

On July 10, Larry and Lorna flew home alone to Canada to stay with their Aunt Esther. We simply didn't have enough money to take them to Australia with us. They felt no deprivation. No. They were half drunk with the joy of new independence as they made their first flight alone.

The day before Larry and Lorna flew to Canada and their parents began their Australian adventure, the family posed in "uniforms." We should be able to identify one another when we met six weeks later (1974). The two shirts and two dresses were made from the same burgundy Thai fabric.

On our last day in Manila (Wednesday, July 1974) we ran out of packing containers. All we could do was push the last of our junk into Larry's tiny bedroom off the garage and lock the door. A steady stream of friends and students, flowed through the house all day. The entire English Department staff came to say goodbye. Beth and Lolita made brave little forays into cheerfulness, while the dogs crept around under the furniture, tails drooping and ears flat. They knew.

Ultimately, we got away to the beautiful new Manila International Airport, floodlit and replete with fountains and palms. (Finally, it had been resurrected from the ashes of the 1972 fire.)

Even though there were six of us, we were hugely burdened with hand luggage. I had created at least half a dozen multi-media programs for use during our travels. In the days before computers and power-point that meant toting many boxes of slides. While the usefulness of these "for-mission" programs very quickly became evident, hauling the equipment around the world immediately became a nuisance.

At long last, we boarded the plane with the Flying Red Kangaroo on its tail. I remembered how many times over the past years I'd stood on the observation deck watching people take off to Australia. How I ached to go with

Left. A postcard of the Indian Pacific train. It offered a ground-level view of Australia on its coast-to-coast run between Sydney and Perth. A very pleasant revival of the golden days of passenger rail service.

them. Tonight it was my turn to fly with the kangaroo.

In the final moment, Leona hugged me wistfully. "Could I find a place in your luggage somewhere, do you think?"

In mock anxiety, Norman clutched her arm. "Well, I'm hanging on, just in case!"

With that we were gone. Our great home-going adventure had begun.

The next morning we had a few hours in Port Moresby, Papua New Guinea, and then away to Australia. We flew in over the reef islands, sunny blue-white-and-brown. The Cairns airport was small and unimpressive. Lying in the arm of the bay, the white little town sort of leaned against the brown hills. No matter. At 2 pm on July 18, 1974, I set foot in my father's land for the first time in more than thirty years.

My cousins, Grace and Charles Sommerfeld, headed up the welcoming party. It included their daughter's family (with new baby) and in-laws. They had driven all the way up from the south to the Great Barrier Reef to be there to receive us. For me, the next four weeks would be a continuing reunion with my cousins and friends all over Australia and New Zealand. My dream, in *toto!*

We made the one-hour ferry trip out to Green Island. It seemed to float over the shadowed sea, with the multi-blues of coral swimming under the high tide. Because the Canadians lived far inland, they were pleased with the glass-bottomed boat. So we peeped into the submarine privacies of anemones,

Above left. For the first time since they were kids, Dorothy and Eileen sat for three days just watching their homeland, Australia, streak past the train window. **Above right.** Leona Minchin's birthday was publicly celebrated in the dining car. **Right.** We spent lively evenings in the club car as the train streaked across Australia's Nullabor Plain.

turtles, corals, mollusks and fish. Walt and I, however, remembered our Caribbean days and longed to join the snorkelers instead.

In due course we started south, taking time for a stopover in Brisbane. Cousin Joanne Sommerfeld and her husband Dieter Werner (both medical doctors) and four-month-old Baby Justin met us at the airport. They ran a shuttle service to get all six of us and our baggage to their 'hut" as they called it. A wispy twenty-three-year-old blonde, Joanne was as charming a doctor as you could ever wish to have standing over your sickbed and giving orders. She and Dieter were both busy with internships in Brisbane General Hospital.

They gave us all the beds in the house while they slept on the living room floor. Walt and I had never before slept in jet-black bed-sheets. The kitchen was painted dark purple, and the baby wore purple nappies (diapers). No question! Joanne had personality plus! That night we had a vast generation

Ever the animal lover, Dorothy cuddled a winsome bush-baby. The koala bear smelled like an uncorked bottle of eucalyptus oil.

gap in the house, but it immediately became so narrow as to be non-existent.

The Lone Pine Koala Bear Sanctuary near the city accommodated Australia's iconic "bears." Also squalling cockatoos, giant lizards, kangaroos and emus (ostrich-like birds). The koala bears had calluses on their rumps from always sitting in the crotches of the trees. One koala that I held in my arms wrapped his paws around my neck and slept on my shoulder. He smelled like an uncorked bottle of eucalyptus oil. The scent of the gum leaves (his only food) was on his breath, seeping through his skin and out of his ears. An adorable bush baby! No question! We had arrived in Australia.

We landed in Sydney early Monday morning. In addition to several cousins, my old schoolmate, Elva Bade was there to greet us. Also, my sister Eileen had just arrived from Germany, ready to join us for the rest of the trip.

After parking our twenty-one pieces of luggage at Central Station we spent several hours in downtown Sydney, climaxing with lunch at the Sanitarium Café. That day (July 22) being Walt's and my twenty-third wedding anniversary, we were presented with a fruitcake (as only the Aussies know how to make it), decorated with silver maple leaves.

At 3:15 that afternoon the seven of us boarded the slim, silver Indian-Pacific train for the three-day journey to Perth. We occupied three "twinettes" in Coach 5 (for Walt and me, Harvey and Helen, and Mum and Eileen). Rather morosely, Mary accepted her single "roomette" which happened to be in another coach. Unfortunately the arithmetic worked out that way.

Our accommodations were, nonetheless, quite astonishing, with every

Left. In Perth Dorothy and Eileen joined three of their cousins at the grave of their Grandmother Martha Ellen Minchin, Middle Swan, Western Australia. Right. Looking for antique square nails, the cousins raided the mud-brick ruins of their great-grandparents' homestead (Alfred and Lucy Minchin, Upper Swan, Western Australia). L-R. Allan Laird, Jess Barrett, Eileen Eckert (Davis), Dorothy Comm, Ellen Henley.

convenience compactly built into the tiny cabins. Even the aisles in the sleeping cars were curved, making the five-coach walk to the dining car quite rhythmical. We waltzed our way down the passageways with the sway of the train, the curves fitting our every lurching step.

Despite our plans to do some work during the trip, we invested most of our time in watching the Outback and then the mighty desert sweep past our windows. We constantly hoped for glimpses of kangaroos and wallabies.

Elva had prepared a birthday cake for Mum, decorated with green gum leaves, a brown boomerang, and a porcelain koala bear. We smuggled it aboard, and hid it in Harvey and Helen's room. When the day (July 24) came we were out on the *Nullabor* (Aboriginal, "not any tree") Plain. Just a little east of the Western Australia state line, the "Long Straight" began. The tracks neither rose nor bent for 478 kms, the longest straight rail line in the world. The whole dining car sang the birthday song for Mum, and the train-wide P.A. system lustily greeted the "lady passenger celebrating her 67th birthday on the train today."

Going to and from the dining car, Eileen and I often lingered in the lounge car where many of the passengers—most of them beyond middle age—spent most of their time. One chap, happily full of drinks, turned the little spinet piano in to a real honky-tonk instrument. The crowd roared out "Clementine" and like songs for hours. Altogether appropriate as we

Left. For the only time in their lives, the three siblings were together: Dorothy, Eileen, and Baby Brother Keith. (Avondale Memorial Cemetery). Right. The old "Amen Gate" at the end of Avondale Road led through the bush to the College campus.

approached the old gold-mining town of Kalgoorli.

Another contingent of cousins waited for us at the railway station in Perth. Also, there were several old men who announced themselves to me as "school mates of your Dad" at Carmel College. Although I didn't know it at the time, in years to come I would become deeply involved in the history of my Australian family, going back over 500 years.[1] This, however, was my first trip home. Mainly I just wanted to revive the places and people I had known as a child. The serious research still remained in the future.

Meanwhile, we'd landed in the Aussie mid-winter. As newly expatriate "Filipinos," Walt and I felt cold. We each bought lambs-wool sweaters at David Jones department store. Australians have smart electric blankets underneath instead of on top. You turn your bed on half an hour early, and then can crawl into a toasty warm nest. So who needs central heating, after all?

We resumed air flights on July 31, working our way back East and allowing ourselves stopovers in Melbourne and Canberra before we reached

Sydney. Along the way Walt and I had numerous speaking appointments, and we used the slide programs often enough to justify the burden we had in carrying them.

The day we reached "Auntie Ruby's House" on Avondale Road in Cooranbong, time telescoped for me. My cousin Ray Britten (her son) had died just a few months earlier. Now his widow Betty and the children lived in the home that I had loved so well. Son John, young as he was, had reliably become the man of the house.

For many years, Comms and Liskes jointly owned a house on Timberland Drive on the edge of Andrews University campus. During their winter tenure (1974-75) Walt and Dorothy bundled up against a Michigan snowstorm.

I recognized the same furniture. The piano still stood in the same spot, opposite the fireplace, across the corner. On our last evening in Australia, we watched television to see the final disgrace of President Richard Nixon amid his Watergate disaster. Despite the high media interest in that sorry affair, we soon turned off the TV. We chose rather to spend our few remaining hours just talking to one another.

Up at 2.30 the next morning, we formed a convoy of three cars (belonging to Charles, Verna, and Betty) to get us to the airport. A real test of family loyalties. The Qantas flight to Christchurch departed at 7. a.m. By sitting on the right side of the plane, I caught the first view of New Zealand's Southern Alps. The mountains rose from the east coast, as we flew across Hokitika. Then the snowy peaks, gorges and glaciers stretched down toward the southern horizon and into infinity. Suddenly it all gave way to the vast Canterbury Plains. Christchurch came up last, facing inland toward its great sheep meadows.

We didn't know whether to expect anyone to meet us or not. After half an hour, just as we were about to get taxis for the city, Kyrill and Gaylene Bland introduced themselves. The young pastor and his wife had been asked to meet "an Adventist mother and two children." That would have been Mum,

Eileen and me. Obviously, they couldn't find anyone to fit the description. They discreetly circled our luggage in the middle of the waiting-room floor and got a glimpse of a name tag. Mum, at the moment was standing guard over the pile. When they presented themselves to her, they were understandably shocked to find that there were, in fact, seven of us.

The Blands made two trips to get us hauled into the Tall Trees motel in Papanui. They brought over pumpkin soup, a salad, and kiwi fruit (giant gooseberries). The proprietors were an elderly Scots couple who ran the motel family style. Fruit cake, biscuits and fresh milk awaited us in our refrigerator. Later, I wrote a letter thanking them for their unusually gracious hospitality. They were surprised and their response warm. We remained friends-by-mail until they were no more.

We rented a Toyota mustard-colored mini-bus for the day and explored the Canterbury Plains. Sheep, sheep, sheep, and sheep—shoulder to shoulder and fence to fence—all day. They were eating turnips, of all things. Grown just for them. The green fields stretched away to the snow-peaked Alps.

At the end of the day, Christchurch's weather went soggy. The next morning, however, our Air New Zealand flight lifted us into the bright morning air, and the sunshine followed us all the way to Wellington. There we had to re-negotiate our car rental and take two Holden station wagons instead of the mini-bus we'd originally ordered. Walt drove one and I the other. Getting to Auckland took three days with stops at Palmerston and Rotorua.

On Thursday night we put Walt on a flight to Los Angeles. I watched the Air New Zealand DC 10 take off, a big bird with glowing eyes from 100 gleaming windows. Sadly, he was going to miss Fiji. He had to take care of his U.S. immigration, buy a car, and get ready for the next segment of our headlong eastward journey

The rest of us had time to love Auckland. From Mt. Eden, one of the city's many little volcanoes, we got a view of the city and its harbors on both the Tasman Sea and the Pacific Ocean. Mt. Eden is a perfect little volcano with a grassy cone on top. In a wonderful sheepskin store, I bought a white fleece for me, a natural brown for Larry, and dyed purple one for Lorna. (She was currently stuck with that color.)

The Friday afternoon flight to Fiji provided us with Maori choir music all of the way. Although a rainstorm circled saucer-shaped Fiji, we made a perfect instrument landing. Then, the heat, rain, and humidity smote us. Had we overshot Nandi and landed back in Manila?

At the Air Pacific counter I was singled out because my handwriting didn't look right. Actually, it never does. Nor does it even look the same from one moment to the next. A pompous officer in a *sulu* (long skirt, known elsewhere as a 'lap-lap') made me sign my name a dozen times. It worsened from illegible to hieroglyphics as I came increasingly more angry. Finally, after having asserted his authority to his own satisfaction, the man let me go.

Our hosts at Fulton College were the Bill Driscolls. Did he remember what we kids had done to him in the Avondale Central School? I confessed to having been among the troublemakers. In thirty years we had both crossed many bridges and endured the many vicissitudes of teaching. So that weekend we found much in common to chat about. We awoke Sabbath morning to the beating of the *lali* drums.

On Saturday night we all ate supper in the wildly painted dining hall—bean soup and basins full of boiled cassava roots. Not rice. The boys provided the entertainment, characterized by much volume, vigor and rhythm. The girls laughed and screamed in a most gratifying way.

On Sunday one of those pleasant "flying hotels" (a Pan Am 747) carried us from Fiji to Honolulu. Although we had a buffet supper, I still got a little frantic with so many people packed in close around me.

The next day we drove around the island of Oahu, and visited the Polynesian Cultural Center and Pearl Harbor. We ate supper in Waikiki at the International Market—under a banyan tree, amid lanterns and fountains. That would be the last taste of exotica on our long home-going trip. From now on life would be serious business.

After we put the Canadians on a flight to Vancouver, Mum, Eileen and I took off to Los Angeles. We arrived to find Uncle Len and Auntie May and the Tom Bradleys waiting for us. Also Walt. He had his U.S. immigrant visa in hand and was driving a smart gold-and-white Plymouth Valiant, only two years old. We reached Loma Linda at 3 o'clock in the morning.

Our study-leave year at Timberland. **Above.** Walt at one of our double desks in the family room. **Above right.** We virtually lived at the fireplace. **Right.** With body-language that spoke of boredom, Lorna washed dishes in the kitchen.

Thursday, without time to draw a breath, Walt and I, Mum and Eileen drove to San Jose, 475 miles north. Typically, our furlough years were marked by several furious road trips. Now, in our calendar-crazed mode once more, this journey became our first marathon for 1974. We arrived—you guessed it—at 3 o'clock in the morning at Auntie Norma Youngberg's home.[2] The next night, after she served us a curry supper (with many *machams),* Walt and I headed off to Walla Walla, Washington. After driving all night, we reached Vic and Gem Fitch's place the following afternoon.

We had to stop for one day of rest. For the offertory in the College Place Church, Gem played "my piece," Haydn's "Truth Divine." At sundown Walt and I took off again, like fugitives on the lam. Hours later, at midnight Sunday, we reached Esther's house in Lacombe, Alberta. Barely coherent, we sank into bed under her comfortable old quilts.

Larry and Lorna seemed genuinely glad to see us. (Thus the labors of parenting are rewarded.) We'd been apart for six weeks and four days, as Lorna carefully reminded us. The very next day, however, we drove to Edmonton International Airport and put the kids on a plane bound for Chicago. Their school had already opened. They would stay with their "Jamaica parents," Uncle Wilf and Auntie Annamarie Liske who were now both on the faculty of Andrews University.

This time Larry and Lorna strode off to the plane taller, more independent and older than when they left us in Manila. Larry wore his new red Australian sweater and Lorna her new blue Canadian one.

Walt and I reserved a little more time for ourselves. Just to see a few more Canadian sunsets reflecting themselves in the ponds in the grain-fields and making silhouettes out of the bluffs of trees. On Sunday morning, September 8, we packed up the car in a flurry of rain

Leaving our Philippine home for a year was one thing. The dogs were another. Our girls took great care and wrote frequent letters about them. (L-R. Lolita, Zeny, and Beth) They also nurtured Bobo who became fat and sassy.

and/or snow. Could hardly tell which. We headed out for the prairies, past the red and white grain elevators, and on down to Michigan.

Once landed at Andrews University, we faced a whole new set of decisions. At least, we'd arrived on time.

First, we spent a couple of nights with Liskes and reclaimed our Larry and Lorna who were now entrenched in their Grade 9 work at the Academy.

Our housing arrangements now passed through three distinct phases. First, we moved into the two-bedroom apartment reserved for us in one of the graduate housing buildings. There we rapidly developed "people fatigue." Larry had to sleep in the tiny dining room area. Emotionally, if not physically, we seemed to fill the whole apartment and leak out through the cracks. The people next door had seven kids (same size apartment). So what was wrong with us? Walt kept house hunting.

Next we moved into an old farmhouse, offered to "reliable missionary families." Now we had more room than we needed. The place was cold.

Sleeping in her huge room upstairs spooked Lorna. On the contrary, Larry loved the cubby-holes and odd staircases. He didn't want to move. Downstairs Walt's and my bedroom looked and felt like a viewing room in a funeral parlor. The whole house was depressingly dark, and I really didn't like it. Walt went on searching.

Finally we bought a pleasant split-level house on a wooded lot, eight minutes' walk from the center of the campus. It had a rental apartment downstairs. It was warm and easy to live in! Liskes became one-third owners with us, and they would become the landlords when we returned to the Philippines the following year.

Unable to afford anything new to furnish our house, we made an intense search in all sources of second-hand furniture. Even after our best efforts, the place remained minimally furnished. Even Spartan. We just told visitors that we'd gone Oriental and liked sitting on the floor. Liskes lent us two old reclining chairs. We lolled in them occasionally, our heads sunk into those thick New Zealand fleeces that covered up the worn spots.

Actually, I didn't mind our lack of furniture. My relationship with money had long ago been established. In a way, money didn't even matter much in our house. Because of his privations during the Great Depression, my Dad had major anxiety even in owning a piece of real estate. Not that we obsessed about bargain hunting. In fact, even today, I rarely think about shopping, unless someone wants me to take them somewhere.

Looking back, I realize now that—with the exception of books—I have spent what money I've had on experience rather than stuff. Surprising how easy it is to lose interest in material goods once you accustom yourself to that lifestyle. Real contentment can often come at an astonishingly low price.

At the front, our bay window with its eighteen panes looked out over the evergreens between us and Timberland Drive. Upstairs, the bedroom windows opened into the tree tops—almost like a tree house. The rather elegant bathroom had Mediterranean cabinets, two sinks, and a huge mirror. Even two teenagers could stand at the counter at the same time without conflict.

Downstairs the sunny family room had French doors on one side, a wall of high windows on the other, and a big stone fireplace in between. Walt and I each had a desk under the windows, side by side. Somewhere (for only $50.00) Walt found an old washer and dryer (circa 1948). At the end of its cycle, the dryer dinged out an old drinking song, "How Dry I Am."

In general the house tended to uninspired colors—gray, beige, off-white, off-pink. Indeed, all of it seemed morbidly "off." In the spring, however, we managed to liven up the kitchen and breakfast nook in yellow daisies. I would have liked to have colored up the whole place, but that makeover would have to wait until Wilf and Annamarie Liske moved in themselves, years later.

When our roll of posters mailed in Canberra arrived, we had wall-covering aplenty. A koala and Western Australian black swans in the dining room, Kangaroos and the Sydney Opera House (fish-eye lens) for Larry. Another koala and Barrier Reef fish for Lorna. Melbourne's Athenaeum for the family/study room. I relieved the greenly cold paleness of my office in the English Department with a pair of handsome kangaroos, unimaginatively labeled "Australian Red Kangaroos." The caption should have read: "Shall We Dance?"

Relishing our social opportunities, we took Thanksgiving vacation-time to head south out of what was turning into an oppressive Michigan winter. We visited friends in southern Tennessee and were back home on duty exactly when we were supposed to be.

The call of the open road invariably intoxicated us.

Valmae and Peter Read drove up from Ohio to celebrate Christmas with us. After spending Baguio Christmases with Leona in the Philippines it seemed quite proper that this year, we should be with her twin sister Valmae. Well supplied with firewood, we kept the fireplace going constantly.

Valmae and I also turned out a festive meal. We contrived to have the buns, veggie roast, gravy, mashed potatoes and vegetables arrive at the table simultaneously hot. Then, at the last minute, I remembered the jellied salad in the refrigerator. A rather elegant thing with pineapple, cranberries, walnuts, all layered with thick sour cream. I handed it to Valmae, "Here, you un-mould it." I envisioned the ruby-red ring as the *piece de resistance* for the whole meal.

Suddenly a sharp cry of pure pain emanated from the area of the kitchen sink. The salad had vacated the mould prematurely, and most of it had sloshed into the dishwater. Ve caught about a third of it in her hands.

"Now then, Mother!" Peter peered across the counter from the dining room side. "Will I have to take you aside and speak to you?" he pontificated.

The loss of the salad was a small price to pay for one of the biggest laughs of the whole day. Walter simply relabeled the dish a "tossed jello salad," and we ate the remains. Still it did look pathetic, lying there in a heap in a soup bowl.

At the end, we employed our three teenage daughters to clean up the kitchen. For at least a day-and-a-half we abdicated our present identities and gave ourselves up to remembering old times and places when we were the kids.

Three months later, we returned the visit and drove down to visit the Reads in Springfield, Ohio. Having just acquired his driver's license, Larry sat at the wheel most of the way. I could see that I was being displaced and could look forward to many years in the back seat. While I prized the independence of driving my car, I have never had any emotional investment in the act. Therefore, I didn't care.

These renewals that come with spending time with family and friends is, of course, one of the major benefits of furlough. Having Wilf and Annamarie Liske near at hand had to be a highlight of that whole year at Andrews University. Most events centered on our big stone fireplace.

For her sixteenth birthday, Lorna invited in a dozen or more of her high school friends. I remember a lot of giggling and games. Walt and I served pizza buns—at the fireplace, of course. They disappeared so fast, however, that neither of us tasted even one of them. A month later, for Larry's sixteenth, we did the same. Again, pizza buns at the fireplace. With Liskes. Just us, quietly together, doing what we'd been wont to do ever since we first met twenty-five years earlier.

In mid-winter, I fell victim to the flu epidemic. Although I managed to keep my classes afloat, I spent my convalescence lying on a mattress that Walt dragged down and placed in front of our ever-warm fireplace.

About the same time, Annamarie and I decided to become healthy by going to the University swimming pool as often as possible. As it turned out, the night crowd rather overwhelmed our matronly tastes. Kids jumped off the high board, athletic youths swam their laps, and little boys in their underwater maneuvers knocked people off of their feet. Just being in the water was something like swimming through a meat stew.

When we met at 12.30 on Mondays, however, we had the place to ourselves. Sometimes Walt or even Wilf might join us. We lolled about in the warm water, looked up through the floor-to-ceiling windows, and watched the snowflakes flutter down. While I have never done fancy swimming, I thought that Walt's and Annamarie's dog-paddling looked utterly exhausting. "Oh well." Walt sighed philosophically. "I suppose we must both have learned from the same dog."

In late March the combined families of Liske and Comm spent the weekend in Toronto, Canada, where Annamarie's brother, Henry Feyerabend, had opened the Portuguese church and founded ARTS, the television studio that became "It is Written Canada."

In Pioneer Memorial Church one day Liskes and we were sharing a pew. Someone asked if we were related. "No," we replied, "but after these many years of our kind of friendship we know that we really are." Can any possession in the world be more lovely than that of having friends who are real people?

Our joint house-ownership, of course, gave us some headaches that could have been avoided, if we had simply moved into that graduate housing apartment at the beginning of the year. Of necessity, in a day's work, all of us were away from the house for five or six hours at a stretch.

One morning Walt was working at his desk in the family room when he heard an odd "pop" somewhere upstairs. Seconds later a torrent of water burst into the utility room, a waterfall pouring down the laundry chute. He rushed upstairs to find that the toilet tank had split open from top to bottom. He turned off the water and prevented the flood from ruining the carpet in other rooms. If he hadn't been home, however, the water could have flowed unchecked for hours. We'd heard of "metal fatigue," but who knew about "ceramic fatigue!" Indeed, we had identified a new thing, "toilet fatigue." Whoever would have thought to worry over that!

For those living in the tropics, being home for the changes of seasons has always brought yet another kind of renewal. I derived little pleasure, however, from the Michigan winter. We had a late blizzard on the first of April.

The fat robins who had returned from the south the previous week bounced around looking very confused. No doubt they were wondering whose idea it was to return to Michigan for Easter anyway. I could understand their distress perfectly. That night we had five inches of heavy, wet snow, and I would happily have traded places to be back in Manila.

By mid-May, however, spring was bustin' out all over. Once again we could have all of the windows in the house open. I loved the sounds and smells of stirring, living things. Long residence in the tropics does breed rebellion against the sealed-in atmosphere of cold-weather living. The campus rapidly became a mosaic of tulips, pansies and daffodils. We had scores of multi-colored trees and bushes, heavy with buds and blossoms, all set in a framework of living green.

Like everyone else, of course, we fought the dandelions in our lawn. In the mornings they hid discreetly closed in the grass, but by midday they flung modesty away in the noontime warmth. They opened and turned up their sassy yellow faces to the sun. If dandelions were rare, we'd nurture them, treasure them, and keep them in greenhouses. Instead, because they're so common, we go all out to crush their carefree exuberance. Why?

At the end of May Michigan got ten days of thundery, cyclonish weather. Indeed, a reasonable facsimile of a Pacific typhoon. Torrents of rain poured through the sundeck and down onto the downstairs patio. The kids jumped into their bathing suits and rushed out. Fortunately, we had many maple trees in our backyard, already in full leaf. I was glad, because the neighbors might not understand how we enjoyed the wild freedom and refreshment of bathing under the eaves in a rainstorm on a hot night. If this were happening in Manila we'd have had no water or electricity, perhaps for days. I was sure that it would take Larry and Lorna quite a while to outgrow that pleasant tropical pastime.

Throughout the year we had messages from our faithful Beth. She always had news of Bobo and the dogs. Her letters reminded us again of just how much of ourselves we had left behind in the Philippines. "I always think of them," she wrote, "and pray for them every night."

I thought of whole generations of the other poor dogs in the Philippines who have no one to feed them, let alone pray for them.

Yes, we had settled ourselves into a viable routine at Andrews University. But never for one moment did we forget that we were still only transients in our homeland.

Notes

1   See Dorothy Minchin-Comm, *The Book of Minchin: A Family for All Seasons* (Victoria, B. C. Canada: Trafford Publishing, 2006). Illus., 671 pages.
2   My mother Leona Minchin spent the winter months among the California relatives, dividing her time between her brother James Rhoads, her sister Norma Youngberg, and her daughter Eileen.

CHAPTER 4

Academics, Bonding, and Culture: The ABCs of Furlough

With study as our purpose for being at Andrews University virtually all of our time and energy went into academic enterprises. Deep into the Doctor of Ministry program at the Seminary, Walt had his life pretty well laid out for him. Teaching two-thirds time, I was back among old friends in the English Department.

Since this was our third time at the University, we anticipated a rich, full year ahead. "All systems go" for us. We were also pleased—even a little surprised—to find a new spiritual tone on the campus. Most of my students seemed to be articulate Christians, willing and able to write and talk about their commitment and beliefs.

Along the way, our Timberland house anchored us down in domestic responsibility—which we loved. Just before Christmas Walt and Larry cut down a 75-foot elm tree by our driveway. It had a rotten heart and was plotting evil against us. Since it reminded him of his lumberjack days in British Columbia, the job rather appealed to Walt. Some nice solid sections would become benches in the backyard, come spring. The rest was stacked in the garage for the fireplace.

Above all, the campus offered some opportunities that we'd have been hard pressed to find anywhere else. In November Walt and I, along with six other couples, had a weekend retreat at the home of Ed Banks, a retired Seminary professor. Two retired couples, one middle-aged (Walt and me), two thirty-some, and two newly-weds (within eighteen months of their marriage). We began as total strangers, and ended up, I think, with a kinship something like what the first-century Christians must have enjoyed. Now when we would

In its rotten heart an elm tree by the driveway threatened our Timberland house. Left. The task of felling the tree appealed to Walt's and Wilf's innate Canadian lumberjack instincts. Right. Their efforts supplied the fireplace for the entire winter, and more.

see one another on campus, a kind of quick-fire responses passed between us. "We've known something good together!" One might thus hope to be preserved from ever taking life for granted again.

I found the classroom climate invigorating. Sometimes in overseas colleges classes tend to too much lecture and can become too passive. Here I thoroughly enjoyed the lively give-and-take attitude that prevailed. I needed that refreshment.

Bernice Reynolds, for example, contributed much to all of her classes. She came in as a sixty-five-year-old freshman and stimulated some memorable classroom exchanges. Recently widowed, she decided if she didn't want to sink into a miserable, lonely old age it was up to her to change her situation. Early in the term she wrote in her journal: "The young people are so kind to me, as if they thought I was some sort of important person." Indeed, to see how the students loved her was pure delight. The young men contended, almost physically, to carry her books for her.

At Christmas a favorite nephew gave Bernice a navy blue sweatshirt emblazoned with the words: "Senior Citizens Too Can Be Freshmen." She expressed herself well, and her extra years of living often gave her the edge over the others when it came to free-writing assignments. The *South Bend Tribune* even picked up her story as a Sunday feature.

Just being part of the Andrews faculty landed me in a virtual hotbed of ideas. That year the thirteen films of the "Civilization" series by Sir Kenneth Clarke were released by the British Broadcasting Corporation. Clarke set the pace for many other television "stars" who would combine scholarship, travel and photography to provide a new media genre. When the "Civilization" series became part of Andrews' Honors Student Program, I worked with both the music and art departments in lecturing and discussing the topics. That opportunity became the foundation for my future years of interest in interdisciplinary studies

Time-pressed as we usually were, Walt and I prized the cultural riches that the campus offered. Take, for example, the magnificent pipe organ in Pioneer Memorial Church. It lifted weekly Sabbath services to the very gates of heaven. One day, Dr. Warren Becker told me, "I never put my hands on this instrument without thanking God again for the privilege of being able to minister with it."

What an instrument it was! Above the manuals and controls, towered thousands of pipes, rank upon rank. At one moment, the gentle tones of the little flutes floated over a thundering bass. Or the brassy, martial En Chamade Trumpets summoned us from the horizontal pipes. Under the central Gothic window, they pointed boldly forward over the heads of the congregation.

Other cultural feasts were also served up at regular intervals. Stan Midgely brought his "Chucklelogue" on Hawaii. The sixty-man National Band from New Zealand included us on their tour, as did a Rumanian Folk Ensemble and the thirteen-man Moscow Balalaika Orchestra. Then came a Danish gymnastic team and the Norman Luboff Choir. Also the virtuoso violinist Ruggiero Ricci. (He was a very small man but his music was huge!)

As I scan my journals of that year, it might appear that we spent most of our time going to concerts. Actually 95% of our existence was consumed in class preparation, paper grading, counseling, studying, and writing, to say nothing of the regular household chores. It was really only that remaining 5% that could be of public interest. It also proves that Walt and I were passionately fond of music.

We also supported our local talent. When the Academy Band Concert performed, we sat proudly watching Larry in there with his cornet. With all the percussion trimmings, the kids blew up quite a storm.

That same year, the English Department staged their first Bobbie Burns Day celebration. Stella Greig (a Mexican) arranged it, and her Gaelic husband Joe (from the Seminary faculty) "piped in the *haggis.*" That was an ethnic Scottish dish that she had cleverly vegetarianized. She also rounded up the local Scots, like Dr. W. G. C. Murdoch, to socialize with us and to read Burns' poetry to us correctly.

On my own time, I spent as many spare hours as I could find in the Heritage Room in the Library, pursuing some research plans that I was hatching. It was there that Louise Dederen expressed an interest in keeping my journals in the archives. "We think," she said, "that your journals contain some of the best grass-roots mission writing that we have." Henceforth, whenever I mailed out my journals, a copy went to the James White Library.[1]

Meanwhile, Walt got bogged down with his Abnormal Psychology class. He complained that he didn't even have a background in normal psychology, whatever that might be. At first, he tried to "run with the horseman." That is, the psychology majors. In the end, he fell back to "running with the footmen," his Seminary colleagues. (This became a favorite metaphor of ours.) Under this stress, he actually had to give up several concerts. Truly a major sacrifice.

In March, Mum came to Michigan for a few weeks. We actually hadn't seen her for eight months, so we were happy to have our resident Grandma with us again.

Then I received an unexpected invitation from Atlantic Union College. For the Alumni Homecoming Weekend in April I was to be the speaker at Friday night vespers. The destination was 1,000 miles away, but Mum and Dad had worked there for twelve years, and it was my school. Having parked Larry and Lorna with their other parents (the Liskes) Walt, Mum and I headed east.

Of course, I felt a lot of soul warmth on the campus I hadn't seen in fifteen years. When I stood in the pulpit in Machlan Auditorium, I remembered that Dad had been the first pastor of that College Church. Here too, in a long-ago time, Eileen and I had brought our three squalling babies to be dedicated by our Dad. When the current students saw us old alumni prowling around the grounds getting sentimental, they were no doubt mystified. They thought it was just their school, but it was ours. In a way that none of them could possibly understand, yet.

Since we were in New England again, we visited a few of our old haunts.

We got thoroughly lost in the colonial seaport of Marblehead. There our California license plates rendered us immediately suspect. A couple of loafing fishermen regarded us with mild curiosity. We asked two blue-jeaned school-girls, "Can you tell us the way back to the Salem road?"

They giggled apologetically. "Uh. We don't know." They really didn't. We might as well have inquired about the most scenic route to Baghdad. Relying on our own resources, we did find Salem.

With the author Nathaniel Hawthorne as its most famous son, Salem was notorious for the 17th-century witch-hunt that carried twenty innocent people to the gallows and persecuted hundreds more.[2] We returned to the rambling House of Seven Gables, with its hidden smugglers' staircase in the chimney. Its "cursed" Well of Maule in the yard, and its rooms full of old china, pewter and period furniture. The house crouched, glowering at the shore, its dark, gabled face looking toward the Custom House and out over Salem harbor.

Down Chestnut Street with its gracious Georgian homes, I found a tiny, dark bookstore. Its main theme seemed to be witchcraft. Could any of those unfortunate victims of the witch-hunt ever have guessed that their demise would turn Salem into a 20th-century tourist attraction? I undertook the purchase of the book, *Historic Salem,* and a few postcards. That transaction became something like Divisoria [Manila] in reverse.

The little book and cards came to $1.85. I make a point of this because of the way that the solemn salesgirl managed the sale. From under the time-blackened counter she took a brass-bound ledger and started writing some kind of receipt. The procedure and the setting were so antique that I looked around to be sure I hadn't been sucked back in the 17th-century. Walt, however, was standing in the street on the other side of the many-paned little window. He had the camera bag, so I knew I was OK.

By concentrating earnestly, the girl arrived at the figure of $1.85. The prospect of estimating the sales tax, however, seemed to bring all of her mental processes to a halt. She withdrew into an inner chamber. Finally she returned with an older woman. "I'm new at this," she explained.

The senior proprietress studied the brass ledger. After several minutes she ascertained

Walt, Lorna and Larry at breakfast in the Timberland kitchen. This was the only space that we redecorated that year. The shabby red-and-white décor displeased us.

that the total was indeed $1.85. "It will be six cents tax, won't it?"

I remembered that we had to reach AUC well before sundown, if I were to have time to get myself put together before the Vesper hour. Already the sun sank low toward the western skyline. At the same time, I wanted to be helpful, because my proposed purchase seemed to have stirred up a crisis in the quiet little establishment.

"Yes, six cents would be right."

Still, she hesitated. "But we have to record it here." After the transaction had been immortalized in the brass ledger, I really couldn't see what other memorial could be necessary. Now the girl brought out an old adding machine. "This is new. We just got it yesterday, and we're supposed to use it." Carefully she picked out the numbers on the console. The scabby old machine (circa 1918) shivered, choked and churned out a slip of paper.

"If the tax is six cents," I reasoned, "that will make a total of $1.91, I believe?" Fifteen minutes had now passed, and I was getting edgy.

"Yes, that would be right." The girl studied the adding machine and then peered into my face, trying to determine, I suppose, whether or not my intentions were honorable. In the fullness of time the six cents was added, and the machine triumphantly clunked out the grand total, $1.91.

Then came the problem of change from $2.00. Ultimately we all agreed that it would be nine cents, and the deal was closed. When I stepped out onto

Chestnut Street again, Walt had already gone back to the car, having apparently given me up for lost.

New England is indeed old! In those colonial seaports one sometimes got the strong impression that the citizens didn't need the 20th century. Thus, we still have tranquil people in the world. To them time means nothing. Now, in retrospect, I do believe I found the little episode more refreshing than frustrating. It just took a while to get there!

Upon leaving Massachusetts we stopped at Hill Brothers Shoe Company in Waltham. That visit had very practical results. I saw serve-yourself rows of shoes, all at half-price, sizes 10-12. Long racks of them! My mouth went dry, and I began to sweat as I reached for 11 AA. (The largest size made in the Philippines was #8.) These were good shoes, not the hard, warped stuff you find tied together with string on bargain-basement counters. I walked out of the warehouse with six pairs, plus two matching purses thrown in as a bonus. Those would be my last new shoes for the next five years.

June 2 was my last official day in the Andrews English Department. Our offices in Nethery Hall were arranged in a "cellblock" around a broad hallway. Most of us worked with our doors open. That meant that any one could enter any conversation at any time. I knew I was going to miss the camaraderie we enjoyed there.

For Dorothy New England invariably meant the revival of a very old tradition—connecting with Harvey and Virginia-Gene Rittenhouse. (Pictured here with their very able assistant, Nettie Boland (right) on the ferry between Dublin, Ireland, and Holyhead, Wales.)

Earlier in the morning a student had presented himself at Grosvenor Fattic's door, opposite mine. Drawing himself up tall, the lad said, "I think that I am worth more than a C."

I'd known Grosvenor for a long time and figured that he had already made up his mind. The exchange was lively, however, with the professor defending his position brilliantly.

At last the student departed,

muttering something about, "I hope you have a good summer, anyway!" No ill will. A lesson in diplomacy.

I, technically, was now free, but Walt still had the summer session ahead of him. Although my teaching specialty had never been American Literature, I did teach it when I was overseas, away from the experts. Then I had the chance to attend an on-location Seminar on Henry Thoreau. With like-minded friends, Drs. Merlene Ogden and Joyce Rochat, and two graduate students, we headed down to Cape Cod. We followed the old stagecoach route from Sandwich, bicycled around Provincetown, went to Buzzards Bay, and saw the Oysterman's House. Then we drove home through Canada. I could hardly have asked for a more basic exposure to things American

I arrived home to find that Walt had brought in more strawberries. All of my life, I have had one clear vision of Paradise. It would be a place where I could eat all the strawberries I wanted. Eat with total abandon. We had come close that summer. We had eaten them, frozen them, photographed them. (We were even leaving some for Norman and Leona Gulley when they came for their furlough year in the fall.) I had come close to strawberry bliss that summer.

By July we had to recognize that our long goodbyes were about to begin. We had our last homemade pizza feast with Liskes. Larry, Lorna and I drove to visit the Reads one more time, and Lorna stayed with them to make the western trek to the August Minchin Family Reunion in California. Back home I lined Nethery Hall at Andrews University, Michigan, is now gone, its "Ivy League" look, however, once suited the English Department very well.

up five barrels and started packing away our winter clothes. They could hibernate in the attic above the garage until we needed them again.

I had to consider every item seriously, because Walt had taken a solemn vow: "We shall not, under any conditions," he said, "drag a trailer or carry anything on a roof rack."

In my spare time, I was typing the third chapter of his dissertation.

During this period, Cousin Kenny Minchin came to visit Larry, and they thoroughly enjoyed one another's company. Kenny, however, opened one of the kitchen cupboards. "How do you manage," he inquired anxiously, "with such a little bit of food around?"

I explained that we were closing up the house and that I had to get rid of leftovers of all kinds. Still, I took care to fill both boys up to the finish line at every meal.

Family reunions have always figured large in my family. One of those Very Important Things that can never be short-changed. For me this was my first step toward our return to the Philippines. I flew to California on August 6 for this purpose. My Dad had died since our last time together, and I had no plans to miss any part of this family gathering. Oddly, while in flight I was robbed of $145. I was chagrined, because I had survived four years in Manila and had never lost one centavo.

By the time I arrived, I found my cousin Yvonne Dysinger coolly managing a household of no less than thirty people. All of the girls in a single room and the boys in tents in the bush up behind the house. Yvonne was always "on top of things." Her survival instincts developed perhaps because she was the middle one in the tribe of "Seven Little Australians" She had to keep up with Party 1 (Kelvin, Joan and me) and also Party 2 (the twins and Eileen).

At the same, Uncle Len and Auntie May were making meticulous preparation for The Wedding. After years of being alone, Kelvin was bringing home a prize, Rosemary. Her loveliness, gentle kindness, and beauty of character won us all. After the ceremony, the reception convened on Uncle and Auntie's little patio, at home in Loma Linda. We literally had to drag the bride away from the sink where she was trying to wash the dishes at her own wedding reception! Such was Rosemary's penchant always for helping.

As the families left, one by one, Mum and I stayed with Eileen. Now divorced she had a pleasant new house with a swimming pool. Her sons kept it in Olympic condition, and it provided high sport for the younger set.

Walt and Larry arrived on August 15, after driving non-stop from

Left. The marriage of Kelvin and Rosemary Minchin (Loma Linda, California, 1975). Right. At supper in E. L. Minchin's home, the bride's new sisters-in-law had to intervene. Ever the helpful one, Rosemary (back to the camera) had to be prevented from washing dishes at her own wedding reception.

Michigan in forty-five hours. I was grateful to see my two men arrive whole, though they looked like bearded tramps. Our sturdy Plymouth was packed solid. They even had their toothbrushes chinked into the cracks.

Three days later Larry and Lorna flew to Singapore with the Ed Heisler family. Now began their boarding school career at Far Eastern Academy. This time they were leaving home in a new sense of the word. Our house would never be quite the same again.

Now that the "tumult and the shouting" had died down, we turned to the field work required for Walt's dissertation. His research concerned church architecture and its relation to worship and belief. It involved critiquing many churches. Churches by the mile. We did so under the guidance of the very excellent architect, Robert Burman.

In the middle of our picture taking our camera bag was stolen, and we had to use Mum's camera to recover what we'd lost. Two thefts in one month! I began to think it was time to go back to Manila and be safe! By mid-September we had assembled and copied the last chapter of Walt's dissertation and sent back to Andrews University for scrutiny by the examining committee.

Walt and I still had one more irrational trip to make. To visit his family in Canada, one more time. At least the trip enabled me to detach myself from the typewriter for a few days. We headed north on the 1900-mile trek into the Peace River country. We had no time left to write letters, so we just phoned ahead, day by day, to warn people of our coming. We drove day and night. It made little difference whether the sun shone on us or not.

The first lap took us to Seattle, Washington, by way of Lodi and by Mount Shasta.

For the weekend we reached Walt's sister Christine in her home in Kelowna, British Columbia. That is one of Canada's most beautiful and fruitful lake districts, complete with its own legendary water-monster, Ogopogo. Barely paying our respects, we hastened on.

Another 800 miles through the wilderness of northeast British Columbia brought us to Tete Jaune Cache (Yellowhead Pass). We descended down into Alberta and drove another 300 miles to reach Harvey and Helen's farm at 1 o'clock in the morning.

Arguably, frenzied road trips of this kind have their own kind of insanity. The distances themselves, however, seldom deter western Canadians or Americans. As Walt and I drove through that great empty land, I looked at the opaque blue-green lakes in the glacier country. We sped through endless miles of virgin forest, and I wondered how many animal eyes were watching, especially through the long night hours.

As usual, a high-speed visit to Walt's family in Alberta, Canada, was the last item before our return to the Far East. Left. Walt and his siblings: (L-R) Reinhold Comm, Walter Comm, Harvey Comm, Esther Comm-Robertson, Don Comm, Christine Comm-Rexin, Mary Comm-Tegge, Ben Comm. Right. The attraction of farm machinery, however old, always dragged Walt out into the fields with his brothers and nephews

Just then, it was only the two of us. We had no baggage—no books, no kids, no responsibilities to anyone but ourselves. This was, I think, an important interlude, albeit a high velocity one. The smoggy freeways of Los Angeles were behind us and the chaos of Manila traffic was yet to come.

When we arrived at the farm, Harvey was just finishing up the harvest. Walt disappeared among the machinery, and I saw little of him for the next two days.

In one long sunset, however, I rode a couple of miles with Harvey on one of his great grunting beasts, the combine. Something hypnotic about watching it lick up the barley, chomp out the straw and swallow the grain down into its churning innards. At the same time, a great yellow eye began to peer at us over the edge of the stubble field. A real harvest moon. I filed away the image. Something to think about the next time a typhoon hit us.

Because the time of separation would be long and the distance great, we felt a great urgency to live every moment to the full. Any time spent sleeping looked like mere idleness. When we reached Edmonton, Walt's brother Ben took us to visit their mother in the nursing home.

Surrounded by partially or fully sedated patients, Grandma Comm sat alone in her room. A solitary and broken figure. Twelve children and decades of unremitting farm work. She looked at us with dull, clouded eyes. "How many *kinder* do you have?" Ben tried to draw her out into our world. "What are their names?"

"I don't have children," she murmured. Ben repeated the question, hoping to break through her wall of deafness." No response. She went back to making her rag-rug, plying her big wooden hook. She could do that without really seeing.

I walked out into the hallway and left the two brothers with their mother. I knew that Walt would not see her again. Even now, she couldn't see *him!*

When we reached Esther's house in Lacombe we found her kitchen well stocked with fresh apple pies. She always knew what Walt wanted most. Then we took to the road again—more hundreds of miles—until we reached Los Angeles.

There would be no more family days and no more cross-country driving for another three years. So ended our study leave, fourteen months of frenetic activity.

When Mum, Walt and I arrived back in Manila on Sunday afternoon, October 12, 1975, we knew we were very tired. We also knew that we were home. Beth, Lolita, and the three dogs, as well as a campus full of friends emphasized that point.

Work and home. They happened to be the same place.

Notes

1   I began my journal writing in 1970 when we first went to the Philippines, continuing for more than forty years. In the process of writing *The Gazebo*, I computerized the journals for library storage. (I am indebted to Edward J. Heisler who contributed so much to the retyping of the material.) The four volumes are preserved in the archives of three University Libraries: Andrews University, Loma Linda University, and La Sierra University.

2   My subsequent genealogy investigations revealed that three of my American ancestors, the Towne sisters, were victims of this colossal miscarriage of justice. See the TV drama, "Three Sovereigns for Sarah."

CHAPTER 5

Another Term of Service

On Wednesday night, October 15, 1975, the doors of the plane opened to that familiar rush of steamy night air that is Manila climate. As we trudged across the tarmac we could hear the shouting and see a forest of waving arms in the crowd up on the observation deck.

While my mother sailed through immigration with her visitor's visa, Walt and I were detained. "You have no entry visas," one officious interpreter of the law snarled.

"Look at our papers, please." We pushed forward our special permit letters issued by the Philippine Consul in Los Angeles.

Refusing to look at them, he summoned a representative of Cathay Pacific Airlines. "Get their luggage checks and put them on the return flight to Hong Kong." Turning to us he barked, "You can be severely fined for arriving in this country without a visa."

"Please! Just look at these papers," I replied. "The Philippine Consul ..."

"That is nothing. He's over there. He doesn't know anything."

Having begged permission to go out into the visitors' area, I found that Mum had already collected our baggage. She was enfolded in the arms of the crowd, loaded with *sampaguita* leis. Dr. Roda (PUC's president) and Don Van Ornam returned with us back into the lair of Immigration.

By this time a bigger man had entered upon the scene and was examining our evidence. "These papers are all in order," he announced.

Forthwith the instigator of the little fracas started making all kinds of humble noises. "Ah, ma'am, I didn't read that part of your papers!" He now oozed goodwill.

With effort, I restrained myself from saying, "Duh! You idiot!"

Liberated, Walt and I walked back into our world that was waiting for us. "Welcome home, *Balikbayan!*" The cries came from all sides. (This greeting is reserved for homecoming Filipinos.)

Enveloped in a reception as warm as the weather, Mum and I climbed into a van along with the English teachers while Walt was claimed by another party in another vehicle. We all headed home to the campus.

Ironically, ten months later (Aug. 24, 1976), when Leona Gulley and her children returned from their furlough she encountered the same immigration officer. As Walt and I went in to help her and the children, he recognized us. As usual, he was ruffled up like a game rooster and was trying to get Leona back on the plane from which she had just alighted. This time he made Walt "buy" three return tickets for Taipei. Just a paper game, of course, but no doubt the little man found it worth the effort. Silly as these encounters may be at international borders, they still, in a marked way, reduce one's vital capacity. At least temporarily.

When we entered our house again, Beth had the three dogs groomed and wild to greet us. It took several hours for them to finish celebrating the fact that we had really returned. Just being with our pets again had to be one of our great, basic homecoming joys.

By mid-December, however, our octogenarians, Rusty and Mitzi, both needed geriatric care. Mitzi was too thin and had lost much of her hair. With her tonic, however, her hair grew back and she developed a colossal appetite. We'd put out three dog suppers, and, unless we were careful, she would eat all

We were back on our familiar campus. Left. Informal gatherings. Right. Graduations and the festivities that always accompanied them.

of them.

In addition to his recurring liver complaint, Rusty was sensitive to whatever he perceived as abuse. If we laughed at him, he would collapse in a heap on the floor and refuse to get up until we had petted him for at least half and hour and told him what a good boy he was.

One time Zeny gave him a bath. He submitted meekly enough, but the ordeal completely crushed his spirits. He had to talk about it for the next two hours. In fact he grumbled all the way to bed time, crescendoing into a real harangue every time Zeny went past the door of my little study where he held court most of the day.

Bobo turned into something of a rebellious child.

"A five-pound dog," Walt mused. "And four-and-three-quarter pounds of it must be ego."

Besides, he was mortally afraid of the dark. One night Walt summoned the gang of dogs. "Let's go." As usual, they all went out for their bed-time outing. Because Rusty thought that he needed to walk all the way around the house, he got stranded in the back yard. After the other two had come in the front door, Walt found him in silent anguish at the back door. The stress of it all completely blew his mind. For the next half hour he stood in the middle of the living room barking at the ceiling.

When someone suggested that he move on, he marched in to my desk, calling upon the Fates to witness the injustice he had suffered. A brief time of silence. When he saw us getting ready for bed, he lost his nerve again. Remembering the grievous offence against him, he raised his voice in lamentation once more. By morning, thankfully, he had recovered from his trauma.

Our love for our pets baffled many of our local neighbors. Walking my Pomeranians one evening I met Ezekiel. Since our return I hadn't seen his dog

Jinky. She used to lie docilely in the sun in the middle of the road. A veritable puppy factory, she supplied household pets around the community. I missed the amiable old matron.

"The people outside [of our compound] took her and ate her." Ezekiel went on to explain. "With rice and wine. You know that's how they prepare…"

"Yes, yes, I know." I didn't want to hear any more. I gathered up my bright-eyed little trio of tail-waggers and hurried home. Poor, poor Jinky!

So many domestic animals in the Philippines were woeful specimens. Dogs and cats were expected to be self-supporting, subsisting on grass and garbage. Only the *carabaos* really prospered, but then this is their country. They seemed able to absorb nourishment from the mud they rolled in. (Out in the countryside owning a *carabao* was the equivalent of having a car elsewhere.)

Our monkey Bobo was something else. She was the sparkling, prancing clown she had always been, and she had doubled in size. (Testimony to the fact that Beth and Zeny had kept her stuffed with good bananas all year.) Unfortunately she had had too much teasing from passersby during our absence. That had not improved her personality. Ultimately, we decided that she should go to the Manila Zoo and enjoy the company of her own monkey-kind. When the day came for her to leave, however, neither Walt nor I could do it. There she was, swinging by her tail from her tree and scouring the roof of her house with a plastic butter dish.

So Walt repaired her tree house. As he spent time with her, her disposition improved. He also expanded her menu and served her

In the 1975-76 school year a new publication was inaugurated at Philippine Union College, *Spotlight on PUC.* Dorothy, along with other members English Department, found herself involved with the production. In honor of a huge mango tree growing near the front gate, we created a gossipy back-page feature: "Heard Under the Mango Tree."

meals. Onions, pickles, *cala-mansis* (limes), green guavas and ice cubes. She ate anything she saw coming out of the kitchen. One day he offered her a snail out of the hedge. She investigated the slimy carcass, chattering and muttering to herself and wiping her little black hands on the side of her house. She rejected it as unworthy of her status. She knew it had not originated in our kitchen.

In January of 1977 we finally did have to contribute Bobo to the Manila Zoo. As we entered what was our last year in the Philippines, our lives became too complicated

The first edition of *Spotlight on PUC.*

to cater to her whims. Besides, we wanted to be sure that she would be "settled" by the time we left.

Some weeks later we went the zoo to visit her. We couldn't find her anywhere among the bedraggled, spiritless creatures staring back at us with dull eyes from their cages. They were only breathing skeletons. Where was our sprightly Bobo? Finally Walt found her. Her head was full of scars from fighting off the bigger monkeys with whom she lived. She had no interest in the bananas and mangoes that Zeny brought for her. She just crouched trembling, an apathetic little heap in my arms. No toys, no love, and no audience to appreciate her antics.

Sick at heart, we brought her home again. Then, bless him, Dr. Damocles Director of PUC Guidance Services, said, "Give her to me. My children will enjoy her." Before we left, thanks to his best counseling techniques, no doubt,

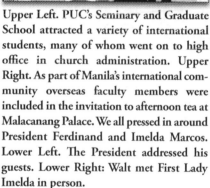

Upper Left. PUC's Seminary and Graduate School attracted a variety of international students, many of whom went on to high office in church administration. **Upper Right.** As part of Manila's international community overseas faculty members were included in the invitation to afternoon tea at Malacanang Palace. We all pressed in around President Ferdinand and Imelda Marcos. **Lower Left.** The President addressed his guests. **Lower Right:** Walt met First Lady Imelda in person.

we saw Bobo rehabilitated, at home in his back yard. She was in a less commodious cage, but once again she could play with her toys and ham it up for her audiences.

Upon returning to Philippine Union College, we found the lawns and gardens strikingly lush and green. Everything had grown! Our coconut palms, papaya trees, the red ornamental hedge, even the creepers on the big santol tree. Also the rains had begun. I found myself often standing at our front door, just to enjoy the view. The campus lay before me, an impressionistic painting in silver rain and living green.

In terms of productivity, however, we didn't have the touch to create a really thriving garden. One time our next-door neighbors, the Alfonso Rodas, had given us some guavas. We truly tried but had little success.

Sitting on the sea wall at Luneta Park and watching the sun set over Manila Bay became a favorite Friday evening treat for the family. Because of its violent weather Luzon provides the most spectacular sunsets on earth, no exceptions.

One day Zeny questioned Lino, their garden boy. "Your trees are so healthy," she said. "See? Ours are not good." Indeed, they had produced nothing but a handful of Bobo-quality fruit.

"Maybe yours," Lino speculated, "are practicing family planning."

Family planning, of course, was one of the most widely discussed topics in the country. (The population had increased almost 25% over the past five years.) Serious trouble! Probably we shouldn't complain, then. if our sad little guava trees were trying to set an example for the nation.

Shortly after our return Walt had to go out and find us another car. He brought home an eleven-year-old Peugeot. "How many miles does it have on it?" I eyed the faded blue vehicle with suspicion.

"Several," he replied tersely. I held my peace and hoped for the best.

Once more we had to adjust to the vagaries of the weather. The summer heat in April could be as destructive as a monsoon flood. One day Walt preached in the College Church. He spoke of Paul's Damascus Road experience and spiritual blindness. He'd said not more than half a dozen sentences when the electricity went off, and, with it the public address system. With the CA, seating some 4000 people, this was no small matter. Now physical deafness became an issue. He struggled to make himself heard in the vast, semi-outdoor auditorium. About thirty seconds after he sat down, the electricity came on again.

Left. Dorothy's office in Jackson-Severens Hall was conventional. Right. Her tiny den at home was different. There she spent her days between two typewriters. The IBM on her left was for professional jobs. The little Smith-Corona (right) did the chore work. Her little radio was permanently tuned to the "Good Music Station"—except when she had to use the dictaphone. Usually, a couple of the dogs sat on the desk, their long golden plumes spread out among the pens, pencils, papers and staples. Their office hours matched Dorothy's precisely.

Thankfully we didn't have to relive the Typhoon of 1970. That time we went two weeks without electricity and water. The campus, as some said, became the largest "dry cleaning establishment in Manila."

A much more cheerful part of our lives was again becoming part of the monthly gathering of our overseas work force for sundown worship, supper, and fellowship. I knew for sure that we'd arrived when we all sat in Ed and Bev Klein's living room eating tropical fruit salad and watching the sun set. Through the wide west windows we watched the rapidly changing rosy-gold horizon. Aqua-tinted streaks of light shafted the banks of curly lavender clouds. If the Philippine islands had nothing else to show you, it would be worth the journey just to see one week's assortment of sunsets.

The youngsters at Far Eastern Academy in Singapore were sent home twice a year to be with their families—Christmas and summer vacation. Therefore we always tried to make something of Christmas.

Larry got sick on the first weekend, however, claiming to have "been up 100 times last night." A somewhat fictionalized report. Still, I stayed home from church to be with him. Not that he couldn't look after himself, but because it's been such a long time since I had any leisure time with my great strapping 6' 2" son. Apparently, he had grown some more in Singapore, for he was now measurably taller than Walt.

We spent Christmas Day with our Filipino children and friends. Our "daughter" Lolita was now in the School of Nursing at Manila Sanitarium and Hospital. She came home as often as she could to tell us stories about her new life. One night her class provided the Saturday night entertainment at the College.

In 1975 Walt and his brother Ben visited their mother in a nursing home in Edmonton, Alberta. We had been away too long. "I don't have a son Walter," she said, looking right past him to the wall.

Along with more than 100 of her classmates, all in cap and uniform, she stood in a line up that ran the length of the huge College Auditorium. After singing and marching in formation they provided skits to demonstrate bad nursing (dumping patients out of wheelchairs) and good nursing

We could not have been more proud of Lolita.

Actually, we had all kinds of homegrown entertainment on campus. For example, I once gave Joe Sarsoza, one of my Graduate Assistants in English, a copy of "Mechanical Jane," a nonsensical play I wrote years ago in Jamaica. Really, it was just a series of comic characterizations. Very successfully Joe Filipinized it, changing the maid's name to "Maura." One evening the kids in the English Dept. played to a packed house. Because the love of fun is universal, everyone enjoyed that bit of silliness.

One day in early January (1976) a guard delivered a telegram to our door. Grandma Comm had died the previous night. In her mid-nineties, she had long been cut off by her deafness. It had locked her into a kind of loneliness into which no one could enter. Naturally, Walt's first impulse was to go home for the funeral three days later. Both time and money were against him. How could he get clearances to leave the country? As many had learned before us, once stationed overseas one simply has to accept the fact that many events at home must be given up.

With her special gift for words, Anne Fighur wrote the perfect letter to Walt. "Oh, we're so sorry. It's never all to right to lose one's mother. Faithful mothers of large families will be in their special place in heaven.... We like Walt, so we know that we like her too."

So our lives went on.

The Gulleys' return from furlough had been delayed. Although Norman came back in June, 1976, Leona and the younger children remained behind. After long years of consideration, Leona donated a kidney to her sister, Valmae.

From a distance we and Norman shared in the family concern over the event, for Valmae was a poor surgical risk. Nonetheless, the operation was more than successful with not a hint of rejection. With typical faith and confidence Leona simply said, "God knew from the start that Valmae would need this, so He just gave her an identical twin sister. Me."

One of my English teachers asked me if what she had been hearing about Mrs. Gulley was true. "It is," I assured her.

She stood silent for quite a while. "That is truly a very great gift," she murmured. Health bulletins continued to be excellent. The "perfect kidney transplant" had been achieved.

In due course, Holy Week came upon us again. The celebrations of Easter week have always been taken very seriously in the Philippines. We knew the format. *The Pasyon,* a very long, epic poem in Tagalog was sung continuously for fifteen days. Choosing any tune of his/her liking, the singer worked through the unspeakably tedious verses, non-stop, day and night. He knelt down with his book, droning on hour after hour. As his strength gave out, others joined in and took over. From time to time they sucked on *calamansis* to lubricate their voices. Loudspeakers magnified their efforts, and the chanting often drowned out our classes on campus.

On Good Friday the *flagellantes* fulfilled their vows. The most reverenced of all the holy days of the year, ordinary life virtually came to a standstill. God was dead! That day we could drive through the streets unhindered by jeepneys and buses. Everyone walked because riding that day would be a sacrilege. With no divine protection one was best off staying in his house anyway. With God being dead, this was the opportunity for anyone who has mischief in mind to get on with it. Thieves, then, pressed every opportunity they got.

Among the various sites in the city where men fulfilled their vows, the church at Malabon attracted many penitents. Their heads wrapped in grimy towels, men prayed at the lace-draped altar in the old Tanza Church before beginning their self-torture. Then they stood around, smoking and waiting for the "cutter" to come. When he arrived, he slashed their backs, arms, and legs with razor blades and broken glass. In the group we saw some first-timers--mere boys who would be doing this every year for most of a lifetime.

On the side were the balloon men, accompanied by the constant ringing of the bells of the ice cream vendors. Eggs were for sale near the altar, for the celebrants would want to suck on them for added strength on the long journey. The endless clack of the bamboo whips and the rhythmic thump-thump of the leather straps went on as attendants beat the penitents, every time they prostrated themselves on the ground. Some flailed themselves with chains while spectators spit on their gashed, bleeding backs.

The heat, the sweat, the wilted crowns of thorns on the dusty heads. The dirt and the blood! Lastly, the sufferers bathed in a river (actually it is an open sewer). How they avoid deadly infections, we never understood.

Altogether, it's such a savage practice carried on in this proudly Christian country. A discouraging prospect. One longs to stand up and shout the good news. "You don't have to do it this way! The dead Christ you imitate is alive! He offers you joy and life!"

Later in the year came All Saints Day. In nearby Holy Cross Cemetery we sometimes visited the all-night vigil-keepers. They kept watch whatever the weather. Families moved in for the night, some even brought cribs for the

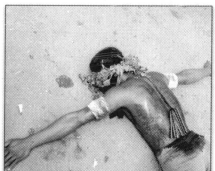

Upper Left. The Easter sequence began with the singing of *The Pasyon,* men and women taking turns. Upper Right. Penitents carry their crosses through the streets, occasionally overstepping reality and dying in their crucifixions. Lower Left. The *flagellantes* inch through the streets, beating themselves and bleeding until they drag themselves into a church. Lower Right. On the island of Marinduque the crucifixion plays out in high drama. Here three Morions pose in their self-made costumes as Roman soldiers.

babies. There plates full of rice, bread and *pancit* were offered to the spirit of a recently dead seventeen-year-old boy. There a widow wept alone at the grave of her husband. The party at yet another tomb had brought transistor radios, packs of San Miguel beer, and a game of *mahjong*.

We felt the pathos of it all—both physically and spiritually.

On campus we enjoyed our own kind of celebration. One of the most memorable to us occurred on July 24, 1976. It was an all-day honoring of Silver Weddings. In the morning Walt and I, along with six other faculty couples who qualified, stood up for a complete wedding service conducted by Jim Zachary. The aggregate of children stood behind us as "sponsors" as we renewed our vows. At noon the Seminary students provided a full Oriental feast. Our neighbors hosted evening worship and supper. In the evening the faculty gave us colorful reception. The Home Economics teacher had made a huge, three-layer wedding cake, and the physics teacher built a functioning water fountain into the middle of it. Altogether enough to make anyone's eyes lean out! I don't think that anyone, not even a Filipino, could have thought of one more thing to make the day more beautiful and festive.

As always contrasts amazed us—literally from one day to the next. About the same time as the wedding celebrations, we were just sitting down to lunch

Left. Several faculty couples celebrated their Silver (25th) wedding anniversaries on July 24, 1976. In the morning Jim Zachary led out in a ceremony complete with a renewing of the vows. (Their collective years of service to the Seventh-day Adventist Church came to 292.) L-R. Bien and Salvador Miraflores, Amalia and Teofilo Barizo, Romeo and Belle (absent) Castro, Dorothy and Walter Comm, Herminio and Lagrimas Reyes, Priscilla and Jose Leonas. Right. In the evening a full reception convened, with the Home Economics Department contributing the cake.

Suddenly our eight-grade Baesa School was not enough. Our kids would come home from Far Eastern Academy just for Christmas and the summer. Left. One day they were there with us. L-R. Lorna Comm, Sharon Gulley, Sheri Van Ornam, Tina Crawford, John Gulley, Larry Comm. Right. The next we were in Manila Airport, shipping them back to Singapore. L-R. Sharon, John, Larry, Lorna, Tina, and Sheri.

one day. It turned out to be as strange a Sabbath day as we ever had. A peculiar figure appeared at the front door. He wore a sweater and was swathed in bandages that seemed to be the remnants of an old pink bedspread. Tall, dark and very thin, he didn't exactly look like a Filipino. I don't think I had ever seen a dirtier person. The odor emanating from him was overpowering, and he had a repulsive skin rash.

"I want to speak to the Bishop," the man said. As it turned out, he had been hanging around since church, looking for the "bishop." Someone directed him to our house.

He said that he was from Bicol and wanted to go home to his mother. Yet when Zeny spoke to him in the dialect he couldn't understand her. "I am three-quarters Spanish," he explained. "My family speaks Spanish." He did admit to having been in jail. That much we could believe.

Although none of his story added up very well, we gave him a plate of food to eat out on the front porch. Then, while he finished a third serving of food, we tried to figure out what to do next.

Walt filled the bathtub with warm water and added some bleach—the only disinfectant we had handy. He took very unkindly to the idea of a bath. "But it will hurt my skin."

Walt thrust a bottle of shampoo into his hand. "You have to do this."

He was in the bathroom a long time. While he was in there, we ran his pitiful little heap of clothes through the washing machine, twice. Then the dryer. Finally he emerged clad in Walt's shirt and pants. They were a little roomy on him, but the overall effect was staggering. His skin was white, and his hair a glossy black instead of rusty brown! The girls had been utterly repulsed by him, but now they pronounced him *pogi* (handsome).

Suddenly he held up his head and started to talk! He said that his name was Jaime Perez Garchitorena. Walt gave him a copy of *Steps to Christ*. "Also I want to pray before I go," Jaime said. Then we gave him the little parcel of his ragged—but clean—clothes.

Near sundown, Walt took Jaime down to the bus station and bought him a ticket for the fourteen-hour ride down to Bicol. Although he promised to write to us, he never did.

Nonetheless, we knew that, at least once in our lifetime we had "done it unto one of the least of the brethren." Indeed, I don't think I have ever seen a lesser brother before or since. Sometimes I have wondered what he did with his life.

CHAPTER 6

Leaving Nothing Undone

Spotlight

On

PUC

Philippine Union College

At the basic, domestic level, we had to be constantly vigilant. The wear and tear of everyday living kept us alert. We had long ago learned not to take anything for granted.

Our two bathrooms, for example, were a case in point. In the earlier part of one night I heard a shattering crash. It somehow fitted into a dream I was having, so I never really woke up. In the morning I opened the bathroom door to what looked like a news photo from the Guatemalan earthquake. The large and long cupboard had fallen off the wall and buried the fixtures in an avalanche of towels, sheets, and bottles. The little floor space that was visible was paved with broken glass. The piercing smell of Listerine pervaded the place. It took a major excavation to find our toothbrushes.

We discovered that the previous cupboard had been held up by just four short screws. How had it endured for the past five years!

Then, just two weeks later, I was in Mum's bathroom searching for a Band Aid. I heard a rending sound, and her cupboard collapsed into my arms. Some things fell into the toilet, but the main structure fell on me, nearly flattening me out. In both cases, Merritt Crawford, our new resident builder, came to carry away the remains, then make us new cupboards.

Crawford's cupboards would probably have endured to the end of the world. The houses on our side of the campus, however, were the ones first targeted for demolition.

The Baesa campus was being sold to be developed as a cemetery. The transaction was nebulous, seemingly too complicated for even the negotiators to understand. In March 1977 two-thirds of the property was cordoned off, and bulldozers began tearing up the landscape, and smoking us out with grass fires. "Your house will be demolished in June," they told us.

We counted on the general *laissez-faire* attitude of the East to delay matters in our favor. We were right. The move to the spacious Silang campus did not begin until a year later, so we didn't have to suffer sudden eviction.

Meanwhile, Walt's dissertation project had been lying dormant ever since our return to the Philippines. Regular classroom events, field work with the students, grad-

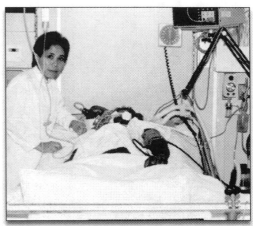

Seeing our "Filipina daughters" finish their education gave us much pleasure. As a graduate nurse our Lolita married and then worked for many years in Saudi Arabia. She supported her parents and educated her own two boys. In this picture she tended a comatose accident victim in Riyadh.

uation, and a rash of weddings. The pressure of end-of-year projects never let up.

For my part, I had encumbered myself with various extras. The most demanding—and most enjoyable—was the founding and editing of *Spotlight on PUC.* It took an enormous amount of time and had to be produced at regular intervals. My English teachers supported me, and together we produced a creditable campus journal.

I had also resumed my movie-script writing with Jim Zachary.

At the end of October I retired from public view to type Walt's dissertation. For the last time. We could not endure the thing lying around unfinished any longer. I spent hours and days hunched over the typewriter, with glazed eyes and swimming head. Occasionally, I would stagger out the door, walk to the gate, and then return to the typewriter. His Doctor of Ministry degree was almost within grasp now. Andrews University was one of only seven seminaries fully accredited for the degree in the United States. We couldn't fall by the wayside now.

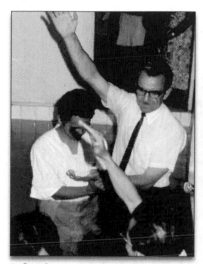

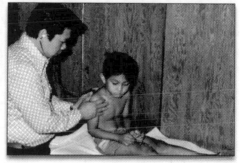

Left. A baptism at the Manila Evangelistic Center. Top right. Evangelistic meetings were aided by singing groups and public health students from the College. Right. Physicians from Manila Sanitarium and Hospital served on outreach teams.

Finally, at high noon on Friday, November 19 we photocopied the full text. Then we drove to the airport and mailed the manuscript off to Andrews University. Next, we gave a vesper program in the Pasay church.

After that, we checked in to Bayside Hotel. We had fled our home in Manila's north suburbs, where books and papers filled every room. We would spend thirty-six hours in a hotel on the south side. We had never done such a thing before. There we were absorbed into a totally neutral environment, among strangers. We were free from every form of responsibility. Soothing! Amazing!

Our 11th-floor room overlooked the vast city and Manila Bay. We slept non-stop for eighteen hours. After a couple of hours eating and walking along Roxas Boulevard, we returned to our room. We slept again, another fourteen hours. After lunching on pizza in the new Harrison Shopping plaza, we went home. We had no more time to spend on our self-prescribed rest cure.

In many ways Walt's professional work ran parallel to mine, but our paths

Left. For sheer pleasure and relaxation, visiting Andrew and Marion Dressler at the U. S. Naval Base at Subic Bay. There Andy supervised the power plant. **Right.** Being on Base rather equated with being back home. The U.S.S. *Tripoli* emphasized what "American presence" means in faraway places.

didn't cross very often. His chief task over our last three Philippine years was the launching of the Masters of Health Science program. He had been working toward this goal for the past six years. Loma Linda University would support the program with faculty members for the next three years. The project started off with twenty-three full time and five part-time students. Included was the first Seventh-day Adventist student to come out of Nepal for higher education.

In order to provide transportation for various Seminary and health field-projects the school acquired three vans. They were all old, and usually they lived in our driveway where Walt maintained them. The worst was the White Elephant. A creaky, disreputable derelict Dodge it had literally been retrieved from the junkyard. I long entertained a prejudice against it. Not because it was old but because it was excessively ugly. It had huge, lumpy curves and had been painted dead white. It would probably take carbon-dating to discover how old it actually was. Occasionally, it worked remarkably well. At those times, I regretted the evil thoughts that I had had. (And had sometimes voiced.)

Being enthusiastic about every facet of the new Health Evangelism program, Walt conducted a Five-Day Plan to Stop Smoking—on top of his summer classes. When he opened the session at Clark Air Force Base, fifty-six military people enrolled.

At the end, one woman announced, "I've been smoking four-and-a-half packs a day. Now I am down to just ten cigarettes a day." Walt made appropriate congratulatory sounds, but he well knew that she really had not yet made the break.

The liquid diet recommended for the first day shocked many. During the fourth session, another girl told Walt, "Well, you've done it again! First, you tell us no tea and coffee, then, diet, and now no alcohol. I know! Tomorrow night you'll tell us, 'No sex.'"

Walt laughed. "You come and see. You'll find out otherwise. There are lots of good things left."

Then Walt turned over some of the questions to a medical doctor who was part of the group. "Here I am a patient," he said. "Not a doctor." He knew the answers, and his talking had quite an impact on the group. "All of this makes me feel pretty stupid," he admitted. "I know all of the medical reasons, and yet I'm here trying to get help for myself. Just like the rest of you."

Any time we left home we had no way of knowing just how or when we might be coming back. One weekend Walt and I drove up to Subic Bay. Our friend, Andy Dressler, was the Chief Engineer at the power plant on the Naval Base. Active in church work, he and his wife Marion had been studying with a twenty-year-old Seabee for the past three months.

Now Michael Barrett wanted to be baptized. The assignment seemed straightforward enough. Spend Sabbath with Andy and Marion and then come home.

Mike had been in the brig (prison) for arson and was due to be shipped home to finish out his sentence. "I went wild and did it all when I got to the Philippines," he admitted cheerfully.

On our way down to Officers Beach, we could see the storm that was to become Typhoon Didang blowing in. Ten-foot surf crashed in, and the whole bay swirled in a muddy fury, full of debris. The storm had eaten away the edge of the beach, so that it dropped off sharply just where the waves were breaking.

To be sure, it was the most violent baptism Walt ever undertook. Mike

Transportation was a constant distress. **Left.** The "White Elephant" was the most pathetic of all of the College vehicles. **Right.** Without a van, however, local buses were the only other option. An unpredictable choice even at the very best of times.

was knocked down twice, but finally he came up the third time with a big smile and "Thank you."

By nightfall the roads had closed in. So, for the next three days we just sat around the Dresslers' house. "We're stuck with you," Andy grinned. "And you're stuck with us." We spent the evenings working jigsaw puzzles and listening to tapes. With such congenial company during our "quarantine," there was nothing for which we needed to be pitied.

By Tuesday, however, we knew that we had to get back home. We abandoned the Peugeot and our suitcase—as well as Walt's last set of wet clothes. Andy took us to the Victory Liner bus station, carrying one small tote bag.

During the five hours it took to get to Manila we had leisure to consider the current depredations of the floods. Splinters of demolished road signs and fragments of houses floated in whirlpools. The rice paddies had disappeared into muddy lakes with treetops waving out of them. Carabaos lounged along the tops of the few rice-paddy dikes that were visible. The water appeared to be a bit much even for them.

People peered out of their upper floors, watching the traffic swim past. Dogs and cats crouched together on the roofs. One house, with the windows thrown wide open, was holding a funeral wake. The place was ablaze with lights. In front of a marble-works shop pallid images of saints stood knee deep in the water making benign gestures over the devastation while living people crowded in among them. Elsewhere pigs, people, and chickens had taken to higher ground, along with snakes and lizards. In some places little boys were busy catching monstrously ugly mudfish.

Obviously, no car could have made the journey. One little Renault came surging by like a half-surfaced submarine, the water dashing up over the windshield. He must have soon stalled out somewhere. Meanwhile, the old bus churned through three and four feet of water as if negotiating the rapids above Niagara Falls. Its sheer weight kept it on the road. Bridges had been washed out under ten feet of water. In Guagua we disembarked and found a Baliwag Transit bus with a plywood body and low roof. It professed to be going to Divisoria Market, so we scrambled aboard and wedged ourselves in behind the driver.

At home Mum and the girls had kept everything under control. Except our bed which was soaked. We were so grateful to be back, we didn't care. Everything was clammy. Paper mushed up in our hands like wilted Kleenex. Shoes, and books grew a coating of green mold in just a few hours.

Six days later the radio announced that the road to Subic Bay was open. Walt promptly boarded the bus again and brought Little Peugeot home.

Meanwhile the monsoon rains had really set it. It became absolutely imperative to get our rusty gutter pipes replaced. We

Typhoons were painfully commonplace. Left. One parked the freighter *Shun Hing* on Roxas Boulevard. Right. Another left Walt frying eggs in the open fireplace in Baguio.

had to divert the waterfalls off the roof and protect our low-lying doorsills. At times like these we knew that we would have been much better off in a high Filipino home instead this "modern American" version of a house.

The repairmen arrived early one morning. Shortly thereafter a mighty shattering of glass summoned everyone from all over the house. The men on the roof had pried off a great, twisted length of old pipe. It swung against the house and broke seven panes of glass in the big dining room windows.

A cheerful, smiling face peered down over the edge at us. If the typhoon currently threatening us that day had actually come, we would have really have been "in strife," as the Australians say. As it was, we swept up the glass and urged the workmen to repair the window before the end of the day. (They actually did.)

That night we went to bed to the sound of the rain on the roof. In full bloom, our Dame de Noche by the window breathed rare fragrance over us. Despite the over-dose of sensory stimulation, we slept soundly through the warm, living Philippine night. A few days later when another typhoon brushed us with its tail, we had an overcast sky with a cool, vigorous breeze. A vast relief from the usual steam heat, and we treasured very hour of that too. This, in essence, is the weather of the tropics.

At church in the College Auditorium (that cavernous old Quonset hut) the wind whistled through the palm trees and rumbled among the sheets of corrugated roofing all through the service. The birds who lived in the rafters had to sing louder than usual to make themselves heard. Recently returned from a three-month public relations trip in the U.S. and Canada, Dr. Roda, the college president, delivered his sermon. He concluded by singing a very moving solo, "Don't Spare Me." The wild bird songs blending with his voice created a heaven-bound atmosphere that was quite indescribable.

Perversely I have always enjoyed tropical storms. Sometimes we dragged chairs out into the front yard to watch the moon play shadow games among our palm trees.

Sometimes we had a full moon in a clear sky, making light sparkles on the palm fronds. Toward Manila Bay we could see curly banks of clouds, shot through with flashes of lightning. Not a sound. Just an endless fireworks display, with the lightning coming in streaks, in balls, and in fans.

Then again, the stars might hang overhead while a cloudbank of thunderheads silhouetted themselves against the clear night sky. They were shot through with lightning, at one moment illuminating the whole landscape and at another emitting jagged spikes of electricity. What a breath-taking show! One had to recall the text in Matthew: "As the lightning cometh out of the east and shineth even unto the west, so also shall the coming of the Son of Man be." (24:27)

I remember also thinking of America's Bicentennial fireworks displays at home. The celestial fireworks we had in our front yard, however, put all of that to shame by comparison.

Although we didn't realize it at the time, December of 1976 was the last time we could celebrate a "normal" Christmas in Baguio. Gulleys and we had only a week left before our kids returned to Far Eastern Academy

We soon jettisoned our original plans for going to the Banaue Rice Terraces. The entire family was too tired, and most of us had been "off color" for several days. One threw up after breakfast and another after lunch, and we had general plumbing problems all round. We arrived in Baguio that Monday night only to find that just one of the two cabins we had reserved was actually available. Some functionary in some office had rented out the living space twice!

Therefore, fusing our two families—and, to a great degree, our individual personalities—the eleven of us moved into a two-room cabin designed for four people!

In the living-room-kitchen area, Grandma occupied a lower bunk, while John's 6' 3" frame more than filled the top bunk. Lorna and Sharon bedded down on a mattress behind the bamboo settee on which Sonya slept. James had a saggy old army cot set on the hearthstone in front of the fireplace. Larry stretched his 6' 1" length out on the settee cushions, and that filled most of the remaining space in the middle of the room.

The little bedroom was filled almost entirely by three single beds. By pushing them together we had enough surface to sleep Norman and Leona and Walt and me. A poll-taking among the four of us the first morning indicated that we should drag the mattresses off onto the floor tonight for more

Baguio will always hold "healing memories" for anyone who worked in Manila. Left. The cabins were plain and simple to a degree. Top right. By day, one of the finest golf courses in the Orient. Right. By night, table games by the fireside.

comfort. Walt's tract of sleep-space on the far northern edge was relatively firm, but Norman at the southern extremity was folded into a slow-slung valley. In between, Leona slept on the cracks. Hers had a tendency to separate and let her down into a chasm while mine resembled a long, uneven mountain range (the Rockies, perhaps). I spent the night scaling one side or the other and balancing on the lumpy peaks.

The single, semi-functional bathroom was accessible only through the bedroom. So the multitudes kept trouping through, across our feet. There had been much burglary in the Baguio cabins in recent years. On this occasion, however, we gave it little thought. It is doubtful that any thief, no matter how enterprising, could achieve much success in that cabin. There were very few places where he could even step without trampling on some portion of a human anatomy.

These crowded conditions seemed to have been a happy accident after all. The kids got a taste of the kind of togetherness we oldsters (Le and I) used to know in other communal family holidays in other years now long gone.

There were, of course, minor physical concerns. In the main, we spent

We drove up to the Banaue Rice Terraces in Ifugao Northern Luzon. At 5,000 feet above sea level, these 2,000-year-old terraces are, the Filipinos say, the "Eighth Wonder of the World."

our time leisurely. Visiting, playing games, sleeping, doing what we pleased. Wisely we academics left all of our books and papers back in Manila. Nothing can deteriorate a vacation faster than their presence.

Back in good form again with hearty appetites, the kids put away the groceries at a great rate. Obviously cooking and eating became popular activities. The cool, upland air, pine-forested roadways, and poinsettia gardens invited walking expeditions.

We always enjoyed wandering through the markets looking at mountain handicrafts, even when we had little money to spend. One day we went down to our favorite woodcarvers' village and made several purchases. Special things we wanted to acquire before we left the country. The Filipinos are so talented in these arts.

With some of our teenagers planning, in a relatively short time, to leave the family nest, it's not surprising that they were thinking of major items for their own homes. After so many years as "MKs" (Missionaries' Kids) it would be too bad not to have a few exotic items to keep for themselves. So our "wealthy bachelors," John (Gulley) and Larry each bought an elegantly carved coffee table for themselves (US$45).

"I'll have the money for that table earned by the end of January," Larry remarked airily. Much involved in electronics and aviation jobs in Singapore, he would keep his word. Lorna bought a handsome pair of large horse-head bookends. She proposed to carry them back to Singapore in her own two hands.

Climbing the hill back into Baguio City in the twilight, we enjoyed an extra bonus. A spectacular sunset laid out in rainbow stripes of rose, gold, aqua and purple spread across the China Sea. We just had to pull off the road to

Left. We became acquainted with almost every wood-carver family around Baguio. **Right.** Sometimes we stood by and watched them make the very piece we intended to buy.

look at it. The black profile of the mountains, with a lone tree here and there, superimposed lively curves against the brilliant, level cloud lines. We spent the rest of the way back to the cabin regretting that none of us had a camera to record the scene.

Then I found a cabinet-maker in Pasay City. I designed an "entertainment center" (though the name had not yet been invented). In three parts, it contained all of our stereo components with storage for records and tapes, plus a few ornamental pieces. It also provided housing for my three Chinese household gods (Longevity, Fortune, and Happiness), carved out of bone. Also a tall, revolving bookcase to match. Benny Dy executed it all in hard *tanghile* wood, a masterpiece of Philippine craftsmanship. My delight was two-fold. I had designed it, and the job was "done right."

CHAPTER 7

Off-campus Ventures

Naga View Academy in Bicol used to be a kind of younger sibling to Philippine Union College. Walt and I enjoyed the occasional necessity of going down there. Such a relief from the seething city that constantly leaned over our compound walls and breathed on us with a foul breath!

On one occasion we would be sucked into a dust bowl. At another time we waded through gumbo mud. The road was innocent of gravel and had no foundation. The rocks thrown into the sludge just disappeared, sinking all the way down through to South America, for all I knew. The cement-block guest room featured spiders, lizards, bumble bees and hornets' nests. And rats, big as cats.

Still, someone always thought to set a jam jar full of pink roses on the table between our cots. Whatever the weather, we barely set down our bags before half a dozen smiling faces crowded in at the door to say "Happy Arrival." Indeed, we loved going to Naga View.

That area of the island of Luzon offers much of interest. Mayon Volcano stands amid the blackened, overgrown remains of the old church and monastery that perished in 1914. Today the green slopes are still grooved with the fresh, long, black scars of the 1968 eruption. Always Mayon sits there, beautiful and dangerous, wearing a curled cloud of white steam on her head while magnificent white cloud banks roll around her shoulders. Surely one of the world's most lovely mountains. I have always felt that I could go there every day and never weary of looking at that perfect volcanic cone.

One time Walt and I rode a "Baby Bus" to the town of Tabaco, a town long known for its *abaca* industry. Every crevice was filled with human flesh, to say nothing of the chickens, bags of rice, coconuts, and all of the rest. Stereo "music" blared out at 500 decibels of sound. Eventually when the driver of

Naga View Campus. Upper Left. A room in the girls' dormitory. Upper Right. Fresh out of the cold showers three young residents dry their hair. Lower Left. A more Spartan room in the Boys' dormitory. Lower Right. Before she entered the Comm household, Zeny de la Roca worked as the summer cook at Naga View College.

the bus decided that the bus was full enough to make the trip worthwhile, we rumbled off.

Every little house we passed seemed to have hemp-rope-making as its own little family industry. Miles of rope lay under the palm trees. Children, youths, and grandpas were all busy twisting, twisting the fibers and then laying up the honey-colored coils on every side. We purchased a few *abaca* handicrafts, including a small rug for our very small sitting room.

Primarily, of course, we went to Naga to make whatever educational contribution we could to the struggling little ten-year-old school. (Since those days, it has grown up to become Naga View Adventist College. Right now the Academic Dean there is Dr. Zenaida Castardo. That is, our own Zeny from the old PUC days!)

When my nephew Kevin visited the Philippines for the second time we took him on the twelve-hour road trip down to Naga. In addition to our school responsibilities we hoped to make the trip an outing for the whole family. That it was.

After passing through a particularly severe rainstorm, our van broke down, about fifty miles out of Naga City. Leaving Walt and Larry on the roadside, Mum, Kevin, Lorna and I found a little white jeep willing to take us into town, explaining that the van was *patay* (dead).

Finally a series of providential encounters enacted in knee-deep mud around the campus got us all together again by sundown. The rest of the

Top left. Between Walt's health evangelism students and Dorothy's English Department, our small living room frequently overflowed with guests. If they came one group at a time, the logistics were manageable. Bottom left. "Grandma Minchin" posed in a celebratory graduation picture with some of her "Voice of Youth" young people with whom she worked untiringly throughout the Philippine years. Bottom right. She conferred with a couple of her "ministerial boys" at the dining room table. (Always fascinated with handicrafts, she hand-crocheted the elegant tablecloth herself.)

PUC's campus provided an amazing variety of international cuisine. Left. One of the graduate student's wives prepares *saging* (fried banana). Right. Comms' house provided the backdrop for the feast. No single house could ever contain the crowd.

weekend included a substantial earthquake, soul-warming church services, and, as usual, round of farewells from our Naga friends. Ever the horticulturist, Kevin discovered a different kind of *gabi* plant to take home and plant in our garden in Manila. The big heart-shaped leaves had soft, fleshy stems patterned like little rattlesnakes.

Naga View was simply the exemplar of the many assignments that, from time to time, took us out of Manila. As Walt and I made our off-campus journeys, however, my mother, Leona Minchin, was not pining away at home. Unless circumstances required that she function as the "commanding officer" during our absence, she had an agenda of her own. She made numerous jungle journeys with the young people she so much loved to be with. Every holiday time and every possible weekend in between, they traveled somewhere conducting their Voice of Youth meetings in the *barrios,* far and wide.

Suddenly our horizons expanded. Having long ago discovered joys of international living and friendships, we highly approved of a bold new venture begun in the summer of 1976. The Seminary (Far East) started conducting extension schools in several places—Indonesia, Japan, and Taiwan for starters. This move injected a new zest to our graduate programs at Philippine Union College.

Walt's first assignment was to teach at the Taiwan Adventist College.

As usual, we had to go through the labors of getting clearances from the military government to leave the Philippines. I involved myself in the dreary affair because I wanted to join him in Taiwan at the end of the month. The College was near the famous Sun Moon Lake and would be well worth the effort to get there.

Therefore, Walt and I set off one morning to start the process. I determined absolutely not to get angry. Actually things went pretty well, considering the hazards of wallowing through miles of government red tape. We could not, however, quite get through unscathed. Near the end we had to rotate through just six more offices. We filled out the umpteenth form and shoved it through a slot in a blue wooden cage. Inside we saw a company of girls and one lone male.

Walt then hurried downstairs to buy documentary stamps off the street. (You had to get them from vendors on the street who made almost 100% profit on the sales.) Meanwhile, when I received our documents, I found that Walt was listed as American. I've always held the conviction—based on some kind of intuitive sense, I suppose—that all of one's documents (however many they might be) should match one's passport in all essential details. I requested the girl at the slot to make the correction.

Since the window was about waist-level for me and eye-level for her, this arrangement made communication a little strained. "American and Canadian are not the same thing." I bent low to peer through the blue crack.

The people inside discussed this apparently new concept among themselves. The word American would be removed, they agreed. The typist typed again. Lo, the word came back the same. American.

I renewed my request. "He is Canadian. I am American. It is not the same." More dialogue inside. By now the entire room was alerted to the crisis.

At this point, Walt returned clutching the documentary stamps in his sweaty fist. He presented his passport. It was blue and mine green. Maybe two different colors would help. More delay and discussion. The typist resumed her post. From where I stood, however, I couldn't see exactly what she was doing.

Presently we received the papers, Walt's on top. Sure enough, it read

Canadian. Score! The girls smiled, we thanked them and departed for the next office.

On the way down the stairs, I glanced at my paper. It also read Canadian. They'd gone all out to make me happy (since I had been so insistent) and had changed both papers. So we returned to the blue cage and took up our burden again. By now, I'm sure the officials felt that we were just being difficult. After all, any white face anywhere in the Philippines was automatically labeled *Americano*. Why not?

When one contemplated the business of getting court clearances in those days, he must wonder—before that task was accomplished—what ever made him or her think that they wanted to travel anywhere anyway. Fortunately, the human psyche recovers from these traumas fairly quickly, especially when it finds some theme more challenging and creative to dwell on other than toiling through government offices.

The most curious part of it all—which really ought to be researched by some social scientist—is the fact that customs, immigration, and city halls all over the world bear a sickening resemblance to one another. It has always been my private belief that The System somehow destroys the humanity of any person who is employed there for long spans of time. It withers up the life forces. It weakens the brain.

In any case, having worked double time in order to earn a few days' absence from campus, I eventually headed toward Taiwan. First, I went to Hong Kong on a glorious flying day in June. There I was to meet Larry and my nephew Kevin who had flown out to meet his cousin at Far Eastern Academy (his first trip to Singapore).

A couple of days earlier I had developed a vicious sore throat and could barely talk. Still I determined to let nothing interfere with my plans. The plane had barely reached cruising level, however, when excruciating pain in my ears struck me down. Surely my eardrums were bursting. The stewardess took one look at me and offered me an airsick bag. All I really wanted to do was open the door and step outside.

The landing was even worse. Then the pain was replaced by a deep-seated ache and about 90% deafness. I took an airport bus into Kowloon and walked

Shopping for bargains in Hong Kong. Above right. One of our favorite merchants was surrounded by modern technology, but, for totaling up the bill, he preferred the more reliable abacus. (After all, it has proved itself for well over 2,000 years.) Above. Kevin grazed around in an antique china shop. Right. The beauty of the display in a jade shop was breathtaking.

to the Grand Company. (In Chinese establishments one encounters an unusual quantity of "Grand" places.) Mr. Lui's photographic supply store was scarcely larger than your bathroom, but it was crammed full of all the shopping thrills for which Hong Kong is famous. I had to open negotiations with him because I had a lot of purchasing to do for the College and other people.

Then I then hurried back to the airport to meet the boys' Cathay Pacific flight from Bangkok. I confess to a great surge of pleasure and pride when I saw our two young giants (both now well over six-feet tall) stride out of the baggage claim area, Kevin looking like a blond Norse god and Larry a hirsute wonder with a red beard.

As we walked through the concourse, we saw a knot of people interspersed among an agitated bunch of photographers illuminating the scene with floodlights and flashbulbs. As we pressed in to look over the heads of the crowd, who should be the center of attraction but Muhammed Ali! A complete babble of twittering females, kids, and adoring men pressed around him. He moved about in a lordly fashion, permitting views of his marvelous physique from various angles. Kevin snapped a couple of pictures to memorialize this surprising encounter. (From the evening newspaper we understood that Ali was en route to Manila. As it turned out, he became a kind of folk hero there.)

Our reservation at the Grand Hotel had been made for us by the Hong Kong Mission hostess, Miriam McLaren. It was designated for "Mrs. Comm and two children." The desk clerk eyed the two "children" towering over me with open interest. He had ordered another cot into the room. Built for a small child, however, the cot was an utter failure, so we hauled the mattress off onto the floor.

It was early evening before we got the Star Ferry and arrived at the hospital. I immediately went to the Emergency Room to find whatever doctor might be on hand to make repairs on my ears. There I found a hairy youth, not unlike Larry. Lately graduated from Loma Linda University, he prescribed medication and desired to see me again tomorrow.

By now my weariness and pain began to overtake me in earnest. When I filled out my questionnaire for the hospital records, I wrote my birth date as October 17, 1976. Larry called that error to my attention. Having corrected that, I then wrote in my sex as "5." Although the boys had a great laugh at my expense, they hung over me solicitously for the rest of the evening as they guided my tottering footsteps from place to place. I learned one lesson today: "Don't ever fly when you have something—anything—wrong with your ears!"

We spent the evening on Victoria Peak enjoying one of the most magnificent night views in the world. Translucent acres of glass in modern skyscrapers, punctuated by neon lights. Later we took the cog railway down the mountain and then the ferry back to our hotel in Kowloon.

At noon the next day we headed for Macau, the tiny (eleven square miles), 400-year-old fragment of European colonialism still clinging to the coast of mainland China. Forty miles southwest of Hong Kong Island, the colony was founded by the Portuguese in 1557. It served as a trading center between China and Japan and between both of those nations and Europe. It also served as a

Left. Kevin Eckert and Larry Comm stood in line for immigration inspection in Macau. Right. The boys descended into the depths of Fortalez do Monte, built in 1616 by Jesuit missionaries. Later, the governor seized the fort for the defense of the struggling Portuguese colony.

vital base for the introduction of Christianity into China and Japan.

We had another glorious day for travel—sunny blue-and-white with magnificent cloud banks rolling over the coastal hills of China. In a long, steady spurt of foam, our hydrofoil, like an agile, blue-bottomed beetle, shot through the inlets and among the islands. The Red Ensign flew proudly from its stern. At that time Hong Kong remained loyally British.

The Macau dock promptly introduced us to a fascinating mixture of Portuguese and Chinese cultures. It's definitely Chinese but with a European colonial twist. The people themselves presented a thorough genetic mixture. Chinese with hazel eyes and long noses and Europeans with Chinese eyes and complexions.

We paused for visas at the Immigration desk. The Chino-Portuguese officer looked at Larry's and my passports. "Brother and sister?" he enquired.

Startled, we both said, "No!"

He studied Larry's beard and ventured again, "Husband and wife then?"

Actually, that little encounter provided me with some leverage on Larry. "Any day you are mistaken for my husband," I remarked later, "it's time to

Bushy animals graze through the grounds of Taiwan Adventist Hospital. Upper left. A large topiary lion rests by the path. Upper right. A giraffe towers over a coiled snake. Lower left. A pair of monkeys show off. Lower Right. Two leafy peasants pound rice.

take a few years off your appearance by trimming up that beard." I really hoped to spare Mum and the PUC campus the debilitating shock seeing him coming home looking like some shaggy prophet come in out of the wilderness.

We spent the afternoon wandering around rich casinos like the gold palace of the Lisboa Hotel. Also, the dog-racing *quinellas* and the ruins of the Cathedral that once mothered Asian Christianity. Then came the Kum Iam Tong Temple (13th-century Ming Dynasty) and Citadel Sao Paul de Monte, the well-preserved fort built by the Jesuits.

We returned to Hong Kong under overcast skies. The junks passed us in full sail along the coast, going out to their night fishing.

Later that night my son casually asked, "Where's that new cordless razor you bought for Dad yesterday?" When Larry came out of the bathroom, he still had his red side chops that made him look Victorian, but we did have measurable improvement. The beard was gone!

The next day the boys and I visited the houseboat village of Aberdeen. The thirty-minute double-decker bus ride out there provided us with the minutest details of street life. Vendors of smelly dried fish and fruit. Butcher shops displaying the carcasses of not only pigs, fowls, and conventional carnivore fare, but also rats! Fortune-telling and street cosmetology of all kinds was available on all sides. Buddhist prayer papers hung in every doorway. On the doorsills slept fat dogs. (Being a fat dog in China does not mean that someone loves you. It means that you're just about ready to be served up as an entrée at the table.)

The scene among the boats themselves revealed yet another world. Families at the doors bargaining with vendors of passing sampans. Squid and fish drying on the roofs. Cats and dogs tied on the decks, with hens cackling in cages suspended over the side. Women toiling at womanly tasks, babies tied on their backs. The children in, under, around, and between the boats, swimming laughing and shouting. Around and through and under it all, the dirty, sluggish water. It's a lifestyle that is almost incomprehensible even to the most experienced visitor.

Then we three parted ways. The boys (with most of my Hong Kong purchases) flew home to Manila, and I went on to Taipei. The pain in my ears remained, but, at least, it was bearable.

No one met me at the airport because, as was usual, Walt never received my telegram. I hailed a taxi and got into it, despite the grumpy look the driver gave me. "Adventist Hospital, Pa Te Road," I said, enunciating clearly. English was a ultra-foreign language here.

He nodded "yes," and away we went. Quite shortly things didn't look right to me. The hospital is near the airport, and it costs only NT$16.00 to get there. Now the meter was climbing steadily into the twenties.

I protested, but the driver grunted and said OK. When the meter reached

NT$30.000, I insisted that he stop. He pulled into a large hotel in a part of the city that I'd never seen before. Providentially the doorman there knew some English, and I explained my predicament to him. He and the driver had a lively exchange, after which the latter gunned up the old motor again. We were off, with him breathing fire and brimstone at every stop sign and inter-section. Not one intelligible word could we exchange.

At last, with a vast sense of relief, I recognized Pa Te Road and the hospital grounds with its famous ornamental gardens. The meter now stood at NT$60.00. I got out, being careful to remove all my luggage with me at the same time.

Inside, late as it was, I found an English-speaking cashier at the desk and asked him to negotiate with the taxi driver. Since the man had said "Yes" when I gave him the address, I didn't see why I should pay him more than the regular fare of NT$16.00. Another noisy exchange outside, the driver stomping in to finish off his rant at top volume inside the lobby. He must have been heard in the most distant patient's room.

I gave him NT20.00, thinking it to be a fair enough compromise. He steamed back out to his car. I thought that was the end of the drama when the front door burst open again, and, amid another volley of oaths, he threw four dollars change at me. Good thing I can't understand Chinese, but everyone in the hospital got a late-evening show at my expense.

When the air cleared a little, I phoned Silva Gryte. She lived on the hospital compound, and her husband was the OB-GYN doctor. The kind, motherly soul hurried over. "You look exhausted! Come to my house and let me get you to bed."

A hot shower and a bed! Paradise indeed!

The luxurious train journey down to Taiwan Adventist College the next day was worth waiting for. Air-conditioned with huge picture windows (with lace curtains, and plush reclining chairs. Uniformed hostesses took us through the Oriental towel routine. The towels arrived on a tray in tight little rolls (hot or ice cold, depending on the weather). Wet and freshly antiseptic. You wash your hands and face and feel alive again.

We were not out of the city suburbs before the hostess brought teabags.

At the Snake Restaurant in the Night Market in Taipei, one of the proprietors slits a highly poisonous snake from top to bottom (for medicinal purposes.) Right. Another mixes snake blood with wine for a customer to drink. To his left hang the remains of the snakes that have already been harvested for blood, gall, and (ultimately) steaks.

The tea-boy followed with a huge teakettle laced into a thick, padded jacket. A marvel of coordination he snatched my covered glass out of the rack by my seat, flipped it open, poured in the scalding water, snapped the glass lid down again, and set it back into the rack. All in one motion. The drink was still warm when I reached Tai-Chung more than four hours later. The piped-in music alternated between Chinese and Western. "O Susanna" seemed a little incongruous as we swept through the lovely countryside with its brick cottages with peaked, tiled roofs clustered in family compounds. "Raindrops Falling on my Head," however, coordinated well with the rain that followed us all of the way.

Walt met me at Tai-Chung station, and we spent the night at the Grand Palace Hotel where the entertainment was gracious, even though we couldn't exchange a word with anyone. Surrounded by so many smiling faces I was able to forget the anathemas of the taxi driver the previous night.

Clearly my husband had enjoyed his stay in Taiwan. A curtain of rain,

A pottery factory in Taipei offers the best in the arts of China. Left. First the molded shapes and then (right) fine hand painting.

however, dropped over all of our plans for sightseeing. We couldn't get to Taroko Gorge, and in the heavy fog I couldn't even catch a glimpse of Sun Moon Lake and its great pagoda. Landslides closed the roads, and we had a very complicated journey just finding our way back to Taipei. In places the floods had washed out the grade to within inches of the tracks, and the four-hour train journey north stretched into seven hours.

Having lost out on the beauty spots in the south, we had two days in Taipei. The China Arts Pottery factory, a glass shop (where I acquired a marvelous little dragon), and the National Palace Museum. Out on the street we even had name chops made for ourselves. Walt's featured a horse and mine a *laohu*, one of those fat, grinning lions that are Chinese temple guardians.

Then came the All Night Market, our last stop after a marvelous Buddhist feast. Silva Gryte suggested we have dessert at the Snake Restaurant. Out front two men worked among cages of very poisonous snakes. The Ten Pacers, the Three Pacers, and so forth. "Ten Pacer" meant that after you're bitten by the snake you can walk ten paces before you drop dead.

The men would take out a snake, crack it like a whip, and brain it on the edge of the table. They hung it on a hook where it continued to writhe, even in death. Then they drained off the bile and blood into two little glasses. After mixing in a little wine, they offered the drink as a cure for "bad eyes." A well-dressed man in front of us paid NT$100 for one glass. He drank it at one drag, but I noticed that he kept swallowing afterwards, just to keep it down. The snake was then taken back to the kitchen to be transformed into soup or steaks.

All in all business was not that brisk, so the snake-men urged the blood-bile-and-wine drink on us. It happened that every one in our group was wearing glasses! Good potential clients, one would suppose. We went home that night not just physically weary but spirit-weary too.

Even so, as we boarded our flight to Manila, we were startled by the headlines in the newspaper put into our hands. Canada had denied Taiwan participation in the Olympic Games. Coming fresh from four weeks of unstinted Taiwanese hospitality, Walt suddenly turned into one irate, embarrassed Canadian.

Having Larry and Lorna at Far Eastern Academy in Singapore, gave us yet one more off-campus responsibility. Actually, it reconnected me with my home town. Of course the first time I visited there back in 1973, I did all of initial getting-back-to-home things. Things I really could not have explained to anyone—lest they laugh me to scorn. Then I wandered around to my heart's content, searching out strange little private things that no one else would know or understand. Even if I listed them, the reader might still be confused. For a six-year-old, however, these places had mattered a great deal.

For Lorna's eighteenth birthday I made a surprise visit to Singapore. On the morning of February 4, I woke her up in her dorm room. She didn't scream, as Larry predicted. In a series of little squeaks and gasps she cried, "Mummy! MUMMY! **MUMMY!**"

I was lodged in a double guest room opposite the dormitory

The long train journey from Taipei down to Taichung is accomplished in perfect, modern comfort.

and Larry and Lorna stayed with me. For the ten days I was in Singapore I became the visiting mother for all of the kids from PUC. This was a job that Ottis and Dottie Edwards did on a daily basis.

I fulfilled Lorna's request. I bought her a typewriter. A pumpkin

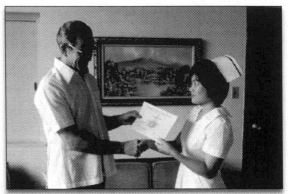

At the end of his summer classes in health evangelism Walt presented students with certificates of completion.

yellow portable Adler. In honor of his birthday three weeks later, Larry got a new trumpet so that he could really enjoy the Academy band. At a somewhat earthier level, Larry showed me around Thieves Market and the All Night Market. Of course, I had to visit my old 10 Woodleigh Close home, over on Upper Serangoon Road. The people living there thought it was their house. No so. In a special way, it will always be mine.

When his day came, Larry wrote a letter that was an anthem of joy. Friends at FEA rented a plane for him to take a flight over Singapore. Once in the air the pilot turned the controls over to him. He cruised over the city for half an hour, circling the Academy several times. The pilot recommended his skills. "I was rather proud of myself," wrote the eternally modest Larry.

I also spent time with old friends. Tony and Josephine Koh made sure that I got to eat

China's first emperor (2,250 years ago) made name chops more legal than a signature. Today, tourists may get their own names thus preserved out on the streets of Taipei.

Swimming around the little volcanic island in Taal Lake has unique possibilities. Dorothy and Larry found that the strange masses of dark green seaweed there could provide a credible wig for anyone lacking hair.

goring pisang (sweet fried banana). Heislers took vacation time and drove down from Penang to see me. Together we drove out to Jurong Cemetery to visit my Dad's grave.

Finally, on February 18, I staggered home to Manila. I was carrying cargo equal to at least three baggage allowances—much of it stuff for the college. I was so burdened I had to look back to see if I was leaving footprints in the pavement as I walked out to the plane.

The letter came in early 1977. I received my official invitation letter from President Norskov Olsen to join the Department of English at Loma Linda University. It was hardly a surprise. The possibility had been under consideration since our furlough year at Andrews University. College teaching jobs are never easy to come by, especially for one straggling in from years abroad. Finding the slot into which to drop can often be a major challenge. Therefore, I was deeply grateful. Walter quite happily expected to return to church pastoring.

Now, at last, our plans to leave the Philippines could become public. Although the needs of our teenagers made our Permanent Return imperative, I knew instinctively that maybe the greatest "mission adjustment" of our lives would be getting used to Los Angeles freeways and the California desert

In August my new chairman, Bob Dunn, phoned me. As usual, the call was transacted with difficulty. Nonetheless, it made me already feel welcome to the Department. I agreed to start my work on January 1, 1978. This would mean the scattering of our family around the earth for about six months.

I had no way, of course, of knowing what it was going to be like even surviving the last six months of 1977.

My last off-campus assignment was to conduct an extension school down at Mountain View College in Mindanao (April 27 to May 25). There I spent one of the most satisfying summers of my life. Indeed, it came as a kind of benediction to all of my work in the Far East.

Walt and I had taught summer school through April. I had weathered through an epidemic of thesis seminars, oral examinations and such. Also, I had promised at least two more scripts for Jim Zachary's public relations movies.

Since our work was going to keep us apart for the next two months, Walt

In a land full of good fruit, nothing ever surpassed the mangoes of Cebu

and I liberated ourselves with a leisurely week's holiday traveling down to Mindanao. As our PAL (Philippine Air Lines) plane headed south over Taal Volcano, we looked on the island within a crater, within a crater, within a crater. That was within a great lake that, in itself, was a vast, pre-historic volcanic crater. Down there somewhere above Lake Taal, we knew, lay the lovely new campus for Philippine Union College. (The campus where we would never live.)

Walt and I lingered through Bacolod, Iloilo, Cebu City, and Zamboanga City, eating mangoes and enjoying the beaches. Finally, we parted in Davao City. Walt returned to his tasks in Manila and then on to his second extension school in Taiwan. I waited for Don Christiansen and the Cessna plane to come pick me up.

Mountain View College is ringed by valleys and mountain ranges. At night it's cool enough for blankets. The old wood-paneled guest house where I stayed had fruit trees and a giant acacia in the back yard. An orchid tree stood

Mountain View College is in the highlands of Mindanao. In addition to its own waterfall, it has a campus limited only by the imaginations of those charged with developing it. Picnic tables in the pine grove invite solitude or communication, attractive for either occupation.

in the front. My meals came in three times a day, and fresh flowers filled the rooms. The friendly people who tended me anticipated desires I didn't even know I had!

I learned to enjoy getting up early, bundling on a sweater, and going to sit on the edge of the campus plateau to watch the sunrise over the Bukidnon Valley. I saw banks of purple clouds along the crests of the dusky, misty mountains, topped with light apricot curls of cloud that turn gold in rapidly growing intensity. When rents and gashes appeared in the purple bank, I could see a lot of activity going on behind. The sun was busy in his dressing room and was about ready to come out. Suddenly he burst over the top. He seemed to have cut himself on the upper edge of the mountains and bled all down through the valley. No wonder people from the beginning of time have been enticed into sun worship. Nothing else on earth is quite like sunrise and sunset. Especially in the Philippines.

Of the forty students in my Biblical Literature class, one young pastor usually came in first. Taking his front seat one morning, he sighed contentedly and leaned back with a big smile. "I always feel so happy when I come here. I start feeling good every time I walk through the door."

Surely that was one of the nicest rewards I have had for years. A real tonic for tired old professors. I had sixteen in the Humanities class, along with many "auditors" who couldn't get credit but who wanted to be there anyway.

Rarely I had known such long periods of solitude. Such large blocks of time to myself. I hoped to finish my current book manuscript, draft another script, and write a couple of articles I had promised. I even found new time

One of Dorothy's last major overseas responsibilities was conducting summer school at Mountain View College (1977).

for meditative personal study too.

One of my graduate students from PUC, Rose Neri, arrived the first week of May. Although she had been delayed in the hospital with a bout of pneumonia, she had made good her promise to follow me to MVC. Not really being programmed to be a hermit, I enjoyed having a housemate. Together we geared the house up for study first and everything else second. She occupied the kitchen table and worked on the examination copy of her M.A. thesis. I used the dining room table over by the east windows, overlooking the fragrant *calachuchi* (temple flower) trees. Sometimes two of us relaxed and just acted like two teenagers.

On my last night at MVC, just before supper I was presented with an elegantly wrapped box. In it lay a new dress that my students had secretly had made for me. "We would like to see you in this tonight," the note said. A kind of Islamic design in browns and lavender in a fine georgette fabric. It was something I might well have chosen for myself.

Supper with students and faculty in the cafeteria, was followed by a meeting in the Chapel for the distribution of certificates for the Extension School. Several students made testimonial speeches for me and the Lester Lonergans who had been teaching a health course for the Seminary. A number of farewell songs followed. Eventually, near midnight, I got back to my room to finish packing.

At 5.30 the next morning I heard singing at my window. "Still, Still with Thee When Purple Morning Breaketh," in close harmony. Indeed, a full-scale serenade! When I opened the front door, some fifty people came in. A number of faculty members made up for the twenty students who had gone home the previous day. "We have come to have morning worship together before you leave."

Sixteen girls came forward, each to put a flower lei over my head. *Calachuchi* flowers, asters and bougainvillea, stacked up to my ears. Then the

The College depended heavily the services of its own little Cessna plane to link itself with the outside world. At that time, Dr. Don Halenz was its pilot.

music—male quartets, ladies trios, plus two accordions. As the sunrise streamed into the living room, Pastor Atiteo gave a little devotional talk about Paul's leaving Tyre and all the people following him to the city gates. They had so many kind things to say. By the time I was supposed to make a response I could hardly speak a word.

I kept thinking of Jamaica, the only other place where we ever had serenades at our window. That had been the beginning of our overseas service. Now this was the end. That morning became much more than just leaving MVC. I was about to leave the Philippines and overseas service altogether.

As many as could pile into the pickup truck came down to the airstrip. Just as the pass was filling up with clouds, at 10.30 a.m., the Cessna lifted off. A heavy downpour caught us over the Del Monte pineapple plantations. I arrived in Manila just before curfew hour that night.

Some three weeks later Walt got home. He desired that his absence not be described as "vacation." His achievements had been many and complex. He taught two crash summer programs for the Seminary, one at PUC and one in Taiwan.

Left. At his 50th birthday party Walt had testified to his long efforts in graduate study by holding a candle burning at both ends. Right. It culminated in 1977 when he received his doctorate at Andrews University.

His non-stop flight from Taipei to Los Angeles developed severe engine trouble, and he had a two-night layover in Tokyo. Once arrived at Andrews University, he spent many days putting his dissertation into final (graduation) readiness. He did come back, however, with his DMin. degree clutched in his hand.

Finally, he spent week in Loma Linda to align his U.S. immigration status, to care for house business, and to help my sister Eileen move to another house. Lastly, he bought me a car to use when I arrived in California. A hulking big green Plymouth, alas.

CHAPTER 8

Some Rain Must Fall

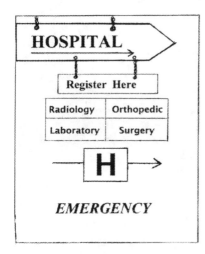

The last six months of 1977, our final year in the Philippines, brought us an astonishing number of afflictions.

I had so many demands every hour of the day, that I felt my feet running before I hit the floor in the mornings. Perhaps that is what went wrong while I was teaching at Mountain View College. With severe pains in my right foot I tried a pressure bandage, hot, cold, and ice. The lot. The misery worsened daily. The only cure seemed to be "Don't Walk." Once back in Manila I was first diagnosed with (and drugged for) gout.

Eventually, it turned out that I was not a Victorian hedonist after all. On July 22 (my twenty-sixth wedding anniversary) I had surgery to remove a large bone spur. "You'll be fine in two weeks," the surgeon predicted.

Two days earlier Lorna had come down with measles. About the same time Leona Gulley contracted a virulent flu and ran a temperature of 104 for a week. They both recovered. I, on the other hand, was still on crutches six weeks later. At eleven weeks I still could not wear shoes. (Was I going to arrive at my new job in California wearing flip-flops?)

Then another problem evolved. For several weeks Walt had been speaking of "arthritis" and "old age." One day in October, after a long, sleepless night with pain and numbness in his legs, he gave up and went to the doctor. Among other possibilities we heard the dread words "multiple myeloma," the disease that had years earlier suddenly killed his father.

Thankfully, that had not happened, but Walt was diagnosed with two slipped discs. They produced raging headaches.

Before I brought Walt home from the hospital, Ed Klein did the neighborly service of setting up traction equipment on our bed. We immediately

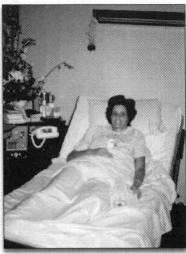

Upper left. Although it was situated on the far side of the city, Manila Sanitarium and Hospital was a good place to be, if you had to be sick. Lower left. "Grandma Minchin" was nursed through her bout with hepatitis. Upper right. Despite being a nurse herself, Leona Gulley had to take her turn as a patient. Lower Right. Dr. Arturo Estuita skillfully saw us through our various bouts with tropical diseases.

fastened Walt into that harness, and he stayed there twenty-four hours a day. Because he had never been sick before, I had to buy him a bathrobe so that he could carry on his schoolwork from bed. Being crippled myself, I had taken to conducting some of my smaller seminars in the convenience of our little living room.

In this manner, life went on according to plan—more or less. Because our time in the Philippines now had a visible cut-off date, we received several special visitors. My cousin Allan Laird and his wife Ivy came up from Perth, Western Australia. Then Dr. Neil Rowland, my mother's cousin, and his wife Marie stopped in on their way to a mission assignment at Mountain View College.

LaVal Comm, Walt's niece from Alberta, had been living with us for several months and teaching a few courses in the Science Department. In October she took to her bed with hepatitis.

The next happening after that was my second round of hepatitis. Walt had to rise directly out of his traction to take me to the hospital. There, I went through eleven bottles of intravenous dextrose in the first four days. For the first time in my life I became wretched enough to wonder if I was going to make it or not. The pain, nausea, and all-consuming sickness! I really didn't care one way or the other. Everyone around me had gamma globulin injections to save them from my fate.

My sister Eileen arrived in Manila on an excursion ticket on what was probably my worst hepatitis day. Blind, inert, and speechless, I probably had never been closer to death.

Ill as I was, I came to think that dying would be an easy and attractive solution.

The jaundice turned me pumpkin orange. Later, on one tottering trip to the bathroom, I inadvertently caught a glimpse of myself in the mirror. Hardly sustaining the shock, I almost collapsed. A face like a dry old leather shoe! I marveled that Walt could stand even to look at me. He just kept hanging around anyway, bless him! Trussed up in traction, he stayed with me through all of my hospital days.

During that time, our traction equipment at home did not sit idle. Leona Gulley kinked up her back. So she harnessed herself into our traction. Then she and Eileen could, at least, sleep together there and have a good visit. Otherwise most of the plans we'd made for my sister's visit were shipwrecked. Under some circumstances, however, just staying home and just looking at the people you love isn't all bad either. At least, we were all still together—alive.

The final act in the drama came when Mum had to lay aside her nursing labors and check into the hospital with her own case of hepatitis. She arrived the night before I was released from medical custody. Although her blood tests were almost as far off the scale as mine had been, fortunately she didn't have the pain, nausea and other evil manifestations that I had suffered. Oddly, her jaundice turned her papaya green.

In December Larry, Lorna, and the other FEA kids arrived home for Christmas. What with all of the sickness and with preparations for my departure to California, our festivities remained rather quiet. Besides, some of our friends (the Van Ornams and the Robinsons) had already moved down to the new PUC property in Silang. They were, of course, living in rather primitive conditions. Still, we couldn't help but feel a little sad about missing it all—the magnificent view, the fresh air, and the opportunities lying open for the new Philippine Union College campus.

Meanwhile I packed most of my books and files—at the rate of about one per day. I had to leave the rest for Walt and Mum, hoping the while that my husband wouldn't get into one of his let's-get-rid-of-it-all moods. Still, I had neither time nor strength to worry about any of it. (I even retained the vain hope of bringing my Yamaha organ home, but that didn't happen.)

I was scheduled to fly to Los Angeles on Sunday, New Year's Day, 1978.

On the Friday Walt had another attack. The pain, numbness and paralysis promptly propelled him back into the hospital. This time traction gave no relief. "If it is going to be surgery," he whispered, "I would like to go home." The barriers, however, seemed insurmountable. It was Rizal Day, and probably no business could be transacted anywhere. No seat on a plane would be available for at least a month. Court clearances to leave martial-law-bound Manila would take a week, at the very least.

Then the miracle began. LaVal gave up her reserved seat for her Uncle Walt. "I really don't mind a few more weeks in the Philippines." Next a phone call to Singapore resulted in a prompt committee vote. Immediately Don Van Ornam prepared a letter to take to the U. S. Embassy, and I wrote a petition to the Immigration authorities.

That Friday I covered twelve offices, dispensing signatures, photographs, and fingerprint substitutes. Somehow, each desk, as I approached it, was idle.

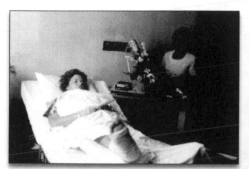

Left. Dorothy's foot surgery. Right. Her connection with crutches became much more protracted than anyone could have guessed.

Although the city traffic was as ridiculous as ever, I somehow oozed through every roadblock. By 4.00 p.m. I was on my way to line up Walt's visa for our overnight stay in Taipei. I ran the whole gamut in a single afternoon!

By 7.00 p.m. I was back at the hospital, exhausted but triumphant. I laid the air ticket, passport, and exit permit in Walt's hands. The poor man passed from surprise and disbelief to as much joy and friskiness as his pain would permit. Whatever the future held, we felt that, at this point, Providence was directing us to go home together the following Sunday.

One more grief faced us. Saturday morning little Rusty suffered a severe heart attack. Although the vet revived him, we left a very sick little dog behind, barely conscious. He and Mitzi were to have gone with me on the plane. Now Sinta and Muffin would occupy the dog crate.

Somehow the trauma of so much illness, along with last-minute tasks, dulled our senses. The momentum of the final events just swept us away before we really knew what had happened. I realized that we'd soon wake up and find that we had left a big piece of our hearts behind in the islands. How could it be otherwise after almost eight years?

On Sunday morning, Larry and Lorna stood among the crowd at the airport to see us off. This really wasn't the way things were supposed to be, and it showed on their faces. Still wearing my slippers, I limped along pushing

Walt's wheelchair all the way to the plane. On his lap he held the box containing the dogs. We had six pieces of hand luggage, and four massive boxes that had to be checked through. Mercifully, all of the officials who might have hindered us looked upon us with compassion and let us go.

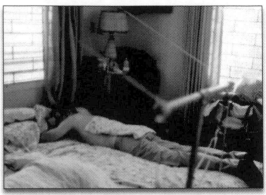

With the onset of his back troubles, Walt alternated between a heat pack (right side of the bed) and lying in traction (left side).

Since our telegram to Loma Linda had never arrived, there was no one to meet us when we arrived in Los Angles on Thursday. In due course, Eileen picked us up, and, like two battered refugees out of The Gulag, we collapsed in her cozy house for a few hours of rest. The next day a van came down from the University to take us to our new location.

Walt and I settled into the little two-bedroom apartment allotted to me just off the La Sierra campus. On Monday morning my teaching schedule and Walt's doctoring began simultaneously. After two weeks, milder methods of treatment proved ineffective. Drawn and pale, Walt looked thirty years older than when we had arrived. At this point he would not even have been able to make the Pacific crossing. Thankfully, we had arrived safely in the right place at the right time.

The morning of January 19 I walked—still in slippers—beside Walt's gurney to the doors of the operating rooms at Loma Linda Medical Center. In the waiting room I sat in a cocoon of isolation for four hours. "We found what we were looking for (a huge herniated disc)," the surgeon announced cheerfully at the end. "He's going to be a whole lot better now." Then, he added, "I don't know how he has lived through this past month." Actually, we had begun to wonder that ourselves.

Walt filled his post-op days with rest, walking, phone calls and visiting

Among visitors coming to see us before we left the Philippines were cousins from Western Australia. (L-R). Allan Laird, Ivy Laird, Dorothy, Walt.

friends and family. I worked through my first quarter of teaching and kept hoping that my foot was not going to keep me lame forever. Together we planned for the house we had fallen in love with and were buying, over on Sunnyvale Drive in south Riverside.

Finally, on Monday, March 5, Walt was able to do what he always hoped he could do. That is, fly back to Manila to finish out the school year at Philippine Union College. Although I had wonderful new accessibility to friends and family, I was still alone with only two dogs to greet me when I came home at night,

Still, I settled into my great new job. New classes with new textbooks, of course. My re-entry into the academic world of the homeland was challenging and, on occasion, wearying. At no time, however, was it unhappy. In four words, "I loved my work."

My colleague, Grosvenor Fattic, summed it up well when he said. "Here it's possible to try out so many new ideas. You have a chance to do that!" Then he added, "Of course, you may fall flat on your face, but they'll let you get up and try again. You'll like it here." After many years of "trench warfare," I found this principle of academic freedom utterly fascinating.

Along the way, I began to glimpse other opportunities. Extras that I really hadn't had time to think about before. Ken Vine, Dean of the School of Religion, needed a writer. (This situation later gave me an opportunity to go on an archaeology dig in the Holy Land.)

Raymond Woolsey called from Review & Herald Publishing: "Do you have a book manuscript to send us?" Me? Another book? I hadn't thought about that for a long while.

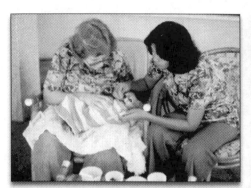

Left. La Val Comm and Zeny treated the geriatric little Rusty. Right. We wrestled with the
problem of getting four Pomeranians back to
the United States.

Meanwhile, ever since I had arrived in California I had had weekly encounters with doctors. The postlude to my latest hepatitis episode involved fierce headaches and agonizing back pains. Most mornings I was able to drag myself to the start line. In the afternoons I became too tired to remember my own name. The night classes seemed hardly do-able.

When I left Manila, Dr. Estuita had advised me, "Don't have hepatitis a third time. You might not survive again."

Therefore I followed doctors' orders with perfect integrity. By the first of April my blood tests had come right, and I got the "All Clear." Even so, for many more weeks, the utter exhaustion smote me down at unexpected times. On occasion, I retreated to my office, switched off the light, locked the door, and lay down on the floor.

Meanwhile, from opposite sides of the Pacific—amid a flurry of money transfers and almost-impossible phone calls—Walt and I closed the deal on our new house in the hills about three miles from the La Sierra campus. A split-level house with four bedrooms set on a half acre of land and surrounded by a dozen productive fruit trees (oranges, peaches, apricots, plums, and nectarines.) Country living within the city limits of Riverside!

Back in the Philippines, Walt was busy teaching on both the old and the new campuses. While convalescing he had to involve himself in the general trauma of an international house move. He spoke of the good days when kind friends stopped by with words of appreciation. "Helps me feel it has all been worth while," he wrote. (Unable to do much sitting, he had to stand up to write me letters.) All of this amid the packing and the selling of the household. I wish I could have been there to help.

So, eighty-two days passed—March 8 to May 25, 1978. Missing one another sorely, Walt and I wrote long letters. Actually journals in which we philosophized on life, discussed *Thoughts from the Mount of Blessing,* and made plans. I from a tiny California apartment and him from our rapidly deteriorating house in Manila. Mum was preoccupied with her young Filipino "children." Larry and Lorna were in Singapore. "I begin to wonder where our home is," I said. "It can't just be packed up in suitcases and boxes."

Together we agreed that keeping it alive in our hearts was the only place we could maintain it. At the same time we dreamed big dreams about when we should all come together in our home at 6732 Sunnyvale Drive. I closed the deal on May 6, 1978. We had fallen in love with it the first sunshiny day when we first saw it in the foothills, surrounded by snow-capped mountains.

During this time I became painfully aware of the problems Dick and Anne Figuhr were facing up at Pacific Union College. Anne and I exchanged several letters. She had been hired at the Academy. Dick, however, had nothing, and his Permanent Return salary would run out in March. He was working hard at landscaping—by the hour—and had said, "Maybe I am unemployable." His stress couldn't help but show through.

I looked ahead at the job uncertainty that faced Walt. As Anne said, "One

Our last Christmas in the Philippines (1978) was a sober one, marked by widespread illness and the prospect of breaking up the family for the next six months.

needs to be wanted in one's own profession." I had always known that when people took up overseas appointments, it was ideal if they could stay there until they retired. Family responsibilities, however, rarely made that possible. The returning missionary coming home! Coming home to what!

Walt refused to talk of anything but faith and courage. I said no more, but a shadow settled over me. It never really went away.

Graduations at Far Eastern Academy have always been a big family affair. I had decided before I left the Philippines that I had to be in Singapore with my family for that occasion. The LLU English Department gave me their blessing and even subsidized my trip.

In order to arrive on time, however, I had to cut my quarter short. On April 15, for example, I did fifteen continuous hours of freshman conferences—followed by three hours of teaching. For my two large writing classes I faced stacks of papers to be graded. One was ten inches thick. (I measured it.)

Still, I made it! With but one little hand-carry tote, my camera bag and purse, I left Los Angeles on an afternoon in mid-May. The past seven months had been a mix of the hectic and the exotic. As I leaned back, Tokyo-bound, I trusted that with just one more push (or maybe two) our family's wilderness experience of separation, sickness and general chaos would end.

For many hours we ran ahead of the sun. Then nature gradually gained on us as the sun steadily leaned toward the western horizon. Crossing this, the largest expanse of air and water on earth, has always tantalized me. Sheer nothingness on all sides!

I sat wedged in with 250 strangers all busy with their whiskey, headphones, business weeklies, and the movie. Ironic! The plane, full of all of these common

Dorothy began to feel at home with her new colleagues at Loma Linda University (La Sierra Campus). (L-R). Grosvenor Fattic (Professor of Medieval Literature) and Robert Dunn (Chair of the English Department).

In 1979, one of the latter years of Far Eastern Academy in Singapore, Larry stood with his parents on graduation day.

ordinary bits of mortality, roared boldly through infinity with no humility whatsoever. One thinks thoughts up here that do not occur quite so easily on the ground.

My journey included three stops. In Japan I had an excellent sightseeing day with my former PUC English major, Shinobu Nakagawa. Then came 24 hours in Korea and a day in Hong Kong. It all related to an Asian Tour that I was contemplating within the next couple of years.

When I arrived in Singapore, our whole family gathered in one place at one time, for the first time in almost six months. We made Larry's graduation from Far Eastern Academy as happy a celebration as possible.

Lorna, of course, had had her packing done and her room spotless for the past month. We had to do necessary excavations in Larry's room in order to retrieve the $50 dollar room deposition. Among other things, I did seven loads of washing. When I saw other mothers toiling at the same tasks, however, I realized that I was not unique.

On June 7 we again became a "house divided." At the airport, Mum and I stood in line for the Garuda flight to Bali. In a parallel queue Walt and the kids waited to board Japan Airlines for Los Angeles.

After an instructive week in Indonesia, Mum and I had just twenty-four hours (June 8) on the Baesa campus in Manila. In the short time I had, I disposed of the leftovers remaining in our house and picked up our last two dogs, dear old Rusty and Mitzi. I spent a last precious hour with my English teachers. I wondered how long it would be before I would eat fresh mangoes and macapuno ice cream again—and in such happy company. I realized again that my Philippine years could never be duplicated in any way.

Left. We had lived long with plans to move to the new campus in Silang. The architect's drawings beckoned us to a new campus. Right. The Comm and Gulley family got to sit on the property and look across Taal Lake, but none of them would live there.

When Mum and I checked in at China Airlines for the Los Angeles flight, we found that the box prepared for the Pomeranians was too big. The dogs couldn't go boxless, of course, so everyone waited anxiously for the last-minute "reduction carpentry" to be done. With all of the other passengers aboard, the box arrived and we stuffed the dogs in—paws, tails, and noses crammed in without ceremony. We would not soon forget the journey—we or the dogs.

A last round of hugs and tears and so ended our years in the Far East. I collapsed into my seat and fell into a stupor from which I barely emerged in time to change planes in Taipei. The twenty-three-hour Pacific crossing involved two more touchdowns—Taipei and Honolulu.)

Now—finally—we could put our home together again. I drifted off into fantasy. From here on we could take vacations, sleep in a couple times a month (at least), and sit down and do absolutely nothing once in a while. The way normal people have always done. I believed that it was the end to the peculiar kind of madness that had been ours. Walt had described the prospect as "feeling like Bobo (our erstwhile monkey) out of her cage."

Settled into our Sunnyvale house, we all launched into our summer tasks. While I taught a full slate of classes, Walt and Larry worked on our former house in Grand Terrace, preparing it for rental. Our new house turned out to have more deficiencies than we had at first recognized and needed repairs.

Just one more mad-cap journey remained for us. We left Mum and her college friend, Ena Young, to keep the house and dogs while the rest of us headed for Michigan —by way of Canada.

Wilf and Annamarie Liske had bought out our interest in the Timberland home that we had shared at Andrews University. Now it was time for us to retrieve the residue of our household goods (including winter clothes) out of Michigan. When I looked at that handsome, red shuttered house set among the maple trees, all lush in summer green, I felt a twinge of regret. With our experience at Andrews University now definitely over, our lot had fallen in Southern California.

Walt visited the "auto-heaven" that used to be Detroit and bought a Chevelle Malibu station wagon. Thus we became a two-car "road train." We took aboard five large drums and miscellaneous boxes. This-and-that-kind of stuff was chinked into all of the cracks—full to the rooflines. Only the two front seats in each vehicle remained available to passengers.

The appearance of our caravan indeed kept us humble. Tied on the station wagon's roof rack were several domestic items that we just didn't feel like throwing out: an ironing board, a step-ladder, a coffee table and five folding steel chairs. Also three chairs that had so much personality, we just had to

The day came when our santol tree stoically awaited its destruction. Right. A carabao mindlessly waited on the road while our home was demolished. What a great amount of living we had done in that house!

keep them too. Wearing this diadem of chair legs, the station wagon did, indeed, have character. The heap of stuff on top was visible from afar and helped keep us together in heavy traffic all the way across the continent. We buried our pride and pressed on. To be sure, no one else in all of North America could have looked like us!

For six transitional months Dorothy occupied an apartment on La Sierra Campus. Here Walt convalesced from his back surgery.

Now with two cars on the road and with Walt and Larry to drive them, I relaxed with Lorna. I happily retired to the position of "relief driver" only, consenting to take the wheel "by invitation only." Only a foolish woman would do otherwise, with two men eager and able to manage the road. Besides, this arrangement left me with 5,000 miles to work on a challenging piece of Persian needlepoint embroidery that I had picked up.

Back in California, I plunged into work again. I had to pay for being away from my office so long. One can go only so far, however, in recovering time lost, no matter what midnight hours he or she puts in.

In September we sold the station wagon to the Security Department at Loma Linda University. They wanted to use it to transport their police dogs. What a noble calling! Far better than anything we could have offered the little wagon domestically.

Walt always loved to "play cars." He also knew my antipathy for the big green Plymouth. One weekend I flew up to Lodi, California, with my mother so that she could visit her brother (James Rhoads) and her sister (Norma Youngberg). Upon my return, Walt met me. As we walked to the airport parking lot, he asked, "Which of these four cars would you like?"

I realized that he had a surprise for me. Knowing the leanness of the

Left. We loved our Sunnyvale house. It enfolded us as if it had just been waiting for us to come home. Right. In a surprisingly short time our freight shipment from Manila was delivered to our driveway. The driver demanded that we—he did nothing at all—unload it all in one hour. Otherwise we would have to pay heavily for overtime.

family exchequer, however, I picked out an obviously second-hand red Pinto. "No, that's not it." Walt chuckled.

It turned out to be the next one, a silver 1976 Mustang with burgundy-red upholstery. With its classy, two-seater lines, it met my desire for a small car very perfectly. I never thought that I could have a love affair with a car. They were all just transportation. This lovely object, however, was mine! Walt had left himself with the old Plymouth that had no personality at all. Visions of the old Peugeots, the White Elephant, and the clumsy Bedford—the whole nightmare of Manila traffic flashed across my mind. That was over. Now this sleek little pony was for me!

To be sure, our years in the Orient had been exotic. Now, however, a flood of happy, new events overtook us as we made merry in our tri-level house on Sunnyvale Drive. Even my cousin Jess Barrett from Perth, Western Australia, gave us several days out of her three-month holiday in America.

Then the Canadians came in force. At year-end, we welcomed six of them, along with some West Indian friends, and assorted nieces and nephews from

other places. My new
Maytag washer labored at
least three times a day. All
five of our double-or-
larger beds were occupied
and eight people slept on
the floor. My now-
divorced sister Eileen and
her four boys came out to
share Christmas dinner
with us. What a bounty
of family togetherness
flowed over and around
us.

Our first year in California we attended the Pasadena Rose Parade for the first and only time. The float from Calgary, Canada, featured a lanky cowboy. We were home, and a new chapter was opening before us.

We quickly became acquainted with many Southern California "basics:" Disneyland, Knotts Berry Farm, SeaWorld, and the Lion Safari. Plus ventures across the border into Tijuana, Mexico. On New Year's Day some of the group went to the Pasadena 90th Tournament of Roses (with its 119 floats). We launched 1979 in a rip-roaring start. I think the last time I had arisen in pre-dawn darkness to see a parade was back in London's Horse Guards Parade for the birthday of King George VI when I was a teenager.

We sat among rows of bodies neatly wrapped in sleeping bags and blankets. Near-freezing night chills. Half a million spectators expected. Filtering all through the mass of humanity came vendors of roses, balloons, film and pretzels, wagons of popcorn, cracker-jacks. Also peanuts, and bird whistles, pennants and tanks of coffee and hot chocolate. Over all rasped voices crying "Cotton candy, fine and dandy!"

A new idea struck me.

After all our foreign years, we had that day participated in something new. The parade was distinctively—even fiercely—"All American."

CHAPTER 9

Our Transition Year

Eventually the year1978, with all of its upheaval, came to an end. As a family we had collectively given up our overseas living. For the last time. We'd moved from East back to West.

Professionally, I had my dream job. Walt's work, as I had feared, was considerably less secure. The previous year when I had first been offered a position at Loma Linda University (La Sierra Campus), he had been very quick to say, "You take it! It will be good for you." His gaze enfolded me with a warmth that he reserved for our most serious moments together. "I want you to have that work."

"But what about you … ?" I countered.

"Don't worry about me. I can do several different things. More so than you," he replied. I knew that he was right on that point. Almost exclusively the classroom was the place where I functioned at my best. At the time, however, neither of us could know how extensively his courage and our security would be tested.

Nonetheless, Christmas found us all together in our beautiful Sunnyvale house in south Riverside, California. My mother, Larry and Lorna occupied the three upstairs bedrooms. Walt and I had the first floor bedroom cozily adjacent to the spacious family room that became our joint den. The four dogs ranged freely around our half-acre, fenced-in back yard. We truly felt that we'd been brought to a very "good place."

All through the autumn, along with our daily chores, we entertained weekend guests from far and near. Southern California is, to be sure, a major crossroads. The sunny, golden winter days in our valley, amid the snow-capped mountains, brought in a detachment of Christmas visitors from Canada. After a lifetime of keeping open house, we simply settled back to enjoy our friends and family in a new way that had been denied to us for the past eight years.

One Sabbath in early February, tragic news visited our campus. I sat in the La Sierra Church one day watching the Zaugg family. Three days earlier the doctor had delivered a death sentence. Dr. Wayne Zaugg had terminal

Loma Linda University English Department faculty. Front (L-R). Winona Howe, Judy Laue, Greg Dickinson. Back. Dorothy Minchin-Comm, Robert Dunn, Frank Knittel, Renard Donesky, Craig Kinzer.

cancer and could not expect to live more than six months. He was a professor in the Chemistry Department, and I didn't know him well. As I watched that little family unit sitting tight together—him, his wife and two elementary-school-aged children. My heart reached out to them.

At such times, of course, one always thinks of the power of prayer and the possibility of a miracle. Realistically, I knew, however, that cancer usually runs its wretched course and moves on to its lethal end

That night I went home to record my thoughts: "It could have been anyone's family. Ours too. Does it take the oncoming of death to teach us how to live? Perhaps. As that family arranges itself for these next six months, they will savor—even the children—a quality of living which none of the rest of us can know anything about. Enslaved to schedules and 'busyness' of all sorts, we lose so much joy that we could have." I longed somehow to break out of those bonds. I wanted to communicate this idea to someone else, but I couldn't find an apt audience. "So," I concluded, "I've said it here in my journal."

Those words would take on a deeper, personal meaning much sooner than I or anyone else could have guessed.

Early spring ushered in a happy event. My sister Eileen re-married. Her "alone days" were over. Once again I was her matron of honor. This time her eldest son, Kevin, "gave her away." Walt conducted the home wedding service for her and Lyman Davis, the tall, peaceable, Welsh-descended man of her choice.

Immediately after the wedding our mother took a trip back to the Philippines. Indeed, I suspect that she had it planned even before we left the islands. Her "boys and girls" received her joyfully, and once again she joined them on their missionary journeys into the hinterlands. Something that had been her life blood for the years that we lived in Manila. She stayed with them for three months. Although Leona Minchin lived to the age of 91, she never for one moment lost her profound interest in those young people. Many of them were recipients of the "Gerald Minchin Scholarship Fund" that she had established in my father's name.

Meanwhile Walt had joined the *Listen* program of the Southeastern California Conference. Although it suited his training and interests in public health, it was, in reality a form of colporteuring (book selling). His income was commission-based and therefore spasmodic. Although he never complained, I worried over the corrosive effects of our uncertain financial base.

At the same time, Walt could occasionally accompany me on some of my professional ventures—something that we'd never shared before. When, in mid-March, Loma Linda University sent me to a Christian Writer's Conference at Warner Pacific college in Portland, Oregon, we went together. Thus, his flexibility with time was a little privilege that we'd never had before.

By the end of the 1979 school year, two major events occurred. Much as we loved our beautiful home, we decided to put it up for sale. Mum felt too isolated out in the hills, so we prepared to buy an older house right on the edge of La Sierra campus. She could then walk to any of the multiple church-and-school activities there that could interest her. To this end, Walt and Lyman painted the Sunnyvale house to ready it for the market.

Although this was only my second year at Loma Linda University, I was granted the summer free for research and writing in England. Passionately eager to see England again after thirty-two years' absence, I begged Walt to come with me. "We could even spend a little time in Europe," I urged. "You could see where your parents came from."

A certified workaholic, Walt did not submit easily. He came up with a depressingly long list of objections. "We'd have to sell the Mustang in order to have enough money," he concluded.

Much as I enjoyed my sporty little car, I knew that Walt considered it too much of a gas-guzzler. In fact, I suspected that he planned to get rid of it anyway. "OK!" I replied. "Sell the car then. But just come with me for at least two weeks. Please."

As I recall, it's the only time I ever won such a bold holiday proposal. Neither of us, however, would ever regret the venture.

Mum returned from the Philippines in time to take charge of the house. The kids both had summer jobs lined up. Therefore, on Thursday night (June 28, 1979) we boarded the Pan Am "Red-Eye Special" to New York. Just Walt and me.

We had an unexpected twelve-hour layover in New York—one of those mysterious mechanical deviations that the airline people studiously try to hide from the passengers. In any case, the next day, we flew into a steel blue-and-apricot sunrise over the North Atlantic. We landed smoothly and safely at Heathrow Airport outside of London.

After a short weekend at Newbold College, we took public transportation down to Canterbury. Europe being our prime destination, we hastened on to Dover for the three-and-a-half-hour ferry crossing to Belgium.

We arrived in Ostend about midnight. Fearfully conscious of our financial limitations, however, we refused to waste $50 for only half a night in a hotel. Therefore, we sat out the hours in the railway station among snoring drunks and backpacking young people cocooned in their sleeping bags. The old building smelled of all of its 100-plus years.

As early as possible in the morning we picked up our rental car, a little blue Opel Kadett. Then we provisioned our lunch box at a local bakery. I have never seen finer baked goods anywhere, before or since. (We assumed that such bread would be the norm for Europe. It was not.) Having lost so much sleep, we felt revived with our marvelously tasty breakfast in Ostend.

Now we were ready for the traditional sightseeing. For centuries, millions

Wedding of Eileen Minchin-Eckert and Lyman Davis, in West Los Angeles, March 10, 1979.

of tourist eyes have rested on these same sights. Millions of pictures have been taken and lectures given. Uncounted friends and families have submitted to long discourses on "What We Did on Our Trip to Europe." Yet, no two people have ever viewed the world through exactly the same windows. Therefore, my impressions were strictly my own and were faithfully recorded in my journals.[1]

In this venue I can offer only a few random snapshots of our journey. In Belgium the sleek cattle grazing among dark clumps of trees in lush pastures thoroughly aroused the farmer in Walt.

In Leyden our *Zimmer mit Fruhstuch* (room with breakfast) put us under a gable roof. We looked out on an immaculate, be-flowered backyard by a broad canal, beside what appeared the "wrecked-car graveyard" for all of the Netherlands.

While we waited for the Rijksmuseum to open in Amsterdam, we watched a large boat being pushed out of a third-floor window to be deposited in the nearby canal.

The very tiny church at Bilzen was surrounded by a very large cemetery. Why the imbalance, we wondered. Near there, Walt for the first time set foot in his *Faderland* (Germany). I photographed him on that spot, fairly bursting with the pleasure of the moment.

The drivers of big Mercedes on the *autobahn* had little patience with sightseeing laggards like us. Anyway, about 75 mph was about the best our little Kadett could do.

Our weekend at the Seminary at Marienhohe in Darmstadt was hosted by Dr. Udo Worschech, then on the faculty and now a well-known archaeologist. Back at Canadian Union College, however, he had been a student in both Walt's and my classes. To be sure, a major reward of teaching lies in the future success and continuing friendship of one's students. No way could we have seen Germany in a more pleasurable way.

Our sightseeing forays with the Worschechs were interspersed with afternoon *kaffee.* Uschi Worschech served us a marvelous Black Forest Cherry Torte that her husband Udo had been advertising for two days. (Germans eat dessert separately from the main meal.)

Our meals on the road were plain but we never suffered deprivation. We usually started each day at a *patisserie* (bakery) where we stocked up on French bread, fresh croissants, hot cheese pies, and the like.

Walt negotiated for a century-old brass cow bell in Switzerland. "It's the only souvenir I need from Europe." He bought it for $25.00 after promising the farmer that he would not let it go out of our family.

Near Lucerne in Switzerland, Walt detoured off the highway to bargain with a genial farmer. He bought a huge brass cowbell. The thick leather strap smelled of cattle and even had some hair caught in the buckle. "Now I have the only souvenir I need from the whole trip!" Walt sighed with contentment as he gave the farmer $25. The man made him promise never to sell the 100-year-old family heirloom to anyone else.

For my part, the best part of Switzerland was an evening with my Newbold classmate, Erica Sturznegger. Over the years, we'd both married and become lost to one another. Nonetheless, we laughed and talked for hours, picking up right where we left off thirty-three years earlier.

Naturally, the stop at Byron's celebrated Chateau of Chillon was obligatory. After observing the standard features of the castle, we especially took note of the two-hole toilet seat suspended over a shaft down into the Lake Geneva. The chilly updraft coming up from the water sixty feet below must have been something of an inconvenience to users.

Finally, at the top of the glacier at Chamonix we saw a sign warning that the path was not suitable for the "Aged and Fatigued." Technically, we knew that we were both. We went down anyway, pleased that we still weren't too late to do it.

On July 16 our European venture ended on the docks at Calais where we left the Kadett. We boarded the ferry *Hengist,* and, in less than two hours we landed back in Dover. The usual entourage of sea gulls attended us all of the way across the Channel.

Picking up another rental car we began the next day at Dover Castle, followed by the nearby Saxon church and Roman lighthouse. There a hoot owl called down to us from the tower. The matter of 2000 years is all one thing to the birds. Even "a cat may look at the King!" Indeed, we need birds and animals to keep us in perspective. Exactly what might the haughty Great Ones of long ago think of the tourist industry here today?

We spent our first night on the English roads in Petersfield, Hampshire. I studied the map closely, determined to make that happen. From there my great-great-grandfather, James Minchin, emigrated to Australia in 1829. While I would visit the town on many other occasions, I have always been glad that Walt was there to walk High Street with me that first time. I hoped that in some way he would connect with them as his people too. With my escalating interest in family history, I decided that he should get used to these kinds of detours.

We followed the lovely country lanes through the Cotswolds and into Wales. We spent our second night in Llidiart-y-parc. The tiny village lies between Glyndyfrdwy and Corrog. I mention these names just to give you the feel of things Welsh. Signs for the public toilets read *Cyfleusterau,* with *Dynion* (men) and *Merched* (ladies). "By the time you get that all figured out," Walt speculated, "it might well be too late."

North through the Lake Country brought us to Gretna Green, one of the most famous border crossings in the world. Since 1710 eloping English couples came up here for quick weddings. No questions asked. Walt and I showed up at the Old Blacksmith Shop on July 22, our twenty-eighth wedding anniversary.

We volunteered from among the tourists present to star in a "sample" marriage ceremony. For my bridesmaid I chose a tall lady about my height. (She turned out to be an Australian.) A bouquet of plastic flowers was thrust into my hands, and a ragged white veil set on my head. I suppose it all coordinated well enough with my slacks, tennis shoes and turtleneck sweater. Walt and his best man were both given silk top hats.

We stood on opposite sides of the big anvil, women to left and men to the right. Since metals are fused on an anvil, it was deemed an appropriate place for a wedding to take place.

We had to answer just two questions. "Are you very certain that you want to marry each other?" and "Are you both over sixteen years of age?" (The old kilted "blacksmith" apologized for bringing up the latter embarrassing question.)

Following the "vows" the best man produced the ring. A large one designed for a calf's nose. Then the smithy banged the hammer down on the anvil and pronounced us "man and wife." We received a certificate and a group portrait of the whole party.

As we exited, the blacksmith, with mischief twinkling in his blue eyes and a thick Scots brogue on his tongue, patted me on the arm. "If he isn't good to you," he whispered, "come back in a week, and I'll give you another one!"

To be sure, Walt and I had never had a more unique anniversary celebration.

By now shortness of time was nipping at our heels. We drove all night back into South England, giving Stratford-upon-Avon a courtesy pass on the way down. That left one day for Walt to see London. We did the best we could.

Then on Thursday morning, Walt turned the car in at Heathrow Airport. We had driven 3000 miles in Europe and 1500 in England. No trouble. Not even a nick of paint lost—and we'd been in some strange, tight places too. After Walt boarded a flight to Los Angeles, I took the train to Chiswick.

Visit to Minchin country in England. Left. As early as 1450, Dorothy's ancestors were parishioners and trustees of the Wyck Rissington Church in the heart of the Cotswolds. Right. The market square of Petersfield, Hampshire, as it looked when her Great-Great-Grandfather left the town to go to the Swan River Settlement in Western Australia in 1829.

Back in Bill and Enid Tolman's Victorian home in Bedford Park our empty room awaited me. This would be my home for the next five weeks (July 26-Sept. 6). Over the years, I would have many more stopovers at Tolmans' place. There I always met an endless stream of travelers coming to London, a high percentage of them Australians. "Some people," Bill remarked, "collect stamps. We collect people." Their three-story house had, after all, six spare bedrooms.

Now, overnight, I renounced tourism and applied myself to my appointed task. I visited the British Museum and various other London libraries to revive my doctoral research. In my present academic world custom demanded writing monographs, presenting scholarly papers, and—hopefully—following with the publication thereof. As a teacher of creative writing, I had a little flexibility. That is, not everything that went to print had to be scholarly. Nonetheless, I resumed my research on the English Abolition Movement with zest. In the stimulating environs of London, I could not have felt otherwise.

I purchased weekly transport passes that gave me constant access to both Underground trains and the buses. Thus I captured the very essence of London. On the double-decker buses I always chose the front seat of the upper deck. Through the treetops I had a superior view of the streets that never grew dull. Every morning, for example, I saw the same woman lying on the grass in Shepherd's Bush Green. At first, I thought, morbidly, that she looked like someone Jack the Ripper might have left behind. I was always relieved to see her move a little.

Every day I waited for #88 bus at the corner of Abinger Road, Bedford Park. I could set my watch by the old man who walked his three smash-faced bull terriers daily. Two white ones on a twin-leash and the black one, going solo.

Top Photo. Walt and Dorothy spent their 28th wedding anniversary at Gretna Green, Scotland, the refuge for eloping couples from England. Bottom Photo. They became the bride and groom for the 'quickie" ceremony over the anvil that the "blacksmith" offered for tourist entertainment. The wedding party was made up of whoever happened to be at the old forge at the moment. The bridal couple stood at the back (left), to be identified by the top hat and a rather worn out veil.

He made the circuit to pick up his morning paper at the corner tobacconist shop. Nothing ever stopped him.

My street journeys also revived my teenage fascination with pub signs, each with its own visual image and its story: Bull and Swan, Drum and Monkey, The Singing Kettle, The Chocolate Poodle, and so forth.

On Sunday mornings I often made a special trip to Bayswater Road where artists displayed their handiwork along the iron fences of Hyde Park and Green Park—a veritable explosion of creativity.

For reasons of poverty I did more looking than shopping on Oxford Street. Selfridges Department Store had a façade displaying Victorianized Greek pillars and graceful stone goddesses with balances and magnifying glasses, casing out the quantity and quality of merchandise. The marvelous Food Halls of Harrods over in Kensington, of course, put ordinary supermarkets to shame for their grossness. Also, gentlemen in gray flannel suits operated the lifts (elevators) that were embossed with bronze lions and gargoyles. Everything there appeared to be "Under Appointment to Her Majesty."

After a while, I felt quite proud when I realized that I'd begun to look like a "local." People started asking me for directions.

During my library hours I occasionally took a little recreational time to investigate my family history. An interest that culminated in a major hobby in succeeding years. In these days of too much change, mobility, and insecurity, the universal quest for roots is a legitimate tie into something past and permanent. Moreover, my findings began to augment my general colonial studies in quite surprising ways.

One afternoon in the British Museum Library I came across a set of indexes to German families. Slowly working through the language barrier, I was hunting for the name Komm. I knew that the family had emigrated to Canada amid revolution and had, perforce, cut all ties. Still, I saw no harm in looking. In a public reading room, after all.

Then I heard a fierce sound at my elbow. A thick, guttural voice growled, "Are you pretending to be a member of the German nobility?"

Utterly astonished I turned to see an intense little blond, be-spectacled man beside me. "Why I'm not pretending to be anything at all!"

He pressed on, assuring me, "I know every family that has ever done anything of importance."

"Well, this family," I replied, "didn't do anything that you would have heard of, I'm sure."

He kept on. Eager, I realized, for me to ask him who he was. By refraining from asking that question, I did, in fact have the last word.

Of course, in such an encounter one always thinks of the really good answers afterwards. I could have said, "No, I'm just hunting up a recipe for *kuchen,*" or "No, I'm checking on the pedigree of

For the summer of 1979—and for many summers thereafter—the reading room in the British Museum Library was Dorothy's academic destination. She spent unnumbered research hours there under the high dome.

my Holstein bull." But suppose I had been the Archduchess of Bavaria or the grandniece of von Hindenberg, or something! What then?

In all of the rest of my travels about London I met with nothing but utmost courtesy from Museum officers to bus conductors. This man was different. It occurred to me that he might be the kind of raw material out of which you could create a Nazi or some such grotesque personality.

Then, as quickly as it started, my first London Idyll ended, and I flew home—just in time to pick up my fall teaching load. Not a day too early. As usual, I have always worked all of my opportunities to their absolute limit.

The homeward flight took me over a new route. From 39,000 feet I looked steadily down first at the icebergs and glaciers of Greenland and then Hudson Bay with the smooth snow patches, blue-and-gold rimmed bays, and inlets of dark blue sea. That gave way to the checkerboard autumn fields of Saskatchewan and Montana, followed by the Rockies and the Grand Tetons. Then, at last, the urban sprawl of Los Angeles. I was home. At least I consciously was still trying to think of the Southern California desert as "home." Not an easy transition.

Walt and I had one surprise treat left before Christmas. In November we left Mum, the kids and the dogs in our lovely Sunnyvale house to take care of one another. Walt and I pointed the nose of the Plymouth northward and drove through to Walla Walla, Washington, to meet Vic and Gem Fitch. The Alumni Homecoming at Canadian Union College was scheduled for November 23-26, 1979.

Walt (Class of '51) and Vic (Class of '55, the 25th-year Honor Class) had been invited to give, respectively, the Sabbath sermon and the Friday night Vespers. How we savored the warm pleasures of being with old friends—in old places. Something we'd inevitably missed during the years of overseas service.

Together the four of us traveled on, this time in Fitchs' green Plymouth. Up through the Rockies and on to the parklands of Alberta. We had years of companionship to catch up on and enjoyed every moment of the journey

That is, until we reached a motel in Cranbrook, British Columbia. From the outside the facility looked fair enough, so we booked ourselves into two rooms. As usual, we turned back the blankets to evaluate the cleanliness of the beds. We discovered a similar deficiency in each room. The sheets were a very pale gray. Walt and I found an indentation of a head on one of the pillows. Fitchs found some hair in their bed.

Too late to dismiss ourselves and find another motel in the very small town. Walt returned to the office to demand clean sheets. In due course, he came back with the bedding. "They were very reluctant to give it to me," he remarked.

The stuff looked and smelled clean, however, so we made up the beds. Even the new sheets, however, were worn thin as tissue paper, almost to the point of transparency.

When we checked out in the morning, Walt and Vic faced close interrogation at the office. "I certainly hope you left the extra sheets in the room," the attendant eyed them severely. Both declared complete innocence. Indeed, if we'd had a mind to steal sheets from anywhere, we would surely have chosen some in better condition. It is enough to face a potential bed-bug threat. It is more than enough to be suspected of absconding with the linen under discussion.

Left. Flying from London to Los Angeles took us over the tundra of Canada's frozen north. Right. When Dorothy saw the island of Newfoundland emerge, she could remember just one thing—being everlastingly COLD down there.

The Homecoming Weekend at CUC was all that it should have been. Seeing friends and family and bonding with the old campus itself. Right down to the pancake breakfast on Sunday morning.

Oddly enough, our motel misadventure made a deep impression on us all. So much so, that Walt and I soon purchased a little travel trailer and bought into a chain of camping sites. Years later, Vic and Gem—retaining the same recollections—bought their own small motor home.

We still had more transitions to make. Indeed, they extended clear into the New Year. In December Lorna moved to Collegedale, Tennessee. She lived with my cousin Ina Madge Longway and worked in a commercial laundry. Although she hadn't finished high school, she had acquired her GED certificate. We kept hoping that some concept of a life work would begin to form in her mind.

Larry had finished his freshman year at the College. but he veered off into aviation mechanics, first and always his greatest interest. He did seem to have a plan.

Our Sunnyvale home had sold. We'd moved into an old "California homestead" style of house right on the edge of La Sierra Campus at 12014

Home once more. As if forecasting the future, instead of standing together Walt and Dorothy allowed the birch tree trunk to come between them.

Raley Drive. With its long, narrow verandah in front it rather resembled an Australian outback house. In any case, it had none of the style that our first "country" home offered. The consolation was that many of us could walk to wherever we needed to go. That, of course, did not apply to Walt. His work with *Listen* program took him out over some 700 miles every week.

Shortly after the New Year, Walt's eldest brother Ben died. Walt promptly flew up to Alberta for the funeral. It was held in Leduc on a sunny January day with a temperature of 20 degrees below zero. After everyone else went home, Walt stayed on with Helen and Orvan, to tide them over into their new life without husband and father.

He himself got home to California just in time to deal with a winter flood. Water poured over the terrace into our two-car garage at the front of the property. Walt worked hours shoring up the wall, and hauling away debris. (I said that this was an old house.)

He came in one night looking exhausted. "Well, I'll write a letter to Lorna," he announced. "Then I want to get to bed early. I am tired."

Actually, I'd never heard him admit that much. Nor had he ever appeared quite that worn. Still, he'd just come home from a funeral. I returned to grading papers and didn't give the matter further thought. I knew he'd get up as usual in the morning and go on with his *Listen* routine.

And so he did.

---

1   I began my journal-writing in 1970 when we first went to the Philippines and continued for the next forty years. Four volumes of the journals of Dorothy Minchin-Comm are preserved in the archives of three university libraries: Andrews University (Michigan), and Loma Linda University and La Sierra University (California). Some readers have generously considered them among the "most useful accounts of grassroots mission service and the affairs of education."

CHAPTER 10

Into a Dark Valley

In the spring of 1980 a very fortuitous event occurred. Walt was assigned to a pastorate and was able to give up the *Listen* program. While I invariably clung to my own kind of security of a college campus, it had been a toss-up with Walt. He always said that he could be just as happy pastoring a church as teaching. In fact, I suspected that he sometimes preferred the former.

His first assignment was in the high desert, Victorville and Lucerne Valley, a 50 to 60-mile commute. He was promised something closer by the end of the summer. From the start he loved the familiar busyness of it all—preaching, Vacation Bible School, children's story time, pastoral visits.

He kept up with the domestic chores too—mowing the large lawn, grocery shopping, washing the cars and all of the rest of the home stuff. With my constant and intense work on campus, day in and day out, I never had imagined doing without all of my husband's efforts. Never once in our married life had he failed to support my academic goals. At this point in time, both he and I appreciated the diminished anxiety that came with his having a regular paycheck. It had been a long haul and stressful for both of us.

At the end of the summer, Walt became Associate Pastor at the Arlington Church in Riverside.

While these events were evolving, an astonishing proposition opened up for me. I became part of the Loma Linda contingent in an eighty-member consortium of archaeologists on a dig in Caesarea Maritima, Israel. I went as a field worker and writer/photographer. (I was charged with turning that experience into a multi-media program)

Had archaeology been a viable profession for women when I graduated from college back in 1950, I very likely would have become a professional. As a teenager, when most girls my age were worrying about boyfriends, I was visiting the mummies in the Smithsonian Institution in Washington D.C. In any case, spending five weeks in Israel now fulfilled a lifetime of dreams for me. Had I lived 800 years ago I might have come there as a crusader, or, at least, a pilgrim. In 1980 I arrived on location simply as a volunteer field-worker.

We lodged at Kayit V' Shait (Heb. "fields and sea"), the beach resort of the old kibbutz, Sdot Yam. It was situated on the sand dunes, virtually within the extensive ruins of Caesarea Maritima. My roommates, volunteers like me, were a Jewish teacher from New Jersey and a nurse from Tennessee. Both snored all night, and one of them talked all day. With all of the heavy outdoor work, however, I slept anyway.

Five days a week I and seven team mates, were assigned to the thirty-meter square, designated as "C26." It had been a graveyard for centuries, and we worked down through layers of skeletons. First Arabs and then crusaders. Finally down to the Byzantine mosaics and, at last, the foundations of King Herod's elegant city, founded in 27 BC.

In the course of the summer we painstakingly removed seventy bodies. Each skeleton had to be deposited in five brown paper bags labeled "Skull," "Ribs and Vertebrae," "Pelvis," "Long Bones," and "Miscellaneous."

With taking measurements and recording locations, the process took up to eight hours. By then, I began to feel a kinship with the poor corpse. We always started our task with trowel, small brushes and dental instruments. Sometimes, as we opened a new grave, I could detect a faint musky odor, but it instantly disappeared in the heat and sea breeze

Once in a while the supervisor of C26 (from Drew University) would get impatient. "Well then, just get him into the bags." The young graduate student was keen to get all the way down to Herod's foundations as fast as possible. The skeletons, however, got in the way.

Being his senior by some twenty years, I once inquired, "Don't you ever stop to think that this was once a real man? He loved, laughed, hoped, and then died in this foreign land." A bit startled, the supervisor just shrugged and walked off. It would have to take a non-scientist, an old woman like me, to

Left. The twenty members of the Loma Linda University archaeology team were part of a larger consortium of eighty people on the dig at Caesarea Maritima, Israel. Above right. Dorothy worked in Square C-26, excavating the nymphaeum. Everyone was in a hurry to get down to Herod's city where some beautiful mosaics ultimately appeared. Right. On weekend sightseeing journeys, Dr. Ken Vine brought the Bible to life right on location. Here where Peter stood on the steps to the house Caiphas, he read of that disciple's denial of his Lord.

think of sentimental stuff like that, I suppose.

Our work day began at 4.00 a.m. with "First Breakfast," and we were in the field by sunrise. "Second Breakfast" arrived about 8.00 a.m, Hour after hour we hauled *gufas* (containers made out of old tires) out of the pit and sifted the dirt for artifacts. After lunch we were granted a short siesta period. Then we washed pottery shards and watched the experts identify them until suppertime. Finally, we attended a lecture until bedtime—which often came much too late.

We knew that much fresh produce grew on the nearby Plain of Sharon, and as we traveled we saw sweet baked goods here and there. The Kayit, however, was trying to keep our team fueled up as cheaply as possible. We ate white bread rolls as hard as hockey pucks. Although there was a great variety of foods, by the time the stuff passed through the kibbutz kitchen it had been pickled, overcooked, smushed, and tortured beyond recognition. About the only familiar thing you could count on were the cold, hard boiled eggs.

Still, happy respite came to us each Friday. We vacated our motel rooms to make them available to holidaying Israelis. Our weekends were spent traveling to either the north or the south of the land. While we stood at various historic sites, our leader, Dr. Kenneth Vine, read an appropriate scripture text and made comments that connected us with the ancient past. In this very immediate way we partook of the Holy Land, all the way from "Dan to Beersheba." Most magnificent to look at were Solomon's Pools where groves of pine trees surrounded the brilliant turquoise water. The reservoirs still supply water to Jerusalem, just as Solomon planned.

Then again, we might spend our two free days at Advent House in Jerusalem. There we could amble through the old streets or stand at the Wailing Wall at sunset to usher in *Shabat* (Sabbath). We walked in the Kidron Valley, climbed the Mount of Olives, and so forth. Strolling through an Arab bazaar in the Old City one day, Betty Vine and I were offered twenty camels for Carolyn, a pretty blond chemist on our team from California.

"Oh," we told the tall Arab with piercing dark eyes, "she doesn't actually belong to us. You'll have to ask her." As might be expected, negotiations forthwith broke down.

The Crepe House in Jerusalem was one place we got relief from the Kayit diet. Every sweet or savory crepe the world has ever seen was available there. A gourmet selection. Naturally, we all went "a-creping" every chance we got.

Although the hard work never ended, each day in Caesarea opened up a new possibility. We couldn't help but share the enthusiasm of the Director, Dr. Bob Bull, when he spoke of the future day when the Hippodrome could be excavated. Meanwhile, as we walked to our dig site, we passed by the Roman theatre. If so minded we could test its very perfect acoustics or pause and sit on the designated seat of Pontius Pilate! (The only place in the country where his name actually appears.) We were all caught up in the constant "rush of discovery" that enveloped us.

A large water conduit, part of Caesarea's enormous sea-flushed sewer system, passed through our square. I hauled unnumbered *gufas* out before I found my great discovery of the summer—a corroded ring, set with a large precious stone. No doubt some Roman matron once grieved over it when she dropped it down the drain those many centuries ago.

Sometimes we found roots deep, deep in the ground, still damp and alive though they hadn't seen light or air for 1,000 years or more. A few days in the sun, these living mementoes from Caesarea's ancient gardens miraculously budded out in green.

At the same time, we had daily reminders of our present situation. Every morning military planes and 'copters flew by our Crusader fortress, just a few feet above the sea and under the radar. Then we'd hear explosions to the north in Lebanon. Some claimed that it was only "sonic booms" while others admitted that it was, indeed, bombing.

Major loss of sleep, heat prostration, and attacks of MET ("Middle East Tummy")! The physical strain took its toll on all of us. Toward the end of the dig I got a heavy cold. Others much younger than I were falling like flies too. Most of us worked ourselves far beyond the point of exhaustion.

When I contracted a killing case of bronchitis, the last two weeks my "gufa hours" were cut back. I worked at registering pottery in the Tech Shed. There I learned about other aspects of field archaeology. As, for instance, the time when Dr. Hornyak, a Hungarian nuclear physicist from the University of Maryland had a particularly bad day. As the coin specialist for the dig he received half a dozen coins sent in the from the field. He found one button, albeit an ancient one. Also one blue jeans fastener, no doubt from some hapless volunteer digger. The rest were too worn for anyone to decipher the inscriptions. The good professor tended to relieve his disappointments by singing. Usually something from an opera. Why not? His wife was the sister of the world famous violinist, Isaac Stern!

Suddenly, the dig ended. We all had to throw the switch and re-enter our "other lives." There's an isolation, regimentation, concentration, and even companionship about an archaeological dig that makes it somewhat like a prolonged hospital stay. Our "release" day Wednesday, July 30, therefore felt quite abrupt.

Next, I launched into a very restorative week.

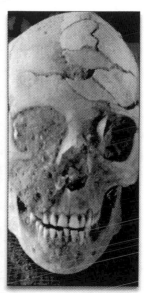

Left. The Muslim dead faithfully lay on their sides, facing toward Mecca. Center. Christian crusaders, arms crossed, faced East in the hope of the resurrection. This Frenchman's hands were missing. Right. Also this Crusader's skull was turned discreetly facing toward Mecca. This hid the fact that the left side of his head had been crushed in his final death throes.

En route home, I planned for myself a six-day holiday in Ireland. Once arrived in London, I deposited my stuff in the airport's "Left Luggage" room and took an immediate flight to Dublin. I departed out of a waiting room decorated in emerald green and shamrock motifs. The cloud cover broke as we came in over Dublin, with fragments of shore and green fields floating up through the mist.

This was just a simple homecoming for me. No academic—or other—responsibilities. (This was to be the first of many trips to Ireland.) I rented a car and drove down into Tipperary to see the four estates that belonged to my grandfather, nine generations back, Colonel Charles Minchin (1628-1681). An English landowner, he fought in Oliver Cromwell's army. That part of the story is not a pretty one, but history is what it is.

All I wanted to do was see Ballynakill, Busherstown, Annagh, and Green-hills—the properties Colonel Charles had acquired for his large family. All by myself, I explored Eire's countryside. Blobs of gray and white, the stout, plain-faced cottages sat in the rich tapestry of greens that made up the hills and fields.

I slept in out-of-the-way Bed-and-Breakfast homes where I met a charming variety of people. The name "Minchin" was not unknown, and I even met a couple of far distant relatives who still shared it with me. Life in

Ireland ends late at night and begins late in the morning. Within this framework, I found ample meals in the pubs and leisure time to visit with the locals. I wouldn't change those private days in Ireland for any sight that was ever advertised in any travel brochure.

Norma Youngberg became part of our family for the last four years of her life. Together the two sisters spent hours at the quilt frames.

I knocked on the doors of the "Great Houses" that were part of my heritage and was welcomed in, as befits "the gentry." In drizzling rain I visited several churches, looked at the parish records, and found significant graves in the churchyards.

Ultimately, a 10 ½-hour flight from London to Los Angeles in Laker's "Skytrain" brought me home. I didn't realize then that years would have to pass before I could undertake such a "normal" journey again.

Once back home, I threw myself into the immediate task of getting ready for another school year. I rather looked forward to opening a new seminar on a theme that had long enticed me. Ironically, it would be on Utopianism.

I found Mum and her sister Norma Youngberg hard at making a quilt for one of Eileen's boys. It was a grand old American art handed down in their family for generations. Looking up from the frame that filled the whole of Mum's living room, Auntie Norma's eyes twinkled, "I don't think there's much of anything about quilting that your mother and I don't know." I knew she was right. Now, some ten heirloom quilts later, we have the evidence to prove it.

Although Larry had passed his FAA examinations, he had not been able yet to get into the aviation industry. As an intermediate measure he had taken a second-choice job as an orderly in a local hospital.

Lorna's case was less predictable. Shortly after my arrival, she gave up on Tennessee and came home, unannounced. Big as our house was we now needed to find more space. We bought a twenty-six-foot trailer and parked it in the back yard. Lorna has always been particular about her living space and has never wanted it contaminated with other people's stuff. This arrangement, therefore, pleased her. She started classes at Riverside Community College.

Back near the trailer, a little pasture had been fenced in for Kandy, a young Arabian-Appaloosa horse that Walt had bought. No kind of occupation or foreign residence had ever lessened his love of horses. Loving dogs as I did, I couldn't reject Kandy although she did make me a little uneasy because of her size. She looked beautiful but acted crazy and needed training. Obviously, Walt wanted her very much, so I tried to be happy

In honor of my homecoming, Walt and Larry had repainted the house— off-white with chocolate trim. Indisputably an improvement over the drab old mustard brown we'd been living with so far.

In those years, real estate still seemed to be a good investment, even for "little people" like us. So, when a three-apartment complex on the far side of the campus went up for sale, Walt wanted to buy it. As such things go, it needed a lot of repair That, I think, made it even more attractive, because Walt perennially wanted to "fix things."

Even though the kids were far from settled, we assumed that situation to be "normal" for our time of life. Otherwise, we seemed to have shaped a livable context for the family in Southern California. At last, Walt and I both had full-time work.

Christmas that year became much more than a date on the calendar because Vic and Gem Fitch and their two boys came to spend the time with us. We did Disneyland and other "public" things together. Mainly, however, we sat around the fireplace and derived our chief satisfaction out of hours of talk—as we have always done.

A few days later Walt and Larry were working together on one of the apartments. Up in the attic, Walt slipped, fell across one of the rafters, and broke through the ceiling. Except for apparently superficial abrasions and bruises he seemed all right. He consented, however, to go to the Emergency Room at Loma Linda University Medical Center.

With that accident our lives took a drastic U-turn, never to be the same again.

During the subsequent medical investigations something very ugly came to light. For some time Walt had been having a slight swelling around the middle. From our viewpoint it seemed quite inconsequential. Now the doctors ordered a laproscopic examination of his abdomen.

The next day, I sat by Walt's bedside, both of us awaiting orders for his discharge.

The ensuing encounter is forever frozen in time for me. The doctor appeared in the doorway. He did not even step into the room. "Well, you have mesothelioma." He fiddled briefly with his clipboard. "Usually it attacks the lungs, but you have the tumors in the peritoneum. You have about a year to live." He shuffled his feet slightly. "Any questions?"

Shocked into speechlessness, neither one of us said a word. Therefore, the oncologist turned on his heel and walked off.

Walt was a man of few words, even at the best of times. Now we just clung together in silence. Neither of us asked the obvious question, "Why did this happen to us?" Instinctively we moved ahead to the other questions, "What are we going to do about it?" and "How will we cope with it all?"

We stared at each other for a long time before words could come. "I am going to fight it all of the way," Walt finally said. I knew he would. I also knew that I would wholly give myself over to help him do that thing.

Later on, I had to ask myself, "Where did that doctor learn his bedside manners?"

Recently, I had given a guest lecture right there on the Medical Center campus in a class on "Death and Dying." I presented the theme of Death as reflected in philosophy, music, and the visual arts. The medical students there

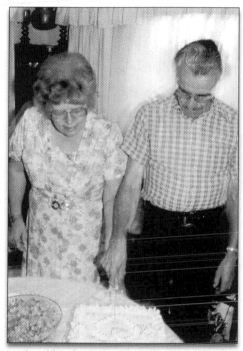

In the old Raley Drive house on the edge of La Sierra University campus, Walt and Dorothy celebrated their 32nd wedding anniversary together. The last.

had been very receptive and sensitive.

I told myself—again—that a physician can not get emotionally involved in the plight of every one of his patients. Our particular case did, however, seem rather far "beyond the Pale." Even now, thirty years later, what happened to us that day borders on barbarity, I believe.

Nonetheless, shortly afterward, Chaplain Jerry Davis, came into the room, seemingly from nowhere. I never knew how he found out about our need. I only know that he was there, the first to hold us up after we had been stricken down. He arranged for me to stay in the hospital with Walt that night. God had not left us alone. We knew that.

The next day we went home to sort our lives out. We had always lived quite abstemiously, so there was not much left to do to improve our case. "I just wish," Walt mused, "that there was something else I could give up that would help."

Accordingly he elected not to take chemotherapy and aligned himself with the Livingstone Clinic in San Diego, an institution specializing in immunology therapy. The dietary rules were stringent. We bought a juicer, and Walt drank carrot juice until the palms of his hands turned orange. As needed we would go San Diego to have the abdominal fluid drained off, liters at a time.

Having a worldwide network of friends we turned naturally to them.

Beginning in March, 1981, letters and phone calls poured in, by the scores and then the hundreds. Some expressed shock, others wisdom. Everyone spoke of faith, prayer, and hope. All mingled together, and Walt knew, indeed, that he was loved. Many letters began with "Words seem totally inadequate ...." Others ended with, "Maybe you

Friends came from afar—the Fitch family. Standing on the steps. Gem, Vic, Vic Jr., Shaun, Larry. Front. Walt, Dorothy, Lorna.

can feel that we care and are reaching out to you." This kind of comfort cannot be described. It can only be experienced.

My dear college classmate of more than thirty years ago, Lynne Kennedy-Schwindt, summed it up so well. "Yes, we are all praying," she wrote. "Praying that God in His mercy will do the very best thing for you—and that whatever that is, you will both have the courage and maturity to handle His decision. Either way might not be easy, because though death is a frightening stranger to us, life can be uncertain and trying in these difficult times. With our limited vision, we cannot demand of God that He heal you, but we do hope with all our heart that this will be His design."

One of the immediate results of our ordeal was that the University granted me tenure. The intricacies of the academic hierarchy are complex. Suffice to say, I found great comfort in this decision—not for ego purposes but for the simple assurance that I could count on having work as long as I needed it.

We now had a thousand new concerns to take up our strength. Not surprisingly, however, Walt carried on as usual, fitting his work around his medical necessities. He talked nothing but courage. I, on the other hand, knew that the end was only a matter of time. For one thing, he obviously had a genetic predisposition to cancer.

The living room held long memories of sadness. We had bought the round, carved table in Baguio, Philippines, years earlier. We didn't know then that it would become a kind of altar. Many, many prayers went up from there while Walt fought for his life.

Secondly, although they found various ways of masking the facts, the medical personnel unanimously agreed that no one survived mesothelioma. Where and when had Walt come in contact with asbestos? Who knew? I suspected that it was in the insulation of the old country schoolhouses he attended in his childhood in northern Canada. The incubation period can be decades long. (Today we are told that it can be as much as fifty years.) Really, it didn't make much difference. Whatever the initial cause, we now had to face it.

Something else underlined the sadness that now entered our lives. Soon after we got home our little Mitzi died. Less than a month later Rusty died. He just couldn't go on without her. They were both seventeen years old. The timing could hardly have been worse for me. I still had three Pomeranians, Sinta, Muffin, and Ziggy (a new stray had found us). In their shining eyes and wagging tails, however, I tried to read "hope."

We also had the canaries, Orphy (for the Greek musician Orpheus) and Davy (the "Sweet Singer of Israel"). Every mild California morning their singing literally pulled the sun up over the hills.

Then we went on with each day as it came to us.

CHAPTER 11

A Different Kind of World

THE AGES of MAN

I knew that our family would barely be holding to a survival course. Even so, from the start, we tried to set up a routine that we hoped would "pass for normal."

One piece of furniture took on significant symbolism. Years earlier in the Philippines we had bought a large, round coffee table at the woodcarvers' village, high in the mountains of Baguio. Ever since it has always stood in the middle of the living room. More times than can be counted when friends visited, we knelt in a prayer-circle around it. Thus, the finely carved table took on the aspects of an altar. No one said so, but I think we all felt it.

Meanwhile, my mother's older sister, Norma Youngberg, had come to live with us permanently. Mum not only managed Norma's diabetes, but she helped keep Walt's rigid diet on track. I, who had long ago determined not to have anything to do with things medical, now had to organize pills and fill syringes. Indeed, I always maintained that the best thing that ever happened to the medical profession was that I did not enter it. Now I came home every night to give Walt four or five injections, designed to boost his immune system.

At the same time, I had to keep my university life afloat. For many months in 1980 I had been tasked with setting up a Christian Writers' Conference on the La Sierra campus. I thoroughly enjoyed all of the "shop talk," the consulting with editors, lining up speakers for the conference, and finding those willing to lecture in my writing classes. Then, the very week that the conference opened, Walt was diagnosed with cancer. After that axe fell, I was hardly able to make even token appearances at any of the conference events.

Even so, I was able to keep my feet on the ground. Several things helped stabilize my professional life. At that time, La Sierra published the church journal, *Adventist Heritage*. At first, I worked as Associate Editor with Dr.

For the General Conference Session of Seventh-day Adventists in Indianapolis, (1990), La Sierra University set up a booth for *Adventist Heritage* (published from the campus). For many years, Dorothy co-edited the magazine with Paul Landa, kneeling behind the large poster. She continued as editor after his untimely death. Also pictured are Richard Weismeyer (center) and Don Bender—both from Loma Linda University.

Paul Landa. Later, when he fell ill, I became Senior Editor. Finding themes and matching them with pictorial resources appealed enormously to my sense of history and my interest in the arts. Those "editorial years" suited me well.

That job led to another. Working first with Paul and afterwards Dr. Fritz Guy, I started co-teaching a research course in the School of Religion. I had long held a rebellious notion, gleaned from my own doctoral mentor in Canada, Dr. Hank Hargreaves. Does scholarly writing have to be deadly boring? I needed to do very little investigation to prove that all of the "-ologies" suffer from a lethal writing style. Theology, I maintained, was surpassed only by Law in density and dullness.

As it turned out, my colleagues Paul and Fritz agreed with my idea. That is, if something is written and presented to the world, people have the right to be able to understand it and—perhaps—even to enjoy reading it. Hence, I brought in my creative writing techniques and set them before the graduate religion students. I tried to sell them on the concept of making their writing attractive to the readers. Indeed, over the years of teaching that class, I developed a strong missionary spirit. I actually felt God-called to do the task! Therefore, I can look back on those particular classes with fond memories.

Another undertaking with quite far-reaching effects was my teamwork with a fellow faculty-member, Alan Collins, a talented sculptor from England. Together we created three multi-media programs, "The Ages of Man," "The

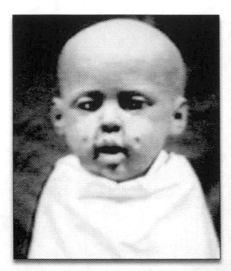

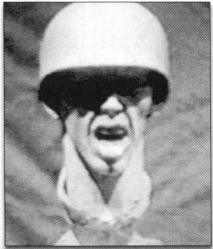

"The Ages of Man" presentation originated at Loma Linda University in 1982. Upper Left. Alan Collins began the sequence in which the audience saw their entire life-span pass before them in just one hour. (Our program was produced before "computer aging" had become commonplace.) Upper Right. The loud soldier marked the mid-point in the life sequence. Right. Alan covered the head of the old man. Next Page. Then, uncovering the head of the now-immortal man in a flash, Alan stood beside the two dramatically contrasted figures. The finale called for the joyful reading of resurrection scripture and Handel's exuberant solo, "The Trumpet Shall Sound."

Family of Man," and the "Passions of Man." All of them involved Alan's live modeling of large, 100-pound "heads" of clay. Calling for at least four readers, my scripts provided the scriptural and literary links to hold the sequences together. Then choral and instrumental music threaded their ways way through each hour-long performance.

Being the most portable of the three, "The Ages of Man" traveled widely. After its initiation in Loma Linda University's Fine Arts Festival in 1982, we carried the program to more than fifty colleges, churches and other institutions—all the way from Massachusetts to Hawaii and Florida to Canada. We ourselves never tired of "Ages." To see your whole life from infancy to old age pass before your eyes in a single hour always had a striking effect.

At the end came the grandeur of The Man passing from death to resurrection, to the glorious sounds of Handel's "The Trumpet Shall Sound!" Even today, the memory of it all still brings tears to my eyes. To be sure, that renewed experience came into my life at just the right time.

In mid-July, 1982, something quite wonderful happened. All the more precious because the event was embedded in a framework of illness and stress. For the first time in two years I even roused myself to write another journal about it. After two decades' absence, Walt and I went back to the Caribbean.

We began it as a road trip in my little "Cherry Tart," a red Plymouth Volare with a cream-white top. Because California to Miami, Florida, was almost 2,800 miles, we were thankful to have Larry with us. His youth, vitality, and driving abilities made Walt and me contented to leave him at the wheel for as many hours as possible.

Three full days brought us to the home of Norman and Leona Gulley near Collegedale, Tennessee. The next morning we added them to our entourage and headed south. Now it seemed that our holiday had truly begun. We had many hours of talk to make up since we'd left the Philippines four years earlier. The miles rolled past without our even noticing them.

After parking our car within the compound of the Inter-American

Division office in Coral Gables, we
made off to Miami Airport, in a
sparkly mix of sun and rain. The
muggy humidity, however, reminded
us that we were back in the tropics.
Modern, airy, and beautiful in wine-
colored furnishings, the new airport
made LAX (Los Angeles Airport) look
like something of a ghetto.

Eileen and Lyman had alighted
just an hour earlier from a night flight
out of LAX. Forthwith, our party of
seven filed onto a Cayman Airways jet.
Together we all flew twenty years back
into Walt's and my past. We'd not seen
the new logo of Cayman before. Sir
Turtle was a very fetching figure, half-
turtle and half-pirate (complete with
wooden leg) in red and green.

In a single hour the green hook of

**Walt's last travel was back to the Cayman
Islands. In the Comms' early days there,
exotic postage stamps had been a major
source of revenue. In a 360-degree about-
face, the islands now prosper with off-shore
banking and lively tourism,**

Grand Cayman afloat in the turquoise ocean appeared. We found that the
former village of Georgetown had now metamorphosed into something resem-
bling a little Miami Beach with high-rise, steel-and-glass buildings at its heart.
Only the sugar-white sands of Seven-Mile Beach remained the same.

Strange as the changes appeared, we knew we were home again. Norberg
and Mary Thompson gave us an air-conditioned condominium at Caribbean
Paradise on the beach at South Sound. Patsy Manderson-Seymour (one of our
Caymanian "daughters") owned National Car Rental. She gave us two
Chevettes to drive for the week. A week divided between the beach attractions
and the hospitality of the old friends who took us all to their hearts.

When it came time to leave for Jamaica, we had to leave Larry in
Cayman. Our meager budget could not absorb another air ticket. He stayed
with my dear friend Cynthia and suffered no hardship whatsoever.

The day we left, it turned out that neither of Cayman Airlines' two jets was operable. We fought (successfully) for seats on "The Pride of Cayman Brac," a non-air-conditioned prop plane intended for local, inter-island service. Hence, it took us three hours to get to Kingston, Jamaica.

As in Cayman, we were hosted by former students and colleagues, all the soul of kindness itself. The day after our arrival, however, Walt's ascites (fluid build up) got the best of him. He went into the Andrews Hospital in Kingston. Unfortunately, the procedure of draining off the fluid was unfamiliar and not efficiently done, so he had to stay overnight. He likened the process to "a snail going in reverse."

Dr. Neville Gallimore gave the six of us a week in the Ocho Rios Sheraton on the gorgeous North Shore. We visited the old haunts from Dunn's River to Montego Bay. Then we moved on to our old college campus in the mountains of Mandeville. Beautiful island, beautiful friends.

My Dad used to look at his slim bankbook and say, "Well, teachers are supposed to wait to get their rewards in heaven." Financially, that's true. Emotionally, never! I have always been amazed at the little things that students have noticed and remembered. Remembered with astonishing clarity. Actually, those West Indian days became a kind of "benediction" to Walt's and my travel years together

Larry met us in Miami, Lyman and Eileen flew home, and the rest of us picked up the Plymouth and headed up to Tennessee. At that point, it became clear that Walt should fly back to California. His physical discomfort had become very great. I think I must have known instinctively that this trip was the last foreign travel that Walt would ever do.

We thought, at first, of leaving Larry to bring the car home by himself. The price of a short-order plane ticket to California for me, however, was prohibitive. So Larry and I brought the Cherry Tart home together. We spent eight days on the road, stopping wherever and whenever we chose.

Christmas, 1982, came around, and we sent out our usual letter. By this time, Walt had lived with the mesothelioma for twenty-one months. While he spoke hopefully of Christmas and Calvary, he admitted that he tired very easily. When people asked him how he felt, he often replied, "Partly fair to cloudy." During the past year his brother, Harvey and nephew Elgin had both died of cancer. The same dark shadow also lived with us every day.

Still, Walt did his best to keep life in our house as normal as possible. Sometimes we'd get up to a real "thresher's breakfast." While his own diet was very restricted, he loved nothing more than making good food and seeing other people eat it. A trait he had inherited his ever-hospitable Dutch-German mother back on the old farm in Peace River, Canada. Imagine starting your day with scalloped potatoes, "terketts," cottage cheese, and fresh tomatoes. You can travel far on that kind of a meal.

We faced other problems, however, that had no material solution. In March we persuaded Lorna to return to Tennessee. We hoped that if she spent time at "The Bridge," a school for rootless young people, she might get on her feet. She stayed, in fact, for just three months.

Back once more in the Jamaican hills, six pilgrims reached the College campus in Mandeville. There they posed above the Mandeville Valley, occupying what has always been known as the "Seat of the Scornful." (L-R). Lyman Davis, Eileen Davis, Dorothy Comm, Walt Comm, Norman Gulley, Leona Gulley.

When school opened in the fall at Southern Missionary College, she wanted to enroll in their one-year Food Service course. The financial strain almost overwhelmed us, so we hoped she could apply for student aid.

Week after week, Walt wrote letters to Lorna. He urged her to find steady work.

To finish what she started. To overcome disappointments. To do the best she could with whatever she had (he recommended the first ten verses of Psalm 37). To consider carefully before she spent a dollar, or even fifty cents. To keep up her study assignments every day. "There are many things that you can do well enough to bring you success and satisfaction," he assured her. Whenever he could, he would send her a little spending money.

Up to this time, however, there was one thing no one understood about Lorna.

That knowledge would have certainly have curbed our expectations. Probably it would have enabled us to do a better parenting job. It would be, however, many years before we had a medical diagnosis. In fact, at the time, the illness did not even have a name! The poor girl had inherited a terrible legacy from her biological mother, Fetal Alcohol Syndrome.

So the days went by. I felt that I was fighting a shooting war on at least five fronts, all at one time.

From time to time friends from our days in the Far East dropped by. It pleased us to be so conveniently situated by La Sierra campus that they could easily find us. Then we found that the School of Health at Philippine Union College had started a scholarship fund in Walt's name. "Kind of a nice honor," he grinned. Then with his usual keen sense of responsibility, he added, "Now I have to get busy and help raise money for it, don't I?" Our years of overseas service would remain our brightest. Partly, no doubt, because we had, in those days, health on our side.

In August we exchanged our trailer for a tiny, ultra-maneuverable Toyota motor-home. Because of its shape and color, we named it "The Little Pumpkin." The first thing we did was spend two weeks camping in the San Jacinto mountains. Thereafter, whenever we could, we retreated to the mountains for a day or two of rest.

We didn't make any ambitious plans. Other than the main one. That was to stand ready for that day what will usher in God's "Peaceable Kingdom." For the time, we could live only one day at a time. Although Walt and I walked in the same direction, our paths were only parallel. They seldom intersected, because he was a man of so very few words. By now we had entered our "last year." I realized it, but I really had no one to talk to about the journey.

In a letter to Lorna, Walt admitted that he might "have to ask for sick leave." That the work was very tiring, and that he had to "take it in small pieces ... with some rest in between." Thinking to spare me, Walt never said anything like that to me. Perpetually courageous and optimistic, he conceded nothing.

Still, I could see him dying before my very eyes. The signs were clear enough for anyone wishing to read them.

With these strong premonitions, I made long-range plans. For two years I had been on duty twenty-four hours a day, seven days a week, between classroom and home. Early in 1983, I wrote a letter to my chairman, Dr. Lynn Foll. From the start my colleagues in the English Department had stood by me through the bleak times. Still, both they and I needed to make a roadmap of some kind. When Lynn replied, he said, among other things, "You are probably our best teacher." I felt that I was barely holding my own, so I deeply appreciated his

Walt 's dedication to alternative methods and to diet extended his life three years beyond the one year he had been given when he was diagnosed with mesothelioma. No one ever figured out where he contacted asbestos.

kind words. I knew that when the end came, I would have all the support and compassion that I could absorb. Also, that I would be given time to heal.

Meanwhile, I did my best to keep my career alive. In the summer I attended the Andrews University Writers' Conference as one of the guest faculty. Before Christmas, I read a paper at the Modern Languages Association Convention in New York City. All good, but with all that was going on at home, I knew that I was barely keeping "my foot in the door" of scholarly enterprise.

In mid-summer we decided to help Larry to further independence by installing him as "landlord" in our triplex. We redecorated one of the well-worn apartments for him and installed a good big refrigerator and a piggy back washer-and-dryer combo. The arrangement, however, didn't last long.

Happily, his training in auto-mechanics school had enabled him to give up his tedious five months of work in a convalescent home. Nonetheless, with the help of a friend he'd known in Singapore, he finally found work in aviation. So, without a backward glance he moved to Guam, where he worked for Freedom Air, a local charter airline.

Our longtime college friends, Jack and Olivine Bohner, lived there, and Larry had, at least for the present, landed in a good place. At 3.15 one morning he cheerfully woke us up to announce that he'd arrived safely. He had a security pass to all of the Guam Airport and had already started work the day he set foot on the island.

As winter approached, Walt's optimism seemed to be as incurable as his cancer. After three years, he grasped at each shred of hope. Indeed, for a few months, the fluid had reduced in his abdomen. The trips to Livingstone Clinic lessened, as did the swelling in his feet and legs. When Lorna inquired about his health, he declared: "The last few months I am doing better, so you don't have to worry. With the present prospect and God's blessing I plan to be around for a long time yet! The treatments are really helping me." He truly believed that.

Full of gratitude for being surrounded by people who cared, Walt maintained a blazing assurance of God's Kingdom to come. I kept my thoughts to myself and said nothing. When someone is terminally ill, you have to let him fight the battle in any way that he can.

So, Christmas, 1983, found our family still together in our quaint old homestead-style house, enfolded in what looked, and even felt, like warm contentment. We had been learning lessons in a very hard school for a long time. We knew that we had to live one day at a time in order to be content within the "cancer world" that we'd been forced into. We made no ambitious plans. Indeed, virtually no plans at all.

Between April and June, 1984, Walt had two surgeries, first at Loma Linda University Medical Center and then at Hillside Hospital in San Diego. Both attempted to "debulk" the twenty-five pounds of fluid he carried. Although they removed six liters of fluid, much more had jelled. It was loculated so that inserting a drainage tube was useless. His liver was also now covered with tumor. Walt described both surgeries as a "complete flop" and had to acknowledge that we were back "to square one."

One evening, when a large group of friends from Philippine Union College came to visit, I discovered how very marginal I myself had become. Someone had closed the sliding glass doors to the patio. (We usually left them open.) Unseeing, I walked straight through them. I collapsed with a twisted back, a sprained wrist and badly cut lower lip.

The next morning, as usual, I drove to San Diego, taking Walt back to the Clinic. He lay in back seat while a strange odor and much heat enveloped the car. Two mufflers had split. By driving slowly and making frequent stops at overpasses to cool down, we limped into a Midas shop in the north part of the city and had repairs made.

I can only remember thinking "I don't have enough strength left even to panic." My own body—and now the car too—were hardly functional. In a general letter Walt confessed: "We are tossed and battered, but we are not overwhelmed or discouraged. God has a thousand ways of which we know nothing."

Yes, a thousand ways. At the moment, however, I could scarcely identify one of them.

At the end of June Lorna came home again. She had not graduated. Larry, on the other hand, had bought his first car (a 1978 Datsun) for $700. He loved his work, and he promised to telephone us twice a week.

By this time, Auntie Norma had suffered a series of strokes, and we had to put her in a nursing home. As she had grown more frail and forgetful, she fixed her eyes ever more firmly on her Lord's coming. She filled the days— hers and ours—with good things. Like the four dogs, sunshine, and quilting. Now that pleasure was gone. Although she recognized us, she couldn't talk to us. The empty space she left behind was a large one, and I felt it deeply.

On June 14, 1984, my colleague, Dr. Frank Knittel, wrote: "I wish I could wave a magic wand and brighten your days ahead with a miracle. I can't do that, but I can tell you that I think of you constantly. You are never away from our prayers." He knew, and I knew. There could not be many days left.

The immunology treatments in San Diego, along with the diet and injection routine had helped, but they had not cured. Day by day, we'd lost ground.

Finally, Walt allowed himself some days (and later weeks) off duty. Retreating with our camping trailer up in the Southern California mountains helped calm frayed nerves and escalating weakness.

Even so, the one year of life that the doctors had predicted for Walt had now extended to almost four.

In the first week of August, another "Minchin Family Reunion" had been planned. Forty of my relatives from all over the country would spend the weekend in a cabin high in the mountains above San Bernardino.

By this time Walt was in a hospital in Tijuana, Mexico. For special treatments recommended by the San Diego Clinic. Nonetheless, he was determined to get out for just a few hours to join the family. When it quickly became obvious that he could not do it, I was equally determined to stay with him there in his hospital room.

"Go! You need to be with your family," he insisted.

So, on Friday night, I crossed the border, back into San Diego and drove north. I picked up Mum and Lorna, and the next morning we headed up to the mountains. Walt had requested three songs from our always music-minded family: "Children of the Heavenly Father," "What, Never Part Again," and "It May be at Morn." I recorded them for him to hear.

I returned to the hospital in Mexico on Sunday morning. When he saw me, Walt threw his arms open. "Don't leave me again." He clung to me in a passion.

"But you insisted that I go." I would never have left him for even an hour, except that he had demanded it.

"Yes, but not now. Not again."

Then he told me about the angel. "He came here Friday night right after you left." He pointed to the bed where I had been sleeping all week. "He sat right there. He stayed with me through Sabbath, until this morning."

"Did you see him?"

"Not exactly. He was a presence." Walt pointed again to the bed. "Right there."

Suddenly I understood why my absence had been necessary. To make room for the angel I had to leave. In pain and increasing incoherence, Walt had been constantly distracted, asking me for this and that. They were useless things that couldn't help ease him anyway, but they filled the time, hour after hour.

I had to believe in the coming of the angel, because there was a compelling reason to do so.

Walt had a very, very private story that he seldom shared with anyone. We'd been married several years before I even knew about it. In the spring of his third year at Canadian Union College he had borrowed a bicycle to ride to the nearby town of Lacombe.

At the end of College Avenue he waited for a northbound truck to roar past. As the dust cloud settled, he launched into the intersection of the old, narrow highway. Another roar and a southbound truck sped around the corner and bore down on him. At that moment, a firm hand on his right shoulder immobilized him as the truck thundered by, inches from the front wheel of the bicycle, almost sucking him into the vortex.

"It was my angel," Walt whispered. "I should have died right there, but … " he shook his head incredulously, "but I knew then that I must have some work to do."

He threw the bicycle down under the trees and fell to his knees in gratitude. "And right there by that little pond, the place was full of angels. All around me."

Now, in that lonely hospital room in Mexico, I stood between the two beds. I humbly sat down on the one where the angel had been. How, I wondered, could I take the place of an angel!

What was it that my friend Lynne had written three-and-a-half years ago? "May you be sustained by shining angels!" It had happened. Walt's life had, in fact, actually been "bookended" by his angel—the beginning and now the end. The two of us looked at one another. We both understood.

Left. Try as he might, Walt could not attend the long-planned Minchin Family Reunion in Lake Arrowhead, California (August 4 and 5, 1984). Right. He died four days later. He was buried on a sunny hillside—the kind of "outdoors" that he always loved.

I had just three more days to go. I was surrounded by hospital staff who spoke no English and left the bedside nursing up to me.

"If this should be our last hour together," I told him, "There are some things we need to talk about." He seemed relieved and was able to say things that he'd held back all the years. He was very tired. As if all of the tiredness that he'd fought for the past four years swept over him in a single wave.

He began to drift in and out of consciousness, and conversation came in increasingly small fragments. "What will you do when I am gone?" he asked.

"I will have time off from work, and I want to go home to Australia for a few weeks."

He managed a small smile. "That's good. I want you to do that."

"Then," I added. "after a while, I will lie down beside you, and we'll both wait together for the Resurrection." We had another one of those very rare moments. "I see," he whispered, "that I have the easy part—going now. It will be harder for you."

I reminded him of the many, many people all over the earth who have prayed for and loved us through these past hard years. "Can you feel their arms around you?"

"Oh, I do! I surely do!" Again, he was almost able to smile.

The next day, in the late afternoon, the doctor (the only one who spoke English) wanted to try one more procedure, a risky one. A couple of hours later, Walt was wheeled back into the room, raving. With one hand he clutched at me and with the other he kept pulling the oxygen tube out. Doggedly, I kept putting the tube back in.

As if it made any difference.

At about 10.30 p.m., the doctor appeared from somewhere. "I want to give you something so you can sleep. You need to." Utterly exhausted, I agreed, and fell on to the bed. The one that I'd been sharing with the angel.

At 1.45 a.m. the doctor was beside me again, shaking me awake. Walt was dead. Peacefully asleep, at last.

I don't know exactly what happened in those three hours that I was drugged. I decided not to ask. I looked one more time at my husband, picked up my purse, and stumbled out into the lobby. It was time for the angel to take charge.

I was still there when they wheeled Walt out on the gurney, but I couldn't look at him again. Someone brought out a couple of bags of our personal possessions and set them down beside me.

I sat alone for another hour before I could drag myself down to the car. I drove up to the border crossing into San Diego. By 4 a.m. I found a pay phone at a motel where we'd once stayed. I called Mum. By sunrise Norman and Leona arrived at the motel. She drove my car home, while I sat beside her, frozen numb.

My family stayed on from the reunion. They were all there with me in the Arlington Church for Walt's funeral on Monday, August 13, 1984. Before we got to that day, however, Auntie Norma died. (Her funeral was on the following Monday.) In just seven days our family experienced a reunion, a baby dedication, two deaths, and a wedding.

I don't have very clear recollections of how it was all managed. Only that I was surrounded by many loving hands that made everything fall into the right places. Somewhere in the middle of those days, Larry walked in. Someone—I don't know who—picked him up at LAX and brought him home.

At the end of it all, I had just one thing left to do. Get ready to go to Australia.

A Prayer for Walt
(Monday, August 13, 1984, Riverside, California)

Today, Lord, we've had a triumph,
A kind of victory and homecoming.
Most people would have called it a funeral,
But for him this day held no fear.
Therefore, he wanted us to celebrate hope—and do it with color!

Of course, he didn't want to leave us.
He fought for life with a courage and perseverance that
Few of us have seen matched anywhere, I think.
Yet, for all that he prayed and had faith, he's gone.
The pain was too much. He just couldn't hold out any longer.

He loved Your Church with a zeal no man has ever questioned.
He filled his home life with so many practical, loving attentions.
You know, Lord, how dearly he loved to serve people,
To wait on them at the table and see them eat—
Even after there was little he could eat himself.

He spoke so often of needing rest.
"Just a little rest, and I'll feel better."
Now he does rest, in the best place of all, Your arms.
He made Your will his own for so long
That he'll be perfectly at home with You.

How he loved the outdoors! Let him run in Your heavenly meadows.
He was always talking to other people about You,
So he'll be looking to see everyone who comes into Your house
Then we'll hear his rich, baritone voice again—singing in Your choir.
I know, Lord, that he'd enjoy serving at Your celestial banquet table too.

So today we call it victory, not defeat.
We make it a time to renew our own pledges to You.
Walt has just gone on ahead of the rest of us.
Watch over his resting place out there in the wide, open California hills,
Until You give him back to us again.

—Dorothy Minchin-Comm

CHAPTER 12

A Prescription for Recovery

The actual preparation required for leaving the country proved to be very complex. The University granted me a three-month leave of absence. That was the easy part.

Convinced that I could not—or would not—manage household finances, Walt had always kept a firm hold on these things himself. For the past several months, however, he had been too sick to keep up with the task. Now I faced his desk, buried in a morass of bills and paperwork. I couldn't even be sure which banks we were attached to. I realized that I should have insisted long ago on being better informed, but it was too late to worry about that now.

A lawyer and CPA, Walt's nephew, Roger Gaskins, drove up from San Diego to rescue me. It took all day, and we filled half a dozen trash bags. When he left, the desk was organized, and I felt truly liberated. Then I went to work on my own desk. At least I understood what was there. I remember being driven by some inner force. Some nights I didn't go to bed at all. During this high-velocity period, I re-vamped my rental properties, set up a retirement fund for myself with the University, and took my financial affairs firmly in hand.

At church I had two friends who loved cars in the masculine way that Walt had always done. I was left with six vehicles on the property. The men disposed of five of them, leaving me with the only one I cared for, my Little Nutmeg, a 1984 metallic bronze Oldsmobile coupe.

Someone else helped me donate Kandy to the University equestrian center. Walt had had such high hopes for his little horse, but toward the end it was Mum and Lorna who had to feed and water her. Such a pretty girl, but she had to go.

I moved Lorna over to one of the triplex apartments and hoped that she would find work by the time I got home.

Then Mum transferred upstairs so that we could rent out her downstairs apartment. Adwen and Karen Yap, a young Chinese couple from Malaysia, moved in. Since our travel plans included my meeting Mum in the Philippines, the newly-weds would manage the house (including three dogs) while we were both gone. (Twenty-five years later, after Adwen had become a dentist, I became his patient. To this day, under his skilled care, I have—and will continue to retain—all of my own teeth.)

With the help of these people—and many more besides—all of the chores were finally complete. Exhausted as I was, I set out upon the long journey that I instinctively felt was right for me. Only thus could I make a clean break away from the painful scenes of the past four years. I wasn't sure exactly how my recovery would take place, but I believed that it would happen.

On Monday night, October 1, 1984, I flew out across the Pacific. I passed the hours amid dozing, drinking, chatting passengers, squalling babies and carefully programmed stewardesses. I was very much alone, however, not yet accustomed to my "widow's weeds."

We ate two breakfasts. One before Auckland, where the city lay green and lovely under a long, red strip of sunrise. The other after we left New Zealand. Then suddenly Australia came up. At Sydney Airport, three cousins waited for me, Betty and Ken Butcher and Peter Pocock. Between jetlag, my emotional disabilities, and the excitement of knowing that I'd landed back home again, we drove right over the Harbor Bridge before I realized where we were.

Since my last visit ten years ago, Betty had remarried. She and Ken lived in a kind of "bush park" out on Matthews Road. Three dozen king parrots, jazzy in their red and green feathers, ate grain in the front yard like chickens, along with the Willie Wagtails. Ducks paddled in the pond, supervised by the magpies. A chorus of bell birds and kookaburras provided the sound effects.

I fell into bed and knew no more. The next day I awoke to see Betty standing in the doorway. "Are you all right?" Well, yes! My mind began to clear a little. "You've been asleep for fourteen hours," Betty smiled.

The days passed. Betty's children took us to the Royal Motor Yacht Club on Lake Macquarie to celebrate her birthday. We listened to dinner music, ate mushroom pastries and took in the nighttime view of the lakeshore.

For my fifty-fifth birthday, Betty, Grace, Verna, and some of the grandchildren had a picnic lunch down by the Swing Bridge at Dora Creek where we used to

Mercifully, Nephew Roger Gaskins, CPA came and spent the time it took to clear the untended desks, pay the bills and induct Dorothy into the world of household finance that Walt had always kept to himself. Only then could she leave for Australia (October, 1984).

swim. Afterwards Charles and Grace gave me a wooden bowl he had made, turned from a knot in the camphor-laurel tree at Sunnyside (Ellen White's Avondale home). Charles Sommerfeld was a very skilled craftsman.

When I stop now to think of it, every social occasion was marked by lively conversation. It just jumped instantaneously from the mundane to the profound. Ideas leaped from head to head like lightning, everyone eager to join in. I can't think of one occasion that fell flat, even for a moment. Yes, that was my family!

Another day we visited "Kirambee," Uncle Len's house in Wahroonga. It looked so small. Shrubs enveloped the place, and a mass of purple wisteria climbed over the back ramp and around the windows of the "Sleep Out " that one time housed us five little girls. I wondered who was lying below those magic windows now! Whoever it was, they only thought it was theirs. In a very real way it would always remain ours.

I spent a few days with Peter Pocock in his bachelor digs at Potts Point. He now had a good job as a classical music consultant with the Australian

Broadcasting Corporation. His bay window looked out over the "yachty" portion of Sydney Harbor. Within three days we went to two operas at the Sydney Opera House. First, Mozart's "Marriage of Figaro" and then Verdi's "Aida." The staging was stunning.

The appearance of the prima donna in "Aida," however, caused a gasp of surprise from the audience. She must have weighed near 500 pounds and was costumed in a kind of parachute. One could hardly imagine her as an object of passion either on or off stage. Certainly, she could have fulfilled no one's picture of an abused little slave girl. The leading man, a long, lean German, couldn't even get his arms around her for the last love scene. Magnificent voices and the grandest of music, but the visual discrepancies proved rather distracting.

I certainly had not envisioned myself as a public speaker on this journey. I assumed, in fact, that I simply was not up to doing it. I was wrong. At Avondale College, John Cox, Chairman of the English Department, asked me to take a class lecture on Hawthorne's *Scarlet Letter.* In the mission story time at the Village Church. I talked about the "mission field" of Loma Linda University and how people in *academe* can contribute to Christian outreach. (I had some ideas, and here was a place to voice them!) In Perth I even preached my Balaam sermon, "The Man that God Called Eight Times." I had not prepared for appointments of this kind, but they seemed to be good for me.

Before I left California Betty had written, "Don't buy an air ticket between Sydney and Perth. I'm getting a surprise ready." It turned out that the two of us and our cousin Grace Sommerfeld were going to drive all the way to Perth. The question after I arrived was whether or not Grace's sister, Verna Britten, would go with us also.

Verna lived in a little house in the village, behind an eight-foot-high wall of pink azaleas (in full bloom). Like her own dainty self, the home was perfection. It took several days, but finally Verna decided to join the rest of us for the long trans-Australia road-trip.

Then she had shopping to do. "I have to find another dilly bag (cosmetic bag)," she told me. "Do you want to go to Newcastle with me tomorrow?"

I assumed that the shopping trip would be simple. Not that I minded walking all over Newcastle. But nothing was right. Not even when we stood before a great mountain of cosmetic bags piled high on a kind of billiard table. Surely Verna would find what she needed there. Not so. We went home empty-handed.

Two days later she asked me if I wanted to go again. I declined. After all, I had already seen every dilly bag Newcastle had to offer, hadn't I?

Eventually, on Sunday morning, October 21, we headed west in Betty's red Falcon station wagon. Betty did the driving. I looked at the map, as necessary, recorded happenings, and took pictures. Grace took charge of the lunch box and catered the meals. Verna regaled us with stories.

Nine hours later, in Broken Hill, Betty and I unloaded the car while Grace organized our food for the next day. It took all of Verna's time to go through her dilly bags, apply her night creams, and so forth. "Nothing wrong with Vern," Betty remarked on the side, "that half a dozen kids wouldn't fix."

Sometimes the car rocked with hilarity. Full of family folklore and entertainment, Verna was also a great sport. "It's all very well," she said as we settled into the motel room that first night. "If I weren't along, you know you wouldn't have anything to laugh at." What would we do without her, indeed!

That was the day that I realized how much I had been laughing. It had been such a long time! I'd almost forgotten what laughter felt like.

People along the way thought we were just four old ladies trekking out into the Never-Never. When we stopped for petrol (gas), they asked where we came from. "Sydney." (Near enough.)

"Where are you going?"

"Perth." Then they'd just about drop their teeth in astonishment. Almost 2,500 miles! Many Australians have never been to Perth, because it's way far out there. But, of course, they knew nothing of us and how we all needed to see our home again.

Road signs warned of kangaroos, wombats and wild camels. We saw nothing, however, but dead kangas. That reminded us of how much damage a collision with a big red kangaroo could do to a car. Therefore, we had decided not to drive the narrow, two-lane trans-continental highway after dark. So, we simply weren't out at the right time to see much wildlife. We did, however,

Three dear, compassionate cousins in New South Wales planned a trans-Australian road trip for Dorothy. Left. The competent Betty Britten-Butcher who bought a red Falcon station wagon for the journey. (She was never happier than when she had a baby on her knee.) Center. The expert homemaker and musician, Grace Britten-Sommerfeld, who saw to it that we had good food all of the way. Right. *Raconteur extraordinaire,* Verna Britten, who entertained us with stories across the thousands of miles.

see flights of cockatoos and galahs. Even a pair of emus loping along the roadside.

On the other hand, the springtime desert was alive. By the third day the trees were shrinking and thinning out. The small gum trees had umbrella tops to maximize the shade. In the early morning, we had heavy dew and fog. Then shafts of light shot through the ragged holes in the clouds, falling into pools of light on the dusty green spinafex (salt bush). Suddenly I saw six 'roos leaping under the graceful umbrellas of the mulga and mallee trees. Flowers banked the roadside like a private driveway. Sometimes we passed acres of violent red and intense black of Sturt Peas in full bloom. To be sure, springtime is when Australia must be seen.

In mid-afternoon we reached the true Nullabor ("No Tree") Plain. At Eucla (billed as the "Gateway to Western Australia") we roved the white sand dunes for an hour. There, waves and mountains of sand were busily burying the old Perth-Adelaide Telegraph Station built in 1877.

We stopped at Mundrabilla, a town consisting of just three entities, a gas station, a motel and a tavern. Our room was furnished with four iron beds, *circa* 1900. On each was an elegantly folded towel with a packet of liquid soap set in the middle. "Quite classy!" we told ourselves.

Grace was the first to take a shower. "The water is very brackish," she remarked when she came out. The special soap packets, then, were intended to make bathing in salt water possible.

Verna was the last to go into the bathroom. She stayed a very long time. Fastidious to a degree, she chose rather to use her own assorted toiletries out of her four dilly bags.

She emerged like a wraith, in much distress. "What shall I do!" Her eyes looked like two black holes in a white blanket. When she couldn't get the soap off, she had tried to dislodge it with her lotion. Then she put powder on top of that. Now she was covered with a fine, apparently non-removable, chalky paste. She looked ready to play a part in "The Mikado."

"You had better just go back and use the packet soap, Vern." Grace always had a practical solution. We tried not to laugh too loudly while Verna went back to make her repairs.

By the next night, we found a pleasant double room in what appeared to be the best motel in Kalgoorlie. Our fourth-floor balcony overlooked the gold mines. By then Verna, not surprisingly, had a towering migraine and needed a "cuppa" (cup of tea).

I left my cousins to get things sorted out (and to take fresh-water showers). I walked some fifteen blocks around the center of town studying the well-kept colonial architecture, iron-lace and all. Lastly, I stopped to pay homage to the statue of Paddy Hannon, the first man to pick up a gold nugget in Kalgoorlie.

The next day, as we pushed on toward Perth, the highway became more lovely by the mile, with the orange Western Australian Christmas Bush dominating the landscape. It stood slender and willowy over banks of muted purples and blues, wavy whites and creams, and sassy little patches of yellow.

We had found our roots. As we turned south toward Quairading, the rock cliffs and salt ponds gave way to narrow red roads running between the wheat fields and "hedgerows" of twisted gum trees. Little had changed since my Dad and Uncle Len rode their ponies, Ginger and Dolly, to school every

day. Nothing remains of Hillcrest Farm except the cistern and sheep shed—containing a dead sheep in a very advanced stage of decay. No one has any reason to go out there now.

For the first and only time, I visited the tiny Methodist Church, alone in the wide spread

Loading and unloading the car, morning and evening, became automatic as we all learned our moves.

of wheat and sheep paddocks. The churchyard has just one grave left in it, that of John Minchin, my Australian grandfather whom I never knew. We had to pull a fallen tree off the tomb so that we could take pictures. He died too early in 1918, only three years older than I was at that time when I stood by his burial place.

We reached the home of Betty's eldest daughter Kaye up in the Darling Range, overlooking Perth. Betty gloried in her new "Nana" job with her latest grandson, four-month-old Rohan. I went off to visit Cousin Jess Barrett. Still living in the old people's community she remained very much her own mistress. Just being with her for a couple of days was, of itself, a tonic for me.

Then we had a great roundup of cousins in Kings Park for a picnic, overlooking our ancestral city of Perth and the Swan River. Sadly, the handsome black swans that gave the river its name are now to be seen only in the old prints that I studied in the West Australia Archives and Art Galley. Or in the zoo.

A week later those same cousins, sons and daughters of the pioneers, celebrated a more solemn event at the annual Thanksgiving service at All Saints Church in the Upper Swan district. The fields that our ancestors had cleared and cultivated surrounded the churchyard. "The First Five Hundred [Settlers]" are Western Australia's equivalent of America's Mayflower passengers or the DAR ("Daughters of the Revolution"). We sat among the tombstones, under

Left. We were going home, so entering Western Australia called for a stop. (L-R) Dorothy, Verna, Grace. Right. Just across the state line, along the Eyre Highway, lie the remains of Eucla (1877) on the Nullabor Plain. While the Great Australia Bight creates a horizon line at the back, the sand hills in the foreground have devoured the long-defunct Telegraph Station. A plague of rabbits in the 1890s destroyed all vegetation, destabilized the dunes, and caused the Station to be abandoned. We added our footprints to the pristine sand. Not many travelers come this way now.

the trees, while two vats of water boiled in preparation for tea. Just past the double grave of our great grandparents, down on the riverbank behind the church, lay the unmarked grave of our Great-Great-Grandfather, James Minchin. He died just seven years after arriving in Swan River Colony in 1829.

Grace, Jess, Verna and I made the four-hour bus trip down the coast to Busselton to see our Cousin Allan Laird and his wife. Their lovely retirement home was within surf-sniffing distance of the beach. We spent hours looking at old pictures. What a lot of laughing we did there!

We took a trip down through the karri forests to Cape Leewin, There the Indian Ocean meets the Southern Ocean in a tumult of currents. The colors of the sea rivaled even those of the Caribbean. Fine Kangaroo Paw flowers, large and healthy in brilliant, velvety reds and greens, lined the roadside.

Then everything changed as suddenly as it had begun. On Monday November 12, Betty, Verna, and Grace headed back east. They would miss me out there in the desert, I knew, but no more than I would miss myself being there with them.

The next night was my last in Australia. Eleven of us descendants of

Pioneer James Minchin went to His Majesty's Theater, to see Lehar's opera, "The Merry Widow." I remember Dad telling of wonderful concerts he attended there as a lad. This beautifully preserved Victorian theater on Hay Street stands on the plot of land that was originally given to James Minchin (1829). Almost 150 years ago, his widow sold it for five pounds! Had the property stayed in the family, we could all be retired on the interest of our investments and never have to work again!

The mid-afternoon flight out of Perth on Wednesday, November 15, took me across farmlands with the sun hazing away into the outback to the east. Soon the brilliant color contrasts of the turquoise, sand-barred north coast with its beaches and reefs came up on the left. I took one last look at the saw-toothed edge of Australia as we veered northwest. Being ethnic Australian, Qantas served a little pavlova for dinner tonight. That would be good enough for those who never tasted my cousin Sue Driscoll's pavlovas back in New South Wales. I, however, gave it a C- grade.

I landed in my hometown of Singapore at 8.30 p.m. Once again, I was set up at the guest room across from Far Eastern Academy. Right where I used to stay when I came to see Larry and Lorna. In the morning, I awoke to rain. The dripping trees and water rushing through the gutters exhilarated me. A total recall of childhood when I learned to love rain amid lush green things, with moss on the walls and lizards on the ceilings. A thousand undefined, nameless sensations have always meant "Singapore" to me. Probably that is one reason I'll never fully adjust to Southern California.

Again, friends surrounded me and allowed me to want for nothing. Socially, my days were climaxed by a breakfast buffet at the Shangri-la Gardens. Surrounded by waterfalls, pools of Japanese carp, and ferns spilling over the balconies, the guests, fresh out of the swimming pools, sat in their white terry robes like refugees out of colonialism. Elegantly appointed tables featured much silver, ranges of cutlery, attentive waiters and serviettes the size of bath towels! We made as many trips as we wished for Danish pastries, pancakes and waffles, scrambled eggs and hash browns, plus meats for those so inclined. Also, huge platters of red papaya, wedges of fresh pineapple and cantaloupe, berries, syrups and jams, as well as hot drinks. Once again, good conversation prevailed, and we all vowed not to eat again until next week.

Then I gave myself a long weekend to Thailand. Bo Morton met me when I arrived in "The Kingdom" at Don Muang Airport late Sunday night. We immediately set off for Cheng-mai, a train journey of thirteen hours up through the jungles. We traveled in second class Pullman coaches. Dad used to make his up-country journeys thus in the 1930s. The dark countryside slipped past us, and the air cooled as we got away from the sweat-bath that is Bangkok. Twenty-five miles down the track two gun-toting soldiers were at my elbow desiring to see my passport. Fortunately I've knocked about the world long enough to know that I must have it with me at all times.

I slept with my camera bag under my head and my little suitcase under my feet. Otherwise, we'd be robbed blind at every stop. All *faren* (foreigners) aboard were warned about this eventuality.

It took three *song tao* (jeepney rides) to get us across the washboard road, first to Mamalie and then to Matan where the school is. This campus is where Dr. Helen Morton was murdered only three years ago. Helen's lovingly tended grave is beside her little hospital. The teakwood cross is inscribed in English, Thai, Hmong and Karen. This morning the sunrise came up behind the shrine like a forest fire.

Next came my stopover in the Philippines. Again I was among old friends, but in a new place. The city-bound Baesa had now completely given way to the spacious Silang site. This must be one of the loveliest college campuses in the whole world. Mum had arrived a couple of days earlier, and I met her in our little guestroom at the top of the hill, just below the water tank. She, of course, would stay on with her "Philippine children" until I finally got back to California.

Actually, I hardly left the campus for the next two weeks. I was occupied with committees, workshop instruction, and so forth. I felt that I'd slipped temporarily back into the slot I left in 1978. My days were, indeed, full and rich. Moreover, I *needed* to be edging back toward the classroom.

Probably the finest and most demanding occasion was the luncheon in honor of Walt. I was presented with a bronze plaque inscribed for his work in founding what is now the International Institute of Health. The music, the

When our Grandfather John Minchin sold his farm on the Swan River, near Perth, he homesteaded land east of the Darling Range. Not a good idea. His grave is the only one remaining at the tiny Methodist Church in South Caroling, Western Australia. After we had cleared off years of overgrowth and debris, we three granddaughters stood together beside the grandpa that we never knew. (L-R). Verna, Dorothy, Grace.

kind words of our former colleagues—he might have guessed the kind of things they would be saying.

Walt, on the other hand would have insisted that he was in no way that remarkable. Yet he worked with utter dedication. All of us who have been left behind know that. One of the songs, "Ordinary People," struck me as a special tribute to Walt's consistent life. Can a man have a more sincere compliment? About then, I wanted to weep but I managed not to. I had been told that more than $3,000 had already come into the Walter Comm Memorial Scholarship Fund.

Last of all, I made room for three idle weeks in Guam. I planned for (and got) some extra sleep. The flight from Manila to Agana provided a glorious seascape all of the way. We passed through three tropical storms—opaque white—to emerge again among the towering thunderheads mounted over the sunlit, royal blue Pacific Ocean.

Friends met me at the plane and draped me with a red hibiscus lei. Among them stood my Larry, in his work clothes and wearing his "GUM" airport pass.

Larry had a good-two-bedroom apartment, just spitting distance from the beach, but with no air-conditioning. So I was established at Jack and Olivine Bohner's place. Olivine's sewing room wasn't large but it was cool.

While Bohners were off to their teaching jobs at the University of Guam, I made a dozen *muu-muus* out of fanciful Polynesian prints. (Ready-made they'd cost from $40 to $60 apiece.) My creations, therefore, were ethnic gifts to take home from Guam. Larry worked long hours but came to spend his nights with us.

Several days I took Larry to work and then had the use of his car to explore the island. Pockmarked with the salt water, the Datsun looked quite leprous, but it performed well enough. The roads were of early postwar vintage. A spatter of rain makes them slick. In

On my journey back to home and my work, I spent Christmas with Jack and Olivine Bohner and Larry in Guam. Fascinated by the wealth of textiles available on the island, I set up my own "sweat shop" in Olivine's sewing room and made ten muu-muus, including a matching set for her and me.

the interest of economy, some creative entrepreneur mixed ground coral into the paving mixture. Now just a small bit of dampness turns the roads treacherous and slimy.

The little island offered more interest than you might at first expect. I especially enjoyed the Piti Rocks. I could hardly tear myself away from watching the grand crashing of house-high surf on the shore. Surely nothing could live in that violence. Once in a while, sharks and barracuda appeared in that huge wall of a wave. Then, just before they should be impaled on the rocks, I saw them turn and swim safely back into the sea. Resistance to such force amazed me. So, survival against great odds is a possibility, I told myself.

For my first Christmas alone, I was not alone. Larry and I spent the day with Bohners' family and friends. Afterwards we played the Dictionary Game. Even so I knew, right then, that Christmas never would the same again. Walt enjoyed it so heartily in the old German traditions that he grew up with. In the time since he left, I seemed to have lost a little more of the "spirit" with each succeeding year.

The next day, as Larry and I waited for my flight home, Jack rushed into the terminal with three warm cinnamon rolls, just out of his oven. "To sustain you on the long flight." He gave me a hug. Then Larry walked with me right out to the plane. As we taxied onto the runway, I glimpsed him silhouetted against the door marked "Freedom Air & Lockheed."

My quest for recovery was almost over.

At LAX Kevin, Lorna and the Leland Wilsons met me with their station wagon. Once home, I found that Mum, Adwen and Karen Yap had supper waiting. The latter had cut a banner out of Christmas paper "Welcome Home Grandma and Aunt Dorothy." We left it in place for several extra days, just to consolidate ourselves.

So it all ended. I had just one more thing to do. On Sunday morning I took Little Nutmeg, my Oldsmobile, out of mothballs and headed the 600 miles north. I spent a very cold New Year's Day with my sister Eileen and Lyman in their new home in Provo, Utah. Four days later I came home.

On the next Sunday morning I was in my office, quite cheerfully preparing for classes to begin the next day.

When I left for Australia, I carried a blank script. I didn't even know what prescriptions Providence had ordered for the healing of my wounded spirit. After three months of treatment, however, I discovered that six remedies had been applied.

The first was Love. The constant, compassionate attention of uncounted friends and family. I used to think that I comprehended the rewards of friendship, but I never realized that it could be like this!

The second had to do with Place. Temporarily free from the old painful surroundings, I had been either visiting happy, familiar settings or exploring new ones.

Then came the rush of new Ideas. I enjoyed so much open, intelligent conversation. It mattered not whether the topic was past, present or future. That enabled me to climb to a level beyond the "Cancer World" where Walt and I had been trapped for four years.

Next, there was simple, physical Relaxation. I didn't have to explain to anyone why or when I wanted to sleep. Long, long hours of rest and quiet descended over me like a prayer.

Finally, came the Laughter. It is possible, under certain circumstances, to forget how to laugh. At first, I was surprised when I heard myself doing it again.

Back on campus, my colleagues were genuinely glad to see me and I them. Fulfilling, creative work is truly a Godsend. Although I had no sure answers for any thing, I faced in my future. I still felt fortified. Work, then, had to be added to the prescription.

The past twelve weeks turned out to be worth infinitely more than I had paid for them. Now I knew that when I had to be strong, I could actually find God-given strength to be so. For that I was very, very grateful.

Chapter 13

Passage to India

My opportunity to go to India came upon me quite unexpectedly in the third year of my service at La Sierra University. The negotiations began in June, 1986. Although the Southern Asia Division requested my services for six months, by the time I became aware of the potential plan it had been reduced to a three-month term for the following summer. My leave would extend from July 1 to October 1. (Later I discovered that India would have had to pay an extra $4,000 for extra time beyond that period.)

Through that winter of 1987 my case rotated within a triangle: Elmer Hauck at the General Conference, Dr. John Fowler at the Southern Asia Division, and Dr. M. E. Cherian, President of Spicer College.[1] Although permission had been granted for me to go to India, my actual job remained nebulous. Yes, I would teach classes at Spicer College. I could also conduct writing seminars here and there. I could ... ?

Before the matter could be settled, however, Dr. Cherian had a heart attack, followed by by-pass surgery. By mid-May of 1987 I was begging to know what my work assignments in India would be. "I can serve much more efficiently if I know what I am expected to do." I didn't want to carry extraneous luggage nor did I want to be unready for what I was actually supposed to accomplish. I decided to offer the administrators a smorgasbord of dishes that I would be able to serve up.

In due course, the matter resolved itself. I would teach three intensive eight-week classes at Spicer College. My teaching load finally settled on Creative Writing, The Bible as Literature, and a seminar in "Christ in the Arts" (Christian Aesthetics). An agenda very much to my taste! Afterwards I would be given a 21-day pass on Air India to travel wherever I wished in the country.

At that point in my career I had a highly ambitious academic book in mind. Building on my doctoral research, I wanted to write about "The Protestant Missionary as a Colonial Entity." I hoped, moreover, to do it within the next three years. I had already had one sabbatical leave in England where I used the British Museum and the Institute of Commonwealth Studies at the University of London. Although the entire book could not materialize, I did write a couple of monographs on the oddly slow progress of "Christian Mission in India" and on "Art as Propaganda."

My arrival in Bombay had been confirmed for July 2, 1987. (This is an important fact to be registered here.) With some fast pedaling I was able to get my grades

A weekend with Dr. Richard and Virginia Clarke in Shannon, Ireland, set me up for my intense teaching assignment in India. Included was our visit to Trinity College Dublin, one of my favorite places—both academic and familial.

in, escape La Sierra campus before graduation, and leave Los Angeles on June 11. Thus I netted several useful research days in England. After a number of visits to the British Museum, I tracked down some new second-hand bookshops. I even snatched a couple of days in the Cotswolds, the long-ago family seat of my father's people.

Next came a six-day detour in Ireland. My friends Dr. and Virginia Clarke had just begun a challenging ministry there. Sabbath morning I occupied the sermon slot at the new Shannon Church. Otherwise, I tried to be helpful with ideas about their new health-evangelism enterprise and the new school. The Clarkes, in turn, showed me all things Irish. From the Ring of Kerry to a Saturday-night *fleadh* (Irish street dancing) in the village of Kilfenora. From Yeats country to a medieval banquet and the sounds of *celli* (Irish music) in Bunratty Castle. From Cashel to an amazing interpretation of pizza, eaten in the shadow of King John's Castle in Limerick. (I have never been able to overdose on Eire.)

Back in London my family and my academic roots came together in a curious blend when I discovered an insightful bit of doggerel that sums up Britain:

As Others See Us

There were the Scots who kept the Sabbath
And everything else they could lay their hands on.
Then there were the Welsh who prayed on their knees
And on their neighbours.
Thirdly, there were the Irish who never knew what they wanted
But were willing to fight for it anyway.
Lastly, there were the English who considered themselves a self-made nation
Thus relieving the Almighty of a dreadful responsibility.

Although my time in Ireland and England had been added as an after-thought, I will always regard those pleasant days as a fortifying prelude to India. Indeed, I needed all of strength I could muster for the chaos that attended my arrival in Bombay. After a whole year of fine-tuned plans, the arrangements for July 2 still fell through the cracks. Nay, they had been swallowed up in a great cavern of miscommunication. Such events often befall the world traveler who journeys below or outside of the usual tourist parameters.

On Wednesday morning, check-in with Air India at Heathrow Airport took only three-and-a-half hours. (At least 30% more efficient than my ordeal in New York.) In flight over Paris we ate hot curry. Later over Greece and Cyprus we had more of it. By that time, we were flying two hours late. Fears of terrorism, even back then, made air schedules nothing but an idea. A dream. Seldom a reality!

Meanwhile, my seatmates took up a lot of space, even though we were on a 747. The two of them wearied me. Truly. Despite a great outlay of cutlery on the lunch tray, they ate with their fingers. No harm done. The *guru,* however, took snuff almost constantly. The *bhagwan* next to me had his feet up on his seat. From time to time, through the long night, a great, dirty bare foot slipped off onto my knee. So the hours passed.

At 1.15 p.m. on Thursday, July 2, I arrived in Bombay Airport. In the steamy air and amid the seething mass of people, I stood alone. There was no one to meet me. Hence, my first hours in India rapidly degenerated into a nightmare. Temperature and humidity both stood at about 100. Armed soldiers lounged about on every side. Never before had I looked down so many gun barrels at one time. Weary to the point of collapse, I staggered through Customs where my little video-8 camera fascinated the functionaries there.

Step by step, I tried to figure out what to do next. When I changed $100.00 travelers' checks, I received in return a great bundle of dirty paper money as big as a roll of toilet paper. The mini-bus to the domestic airport for the flight to Poona proved to be much too mini. I had to beat off a swarm of little beggar boys trying to touch my baggage so that they could get money.

I bought my ticket for the flight to Poona. Encumbered with a heap of luggage containing my teaching materials, I sat down and draped myself over the pile, fearful of thievery. Intermittently I dozed off. Thus I waited for many hours. In fact, I missed one flight. I didn't realize that merely buying a ticket does not guarantee a reservation. That had to be negotiated separately. I'd simply been told to wait for the 4 p.m. flight, so I had no way of knowing that no seat had actually been allotted to me. Alas!

Off and on, I tried to get a phone call through to someone—anyone— in Poona. It was not as if I could just step into a booth. A little man sat at a table with a cardboard box full of coins and a telephone *(circa* 1930). He dialed the number. A dozen people stood by as my audience, everyone yelling above the airport din.

By now, I was entering my third day without sleep. An hour before take-off, however, the Security Check Point looked like the beginning of a riot. That aroused me sufficiently to get myself onto the plane.

Upon arrival in Poona, I hired a *put-put* (auto-rickshaw) to take me out to Spicer College. Near midnight, I stumbled up to the door of Edith Willis's

"The Bible in the Arts" class went well at Spicer College. I was glad, since it remains my favorite subject.

house and virtually fell at her feet. A fellow-Australian, she taught English at the college. (Her husband Lloyd was away in Jordan on an archaeology dig.) She was horrified that no one had met my plane in Bombay. "We were told that you were very sick and not coming to India at all," she cried. Too tired to care, I showered and fell into bed.

By morning I had succumbed to a virulent form of flu. My new friends on campus immediately pressed in to nurse me back to life, and a local doctor gave me a round of antibiotics. In this part of the world you can be smitten down by so many sudden, violent, and nameless tribulations. My arrival really had more drama than I bargained for.

Three days later I started my teaching. I had to work hard to live up to the advertising that had preceded me. Classes were over-full and brimming with enthusiasm.

My bedroom in the Guest House had windows on three sides, and the wide overhanging eaves allowed me to keep them open. I heard birds in the garden. Both day and night, an amazing variety of birds filled the air with odd calls and whistles. One kept saying "Quilk, quilk, quilk," and another answered "Why, why, why?"

I ate lunch daily in a variety of faculty homes, making new friends and savoring a wonderful variety of Indian dishes. Students brought in bread and fruit for my morning and evening meals. After a few days, however, my little refrigerator—named Godreg—died. Workmen brought in an old Amana as a replacement. More impressive, except that it didn't work. I believe it (110) got plugged into 220 current without a transformer. Then all kinds of things happened—none of them good. When the men tried to lay Amana down on his back I protested. "I understand that a refrigerator should always be kept upright."

A time of meditation passed, the maintenance man simply sitting on the floor and looking at Amana's backside. I kept working at the typewriter nearby, until I saw a series of little explosions, sparks and fireballs. More thought. By this time

Poona Railway Station in the early morning. A traveler pays off his *put-put* (motor cycle taxi). Beside him lie three covered bodies not yet arisen

Amana was resting on his face, appearing quite dead. After a while, one of the men excused himself and carried away a box full of Amana's entrails. For biopsy, I supposed. The body of Amana remained at rest in my dining room for many days. Eventually another, rather tired refrigerator was set up in my kitchen. Once more I could have cold drinking water and fresh fruit at hand.

Despite the long classroom hours, I seized every opportunity to explore the local culture at grassroots level. India is so overwhelming it really can't be reduced to a few paragraphs. All I can do here is single out a handful of powerful impressions.

One August morning Edith and I arose at 5.30 a.m. to get to the Poona railway station and board the "Deccan Queen" for the four-hour train-journey down to Bombay. The round trip cost just $5.00. We picked our way among the dozens of people still sleeping on the sidewalks. No way of know whether the wrapped body was male or female, alive or dead.

Then, from our second-class windows we watched the countryside slums stir to life. Small breakfast fires burning in the open. Goats probing the garbage heaps to see if anything new had turned up overnight. Men and boys relieving themselves in cheerful, friendly groups, here and there, and waving to us as the train roared by. (Decency required that women attend to their personal needs before dawn or after dark. No exceptions.)

Slums in any country are, sadly, a state of mind. Cheap housing and a water supply do not necessarily improve the standard of living. Poor people often reject or destroy the very benefits they have received, unable to forsake the life they've known, however bleak.

Next we descended the great Western Ghats (escarpments) where the Deccan plain drops off into the coastal lowlands. In jungled gorges the monsoon waterfalls defined the contours of the green cliffs, and morning mists floated into the little valleys. Unexpectedly, mountains swallowed us up in dark, wet, downhill tunnels. India is a gorgeous, big, beautiful land. Something that surprises most visitors, I think. Too often the grinding poverty and the squalor of the city streets preoccupy us.

Later, as the shacks along the track became thicker, we knew we were approaching the bursting precincts of Bombay, or, as one wit has put it, the "pre-stinks." The city, burst with ten million people, all of whom appeared be on the streets at the same time. Three hundred years ago Britain's East India Company first built a trading post here upon the swamps oozing among seven islands.

Finally, we thundered into the Victoria Terminus, a gingerbread colonial building, and a pompous relic of the 1880s. A cataract of humanity surged over the platforms and among the carts of fruit. In the middle of it all a holy man, in a trance-like condition, did *puja* (worship).

As we waited for a taxi, we watched a couple of uniformed persons leading away a company of some twenty grinning men, loosely bound together with a single rope. They went mildly to the truck awaiting them. They had ridden the "Deccan Queen" without tickets and now had to be led away in public disgrace, like a flock of goats.

To her chagrin, Edith had forgotten the sandwiches she had prepared, so our rather imbalanced breakfast had consisted of a chocolate bar and a package of biscuits. Therefore we felt no guilt when we went to the buffet-lunch at the elite Taj Palace Hotel. The palatial dining room featured uniformed waiters who might have been on loan from a Maharajah's palace of the 1920s. We faced a huge variety of curries, vegetables, and breads, all labeled with cunning little brass signs. An image of Lord Krishna (playing his flute) presided over a very expansive dessert table.

Our main business in Bombay was to purchase the College's farewell gift for Harold and Rita Erickson who had served in India for thirty-four years. (That is a big piece of time out of anyone's life.) We chose a small, pure silk, hand-woven carpet from Kashmir. An absolutely exquisite work of art. When you realize that a 9' x 12' carpet would cost about $30,000.00, you understand why we could afford only a little wall hanging.

Meanwhile the Iranian proprietor of the shop earnestly eyed my video camera. He offered me a carpet in exchange for it! My passport, however, had been elaborately imprinted with a stipulation that I must have the camera with me when I leave the country. Otherwise I would have negotiated an exchange.

At 4.45 p.m. we re-boarded the "Deccan Queen" to return to Poona. The afternoon's spectacular ascent of the tunnels in the Ghats was even better than the morning journey down. Thunderheads moved in over the mountains and wet down the landscape. Long, fine sheaves of green grass framed the black rocks. The stone walls and huts were permanently mossy, and the air felt earthy damp. Farmers planted rice with their patient buffaloes while shafts of the golden sunset reflected themselves in the still water in the paddies.

The following week the Ericksons were farewelled with a festive curry supper. Thirty-four red roses had been woven into each of their jasmine garlands. I had already come to feel so much at home on the campus. What must they have been feeling?

Eva Nonrang, a bright young English teacher, turned aside from her doctoral studies long enough to discuss my literary investigation of the "missionary as a colonial figure." I wanted to define the points where Christianity and Hinduism touch. So I watched Hindi movies, read Indian authors, and had stimulating conversations with my new friends. On the lighter side, Edith introduced me to Asterix, sophisticated comic books written by two Frenchmen. Popular entertainment for European "egg heads," Asterix is virtually unknown in the United States. I soon decided to take some home to share with my colleagues.

My non-classroom hours were, indeed, well filled. Horst Rolly (a young professor from Germany) lent me a tiny tape recorder, and Edith brought over a dozen classical music tapes. Thus I lived a life of rich austerity and high thinking. As I lit my two candles on dark nights I actually enjoyed the "gift of doing without." Most Americans know very little of this matter.

Take Spicer College itself. Plenty of students, plenty of brain power and an abundance of enthusiasm. But so few material benefits. A new science complex stands ready but it is wholly without furniture. Not even blackboards. The old buildings (and I mean old) have blackboards that look like the bottom of a stone quarry. Desks and chairs are in very short supply. Actually we lose the first ten minutes of nearly every class period while students scramble about to bring in chairs. Noise and confusion reign. Unless you are actually sitting in a chair at the moment, it will be carried out from under you.

The "Deccan Queen" train arrived at the main station in Bombay. Amid the surging crowds a holy man—far away in another world—did his *puja* (worship).

Sometimes I could find a table in the classroom, but usually not. Mostly I sat in a student chair, if one could be found. Sometimes the students sat on the floor, but they never allowed me to do so. Back home we take classroom furniture so much for granted. It's always there when we require it. Spicer, on the other hand, needed at least twice the number of chairs and desks. Oddly enough, I didn't mind the deprivation. The liveliness and zeal that ran through each teaching session more than made up for it.

About 8 o'clock one night Gordon Jensen made the rounds of homes and dormitories to invite everyone to come to his house and see his special cactus, the "Night-Blooming Cereus." It blooms once a year for about two hours. As Gordon said, "In the time they've got, the flowers pour out all they have." Anywhere from five to twelve inches in diameter, the flower has slender petals framed like a cup, white with tinges of pink or yellow. It grows directly out of the cactus leaf.

The Jensens had positioned three bright lamps to illuminate the wonderful sight. Between 10.00 and 11.00 p.m. at least 300 people came, most of them with cameras. It was a truly grand show in the fragrant Indian night, with seventeen flowers open in full glory. The perfume was rich enough to make your head light. Had this gorgeous but transient event have been carried to a professional flower show, the connoisseurs would veritably have gone mad with excitement.

The next morning I went back to Jensens' house to photograph the end of the Night-blooming Cereus Story. There they all were, hanging their heads limply in the morning sunshine. All except one. Perversely, it planned to bloom all by itself that night. So I returned at 10.30 p.m. to see that last lone, "Star of Bethlehem." How proudly it shone, all by itself. Then it was gone.

About the same time an interesting little ceremony was being acted out in my own front yard. After the *malis* (gardeners) cleaned up the yard of the Guest House nicely, it was determined that the house should have a new gate. All of the houses on this campus street have cunning little brick gateways— except this one.

Carefully the bricks had been counted out. Then came the mason, with the bearing of a *pundit* (holy man) and wearing a clean *kurta* and *dhoti*. His two assistants were two frail-looking low caste women in ragged saris. They must have been hungry many a day, but it was their *karma* to be street laborers. (They made eight or nine rupees, less than $1.00, a day.) They did the heavy work, serving up the mortar to him in a pan, like gray mashed potatoes. Then they handed him each brick, one at a time, while he squatted before the wall, moving only his hands.

In due time, the Super-Mason then arrived, in a stiffly starched khaki uniform. It took him three more days to put on the finishing touches while the first mason and the women deferentially waited upon him. He appeared to be saying a *mantra* over each brick. Meanwhile, I went to and from my appointments feeling humble and somehow unworthy.

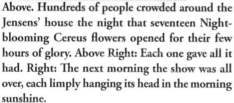

Above. Hundreds of people crowded around the Jensens' house the night that seventeen Night-blooming Cereus flowers opened for their few hours of glory. Above Right: Each one gave all it had. Right: The next morning the show was all over, each limply hanging its head in the morning sunshine.

Next came the "Brother-and-Sister Festival." Sisters tied a *rakhi* on their brothers' wrists, a tinselly, highly colored little ornament. It committed the brother to a lifelong defense of his sister, even to the death. That day I ate lunch at a potluck of faculty and club members and saw a number of little boys proudly showing off their *rakhis*. Eighteen-month-old Jason was intensely excited by the bracelet his six year-old sister had given him. He jitterbugged around until it broke and fell off—much to his distress. Perhaps it's over-much responsibility, anyway, for one still in diapers!

In the interest of making the best use of my twenty-one-day air pass, I wanted to secure a travel permit to visit the tribal lands near Bhutan, Nepal, and the Burma border. I had begun the task on our trip to Bombay where we

Above Left. The Elephant Gate at Aurangabad, the first stop on our weekend venture into Indian history. **Above Right.** Members of our Spicer party included three senior students. (L-R). Zipporah Theuri (Kenya), Edith Willis, Zuali Chuakchuack, Errol Palinpane, Eva Nongrang. **Left.** Breakfast stop, as we practiced the usual roadside economy. (L-R) Samson (van driver), Eva, Zipporah, Dorothy Comm, Lloyd Willis, Zuali, Errol, Mark Willis (visiting home from Andrews University).

spent more than two hours in the rooms of one H. K. Puradupadhuye. I was referred, finally, to the Poona Police Department.

Every trip into the Poona risked life and limb, and I regularly got my "Poona Street Headache" from the heat, fumes, and general stress. Once there I witnessed the bureaucracy functioning more sluggishly than I had ever known. Not even in Manila. First, they held my passport for a week, until I began to feel a little lonely.

At first the officers questioned me about Singapore, Loma Linda, and so forth. *A propos* of nothing, as far as I could see. At least twenty-five people occupied the office, but the Great Ones present were unable to agree on anything. The Chief and his aides discussed my case at top volume, in Marathi.

The sound of their cogitations was deafening. Their filing system consisted of some 300 large, canvas bags stacked on a high shelf above our heads. Labels thick with dust, the documents had been entombed there for decades, it seemed.

On one of my visits, a very pregnant Iranian lady customer explained, by way of encouragement, "They are giving you some of their minds." Affairs proceeded so slowly for both of us that I feared she might have to be airlifted right out of the waiting room and into the hospital.

We stayed until after closing time, however, only to hear, "Come back later." Upon departure, I signed a very large dog-eared document that declared that my passport had, indeed, been returned to me.

We made three more fruitless trips to the police headquarters. On the fifth trip, I told Edith, "I am laying out Gideon's fleece. If I don't get the permit today, I will take it as an indication that I am not supposed to travel up to the Northeast." They were, after all, having a civil war up there, and we heard that dead bodies lay randomly about the streets.

On our fifth visit the furor began again. "Sit down and wait a few minutes," said one who carried a stout billy club.

"What might 'a few minutes' be," I asked.

"Maybe fifteen minutes. Maybe after six o'clock."

I had a class to teach at 7 p.m. Edith looked at me. "Looks like you have your fleece." I agreed, and we stood up to leave.

The policeman stared at us in befuddlement. The crazy *mem-sahibs!* After all of this effort, and they will walk out, just like that? So we did.

Instead we went to the airline office, and I traded my Megalaya bookings for a trip to Jaipur. Anyway, I'd just finished reading *A Princess Remembers: The Memoirs of the Maharani of Jaipur.* The trade-off looked good to me.

"Well," Edith sighed, "I am glad that you're not going to see the war." True, it would have been an interesting journey but there's no use courting danger. Life offers quite enough risks in the ordinary course of events, so who needs any extras?

When Edith's husband Lloyd returned from the archaeology dig in Jordan in mid-August, I got a preview of my travels to come. It came as a gift to me from the Southern Asia Division! They also gave us the use of their "Matador" van for a three-day, weekend journey into the Deccan. (The Matador had an Indian body and a German Mercedes-Benz soul.) Lloyd and Edith Willis, Eva and I, and three senior students, plus our driver (appropriately named Samson) made up our party of eight.

Beginning in Muslim Aurangabad we visited half a dozen historical sites: The medieval fortress of Daulatabad, the (Buddhist) Ajanta Caves and the Ellora Caves, the Panchakki (Watermill), and the Mausoelum of Bibi-Ka-Magrara. The journey was wonderfully rich in culture and history. In the lively company of good friends, the storytelling, jokes, and deep discussions never waned. At the same time, the earthiness of the passing roadside scenery contrasted with the elegance of our hotels. There we relaxed in air-conditioning, took hot showers, and ate in colonial dining rooms that evoked some of the best days of the Raj.

As they had become aware of my passion for history, campus friends made sure that I missed nothing nearby either. The Mughal Fort Simha Gad ("Fortress of the Lion") was only fifteen miles up into the mountains above Poona. After the monsoon rains the valleys greened up beautifully, affording us a breathtaking view of Poona with its reservoir lake. The mountain road clung to the cliff-side, where luxuriant tufts of emerald green grass tucked themselves in among the wet, black boulders.

By the time we reached the Fort with its two elephant gates, we had ascended into the clouds where a cool, misty dampness enfolded us. Wisps of fog swirled around us, like the ghosts of the warriors who centuries ago fought and died on this rocky pinnacle. The ruined walls wore a delicate tapestry of black mold with the finest of green mosses and tiny lacings of fern. Up there I found it impossible to remember that I'd ever been hot and sweaty in my whole life!

The earnestly prayed-for monsoons finally arrived on August 16. It could rain non-stop for twelve or fourteen hours. At Spicer College the grass had started to turn brown and the *malis* had no more to cut to sell to feed the wandering street cattle. Many of the cows were already bone-thin. Only a painted elephant that went by the gate the other day really looked in good

The building of the gate at Spicer College. Left. The Super-mason. Right. His *sari*-clad laborer mixes mortar.

form. India is victimized to an unusual extent by its climate.

Electricity could always turn off at odd times, and during the monsoons it became more erratic than ever. One night I had barely launched into the Christian Aesthetics class when we were catapulted into utter darkness. Suitably, the theme for the evening was "Death." While I can talk in the dark, the students had some trouble taking notes. After thirty minutes someone came in with three little candles to share among forty-five people. My plans for showing slides, of course, had to be shelved. Flexibility is ever the watchword.

Nonetheless, back in my house, I usually appreciated the untainted darkness amid the dripping trees. So many trees in that clean night. (There, you noticed especially when something was clean.) Also I enjoyed the rainy mornings. I dragged my table and chair out onto the verandah and that was quite pleasant. I couldn't waste my candles on the gloomy house. I needed to save them for nights. The rhythms of the rain blended with the morning chatter of the birds. Dancing rain pools filled up the lawn and driveway.

The Ganapati Festival came at the end of August. Ganesh is the elephant-headed god, patron of food and appetite, who often appeared in restaurants. Processions, musicians, firecrackers and general exuberance all round. All color and noise.

The Willis family and I spent some hours "Ganeshing" in Poona's side streets, especially along Lakshmi Road. The images rode around in pushcarts with their heads swathed in dirty rags. "It is not modest for him to see or be seen until he is officially installed," I was told. The average Ganesh is made of unfired clay and brilliantly painted. The images are kept for ten days then they all disappear. After being ceremoniously "baptized," they are dumped in the river to return to their original elements.

A visit to an Indian *sari* store is enough to make one drool with desire. We took off our shoes and sat on the white floor pads while

While Lorna Christo-Samraj and Edith Willis (center and right) dressed themselves, Dorothy needed a lot of help getting into one of the world's loveliest dresses, the Indian *sari*.

the salesmen displayed *sari* after *sari,* each one different and each woven with gold and silver designs. So gorgeous I tred to think, "What could I use that one for?" Then I realized that the answer was "Nothing." So I just looked and loved.

Still, Edith's Hindu tailor, Kirloskar, enabled me to take home two trophies of Indian fashion. An ascetic, high class Brahmin, he truly was a magician. First, he created an absolutely lovely dress for me out of a lavender and magenta silk *sari.* Then, he made me a modest *shalmar kameez* in the Punjabi style for me to wear in the Muslim parts of the country. Besides being comfortable, it enabled me to blend into the landscape quite well.

I spent my life wearing what I happened to like—or, in this case, what would be expedient. I never was "in fashion." I was usually "out," frequently in more ways than one. If I ever happened to be "in," it would probably have

The very skilled tailor Kirloskar is a devout Brahmin, works in the simple setting of his little home. He begins work on Dorothy's *shalmar kameez*.

been quite accidental.

In early September my farewells to Spicer College began. One Thursday morning I spoke to the English Club. That evening, when I tried to dismiss the Christian Aesthetics class, the students hung back. "Am I the only one who doesn't know what's going on here?" I asked.

Everyone grinned knowingly and nodded "Yes." Their program included prayer, many speeches of appreciation, and a tray full of cake. The gifts: a brass *puja* lamp with a peacock standing in a ring of fire, and a delicate wooden plaque with herons "appliquéd" on it.

Three days later my official farewell convened. First came the sweet jasmine garland with red roses. Next, an elegant little teakwood table inlaid with bone and featuring nine elephants. The climax was startling, however, because I had been in India only two months. Not much time to earn the honor. I understand that President Cherian had to give official approval for this rare, ancient rite of respect. On a silver tray, a student carried in an emerald green silk shawl, the design shot through with gold thread. Then, with royal ceremony I was formally wrapped in it.

At that the great crowd in the College church broke into "God Be With You Till We Meet Again." I had to make my final speech short, for I was very much moved by all of that love and grace surrounding me. Words could not come easily. Would I come again to India, they wanted to know. A thousand times yes!

Simply being appreciated for my services was the most precious gift of all. Such expressions may feel awkward, but they're so rare. Formal letters of appreciation went from the College and the Division office to my employers

Farewells. Left. Heavily be-garlanded, Harold and LoRita Erickson displayed their gift, the silk carpet from Kashmir. Right. Enveloped in her special silk shawl, Dorothy receives her gift, a teakwood table featuring nine inlaid elephants and elephant legs. Presented by Dr. M. E. Cherian, president of Spicer College. A smiling Edith Willis looks on in the background.

at Loma Linda. Good. Perhaps I prized the student letters most. Especially the one from the boy who wrote: "I just got so happy every time I came into your class."

My last day on campus brought

me, along with the Willises, to lunch at President Cherian's home. We had a *pukka* (genuine) Gujarati meal and a chance to see the lordly, 150-year-old house that a maharaja once used for his summer retreat. To say nothing of the excellent table talk. Could it be that countries with more privations and hardships provide the most fertile places for ideas?[2]

That night visitors kept coming to the Guest House until near midnight to say goodbye. Thus ended my Spicer Idyll.

1   Spicer College was named for William A. Spicer (1865-1952), one-time president of the General Conference of Seventh-day Adventists. First founded in Tamil Nadu (1915), the college moved to Poona in 1942. The 74-acre estates included excellent farmland.
2   My academic summation of my experience in India eventually became a monograph, "Christianity in India" (1998, funded by the Schrillo Award). It was based on how missionaries have been portrayed in literature. Some specific examples were drawn from nine "Bollywood" movies in which Christian characters became the villains while the ideals of Hinduism were extolled.

CHAPTER 14

Taking the Long Way Home

My See-All-of-India-in-Twenty-one-Days journey began on Wednesday, September 9. The flight from Bombay south to Goa followed along the picturesque edge of the Arabian Sea. It took only forty-five minutes, but it landed me in another kind of India. Because the Portuguese conquistadors arrived here in 1510, brave little white crosses now replaced the usual shrines to Shiva and Nandi.

On the advice of Poona friends I had been booked into good hotels. Arguably, I needed the security, for I was traveling alone. Little did I imagine the elegance that awaited me. To be sure, nothing else could so completely show me the many, many contrasting faces of India. As for the bills accrued? Well, I could pay them when I got home. No worries right now!

It all began at the Hotel Cidade de Goa that is patterned after a 16th century Portuguese hill town. My little iron-railed balcony looked down on the brick-pathed gardens and on to the crashing surf beyond. A very large turquoise-blue swimming pool looped through a coconut grove. A lush, bushy island of palms and flowers sat in the middle of it. Over the past weeks I had accumulated a rather heavy backlog of tiredness. Although I spent a little time in the old city, I basically gave myself up to the pool and the beach. I thought, in fact, that I just might have discovered a Garden of Eden here.

The next morning I lounged in the pool, half hidden among the flowers and trailing vines. I watched two handsome, bronzed men set out the deck chairs on the brick pavement. "So they [meaning the tourists] spend all of that money to come here to sun-bathe so that they can look just like us!" They laughed.

I laughed too. I laughed because I was no tourist come to loll about in the sun. I had worked hard for this vacation. More importantly, I had made friends and seen and done things in India that a mere tourist could never dream of. I felt that I had come close to the real India. Not all the way, of course. But close.

I arrived in Bangalore for the weekend where I spent many hours with friendly people at the small English-speaking church, preached the sermon, and so forth. My hosts were the Assistant Union Treasurer, Sunder Puroshothom, and his wife Devene. Not only did I have a curry dinner at their house, but they also treated me (on Sunday) to a trip to Mysore. A six-hour bus journey, round trip.

Bangalore is a textbook case of the extreme contrasts that make up India. Sunder and his son had met me at the airport on Friday. He hired a taxi for me, and he and the boy and followed on his motor-scooter. Somehow the Bangalore streets seemed a little wider than those of Poona. Thousands of people, of course, but there definitely were fewer cows.

The taxi itself was a study in ingenuity. The courageous young driver had a *puja* arrangement of flowers on the dash, and he needed all of the help he could get. Proudly named Ambassador, the car was, in general black, but it appeared, primarily, to be a random mosaic of paint and textiles. To my untrained eye, it looked like something from the 1940s, but it also had parts from other years grafted on. At first it wouldn't start at all, then suddenly it kicked off with a brave little snort. When the brakes were applied, the vehicle swayed crazily, making deafening shrieks and squeals. Poor thing! We stalled at several intersections, the motor sighing and sobbing in a most pitiful way. The horn, however, worked excellently. The driver used it without intermission for the whole twelve kilometers across the city. All the while a red warning light kept flashing on the dial. Shifting gears was useless, because the stick just kept falling back, inert. When the driver even found the right gear, he had to hold the stick in place by force. So we jerked and chunked all the way across the city, almost failing on the last small hill. At the end, we lurched through the gates of the most beautiful hotel I have ever seen, the Windsor Manor.

Indeed, the Windsor made the Hilton in New York where I recently attended a convention look like a slum. And all for about the same price one would pay for a decent roadside motel in California. It was a magnificent, artfully planned replay of Bangalore's old British days. Since I had been living (professionally) in the 18th century for years, the regency décor enchanted me. Behind a classic white façade was an enormous octagonal lobby, with a large *puja* lamp burning at the entrance. With its pairs of polished teakwood columns and brass-railed balcony/mezzanine, it recalled the central hall of a maharajah's palace. The effects of the brass-light-and-mirror decoration, ornate wall sconces, red-velvet chairs, and bowls of fresh flowers on the coffee tables was absolutely stunning.

My room was furnished in white and rose silk. A carved frieze edged the high ceiling, and the bathroom was tiled with painted roses above a white marble washbasin and a dark green marble floor. My French doors opened onto a big roof garden that would have served the Queen of the Hanging Gardens of Babylon. Imperial names added to the ambience: Lord Hastings Wing (my area), Wellesley, Wellington, the Royal Afghan, and so forth. If I had ever seen a more artistically crafted hotel, I don't know where it was.

Monday morning I flew to Cochin, Kerala ("Land of Coconuts"), where Pastor Thomas Mahaikutty met me. A member of my Christian Aesthetics class at Spicer College, he came all the way down there (his home place) to be my guide. He understood my eagerness to follow in the path of the Apostle Thomas who is said to have arrived in South India in AD 52. The present extensive "Syrian Christian" population proudly traces its heritage back to the ministry of Thomas.

To be sure I needed a guide. Malayalam, the language of Kerala, must be one of the most impossible tongues in the world. Moreover, the people love to talk, and they go at a tremendous rate. Someone at Spicer once remarked, "If you shake pebbles in a tin can, you get Malayalam speech." Now I could believe them.

"What a problem the Apostle must have faced," Pastor Thomas mused, "arriving a stranger in all of this confusion. He had to bring with him the Pentecostal gift of tongues, surely, so that he could start his work here."

We spent a very long day visiting the ancient "Thomas churches" and schools where, invariably, torrents of children poured out of the doors to see the strange *mem-sahib*. We ended up at Thomas's home in Ottapalam, a substantial Adventist mission compound with a large school and 100-bed hospital. His wife and three over-awed children had been waiting all day for us to arrive. A tasty and very polite dinner awaited us.

Before we began the two-hour drive back to Cochin, the pastor wanted

me to visit his father-in-law nearby and "bless" the family. I visited with the very feeble, eighty-year-old man and felt grateful for the good health of my own mother who was the same age.

On my long journeys (like this one), Mum very capably supervised the house and our (difficult) rentals, did the banking and paid bills, entertained guests, and provided for the needs of the

That the Apostle Thomas arrived in India about twenty years after Christ's resurrection is a firm belief in the Kerala district. At one of the early sites the story of the Apostle baptizing Brahmins is portrayed in three-dimensions.

four dogs—whom she loved as fondly as I did. As the pages of my India journals multiplied, I sent them home in two batches for her to duplicate and mail out to our large "fan list." Mum made things work. As she always said whatever the circumstance, "But I don't want to miss anything!!" In that spirit she lived into her 92nd year.

My room in the charming old Malabar Hotel pleased me, overlooking the coastline so full of history and romance. Even so, nothing came near the joy of the day spent with Pastor Thomas and his family. A day given over to following in the footsteps of Christ's Doubting Disciple.

In Madras, I hired an auto-rickshaw (driven by one Gopal) for the day. Cheaper and slimmer, it wove through traffic faster than a taxi. I first spent a hot, sweaty hour climbing the Mount of St. Thomas and back. A fifth century church marked the site of the Apostle's martyrdom. Then, at Mylapore on the sea, I visited his tomb. My last stop was a personal one. One of my ancestors,

James Minchin, served as Master of the High Court of Madras in the mid-19th century. The old building was very Victorian, but, at the same time, so very Indian.

My stay in the Adayar Park Hotel in Madras called for the escape talents of a Houdini. In the morning the lock on my door (#117)

In Calcutta Dorothy met by one of her former students at Philippine Union College, Lalchangsanga Colney. They dined at Megalaya Government House.

jammed and I couldn't get out. Five men came to lead me out through the adjoining room. This took an hour. Given Room #108, I moved my stuff there. When I returned about 4 p.m., that lock jammed, and I couldn't get into my room. It took an hour to move me to #104 and to get the five men back to shift my stuff out of #108.

That night I decided to treat myself to just one more sizzler meal. That authentic kind to be found only in the Orient. A black iron plate, heated red-hot, was set into a thick wooden panel, and rice, vegetables and sauces were heaped on it. The food arrived in clouds of steam, kicking and shouting. The green beans and cauliflower blossoms fairly rattled in the dish. Indeed, I could hear it all coming from afar off. When the volcanic eruption subsided and things stopped jumping, I started eating. There were nice surprises. I found a baked banana at the bottom of the heap. Also a pepper stuffed with rice. When I stabbed it, all kinds of good stuff tumbled out.

Back at the hotel again, #104 had a jammed lock too. More attention from the five men. Finally, I went to bed just hoping that I could escape in the morning in time to make my flight to Calcutta. Everyone was polite and most helpful, of course. It's just that in this part of the world there seems to exist an undercurrent of mishap that no one can control. By the same token, one just presses forward, and, in the end, for reasons that cannot be explained, everyone survives. At least, most of the time. Hence, I made it to the airport just before the plane's door closed.

An hour's flight up the Coromandel Coast brought us to a thirty-minute touchdown at Visakhapatam. Hundreds of miles of empty, yellow beach lay like a long, thin shadow in the blue horizon of sky and sea. At intervals inland rivers spewed mud out into the ocean. Other rivers lay like parched brown snakes with only a few damp spots remaining. Outlying villages of round gray-thatch huts huddled around large *gopurams* (temple-towers). The worst drought in 100 years, I was told.

My host in Calcutta, a major stronghold of orthodox Brahmanism, was Lalchangsanga Colney, a former student at the Seminary in the Philippines. Since I had given up getting a travel permit to go to his country, he came to Calcutta to meet me. He had booked me into a "VIP Room" at the Megalaya Government House. On the way to his lodging, our taxi had two breakdowns. Nervous, I believe. The city was seething cauldron of humanity, blanketed in heat and stench. Listening to Colney talk to his countrymen, I realized how "un-Indian" the speech is. More like Chinese than anything else.

The Calcutta Seventh-day Adventist Church is near the Maidan, a prime location. The congregation, however, was small, for Christianity has made little impression on the city's fourteen million people. Just before I boarded the plane for New Delhi, Colney gave me a rare, beautiful gift—a red-black-and-white Mizor shawl, hand-loomed for the cool, rainy hill-country on the Tibetan border.

Regular airline passengers can be quite dull. On my flight from New Delhi to Agra, however, fifty-two very small school children were on their way to see the Taj Mahal. Turned out in starched white uniforms with blue-striped ties, most of them were having their first plane ride. Energized by pure adrenalin, they squealed, crowed, and chortled for entire thirty-minute journey. They left the windows only long enough to sample the aircraft toilets, an endless, jittering line of them.

Ultimately, I too reached the Taj, that "Dream in Marble." Unlike other buildings, it seemed not to stand on its foundation. Rather it appeared to float. Very fitting for the almost-four-hundred-year-old love story of Shah Jehan and his beloved Mumtaz.

The next day I went out to see Fatehpur Sikri, a red palace-mosque complex built by the Great Akbar (mid 16th century). On the way back to Agra the taxi stopped so I could watch between 200 and 300 vultures tearing into a dead buffalo. "It will be all finished in about twenty minutes," the driver remarked.

The younger, smaller birds stood around in a plaintive circle while the big boys did the eating. Still, three skinny dogs managed to hold their own in the midst of the melee. Almost instantaneously the bare bones were left to bleach in the sun. Actually I was not in good condition for this treat that the taxi driver had given me. Having picked up some kind of malaise in Calcutta I still kept to my travel schedule, perpetual fever and chills notwithstanding. To say nothing of being nauseated to the bone marrow. Unfortunately, I

A "rare sight," her taxi driver assured Dorothy. They watched an enormous flock of vultures strip bare the bones of a just-dead buffalo. It happened in minutes. The birds have sometimes been described as the "sanitation inspectors" of Third World countries.

shall always have to remember my visit to Agra with being really quite ill.

I had a decent room at the Mughal Hotel, but had not the strength to avail myself of the other amenities A surly camel name Doori. The elephant Lakshmi and her *mahout*. A snake-wallah with baskets full of snakes and a mongoose. Two ponies ready to offer rides in Victorian "royal" coaches. And an astrologer-on-duty at the front desk.

In Jaipur the road traffic consisted of camels and elephants that outnumbered the cows. Red forts and palaces scattered across the Rajasthan Desert, and I fought down my illness and went as far as I could go in the time I had. At the Amber Palace the harem was open to all. In the Sheesh Mahal ("The Winter Palace of Mirrors"). A single candle flame made the whole "jeweled" chamber burst into galaxies of stars. Most of the glory, however, was departed. A company of large, very long-tailed monkeys supervised the royal suites. So, where the *maharanis* and their ladies were once imprisoned, as in a gilded cage, both men and monkeys alike may now look.

Thursday night, at 3.00 a.m. I reached the guest room at the Union Compound, after having to beat off an amorous Muslim businessman at the New Delhi airport. "You're home with friends," Gullu and Yvonne Bazliel assured me. I was about ready to weep with gratitude and exhaustion. Dr. Yvonne (an old friend from my years in Jamaica) treated me with a walloping dose of drugs so that the dysentery and my fever finally abated. I spent a restful weekend, undertaking only minimal sightseeing in the city.

I had used my twenty-one-day pass to its limit. I had just one more place to see. My flight to Srinagar, Kashmir, on Sunday gave me first glimpse of the Himalayas. White peaks under a layer of white cloud, all afloat over the river-laced valleys. The very "roof" of India.

Then the pilots cut back the engines, and we flew straight into the eighty-five-mile-long Vale of Kashmir. We set down in a landscape unlike any I had ever seen before. The gold-and-green rice paddies lay in graceful, natural curves. Long rows of Kashmir's distinctive trees—the *chinar* and the tall, thin *babula*—intersected the fields.

The people there were careful to distinguish themselves from "regular Indians" who weren't allowed to immigrate into this valley. The Aryan blood of the Kashmir people was evident in their height, fairer complexions, hazel eyes, and very large noses. The policemen wore flamboyant uniforms—red-and-white sleeves, white gloves and spats, and red-white-and-blue turbans with high red 'rooster' crests that had long, flowing tails hanging down the back.

For two days I stayed in a Gurkha Houseboat on Lake Nagin. Firdous Ahmal was my guide. Handsome with a mop of dark brown hair and an almost-red beard, freckles and green eyes. He was just about what I thought King David must have looked like. (David, however, was fortunate in not being a chain smoker.) Firdous spoke moderately good English.

Moored in reedy, grassy water, my boat was about 150 feet long and twenty feet wide, curved up at both ends. Inside the natural wood was literally

carved into "lace" with furniture also fashioned in
intricate detail. Window and
door hangings were made of
fantastically embroidered
calico—with bold birds and
flowers in bright wools.
Kashmiri carpets covered the
floors and even the outer
decks. Chandeliers and brilliantly painted papier-mache
vases blended into this regal
display. A houseboy cooked
and served my meals. All of
this for about $20.00 a night.

**Dorothy spent a pleasant weekend in New Delhi.
Gullu Bazliel (hospital administrator) and Yvonne
Stockhausen-Bazliel (physician). The latter was an old
friend from Jamaica days.**

The next day I hired a *shikara* (boat) to go to Nishat Gardens on the far
side of Dal Lake. The boat, canopied and pillowed, floated me away like a
Mughal princess. A solid field of lotus plants separated the two lakes. The waxy
surface of the lotus leaves trapped the water droplets, like diamonds on a bed
of green velvet. Saucy blue kingfishers dived into the lotus beds for their supper
while the ducks water-skiied through the reeds. A world of perfect, unspoiled
loveliness.

Later came a visit to the hill-resort of Sonamarg, in the alpine meadows
at the top of the Sindh Valley toward Tibet. On the way, we passed a sign
reading: "Accidents Prohibited in this Area." What a grand idea, if you could
make it work!

On my last night, Gulam Wangnoo, owner of the Gurkha Houseboats,
came down from his house on the hill to visit me. He used English deliberately
but very well. He spoke proudly of the generations of his family who have
kept houseboats on Nagin Lake since the early 1800s. He showed me his big
red-plush guestbook. "See! Three Amercan Roosevelts, stayed on our boats in
1925. One American president, yes?"

Mainly Mr. Gulam wanted to talk—in that curiously imaginative way

Kashmir. Top Left. Lake Dal is thick with lotus plants. Left. The carved deck canopy of a Gurkha Houseboat. Above. A mirror reflects the opulent interior of the houseboat, complete with silk carpet. Remnants of the Raj! The houseboats are docked at carefully tended gardens.

that you find only in the East. About creation, faith, love, mercy, and judgment. "I am a happy man." His fine, sensitive face fairly glowed. "I have much inner peace."

Then the houseboy served me my dinner. On a white cloth with antique dishes, and heavy Victorian silverware, and a serviette large enough to diaper a baby. On that genteel note, I went to bed—for the last time in India.

From there on I had mapped out a killer schedule. One that would involve fifty-hours hours of non-stop travel. From Kashmir to Poona, to Bombay, to Dubai, to Rome, to London, to New York, and finally to Los Angeles. I would be back on the La Sierra campus to start classes the morning after my arrival. Only an idiot could have thought up such a plan. I have, however, always been one to wring out the last drop of usefulness from whatever opportunity came my way, whether it was research time, simple sight-seeing, conversation, or the air-ticket itself.

To severely understate my case, by the time I reached London I was rather worn. At Heathrow Airport I stood in line waiting to re-board the Air India flight from which I had been evicted an hour earlier. Tired beyond reason, I had no idea that I was about to have one of those faith-confirming

Barry and Janet Sillitoe in their little home in Exminster, Devon. When we first met on the Air India flight, we did not realize the fulfilling years of friendship that lay ahead of us. How many times I would sit with them in this little solarium and how many times they would visit me in the California desert.

encounters that comes only once or twice in a lifetime.

I watched a couple of Hassidim Jews in their prayer shawls. Off to the side, they earnestly pursued their devotions. Brain-weary as I was, I made some trivial remark to the little couple standing beside me. Speculating that the prayers would "cover all of us."

The sharp-eyed man replied with some scriptural allusion, and his dark-haired wife smiled and put in a word or two. Instantaneously I woke up! We chatted amiably all the way down the jet-way, wholly unaware how we appeared to the public.

A few minutes after take-off one of the flight attendants approached me. "If you wish, I can change seats so that you can sit with your friends." My friends? We had met for the first time as we were boarding the plane!

So I sat down beside them. As I fastened my seatbelt, we picked up our conversation where we had left off, virtually in mid-sentence. For the five hours that it took to reach New York, we "old friends" became acquainted. Barry was an engineer, and Janet worked as a visiting community nurse. They lived near Exeter. Me? I'd been in India for three months and had to be back in my office at Linda Linda University tomorrow morning.

Committed Christians, the Sillitoes were going to attend an international gathering of "home-church" people in New York. Afterwards they would visit one of their three sons who had recently married an American girl.

This friendship that had such an astonishing beginning has held fast for twenty-five years. Often, along with other friends, I have been entertained in Barry and Janet's hospitable home in Devon. Sometimes we have met in London. They have also come several times to stay with me in Southern California. We still marvel at how it all began, but we agree that our meeting was far more than a mere coincidence. It had to be a kind of "God Thing," we think.

This lovely, so-satisfying event, then, turned out to be the last gift I received on my unforgettable "Passage to India."

CHAPTER 15

Testing the Outer Limits

I can assess the seventeen years between Walt's death and my retirement only in hindsight. On the domestic front, I had a house right on the edge of the La Sierra campus. My mother continued to live with me there, while Larry and Lorna came and went. Professionally I reached the high point of my career. La Sierra University had given me tenure as Professor of English. That meant that, barring some colossal stupidity on my part, I would have a job as long as I needed it.

Teaching on a college campus is actually a very "daily" affair. Not a lot of glamour but still a great deal of satisfaction. I attended faculty and departmental meetings, committees, and self-study projects—world without end. I constantly faced the reading of numberless stacks of essays and term papers followed by testing and grade evaluations. All of these labors, however, were offset by the adventures of research and preparation of lectures and lively classroom discussion. Along with mentoring students. Nothing equaled the joy of watching some young person literally wake up, during an exchange of ideas. That was my basic job description. As the poet, William Butler Yeats, put it: "Education is not the filling of a pail, but the lighting of a fire."

About the time of my arrival at Loma Linda University, I became increasingly aware that I wanted to write. Years later my colleague, Neurologist Dan Giang (of Loma Linda University), explained that I had a medical condition called "Hypergraphia." That is, the compulsion to get things down on paper. Therefore, since my brain must be wired differently from others' and since I did teach a wide range of writing classes, I had to accept the fact that I needed to write

At the end of my first year at La Sierra, however, I realized that I had not been writing anything. Forthwith, I decided to "keep Tuesdays" when I had no classes. One of my fellow teachers said, "Remember Tuesday to keep it wholly and do all thy own work."

My family was all self-sufficient and independent. "What you eat or wear, where you go and how you get there—on Tuesdays it is no affair of mine." After taking this vow of abdication, I found that I really could drop out a day like this, and the world went on just the same.

I enjoyed only a short period of success, however, until Walt's illness brought this arrangement to an abrupt halt. I couldn't even begin to pick up the pieces until five years later.

My three months in India in 1987 were followed the next year, by almost three months in Britain. It proved to be a forecast of things to come. Through June and July Bob Dunn (the Department Chairman) and I conducted a four-week "London Center Tour" for Loma Linda University. Since the class was titled, "Restoration and Eighteenth-Century England," most of the lecturing fell to me.

In London we lodged at 48 Harrington Gardens, Kensington, a five-floor Victorian townhouse just two doors away from the home of the poet, W. S. Gilbert (of Gilbert-and-Sullivan operetta fame). Among the students was my lifelong friend, Fern Penstock. We shared a room and much more for most of the summer.

In addition to the classroom hours, our London days included several walking tours, a Thames River trip to Hampton Court Palace, as well as theater performances and concerts. Then our coach

Appearances to the contrary, Dorothy's life at the University was actually very "daily." Connecting with students in the classroom and keeping office hours for counseling students and reading papers.

Left. This address, 16 Priory Avenue in Chiswick, was the destination for Dorothy and her friends on repeated visits to London. **Right.** Here in their pleasant Victorian drawing room Bill and Enid Tolman hosted guests and boarders from all over the world.

took us away into the countryside: Stately homes, Cambridge, Oxford, Lincoln, and finally to Edinburgh and Robert Burns' home places. All of that was followed by Wordsworth country, Stratford-on-Avon, Wales and Bath. Strictly speaking we strayed out of the confines of the 18th-century, but we gave the students as rich an English experience as possible.

During our time in London, I received the news that one of my book manuscripts had been accepted for publication. The students cheered me on. "We're taking you to the Hard Rock Café to celebrate!" They must have detected a twinge of anxiety in me. "Oh, it isn't bad," they promised. "It's really more soft than hard, you know." A confirmed classical music devotee, I endured the heavy beat and loudness with difficulty. Nonetheless I appreciated the honors.

When the official study tour ended on July 14, Fern and I lodged ourselves on the top floor of Bill and Enid Tolman"s town house in Chiswick. I returned to my academic research while she roamed London (with her sketchbook). Weekends we visited London churches and strolled the art exhibits in the parks on Sundays.

During the first half of August, we had another intermission. Fern's husband Floyd and my mother arrived together at Gatwick Airport. We met them with a car I had rented, and the four of us struck out into the countryside for fifteen days of sightseeing. By now I had become familiar enough with Britain to pass for a guide.

We spent three days with friends in Newport at the Welsh Eisteddfod (ancient music festival). Amid swells of magnificent music, elfish dancing, and manifestations of the iconic red dragon, the event climaxed with the "seating of the bard."

Promptly we headed off to Ireland. At this point we began an odd relationship with our rented cars. We had turned in our first one because it had a faulty speedometer for which we did not wish to be responsible. The next one we locked up and left on the dock at Fishguard when we took the ferry *St. Brendan* to Ireland.

After a scenic but uneventful driving around Tipperary and the Ring of Kerry, we headed back to Rosslare for the return to England. Floyd had left his jacket in a restaurant in Cashel. During the sea crossing he realized that the car key for the car in Fishguard had been lost with the jacket. Upon arrival, we had considerable difficulty getting another car, Fishguard being isolated on the coast and lacking even a locksmith.

After almost a day's negotiation we got another car (with less than 200 miles on it) and headed up into the Cotwolds. Now we were deep into the "lands of my fathers" on a narrow road between Upper and Lower Slaughter. At the wheel, Floyd crowded left into the bank of the hedgerow while a fish-delivery van rounded the curve, went into a sixty-foot skid and slammed into us. I can still see the wide-eyed, terrified young driver in the truck. It was his first—and probably his last—day on the job.

Hours passed while the police made their report. "You are fortunate," they told the youth, "that they are tourists. They won't want to stay around to sue you."

An eccentric, ungracious tow-truck driver picked us up. Eventually, he delivered us to Banbury Cross—where the fair lady of the nursery rhyme came "in on a white horse." At the rental agency we had to ask for another car. I felt small enough to crawl under the door without even opening it.

"Each car we get has lower mileage than the last one," I told Floyd. "Why don't we just take this one straight from the factory." He was not amused.

Happily, we had paid our insurance and the staff gave us another car. Indeed, they revealed none of the horror that I felt about our situation.

In it, we drove north to attend the Edinburgh Tattoo in Scotland. I had carefully juggled the dates around so that we could do this. The hotel where we stayed lent us blankets to keep warm up in the bleachers. We watched the precision of the colorful exercises through a blinding curtain of rain. The woolen blankets became so heavy

Outside Gatwick Airport Fern Penstock and Leona Minchin loaded luggage into the first of the car rentals we went through in two weeks.

that we could barely haul them back to our rooms. Nonetheless, with true Celtic commitment the show had gone on, the downpour notwithstanding.

Ultimately, we got the car back to Gatwick Airport without further incident. We had used seven rental cars in fourteen days!

With Penstocks and my mother en route back to California, I returned to my library work. I punctuated that with a weekend in Devon with Sillitoes. Then a trip to Greenwich and another to St. Albans. I also spent some hours with the Spanish Armada Exhibit.

Over the next several years I would have three "sabbaticals" as well as other opportunities to study in the London libraries. I would become more familiar with and more at home there than I was where I lived in Riverside, California.

At first, getting permission to enter those sacred halls required a great deal of busywork. At the British Library, for instance, the photograph for my pass had to be taken with my eyes shut! Thereafter, I supposed, I would have to be sure to prove that I was alive and fit to use the Library. Then I had to go to the U. S. Embassy for a letter of recommendation to allow me into Manuscript Room of the Museum.

Next, I went to the High Commissioner for Jamaica to gain entrance to the library of the West India Committee. On my first day there I found a full-scale Jamaican quarrel going on in the lobby of the great old house in St. James. The doors had been locked for security. That put the combatant into a mighty rage. Totally out of control, he shifted from Oxford English to *patois*. I hung around for an hour, but when I left he still hadn't finished.

One finds all sorts in museum reading rooms. A marvelous place to be. Some people stay too long, and they dry up and blow away. One can encounter persons in a large library who, out on the open street, might have wholly escaped one's attention.

I tended to loiter in the English streets listening to the buskers. I thoroughly enjoyed their music skills, even though it appeared that their activities were only marginally legal. These phenomenal musicians don't appear to be begging nor are they handicapped. Still, they all look as if they could do with a handout. Their talent and choice of classical music never ceased to amaze me.

I always stopped to hear a flute player on a corner of Tottenham Court Road. Exuding a kind of "class" even in his tattered overcoat, he played with amazing volume, traffic blasting through around him on all sides. What did he perform? I loved the irony of "Sheep May Safely Graze."

Then in the Underground Station at St. James, I heard the strains of a Beethoven violin concerto at the bottom of the long escalator. The sound resonated and amplified marvelously through the cement tunnels as the trains roared by. In rags, he played as if he were on the stage of Royal Albert Hall, his violin case open beside him.

I concluded that the buskers say something good about English culture in the hectic, inflated days we live in.

I ended my 1988 three-month-long British excursion with a weekend at Newbold College, attending the Pope Tercentenary. When he was only twelve years old, the poet Alexander Pope had moved from London to Binfield. The family was Catholic, and no one of that religious persuasion was supposed to live within ten miles of London. Part of their property, Popeswood Lodge now belonged to the College. (That is where we had lived back in 1946 when my Dad taught at Newbold.) This convention made a suitable and convincing conclusion to my British summer.

The next year, 1989, my cup truly overflowed with joy, challenge, excitement—and, at the end, crushing sorrow. In addition to my official, "paid" travels, another opportunity had opened up to me. I had to take care lest I become completely intoxicated with it.

By this time Larry was working with Continental Airlines. Some quite astonishing travel privileges accrued to me. I could fly stand-by for $20.00, anywhere in the country. I tested it out the first weekend of March by flying across to spend the weekend in Washington with the Bill Dysingers and the Kelvin Minchins.

Next came Spring Vacation and I had a week to spare. When I offered to conduct a Writers Workshop at West Indies College (free of charge), the idea was received with enthusiasm. The first leg of the journey from Los Angeles to Newark was easily accomplished. I knew that the Newark-to-Montego Bay segment was overbooked. No matter. I was on a missionary journey, and if it didn't turn out I could just come back home. Nonetheless, my old friends had planned a whole week. "They're expecting me," I told God. "Please find me a seat, somewhere."

I watched while what appeared to be the entire population of New York boarded the plane bound for Jamaica. I was busily forming a back-up plan if I didn't get on. Just as the door was about to close, I sidled up to the attendant. "Do I have any hope of getting on this flight?"

The girl smiled and handed me a boarding pass. Lo, I sat in the first row of First Class, with all of the rights and privileges appertaining thereto!

A car from the College awaited me. For the next three-and-a-half hours, we wound across the island and up into the mountains to Mandeville. Yes, I worked hard every day, but I thoroughly enjoyed my old friends from twenty-five years ago. And Mandeville itself, especially the cool, green mornings. And the snowy egrets strutting around the gardens. They were new, blown in here from Florida fifteen years ago by a hurricane.

The next month I flew standby again to spend a weekend with Virginia-Gene Rittenhouse in one of her early Carnegie Hall concerts with her New England Youth Ensemble. (I sat through fifteen hours of rehearsal with the great John Rutter.)

In June, after lecturing (per appointment) at the annual Writers Conference at Andrews University, Michigan, I played my "stand-by card" again. I spent three weeks with friends and family in England. In July, Eileen and

Lyman joined me in Alberta for the Calgary Stampede. From there, I headed to Omaha, Nebraska. I promised to help my beloved Aunt Mid (Mildred Bennett) for the first Writers Conference sponsored by the Willa Cather Foundation in Red Cloud.

The configuration of the "College on the Hilltop" changed much as it grew into a University. What never changes is the refreshing view of the cool Mandeville Valley. For this and many other reasons Jamaica has remained a destination worth getting to.

By the time I arrived, I had a hacking cough from days of exposure to cigarette smoke in public places. Auntie had severe bronchitis too. We joked about coughing in counterpoint and barbershop harmony. At the same time I thought she seemed unusually tired. She didn't admit to anything, however, and the Writers Conference went forward as planned

I was home for just 48 hours and off to the Orient. Away to LAX at 4 a.m. I was to work on the movie ("We're Beginning the End") that would be used to represent the Far Eastern Division at the next General Conference session. I would tour the entire Division in twenty-two days and then stay in Singapore to write the script. A photography team from Australia followed my itinerary.

So I was suddenly dropped back into my familiar context. At each stop I was entertained generously and taken to significant places. I interviewed the people who were to be featured.

I was first greeted with "Hafa Adai" (Welcome) in Guam. Then came four days in Japan and Korea.

In Bangkok Ray James, Communications Director for the Far Eastern Division, met me and became my guide for the rest of the journey. I surprised

Left. Kevin Eckert and Ottis Edwards (Far Eastern Division president) wait for *murtabak* **to be made at an Indian restaurant in Singapore. Right. Dorothy worked almost round the clock some days to finish the video script. That's when her childhood playmate, Ah Ching Tan, brought her a delicious lunch of** *mee-goring.* **They had not seen one another for almost fifty years.**

my cousin Ina Madge Longway, Professor of Nursing, currently stationed there. Together we received the heart-rending news that our Aunt Mildred had lung cancer. I had recovered from my bronchitis, but we knew that her coughing would ultimately bring her down.

The Bangladesh part of the journey was new territory for me. Ray and I were met in Dhaka by Judy Whitehouse (another one of my American cousins) whom I had not met before. She and her husband Jerald represented ADRA (Adventist Disaster and Relief Association) there. I was fascinated by Pollywog Handicrafts where thirty-five basically illiterate women did the finest of cross-stitch embroidery. They perfectly reproduced English words in the little greeting cards, words that they did not understand. Out at the Bangladesh Adventist Seminary in the flood-lands, 400 smiling students greeted us. The very barren setting was offset by bright smiles and the curiosity of the children. Even the flowers along the paths became more prominent.

While in Hong Kong, I spent one evening with Uncle Melvin Milne in his high-rise apartment at Stubbs Road Hospital. One of my "uncles" from my Singapore childhood, he was being cared for by his foster-daughter—and my playmate—Eunice Mill. We had good food and much talk of old times.

The unique part of the story in Taipei that I chose was that of the tree-sculpting artist Ching Iin. For the past thirty-one years he had populated the hospital gardens with "bushy" people and animals. Some of them were lost in the building of the new hospital, but the rest now lived around a fountain, a watering place visible from the main street.

I arrived in the Philippines in time for the monsoon rains, and my story-finding journey took me from Manila, through Cebu and down to Mindanao.

I reached Singapore on August 11, worn out with the pace of the past three weeks and painfully aware of the staggering amount of writing that lay before me—a movie script plus twenty-six mission stories. It was well that the Far Eastern Division hadn't employed a novice to do the job. At least, for me it was familiar territory.

I had an optimum situation for the work. I used Gordon Bullock's office desk (the size of a garage door) and had two or three secretaries I could call on. The computer was unfamiliar. Knowing that I have only a tenuous grasp on the computer world, I hoped to be able to hide my ignorance and just get on with the job. Only one thing was missing. No one could give me extra time to do it all! On the recreational side, I was, after all, in Singapore. So most of my dinner hours were given over to feasts with friends, both old and new.

Although I no longer had direct connections with Far Eastern Academy, I was pleased to be invited to give a vespers talk. I looked at all those fresh-faced young kids and took my text from Nehemiah: "I am doing a great work, and I cannot come down." Perhaps my last month of travel and unremitting work had influenced me over much, but I decided there was no point keeping it a secret. Life is hard work, and you do need to set a goal in order to get through it. I thought they should know!

After a week of steady work—morning into the late nights, I went to Indonesia to glean more interviews. In four days I visited the high spots from Jakarta to the Celebes. Some were amazingly high. At one feast I had nineteen dishes set before me (not counting all of the rice).

The ADRA jeep took me up into Minahasa territory (North Celebes). At one *kampong* (village), the chief's wife gave me an orchid corsage. She was presiding over an ADRA-sponsored Child Survival program. Our meal consisted of fried bananas and boiled corn, washed down with green coconut water. Some 120 women had brought in their babies for health care, and the schoolyard was alive with other children underfoot. "Please, Doctor, give us some counsels about our children," the chief's wife implored.

"Oh, but I am not that kind of a doctor." I cast about how to explain, out there in the hinterlands of Sulawesi, why I couldn't say anything about children.

No use. I was a doctor, and therefore I had to say something. Hastily attempting to disguise my medical ignorance, I assembled some general wisdom concerning children. It was received very reverently.

When I got back to Singapore, I found my nephew Kevin waiting for me in my little apartment. Also an employee of Continental airlines, he had flown in by way of Copenhagen to spend some Singapore days with me

He had brought in durian. The overwhelming stench struck me when I walked in the door. "You can not keep that thing in here, Kevin. Out with it." He seemed a little surprised that I didn't want the odiferous food in my sleeping quarters. Although he bought durian all week, he did keep it outdoors, and whenever he needed a "fix,' he did it out on the street by himself.

Being that close to Australia, I couldn't see going home without visiting my cousins in my other home. When I flew to Perth on September 1, my writing was still incomplete. An air strike further frustrated me. Too late to get a seat on the train. So, after four days, I boarded "Bus Australia," bound for Sydney—a three-day time commitment. Non-smoking, fortunately, but that didn't take care of rock music all day long. Nor did it purify the loosely assembled fellow who took the seat in front of me in Adelaide. He smelled like something dead that had been rotting in a swamp for a month.

During the two weeks I had in Sydney and at Avondale College, I worked on my writing assignments. The rest of the time I spent showing Larry around Sydney when he came down for his first trip to Australia.

I arrived back home on Saturday night, September 25. Mum had "held the fort" well during my long absence. She and the dogs gave me a rousing welcome. I of course plunged directly back into my teaching program.

One thing was, however, seriously amiss.

September 7 had been Aunt Mildred's 80th birthday. Just in time for that occasion, her autobiography, *The Winter is Past,* came off the press. She was to

Dorothy's script-writing interviews took her among the bullock carts of Jogjakarta's streets and into rural Indonesia where she had to prove that she was not a medical doctor.

receive special honors at the forthcoming Western Literature Convention in Idaho. With my ever-so-handy airpass, I planned to go up there for the weekend and surprise her. It turned out, however, that she was too ill to attend. Her daughter Alicia had to read the paper that she had prepared for the occasion. I knew that my dear Aunt Mid was on a rapid downward spiral.

Along with Mum and my sister Eileen, I arrived in Red Cloud on October 12. Although Mid seemed so much her dear self, it was, at first, hard to believe that the demon at work in her body was now part of our circle. The moon rose full and very beautiful that first night in Nebraska, but she was too tired to join us on the front porch to look at it.

So, we puttered around the house, and I helped her go through some old files. She gave me the worn brown leather notebook that contained the many poems she had written over her lifetime.

One afternoon, as we sat alone, I asked Mid, "Have you given up the fight?" I had to know.

"Almost, I think." She looked so tired. I wanted by the sheer vitality of my own health and courage to reach out and rescue her. I laid my "alive" hand on her pale ivory one. I wanted to seize her and drag her back into the mainstream of life.

"I want to come see you once more." I said.

"But everything's so hard," she sighed. "If it's just too much, and if I can't hang on, you'll understand, won't you, sweetheart?"

To Dorothy,

When I approach the place of our meeting,
Creative juices begin to flow.
My heart chokes with words I mean to tell you.

The warm flood of mutual love, understanding, thinking,
Draws us into its wet warmth
Where flowers grow, flourish and blossom,
And no weed appears.

Love, Auntie Mid

(January 3, 1986)

I prized none of Mildred Bennett's poems above the little one she had written just for me, three years earlier.

Then she went on talking about her funeral. "I love Elgar's 'Pomp and Circumstance' march. I want that at my funeral, for celebration and rejoicing. A graduation, you see." She looked at me intently.

"Yes, of course. That's what it should be." I agreed.

I had to pray that I would know just the right time to return to Nebraska. We had been back in California just ten days, and telephone calls had criss-crossed the continent daily. One evening I had the overwhelming impression. "Time to go. Now." At 3 a.m. the next morning, I drove into Los Angeles and took the next flight to Omaha.

By this time, Auntie Mid was in the hospital. When I walked into her room at 10 a.m., she recognized me with a lovely smile. On the side, Uncle Wilbur (Red Cloud's long-time family doctor) told me, "Her last scan is one of the worst I have ever seen."

To know what dying is really about, you have to live it. It's never neatly packaged to fit into the time slot dictated by movie or television. It is pure

In 1992 Dorothy and her mother, Leona Minchin, had only one formal portrait made in the many years they lived together after Gerald Minchin died. The stage props symbolized the beautiful things they most enjoyed—books, handicrafts, a globe (travel) and the Gold Teddy Bear (animals). (Courtesy of Adair Photography, Redlands, California)

agony, and one can choose neither the time nor the way of going.

I spent four days at Auntie Mid's bedside. We talked. Then we talked less. Over the years we had said so many things, that at this point we understood without many words. She knew that she was fighting an earthly enemy too strong for her human body. "Now I want to go home," she whispered. "I've fought the good fight. I have finished my course. I have kept the faith. Everything is all right. It's all right."

Then I had to leave. At the door of her hospital room, I turned and said my last goodbye and walked out, quickly. My classroom and office awaited me. I couldn't stay longer. I knew I couldn't come back for her "graduation," but there would be many others there at the funeral. Having made that last visit, I knew that I, like Mary of Bethany, had chosen "the better part."

She lived eleven more days. Just before midnight on November 7, that merciless intruder, Cancer, finally stepped in and snatched her away.

As I prepared Mildred's obituary, I tried to comprehend all of her, one of my very best friends. Academic achievements? (There had been many.) The spirit and energy that enabled her to turn the little town of Red Cloud into an American historical monument and to open up the world of Willa Cather to scholarship. (Important, yes.) Still, the mere statistics of her life left much unsaid. She loved ideas, and there was no subject she was afraid to investigate. Her mind never rested from exploration. Above all, because "Unconditional

Love" was a life-theme, she had lived a life of wonderful compassion.

At last, I could review that year of 1989. Had I really done all of that? The height, depth, and breadth of it all seemed beyond reach! Had I actually traveled to all of those places? Besides, that was the year I had my sixtieth birthday too! Maybe I should start practicing a little temperance. Soon. I believe that I had pretty well tested the outer limits of my endurance.

Mildred Bennett (1909-1989), of Red Cloud, Nebraska.

CHAPTER 16

The Music Mix

While 85% of my university work was routine, the other 15% was pure academic adventure, interspersed with delicious, just-for-fun features. Indeed, a number of exotic experiences punctuated my campus life. I traveled, taught classes, did research and writing, and more. World wide. I made seven teaching tours and worked through three "overseas sabbaticals." And much more. At those times I literally flitted among the mountains tops of academic enterprise. A heady experience that I could never have envisioned at the beginning of my teaching career.

My three tours with the New England Youth Ensemble forever remain in a class of their own.

In 1992 the journey to China followed on the heels of the five-week research trip I had made to Britain. I didn't believe I could find the time. Still, who could resist Virginia-Gene Rittenhouse's invitation: "Our New England Youth Ensemble is going to China. Would you come along and give us an on-tour seminar?"

Thus, I found myself in the West Coast group leaving Los Angeles and bound for the Orient on May 20. In Narita Airport, Japan, we joined the Boston contingent of musicians, making up a party of ninety-two travelers. I streamlined my lectures to keep pace with the very ambitious concert schedule and labeled my for-credit package "Backgrounds in Asian Culture." I had to fit in ten hours of class lectures. Research, term-papers, and a final exam would follow at home.

At midnight the immigration officers released us into the streets of Shanghai. We boarded the three waiting buses and set off into that teeming city of thirteen-and-a-half million. Although we practiced the customary economies of the NEYE, some mission-minded physicians had sponsored this tour. Unexpectedly, then, we lodged in fine tourist hotels. Thus, under the cool but intense scrutiny of our six guides, we would live within the grand showcase of Communism, effectively removed from the "real" China.

Nonetheless, of the 200 other music organizations who had applied to concretize in China, the NEYE and the Atlantic Union College Collegiate Choir were only the second group to be accepted by the communist government. Besides, large numbers of young people from America were highly suspect. China didn't want more drugs. So while aging tourists might dodder around the country, university types were inevitably under suspicion. Moreover, a whole Chinese generation had grown up knowing almost nothing of Western classical music.

Tensions rose after our first concert at the Shanghai Conservatory of Music. No religious references of any kind would be permitted. Handel's Coronation Anthem caused immediate consternation. "But," we explained, "'hallelujah' is simply an exclamation of praise, and 'amen' only means 'so be it.'"

Would the tour be cancelled? Would our colorful Chinese-English brochures be confiscated? The jury was out for several days. On Saturday we attended the Mu Ena Tang Church under the auspices of the Three Self-Help management.[1] We sat in isolation in the balcony looking down through the high arches, not allowed to give music or to speak to anyone.

We were treated to a visit to the exquisite Yu Gardens, to a commune full of happy peasants and a "Children's Palace." Then they entertained us with an excellent acrobatic performance.

When we boarded the train for the four-hour journey to Hangzhou, our young people hailed the event with wild excitement. Most of them had never been on a train before. We passed miles of gardens and rice paddies flanked by spiritless gray cement buildings. No cattle or machinery. Just two bare hands with which to work.

This journey, however, became the turning point in our affairs. The chief guide, Michael, came to the compartment shared by us "geriatrics." "I know now who you are. I want to do all that I can to make the concerts successful!"

Left. The celebrated English conductor and composer, John Rutter, and Virginia-Gene Rittenhouse confer backstage at Carnegie Hall, New York. Right. Dr. Virginia-Gene Rittenhouse in her dressing room at one of her many concerts at Carnegie Hall.

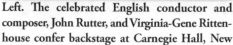

Forthwith, he cleared a broad path through all of the communist bureaucracy. He even agreed to let Alex Henderson sing "He's Got the Whole World in His Hands." That solo repeatedly sent the audiences into paroxysms of applause. We took care not to discuss the identity of "He." (I have always wondered who the people imagined he was.)

Americans take total mobility for granted. They expect the freedom to try anything they please. At this point the students did a lot of observing and thinking. At last, in the evening concert in Hangzhou, they relaxed enough to do what they had come to do. They performed for a very sophisticated audience. Despite the language barrier, everyone followed the whimsical story of "The Laughing Song," Our charming young seventeen-year-old soloist won all of them over with that one. Shawn Cabey's flashy Rachmaninoff piano concerto likewise also pleased the crowd. By this time our guides were alluding to "the next time you come and we will give you much more."

Our domestic flight to Beijing was Spartan. First we visited the elegant (but run down) Forbidden City, truly a national treasure. This, even though the emperors are now roundly despised. Seeing the huge palace makes you walk your feet off, down to bleeding stumps.

For the next day, I discussed Chinese folk tales and tried to prepare everyone for walking along a tiny fragment of the 3,000-mile-long Great Wall. I wanted to make all of my lectures as relevant as possible.

Our drinking water, of course, had either to be boiled or bought. The bottle labels promised us almost everything short of eternal life. ""Natural Mineral Weter to Rare Quality." "From the spring of

The government discouraged foreigners' mingling with local people. At the Three Self-Help (Christian) Church, however, we stood proudly (and briefly) beside one long-suffering pioneer of Adventism in China. (L-R). Harvey Rittenhouse, Virginia-Gene Rittenhouse, David Lin, Dorothy Comm.

the famous Mt. Laoshan nutritive for infants." "Contains twenty beneficial elements." "Protect life function of human body." "Holy Water" of "Precious and High Quality."

The best one offered "trace elements whice [sic] accelerate intellect of the human pody [sic]." Young Melville Andrade lingered over this one. "Ah! Let me get several gallons of that," he sighed wistfully.

By the time we reached Xian, our fame had preceded us. A large red-and-gold banner across the front of the lovely Golden Flower Hotel read: "New England Youth Ensemble and Choir." We learned that, unknown to us, 200 Seventh-day Adventist members had been able to get into the afternoon concert at the Xian Conservatory. Another 150 joined the audience at the hotel in the evening. Of course, we could only look at one another across the empty space.

I stood on a balcony looking down on the lovely evening scene: guests at the tables, enthralled. The young musicians as smart and professional as always. Plus the uniformed guards and plain-clothes informers crowding in on every side. They stood right in among the replicas of the terracotta warriors that were part of the décor. A whimsical scene, for those soldiers of Emperor

Chin (221 B.C.) looked so much at home among the living people. And the horses too, with flowing manes and perked up ears. Let no one say that China was primitive 2,000 years ago.

The guides regularly set wonderful shopping opportunities before us. Perforce, we had a kind of counterpoint going there. While we appeared to be tourists, most of us were, in fact, paupers. A great mystery to our tour guides, hotel staffs, and street vendors alike!

On the other hand, the four-hour cruise on the River Li proved to be the very best Guilin could offer. If you never visited China, you might think that the painted scenery was nothing but the imagination of generations of artists. The lime stone mountains of Guilin have been as sacred to Chinese art as Mount Fuji has been to the Japanese. The slender mountains on either side of the river fade into the distance, range upon range. In the foreground cattle graze in green meadows beside the broad river bank. Occasionally a house looked out at us from among the bamboos, with stone staircases leading down to the water.

We literally sailed through a Chinese painting. We stood for hours on the upper deck, breeze in the hair, with a feeling as spiritual as a prayer in the heart. Overdosed on crowds, cities, and civilization, some of the kids murmured, "This is where I could live for the rest of my life." Our four-hour journey ended at the village of Yangzhou where our buses mercilessly waited to haul us back into the 20th-century.

The Reed Flute Cave of Guilin was named for the stand of bamboos that grows around it. Although it compared with America's best in the line of caves, the Chinese formations were much finer—like trees and rocks in carved jade. An underground microcosm of the mountains that we saw on the previous day's river trip.

Meanwhile, the emotional response to the music escalated throughout the two weeks we were in China. In Guilin, the local guide declared it to have been "a very perfect performance." At the same time, the young concert-mistress, Rachelle Berthelsen, spoke despairingly of the "noise we make!"

"But," I countered, "somehow no one out there in the audience even hears the mistakes. Never." It recalled the early days back in Poland and com-

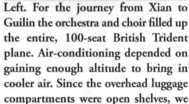

Left. For the journey from Xian to Guilin the orchestra and choir filled up the entire, 100-seat British Trident plane. Air-conditioning depended on gaining enough altitude to bring in cooler air. Since the overhead luggage compartments were open shelves, we took care to be sure than no one got brained with a backpack or a violin case. Above Right. Without ceremony the group was set down on the Guilin runway and left to look after themselves. Right. When they reached the Golden Flower Hotel (Guilin), however, a red banner welcomed their arrival.

munist Russia.[2] Back then the musicians used to say "The angels play with us." We could hear that the angels were still playing in China too.

Departing out of China for Hong Kong occupied two sweaty hours. Our group visa listed us alphabetically. Fair enough. We were required, however, to line up, physically, by our assigned numbers. All in a very small space. Moreover, we had to have every piece of our luggage with us. So ninety-two of us scrambled around among bags and boxes, amid tuba and trumpet, tympani and cellos. One of the bass viols reared up like a dinosaur in our midst while the other had to be inched forward along the floor in its coffin-like container. Moreover, the entire airport provided just twenty-five luggage carts to facilitate this escalating fury.

Although I found my "A26" ahead of A17 and definitely behind A67, getting into position took some time. I suppose the numbers must have somehow been related to the list of our names, but the connection was never clear. Ultimately our cargo—and we ourselves—had to filter through a single, narrow, one-person-size gateway. Almost it could not be done.

The common-sense solution to this riot would have been for the officials to look at the list of our names, which lay plainly before them. They could simply have checked off each passenger as he/she staggered through the bottleneck. Instead, tranquil Chinese officers watched us from the sidelines and derived the same satisfaction, I suppose, that people get from watching Kung Fu.

The entire one-hour flight to Hong Kong's Kai Tek Airport really wasn't long enough for us to recover from the trauma of our exit from China. At the same time, we would never forget our guides, very near tears, as they bade us farewell.

A sudden sense of liberation enveloped us. The doors of MacDonald's stood open. Fresh fruit abounded. We needed no guides. I was well able to show my friends around and get them to Victoria Peak for that breathtaking view of the city's nightlights.

Then away to the concert-hall in the Hong Kong Center for Performing Arts. With fire and freedom the kids plunged into their sacred repertoire. David Workman's virtuoso trumpet. Alexander Henderson's solos. The choir in full voice. The evening ended in many encores and three standing ovations.

Later that night half a dozen kids came to me, wide-eyed. "We didn't know it could make such a difference," they cried. "I mean, not being able to sing religious music in China all of this time."

Culture and Classics. That's all that we could give China. Now it was "Culture, Classics and Spirituality." No one had to explain the difference. Probably none of us could ever be quite the same again.

We flew to Thailand on Hong Kong's own Cathay Pacific. Marvelous! Even room for people with legs. We explored exotic Bangkok—the temples, the *klong* (canals) and all of the rest. A new consciousness flowed over the students. We had arrived once again in a land of belief. Even if it was not our own belief.

With Singapore as the end of the tour, I really wanted to share my hometown with my friends. Alas, great changes were occurring. Visiting the Far Eastern Division office at 800 Thomson Road was like taking part in a wake. That lovely old mandarin mansion, along with Far Eastern Academy (which closed its doors a few weeks earlier) are destined for destruction. Already the compound looked like a ghost village. Empty buildings. Friends gone. No future in that town.

At the same time, the city of Singapore remained its brilliant, modern self. Changi Airport was stunning. Where else have you seen full-sized palm trees set amid the marble planters? Or a two-storey-high waterfall. Or when have you collected your luggage off conveyor belts that circle around orchid gardens and bonsai trees. Moreover, the luggage carts are plentiful and free. I have always resented the miserly policy in Los Angeles that requires $1.00 per cart from people who have just disembarked from Rio or Algiers and don't have dollar bills in their pockets.

Our last night was given over to goodbyes, wisdom and honors. We crowded around Rittenhouses' room on the twelfth floor of the New Park Hotel. For my services, Virginia Gene gave me a folk painting from Xian. She had seen me admiring this water-color panel of a great flock of geese among the bamboos in the moonlight, all of them asleep. The Chinese caption read "Peace and Quietness." That image aroused an instinctive response of my often-too-busy life.

I sandwiched in my last lecture during our six-hour flight from Singapore to Tokyo. In discussing their proposed term-paper topics, we drifted into stimulating conversation. Many of the non-credit students joined in what became philosophical review of our twenty-five days in Asia. No one can ever tire of bouncing ideas around among inquiring minds. That is why I never thought of looking for another kind of job!

Probably we will never know how closely we were scrutinized in China. We all had limitless possibilities for getting it wrong. To have instantaneously become *persona non grata,* the Ugly Americans. Therefore, I was so proud of

Well-to-do peasants on the River Li had two or three trained cormorants as fishing partners. The large, sassy birds would catch the fish, but their collars prevented them from swallowing.

our young people. Their cheerful friendliness, their commitment, and their grace. Indeed, they won the day—every day.

A highly contrasted journey came up just six weeks after I got home to California. I had treated myself to a new little ruby-red Honda Accord LX (with a moon-roof), and it was ready for a road test. So when Vern and Mary Stellmaker came up from Australia we struck out north on the Pacific Coast Highway. In twenty-six days we covered nine U.S. states and two Canadian provinces (6,270 miles).

All through the eleven national parks we enjoyed eating, chatting, sleeping, and looking. (Mary never ceased, for a moment, searching for bears!) Rarely did we drive more than 300 miles in a day. Riding, day after day, through the mild, clean countryside we absorbed the blue sky, open vistas among mountains and rivers, and fresh stands of trees. Absolute freedom to do as we pleased. The irony of it all struck me. The inevitable contrast with the stringencies of my recent China Tour.

Three years later I made my second teaching tour with the New England Youth Ensemble and Collegiate Choir. That time Wilf and Annamarie Liske came out to spend the thirty-five days of my absence with my mother. They did a warmly, wonderful job of taking care of her. How many friends like that do you make in a lifetime? A family reunion for us all!

My Royal Jordanian flight on June 20, 1995, landed me in Schiphol Airport, Amsterdam. (That airline agreed to fly all 93 members of our music group to the Jerash Festival in Jordan at half price!) From there I backtracked to Heathrow Airport, reaching the Tolman's fireside in Chiswick by supper time. The next day I had myself at Gatwick Airport to meet Vic and Gem Fitch, flying in from Calgary.

I planned this as a one-week prelude to my official summer assignment. We three took possession of a little green Renault car rental and headed off on our little tour of Britain. A venture that we'd been talking about for at least

In the rotunda of the Media Hotel in Beijing Shawn Cabey enchanted the audience with his rendition of the Rachmaninoff piano concerto.

fifteen years. We started with a parish church in Essex where Vic had the chance to kneel on the grave of his grandfather (generations removed) and make a brass-rubbing of the engraved figures on the tomb-top.

We drove through the Cotswolds, Wales, and finally ferried across to Ireland. This destination belonged to Gem. As an O'Brien she is descended from the legendary Irish High King, Brian Boru. (Vic and I paid her due honors.) The Celtic designs fascinated her, and she stood in reverent silence before the Book of Kells in Dublin.

Upon our return to Wales, we had to rent a tiny Fiat, about the size of a baby carriage. (We had been promised a Ford Fiesta.) By the time we reached Chiswick, we and our luggage were literally oozing out of the cracks. Bill Tolman gave the car one cynical once-over, "Ah, yes! Fix It Again, Tony."

Years ago during an unfortunate interval of car-ownership, Walt had bought a Fiat. From then on, I vowed that I would never willingly or knowingly have one again. Still, one does what one must do.

Nonetheless, we did reach the airport in time, and I waved Fitches off to the Netherlands where he was a delegate at the forthcoming General Conference session in Utrecht. I finished up the paper work for the car and then took the bus down to Exeter to spend a weekend with Sillitoes before my responsibilities began.

A flight out of Heathrow set me down again in Amsterdam Airport where I was supposed to meet Rittenhouses. I missed them, however, and had to find my own way out to the Hostel Slot Assumberg in Heemskerk. I instantly felt at home with all of my musician friends again. I was pleased to find the personable Janusz Bilinski (bass viol player) in the group.

The weekend inundated us with 50,000 people in the Utrecht convention facilities. Chances of meeting anyone you knew were minimal. Fortunately, however, my old college friends, Jack and Olivine Bohner found me straying among the exhibition booths. Fresh from visiting relatives in Germany, Olivine was to become my roommate for the rest of the tour.

Their concretizing complete, the Ensemble and Collegiate Choir now headed east in our two English coaches. We had three drivers, "Big John" Lake, JR ("Little John"), and Paul (a congenial Londoner). The tour began with the all-night journey to Salzburg, Austria. We circled Brussels, Luxembourg, Stuttgart and Munich and missed all the lovely forest scenery of Germany.

Nevertheless, we were all deposited in front of the 17th-century Dom Cathedral for the first concert—just in time. Everyone scrambling to find their instruments and concert clothes created quite a stir in the square, and several tourists paused to watch, believing us to be one of the local attractions.

Finally, Olivine and I found seats in the stony, cool Dom to hear the Kodaly 'Missa Brevis." Tired as they were, the orchestra and choir were thrilled with the music they could make under the magnificent Romanesque arches.

We slept that night at the large Landesberufsschule (vocational school) in Obertrum. Tired beyond limits, Olivine and I chortled over our big, double room. Spanking new with a huge shower and endless hot water. Bleary-eyed we stared at one another across the clean, airy space. "Ah, well! If you put us both together," Olivine speculated, "I think you could find enough good parts to make one whole woman." We well knew the pace we would have to keep up in the coming days.

En route to Venice I tried my first bus lecture. Along with Lyn Bartlett (Academic Dean of Columbia Union College) I was to teach an on-tour course on "The East-West (Muslin-Christian) Encounter."

Our hostel in Venice turned out to be a barracks. At the entrance the women were herded off to the left and up to the fourth floor. Men to the right and the lower floors. (I got the distinct sense of entering a concentration camp.) A few of us rushed by the windowless cubicles and found a room with a window. Besides, it had only three bunk beds.

Our Australian concert-mistress, Naomi Burns, seized one of the top bunks and then sat down on the sill of the arched window. We stood watching the moon over St. Mark's plaza. "How lovely!" she pointed to the moon-streaked water of the Grand Canal, determined to salvage the aesthetic joys of being in Venice. "This will be one of the loveliest nights of my life!"

In that spirit we bore up under the merciless heat and lined up for the three available showers. (None of the shower doors would close, and we had access to just three semi-functional toilets.)

Most of the girls floated about like mummies in sheets and went to bed naked and wet, just to keep cool.) Eventually, we all got sorted out, the conversation simmered down, and we lay very still, just to stop sweating. Modesty was not one of our concerns.

Suddenly a man appeared in our midst, scanning us with a large flashlight and yelling in Italian. We assumed that he was telling us to "shut up." This extemporaneous, self-appointed "Dean of Women" must have come upon several unclad bodies while he made his rounds. I wondered how matters might have gone in a private room with, say, just one or two girls in it.

On the other hand, our entertainment at Bogenhofen Seminary was above reproach. At that point we lay very near the village of Braunau where Adolph Hitler had been born. How, I asked myself, could someone be reared in such lovely surroundings turn out to be so evil?

From this point onward the border crossings became increasingly more complicated as we drove toward Prague. Janusz chose to withdraw his Polish identity and took a back seat. "I know these people," he murmured darkly. "I don't want to talk to them."

Experienced in these matters, Big John managed, more or less, to keep us moving forward. He helped things along by shrewdly dispensing six-packs of sodas, cold out of the coach refrigerator.

When we arrived in Czech, we saw simple, steep-roofed cottages. Often

Australians, Vern and Mary Stellmaker, thoroughly enjoyed the comprehensive trek through America's Northwest in Dorothy's new car. Never, for a moment, did Mary stop looking for bears. Right. A primitive lunch stop on the Bozeman Trail, a relic of the Montana gold rush (1863-1868).

in disrepair, they looked displeased with themselves, buried in weeds but sometimes attempting a few flowers. The whole landscape seemed to say, "We are trying, but we're so tired."

Some twenty-five miles across the border we came upon an enormous traffic jam. Cars kept coming at us on the wrong side. A lethal accident? No. Three small planes had just landed on the road and were being hauled off by tractors. The highway was already there, so why bother building an airstrip?

Long delay at the Polish border, even with Janusz now translating, made us late for the concert in St. Mary's Church in Krackow. The two huge bouquets of flowers that Virginia-Gene and James Bingham (choir master) received at that concert, however, were saved for the death camp at Auschwitz the next day. Virginia laid one in the crematorium. The other went to the shrine of the martyred priest, Father Maximilian Kolbe (d. 1941), who sacrificed his life to save another prisoner who had a large family of children.

We sat on the grass in front of the prison to eat our bountiful lunch. It felt almost irreverent to do so. We ate quietly, almost as if at communion.

Crossing the Czech border again almost destroyed us. Six packs of soda didn't help any more, and our drivers became very uneasy. The border guards had checked us in incorrectly, and now they impounded our buses and refused to let us out. "They can strip the bus, if they want to," JR said. Flying in and out of the airport would probably have been without incident. Having almost

100 people melting down on two buses was, apparently, an opportunity not to be missed.

This time Janusz *had* to negotiate. Then suddenly—after three hours and for no reason that we could determine—the guards let us go. "You must cross the border into Austria before midnight or you will be arrested for trespassing without visas," they growled.

It would be a five-hour journey, and we were allowed just one rest stop. "We have just thirty minutes here," JR announced, when we finally found a place. The facility had just one seat in each restroom, and our line of people seemed to stretch into infinity. We had not been off the bus since Auschwitz.

"All right!" Virginia-Gene took command. "Men to the bushes. The rest line up for both toilets." The station, fortunately, was surrounded by a dense stand of trees.

"Please, ma'am!" one of the boys whispered, "Not everything can be managed in the forest." She suffered him to stay.

That interlude took a full hour. (No doubt the police had us under surveillance the whole time.) As the clock eased on toward midnight, our unbelievably skilled drivers maneuvered us through village after village.

Near the end, JR made a wrong turn at an un-signposted fork in the road. That detour on to an unfinished road almost ran us into a lake. We lost forty-five minutes.

Before going on to the General Conference in Utrecht, Fitchs and Dorothy toured England and Ireland. In an old parish church in Essex Vic made a brass rubbing off the tomb-top of one of his ancestors.

Finally, literally panting for breath, we wheeled into the border-crossing at 12.15 a.m. Providence knew that we had endured enough. Nothing was said about being fifteen minutes

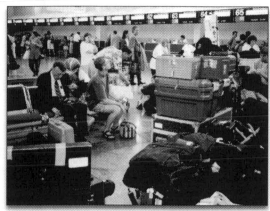

This picture of the New England Youth Ensemble in transit could be in almost any airport in the world. Managing the aggregate heap of luggage, instruments, trunks of music files, and food boxes was not a task for the faint-hearted. In the middle of it all, Dr. Harvey (his vital briefcase of documents and money at hand) sat down to grab the chance to get a bite of food.

late, about speeding, or about driving on a limited "three-and-a-half-ton road." The sullen guards just waved us through.

Another four hours to reach Vienna. We reached the Academia Hotel at 4 a.m. scarcely realizing that we had arrived. One look at our beds and we crashed.

The next day, our coach drivers headed home to England. Lyn Bartlett went with them, leaving me to finish the class lectures in Jordan. (With normal border crossings we could have had the class work done by then.)

Not unexpectedly, confusion attended our arrival in Amman, Jordan. We all stood in utter silence as we were moved from here to there, like sheep for shearing. (One anomaly created crisis. Why should there be two people in the group named "Dorothy?" Me and the mother of James Bingham.) Eventually, after an unconscionable amount of time, we were each presented with a handsome laminated card (our own photo ID) for the Jerash Music Festival. We were in.

The military buses set us down at the large, elite suburban school of Rawdat el Ma-aref. Midnight notwithstanding, the chefs had a handsome meal waiting for us. Artistic platters of humus, yogurts, bean sauces, and pickles accompanied the rice. Stacks of pita bread waited to be stuffed with whatever we chose to put into them.

Beforehand, however, we had concerts in Israel. The first day, as we headed to Galilee, Virginia-Gene asked me to give a morning worship talk. Fortunately my new devotional book *(Glimpses of God)* was already under

construction, so I found something to
say about "The Balm in Gilead."

Four small buses trundled us over
the blinding white desert roads. Chaos
at the border, of course, and everyone
fretted while the music instruments
baked in the back of the police truck at
a temperature of at least 130 degrees.
No one who has been to Palestine in
the summer will ever take cool air and
water for granted again. Along with the
buses we acquired two guides, one
Christian and one Moslem. They
appeared not to care for one another
nor for any of us either.

Nightfall brought us to the Karei
Deshe Youth Hostel, north of Tiberias
where a tasty and generous supper

No matter what time of the night the group
came in, the gracious chefs at Rawdat al-
Ma'aref School in Jordan had a meal ready
for us.

awaited us. While the orchestra and choir gave an evening concert in the
fountain courtyard, I sat by the lake. With Mozart music behind me and
Galilee before me, I sat for a long time with my own thoughts. A light breeze
flicked away the heat of the day.

To the disgust of "Napoleon" (our name for one of the guides), I
attempted a class lecture on the long road south to Bethlehem. Thinking that
we had to be among the Big Spenders, he was eager to herd us into the souvenir
shops and resented the distraction.

We lodged that night in Mor Sharbel House (a convent). It overlooked
a deep valley with row upon row of square-jawed little flat-roofed houses on
the hillside. Immediately below our window was a derelict house, mud
returning to mud. Burned rubbish surrounded it and fresh garbage sat on top.
No one will clean it up because, probably, it is the will of Allah that it should
be there. Chickens picked through the junk, dogs yapped, and children
screamed. Noise is part of the culture. Everything hangs out. Late at night,

however, when I lifted my eyes to the little hills of Bethlehem and the stars shone above, I managed to rise above it all.

In addition to public concerts, we also created our own private memories. Singing in close harmony, we had "Amazing Grace" on Galilee. "I Walked Today Where Jesus Walked" on the Mount of the Beatitudes. "Let Us Break Bread together on our Knees" echoed up into the stone vaults of the Upper Room. "He Lives" at the Garden Tomb.

Upon our re-entry into Jordan, the guides demanded "tip" money before we even reached immigration. Because of their attitude, Virginia-Gene had cut it in half. Even so, they and the bus drivers were going to collect about $1,000. At the border, they walked out of our lives. Hardly anyone saw them go, and no one cared.

Our last sightseeing extravaganza was Petra. The home of the Edomites (children of Esau) as early as 800 B.C. We could have spent hours in the rocky labyrinths. In places the trail was barely ten feet wide, while the pink, beige, and mauve stone walls rose at least 100 feet. When Virginia wanted a sundown talk, I had to cast about among my still embryonic devotionals for something about rocks.

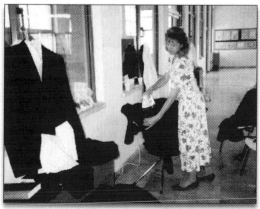

Practical helpers like Rosemary Sprague were part of the orchestra's necessary support. In Jordan she kept concert clothes in stage-ready condition—laundering shirts, pressing suits, sewing on buttons. Whatever.

Our return to Amman became life-threatening. The militiamen drove like madmen, playing 'chicken" with one another. They narrowly missed robed and veiled pedestrians on the roadside, swung around corners on two wheels, and sometimes became completely airborne. The wind and sand desiccated our skin. We bounced up and down on the seats, hoping not to shatter vertebrae as we slammed down each time. The soldiers' handling of the buses was a cross between the skills of Bedoins on horseback and kids on skateboards.

Moreover, our driver's hospitality included at least 70 decibels of raucous Jordanian music. "Like a fly trying to get out of a bottle," Olivine muttered. Still, the ride almost obliterated the sound. Finally,

A highlight of the 1995 NEYE tour was concretizing at the Summer Festival in the 2,000-year-old Roman amphitheater at Jerash, Jordan. Afterwards we walked the ancient plazas and colonnaded streets.

she jumped up and shouted to the driver. "Stop racing."

"Do you want something?" the girl-guide inquired mildly. (She had contributed nothing for the entire day.)

"Yes." Olivine spoke with the hard-earned authority of forty-five years in the classroom. "Tell him he is driving like an idiot." The fact that the man carried a revolver didn't deter her in the least. Not for nothing is she descended from King Louis IX, the last of the Crusader kings of France. She had "presence."

Apparently the girl communicated the message. Things calmed down for at least fifteen minutes. Later, NEYE's music librarian had confronted one of the other drivers about his smoking.

Surprisingly, we all did arrive back at Rawdat El Ma-aref at midnight, alive. Supper waited for us—the chefs smiling and patient as always. Virginia Gene complained to the young Jerash Festival manager whom she found waiting in the school foyer.

The next morning none of the former bus drivers showed up. The school generously offered the use of their buses and drivers. Two of the vehicles were even air-conditioned.

I managed to get in my last two lecture hours between breakfast and rehearsal time. On such a high-octane tour, of course, one is fortunate to find the kids awake, much less capable of assimilating knowledge.

Then on to the famous Festival of Culture and Arts, inaugurated by Queen Noor in 1980. Apart from the Eugene Ballet Company, our group was the only representatives of the United States. Founded in the 2nd century B.C. Jerash became one of the most important Roman cities in the Middle East.

Ultimately, we filed into the South Theater, up against the Zeus Temple, to find the jagged stone seats in the semi-circular curve no softer than when the Romans set themselves down there.

Security-armed soldiers stood every ten yards along the upper rim of the theater, and swarms of uniformed people crowded around the stage.

Then, the baton when up on the drum-roll of Handel's "Royal Fireworks," NEYE's signature piece. The very air exploded with sound so pure and clean that it defied description. Naturally, the kids had never heard themselves play in such perfect acoustics. What a gift the Greeks gave us in their

Left. In her latter years (in addition to managing the house and the dogs) Grandma Leona Minchin spent hundreds of hours cutting felt sets for children's ministries, worldwide. Right. A beginning and an ending. Grandma Leona Minchin (1907-1999) held her three-week-old great-grandson Gary (Larry Comm's firstborn). Three weeks later she died at age 91.

Left. Travis Losey (viola, first-year medical student) and April Bellamy (violin) were the thirteenth couple to meet and marry out of the New England Youth Ensemble. (The total number of matches, as of this writing, stands at approximately twenty-five. They married two weeks before the beginning of the 1999 tour. They volunteered to spend their honeymoon serving on-the-road meals to 45 people. Their careful shopping resulted in virtually no waste of food. **Right.** The Ensemble's two Icelandic "Vikings," Ingi Erlendsson (trombone) and Sturlaugur Bjornsson (French horn) attempted to confiscate Muireadach's great cross (900 AD) at Monasterboice, north of Dublin. It was the least they could do for their ancestors who persistently raided the Irish monasteries and stole precious church vessels.

outdoor theaters. We have never yet produced enough acoustical tile to equal what they did.

Tewfic Safieh came to the concert. From his office in Fort Lauderdale, Florida, he had made all of our travel arrangements. After the concert he had good news for us, "I own five travel agencies. I cannot employ such people as this. I have fired the guides that you had in Israel."

On the way back to Amman one of our buses stalled on a hill. Deliberate and classy as a duke putting on his tuxedo, the driver divested himself of his gun-belt and donned overalls. He went to the back and applied some kind of potion. Then he returned to the front, removed his overalls, picked up the revolver, turned on the ignition and drove off. Such grace and expertise! Real class. Once again, the chefs at Rawdat had a full scale meal waiting for us.

At the second night's performance, Olivine and I sat behind the U.S. and German diplomatic corps. They were nothing short of ecstatic. "Truly," the U.S. ambassador exclaimed, "this is the very best kind of diplomatic contract the United States can send overseas." Virginia Gene came away laden with three enormous flower arrangements.

On our last night, the kids made no attempt at sleep. The mid-night meal began at 1.30 a.m. Our luggage had to be out in the halls for pick-up at 4 a.m. Our bodies had to be down in the dining room for breakfast at 5. Olivine and I just changed into our travel clothes, lay down on our beds and listened. The noise level among us rapidly rose to Arab proportions.

Ever the astute businessman, Tewfic saw us off on our homeward flight to Amsterdam. "The palace was thrilled with the concerts," he urged. "They have already issued an invitation for next year."

"Very good." Virginia replied. "But we're bankrupt now."

"And tired," she might have added. As we boarded the old Tri-Star, our whole crowd simply slumped forward in their seats. The attendants wondered. Why do so many people, at one time, appear to be incapable of resuscitation?

During this phase of the journey I had one empty seat beside me. My seventeen students took turns coming and sitting with me. I gave them about half an hour apiece to discuss their research plans. While the kids slept before and after, I had to stay upright the whole way.

By the end of the ninth hour I was thoroughly spaced out, almost in an "out of body" experience. By the time I reached Los Angeles, I had been awake for fifty-two hours.

Consequently, when Larry met my plane, he just scooped me up and took me home.

At the end of the summer, I recharged my own batteries at a Writers' Conference in Colorado Springs. I deeply appreciated my personal benefits: my own car, air-conditioning, and potable water. Best of all I had the luxury of sitting back and having someone else teach me something.

On March 26, 1999, my mother Leona Minchin died, following a series of debilitating strokes. Almost to the end she cut felt sets for Bible storytelling around the world. She faithfully wrote letters to the young people she loved so well. She kept house during my absences, and lovingly ministered to the Pomeranians we always had in residence. She had lived with me for the more-than-thirty-years of her widowhood.

Although I was near retirement, I had not yet arrived. I could not do all that she needed, and she spent her last months in a nursing home. A sad move that I had always hoped I would not have to make. I really felt defeated. I often recalled that when people came to the house, she never wanted to go to bed, no matter how late the hour. "But you don't have to stay up," I would say.

"But I don't want to miss anything." Her blue eyes begged, and she would stay until she couldn't sit up another minute.

Of course, it took time to deal with the emptiness. The thought would recur many times a day, "Have to hurry and do something for Mum." Then reality would strike. I had no more reason. No place to go. Nothing to tell her—ever the eager listener. I realized how very much I had been my mother's daughter. I never wanted to miss anything either.

So, four months later I flew to London again. My series of unsuccessful back surgeries had begun. Now, I needed a little "test trip" to ascertain how travel-fit I was to lead one more teaching tour for La Sierra University

For the third time, I joined the New England Youth Ensemble. I met the group at the International Workshop at the Scottish Academy of Music. Along with several hundred other students we were housed in art-deco Baird Hall in Glasgow. For a few days I just sat back and enjoyed a constant diet of classical concerts.

"Off-the-bus eating" had always been a money-saving tradition of New England Youth Ensemble from its beginning thirty years ago. The multiple role of buyer-cook-server-clean-up personnel had been filled by parents, friends, and sometimes the students themselves. This time we had a bride-and-groom team, Travis and April Losey. They were the thirteenth couple to meet and marry out of the Ensemble. Wedded just two weeks before the beginning of the tour, they volunteered to spend their honeymoon serving on-the-road meals.

When the Workshop ended, I began service as an "academic tour guide." Our five days in Ireland began with the stone crosses and round towers of Monasterboice (thirty miles north of Dublin). At St. Michans Church Dublin they saw the organ used by Handel for the first performance of "The Messiah." Also the mummies in the burial crypts—including a tiny nun and a big Crusader who had been 'trimmed down" to fit his coffin.

We visited Glendlough in the afternoon and reached Cashel just in time to find beds in a youth hostel for the night. I knew that the orchestra was accustomed to a breakneck schedule, so I crammed everything into the agenda that I could manage. The Killarney Lakes and Ring of Kerry were simply for sightseeing, the rain notwithstanding. The cheeriness of multi-colored house and store-fronts with their bright window boxes and hanging baskets of flowers defied the gray weather.

Near Limerick I explained the verse-form and invited the students to write their own rhymes. John Lake (coach-driver) offered some pithy samples of his own. Soon the kids came forward every few minutes to get the microphone and read their limericks. A friendly friction rapidly developed between

The NEYE boys prepared to roll out their sleeping bags in a side-room at the Celtic Seventh-day Adventist Church in Dublin, Ireland. All part of touring with NEYE—no one ever asked how many stars a "hotel" like this rated. Practicing such economies enabled the orchestra to make incredibly long, complicated journeys.

those as the back and those at the front of the bus.

The medieval banquet at Bunratty Castle offered the best in Irish fiddling, singing and harping entertainment. We had a delay at the Dun Laoghaire ferry port. The kids climbed the walls to see the sunset over Dublin harbor. Naomi Burns and some of her friends set themselves up beside the bus, playing

At Bunratty Castle. Ireland, the musicians went into a time warp and ate a medieval banquet. Left. As part of the entertainment the "butler" arrested Dan Malarek (violin) for "alienating the affections of the ladies of the castle." In a convincing way, Dan kicked and roared his way down into the dungeon. Right. Then the butler persuaded the presiding "Earl" to allow the prisoner to redeem himself with a song. The prisoner sang "O Canada," to the boos of the Americans and the screams of the drunks. "Only someone from the United States," the butler remarked, "could feel threatened by a Canadian."

Gaelic folk music. Their busking attracted several onlookers.

After two days in Wales, the orchestra went off to concretize in Russia and Siberia. I used the five-day interlude to visit Janet and Barry Sillitoe in Devon. The orchestra returned looking "green." Many of them quite ill. Nonetheless they kept two more concert dates in Scotland.

Finally, most of us gathered at Heathrow for the flight home. As usual, I looked over the display of Cadbury chocolates. I would spend my last English money, as always, to buy a box of sweets for Mum. Then I remembered. This time she wouldn't be waiting at home to receive it.

That sorrowful awareness went along with another sobering conclusion. Several of the young NEYE men had always faithfully looked out for me. Finding my bag, getting it off and on the bus, and steering me through the airport. I realized that while I might travel some more, physically I was becoming more and more dependent on others. I also was getting old.

I had always envisioned retirement as time when I could undertake some overseas teaching appointments. Do some more international living. Now I had reason to suspect that my retirement was not going to be what I first imagined.

Even so, I couldn't foresee how crippled I would actually become.

1 Three Self-Help required all Christians to worship together. They had to be: (1) Self-propagating, (2) Self-financing, and (3) Self-indoctrinating. These rule precluded all contacts with foreigners.
2 See Dorothy Minchin-Comm and Virginia-Gene Rittenhouse, *Encore* (1988) and *Curtain Call* (1995).

CHAPTER 17

Skipping Across More Mountain Tops

One of the additives to my teaching at La Sierra University was the way my ordinary academic enterprises kept bringing me wholly unexpected adventures. The exciting exchange of ideas. The discovery of surprising information. Odd domestic situations. A constant blending of past and present. Warm association with friends in scores of different contexts.

When my sabbatical quarter began in 1993, I committed myself to some really forensic research. I proposed to bring the famous but tragic poet, Archdeacon Thomas Parnell (1679-1716) "back to life." Once such a popular figure on the literary scene in 18th-century England almost 300 years ago, he has been almost forgotten. Another footnote to history was the fact that he married—and remained devotedly in love with—Anne Minchin of Ballynakill, Co Tipperary, Ireland. Therefore my professional interest in the 18th-centruy literature intersected with my own family history. I was off and ready for the chase. I had to discover all that could be known of the elusive Parnell, and I determined to "miss nothing" along the way.

I began in London with the parish records at Westminster Public Library. Then St. James Piccadilly, an affluent church near the city lodgings of the equally affluent Parnell. Next I read, so to speak, several miles of microfilm in the British Museum Library.

Throughout my journey, whenever and wherever the facilities permitted, I spent evenings typing, transcribing and organizing my library findings. Not only did I need to control the amount of paper I was carrying around, I also had to be ready to write my monograph when my research time ended.

I made the most of my last Sunday in London. First, I visited John Wesley's Chapel and his home next door, and his burial place in Bunhill Fields nearby. I even dropped by the Angel Pub for lunch and wondered how often the aged Wesley might have gone there to take a pint with his some of his parishioners. I remember how my Dad talked about his pilgrimage to this place where Methodism began. He used to be proud to bear the name of Wesley himself.

Next, I stopped at St. Paul's Cathedral, whence the Wesleyans were evicted. I heard Evensong and listened to the fifteen-minute long peal of the bells. Enough to move even the veriest atheist, I do believe. Today a fine statue of Wesley stands under the shadow of St Paul's dome, so all must be forgiven. Finally, I attended the service at All Souls Church in Regent Street.

Meanwhile I had bought a Brit Rail ticket. Being wholly alone and planning extensive travel it made more sense than renting a car. My serious rail journey would be punctuated by several pleasing, personal interludes. The first part of my journey took me from Paddington Station to Newport, Wales. There I turned aside to visit Michael and Wendy Sammons and see Penhow Castle, the oldest "lived in" castle in Europe.

Another digression when I made the two-and-a-half hour ride down to Exeter and weekended with the Sillitoes. During that time, I turned aside for an unusual exhibition in the town of Topsham, a competition for "The Ancient and Honourable Guild of Town Criers." (Centuries earlier, William the Conqueror instituted the medieval form of media, crying.) They were in full cry and full costume, each shouting the best features of his (or her) town. Judges awarded prizes for both the "best cry" and the "best costume." A huge amount of color, noise, and vitality.

By Monday I had myself back to work in Chester. Parnell died here, suddenly and mysteriously. I walked the city streets all day, resting only to listen to a jovial, bearded busker with his jazz clarinet at The Cross. I combed through the Public Library records. There seemed little to discover, however, and that supported the supposition I had begun to formulate—that there had been a "cover up" by the Church of Ireland. Parnell's death had been sudden and unexpected—from manic depression and possibly suicide.

En route to Belfast, I turned aside a half day with Steve and Cindy Kuan right in the middle of Glasgow. I had not seen them since our days at Philippine Union College. They had just brought their five-day old son home from the hospital. She was a nurse and he a doctor (currently taking his ENT specialty in Glasgow). Nonetheless, little Shawn was the first, best, and only baby yet born. A delight, seeing the little family together, so far from their home in Penang, Malaysia, but so happy.

My rail pass included the Sealink ferry, *Stena Antrim,* that took me across to Larne, Northern Ireland. Now I was in hot pursuit of all that I could learn of the Church of Ireland in which Parnell served as a priest in Clogher.

PRONI (Public Records Office of Northern Ireland) proved to be one of the most efficient libraries I had ever seen. I spent many hours in the archives. Near the Library my lodging was in the Protestant section (marked by red-white-and-blue curbs), and I stayed within the lines. Daily, however, I read about the conflict in the evening papers.

I spent the weekend with Richard and Virginia Clark. They were working in Ennislkillen under the auspices of the Emerald Health and Education Foundation. On Friday evening we walked through woods of elm and hemlock around Lough Erne. The setting sun filtered through multi-textured underbrush to highlight a dozen shades of Irish green. Ducks skimmed the water, and birds fluttered overhead, arguing over last- minute bedtime arrangements.

A soft luminescence settled into the background, making the islands and promontories seem to swim in a cool, gray mist. No wonder so many British myths center on lakes. Nearby rowboats lay among the reeds, as if waiting for the Lady of Shalott to pick one of them. If we had looked hard enough, we might even have seen the Lady of the Lake reach up to receive King Arthur's sword, Excaliber.

More importantly I thought of the ancient communities of Celtic Christians who lived on these shores, in the ancient abbey ruins that floated in the dying light, just beyond our reach. The three of us stood there in the same picture frame, as it were, with a Gaelic Christian of 1500 years ago, seeing exactly what he saw and sensing the same presence of God as he did.

The next day Richard took me to Clogher to interview Jack Johnstone, the town historian. We drove south just over the Ulster border to Clontibret and Aughnamullen, two more of Parnell's parishes. Back in the woods we came

Dorothy wasted none of her non-library hours in England. Walking around Dartmoor, joining sky-watchers on the south coast to see a mid-morning eclipse of the sun, wandering through John Wesley's home in London, and much more. One time Sillitoes took her to see a competition among Town Criers. Ultimately she came to know Southern England almost as well as Southern California—and loved every inch of it.

to dour old "Carnaveagh House" where two more (bachelor) historians lived, with their middle-aged spaniel, Sue.

The Montgomery brothers, Nixon and George, were close relatives of Field Marshall Sir Bernard Law Montgomery of Alamein (1887-1978), my childhood hero from World War II. Indeed, I found their resemblance to him quite astonishing.

Their father had served as rector of Aughnamullen. In the churchyard they showed us a large grassy mound where a company of Cromwell's soldiers had been buried. They survived the Battle of the Boyne, only to die of scurvy. Not a single word was spared to identify them. I was careful not to mention that my great-grandfather (several generations removed, fortunately) had been a colonel in Cromwell's army. It did not seem the time or place to speak of the matter.

At mid-week, I took the train from Londonderry to Dublin. A distance of only 150 miles, but it took the better part of a day. Along Lough Foyle toward the North Sea we passed fields of frolicsome young cattle and phlegmatic sheep. The sober streets with gray-and-white row houses were an incarnation of Newfoundland as I had known it more than forty years earlier. At low tide the sea birds wheeled overhead in great flocks to welcome the rainy sunrise. Then the railway turned inland. The rail lines met the sea again south of Drogheda. White surf on a gun-metal gray ocean. More cows and sheep in pastures bordering the beach. Alternating yellow grain fields and plantings of potatoes.

That night I reached my lodgings in Trinity College Dublin. I ate my meals at the Commons, set in a square of old ivy-clad university buildings. The main quadrangle is paved with distinctive cobblestones. In the rain they form an artistic montage of lights and textures. I have always enjoyed TCD. Besides "my poet" was one of the most brilliant alumni to pass through those gates. He entered the university at age eleven.

As I tracked Parnell's Protestant roots I realized, for the first time, the full implications of what happened when the Public Records Office in Dublin was torched in 1922. The loss of the parish records irretrievably took centuries out of the lives of many people. Therefore, no one can ever find where Parnell's wife died and was buried seven years before his death. Having discovered what Anne did not do, I now had to piece together some of the existing possibilities.

One day I walked along the Liffey River to the fashionable St. Michans church (dating from 1046) where the Parnells worshipped. Their house nearby on Mary Lane by now had evolved into a market place.

I cased out three items of interest for use on future teaching tours. St. Michan's church houses the organ that Handel used for rehearsal of his first performance of

While tracking her academic quarry, Thomas Parnell, around Ireland, Dorothy met the Montgomery brothers, local historians. They were close relatives and look-alikes of Field Marshall Montgomery of World War II fame. He has been a hero of Dorothy's childhood, so she recorded her visit by standing with her hosts on the steps of the old family home.

the "Messiah" in 1724. It stands in a balcony railed in with a wonderful piece of woodcarving that features a variety of musical instruments, all out of a single piece of wood.

The second was a "confessional chair," partly chair and partly lectern. Here in front of the congregation, sinners had to publicly "set their lives in order." Rather heavily Calvinistic in tone for an Episcopalian church, I thought.

Third were the famous burial vaults that honeycomb the ground under the church, available only to select, well-born people. The Parnells, de Burghs and others occupied the dozens of chambers not open to the public. Visitors climbed down through a heavy iron door to one of the open vaults. The chemical properties of the stone walls and the dry air have long since mummified the bodies. One large Crusader (800 years old) had had his legs broken to fit him into his regulation-size coffin.

On my last evening in Dublin I strolled through St. Stephen's Green and watched the ducks on the little lake going to bed. Tree branches trailed almost into the water. Then, at the last moment the weather cleared, leaving behind just enough clouds for the sun to paint pink. That was my last night in Ireland.

I worked my way back toward London. First on the ferry and then on the train. As we left the little station of Rhyl in Wales I noticed the peculiar hairdo of a woman up at the front of the coach. Remarkably thick white hair, I thought. The tight curls, however, seemed an odd choice for an elderly woman. The man next to her seemed quite detached, and the two of them sat there in total silence. Just as I rose to disembark, the old lady turned to look across the aisle, and I glimpsed the profile of a long, slim nose. A big white poodle! He/she had been the soul of decorum the whole way.

I had one last visit to make before going home Dick and Wendy Sawyer met me at the station in Winchester. They had spent a lifetime on Minchin family history (Wendy's heritage). I knew that they were keenly interested in my Parnell studies. We ate dinner together in a roadside restaurant, lingering at the table talking non-stop, as usual. Indeed, we were the last out of the dining room, leaving just before formal eviction proceedings would have begun.

Arriving at their home, Horsebridge House, in Kings Somborne, we made firm plans for the next day. To go nowhere. To see no one. To do nothing but what we chose. That is when I presented them with a bagful of questions for which I had no ready answers. Dick and Wendy would work it out, if anyone could. When I finally got home to California, all I had left to do was unpack my suitcase full of books and papers and write the "book" that my sabbatical committee required.

Two events bracketed the year 1997, one hoped-for and the other a peculiar kind of surprise. In February Larry married Meriam de Belen, the younger sister of former students of ours in the Philippines. A quiet little family affair in the home of Jack and Olivine Bohner.

Then, late in November, cyberspace invaded my life. The Excite Company conducted a world-search to see if anyone on the planet actually bore the name of Dot Com. Some of my students (never identified) turned me in. As it happened, I was the only person in the world actually bearing the name.

This circumstance set a surprising chain of events in motion, climaxing in a "business class" trip to New York. I gave my second air-ticket to Joan Patrick, a visiting cousin from Australia. Off we went with a little stuffed eagle, La Sierra University's mascot, in hand. The Excite people lodged us on the 47th floor of the Sheraton in mid-Manhattan and gave us tickets to the new Broadway musical, 'The Scarlet Pimpernel."

The next day I had to face the ordeal for which I had come—the Rosie O'Donnell show. I had insisted from the start that I wouldn't be able to "fit in." How right I was!

When everyone had settled in the studio, a little man in overalls ran up and down the aisles. With a small switch he whipped the audience up into a towering passion. They screamed and stomped to the roar of two rock bands. Enough to blow your brains clean out of your head.

My turn came, and I presented Rosie with the little mascot. She set him down right in front of the camera. With "La Sierra University" emblazoned across his chest, he remained there for the rest of the show. "What do you teach," she inquired.

"Literature and writing." A sudden pall fell over the howling multitude. As if I had claimed to be a mortician or the Angel of Death. I suppose it would

St. Michan's Church, Dublin, Ireland. On tour with the New England Youth Ensemble in 1995, one of the boys stepped cheerfully into the box where devout parishioners were expected to publicly confess their sins for the week. He convinced us of his sincerity—almost.

have been easier to call myself a drug dealer. The fellow with the whip had to rush in and work the room back up to the high-voltage level of excitement they wanted to maintain.

As expected, I tried to say something about Excite, but I couldn't get a word in. Robin Williams took up most of the rest of the show. Anyway, Rosie got what she wanted, novelty. Excite, unfortunately, got little for their investment.

The next afternoon Joan and I waited for the car to take us to the airport. I guarded our bags in the lobby while hundreds of black-clad convention attendees poured out the front door. Because of my on-going back problems, we had put all of our valuables in Joan's tote bag that I had wedged firmly between my feet. That bag was stolen.

Everything went with it—wallets and $300 cash, air-tickets, car keys, and cameras. We stared at one other in shock—she in a blue jacket and me in my old mauve coat. The colors made us stand out like aliens amid the standard black stirring all around us. No wonder the thief got us.

Of course, we missed our plane because we had to go to the police station. With no documentation we had to make a report, work out who we were, and negotiate new plane tickets. Hours later we stumbled into our Economy seats.

During the layover in Chicago, Joan briefly disembarked. Then she came back. "All of them out there," she said with a knowing glance. "They look just like us."

"What do you mean? They've been robbed too?"

"No. They are wearing all kinds of colors." A sobering thought! Properly clad in black we might have been spared the New York ordeal.

So we winged our way back West. "Probably," I told myself, "that is where I belong anyway."

For weeks after my Rosie O'Donnell appearance I found myself awash in a sea of telephone calls from all over the planet. My original visit to the Excite Company in San Jose, California, appeared in several video clips on CNN and other television channels. "Dot Com" was, indeed, news for a while.

One evening I sat in the Jacuzzi at my condo in Palm Springs where I was living at the time. The two women literally fell upon me. "You are the one!" they screamed. "We saw you!" Instantaneously, they worked themselves up into a great "fan club" kind of frenzy. They carried on until I craved to be delivered from what had become an utterly ridiculous scene.

Indeed, the whole affair befuddled me. I still subscribed to the obsolete notion that you should become "famous" because you had accomplished something. My Dad had chosen my first name, and my husband gave me the surname—that is, Dot Comm. I had not contributed to any of it. Nothing made any sense.

Eventually the sizzle and froth did subside. I was left with just one regret. I wish I had caught on to the situation early enough to copyright my name. What if I could now collect say 1% royalty every time someone used "dot com." Then I could sink into a heretofore unimagined nest of financial security. Instead, I just had my fifteen minutes of fame, and then it all went away.

The next year I made a trip that turned out to be a kind of post-graduate course in influence. A couple of my former students from West Indies Training College phoned me. "We are going back to Jamaica for the fortieth anniversary of our graduation. You were our senior class sponsor," they insisted. "You must come with us. OK?"

Many of the members of the Class of 1958, I knew, now lived as profes-

Left. Upon being "discovered" by the Excite Company, Dorothy received a check for $500. Right. The "dot.com" excitement included a trip to New York. Along with her cousin Joan Patrick, Dot was entertained by former student Blake Foster and her husband, Dr. Craig Foster.

sionals in the U. S. and Canada. To be sure, I was easily caught up in their enthusiasm. My air-pass, however, did not include Jamaica. Moreover, the homecoming would be Thanksgiving weekend. I could not risk the uncertainties of standby anyway, lest I be late getting back to work.

The calls kept coming from several different directions. "We want you to be with us. Why can't you just come." Hazel and Cecily were not taking No for an answer.

Forced to the wall, I replied, "If you must know, I just don't have the money for the trip. But I'll write something that you can read when you're all together on your sentimental journey."

"Oh. That's good, but … " Silence.

Within a week, I received an air-ticket in the mail. Twelve of my students had made sure that I would be back in Mandeville with them.

We all met when we checked into Tai Center, the recently opened guest-house on the University campus. After forty years we sized up one another. "Goodness! What a way he/she got old!" Then, in a moment the voice, the smile, the old personality came through. "Whatever made us think that we had changed?" we asked ourselves.

Soon we were lounging about in one another's rooms, laughing, talking *patois,* and acting like silly kids in the dormitories. I gave each of the twelve of them the only gift I could think to bring, a copy of my new devotional book, just off the press *(Glimpses of God)*. Randy White clutched his book to his heart. "Ah! Teach," he hugged me, eyes shining. "I am going to take this to heaven with me!"

"No, no, Kiddy," I replied. He had been such a little fellow that he earned the name. Now, however, what he may have lacked in width he had more than made up for in length. "You won't need it up there, Kiddy!"

At Friday evening vespers I read my promised "Forty Reminiscences for the Homecoming Class of 1958." Horace Newman followed that with a tribute to my sponsorship. I had to respond. "Now how am I supposed to live up to all of that and make it be true?"

"Oh, Ma'am," the irrepressible Horace returned. "It is true already. It must be. Because I was born totally unable to tell a lie."

So our days flowed on in music, food, friends, and endless celebrations. I got myself home on time, Tuesday evening. Even now, I remember those reunion days and feel that I might never really never come down off the mountain top of that weekend experience that my students gave me.

The Celtic Study Tour in 2001 would be my last official service to La Sierra University. John Jones (Dean of the School of Religion) and I co-directed the fifteen-day exploration of the sites of Celtic Christianity in Britain. The

Happy 40th-Homecoming at the old college (now North Caribbean University) in Mandeville, Jamaica. In our non-public hours we gave ourselves up to the good fun that memories of old college days inspired in us now-more-than-middle-aged people.

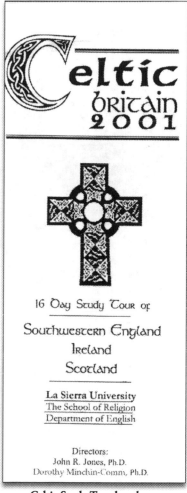

Celtic Study Tour brochure

plan had been two years in the making

As our Air New Zealand flight winged in over the Hebrides and Glasgow I looked down at the dense cloud-cover and sighed. "I see what kind of weather they're planning for us down here." We would not be side-tracked by rain, however, and we were running when our feet hit the ground.

Charlie Zendai, our long-suffering coach-driver, waited for us at Heathrow with his coach from "Gulliver's Travel." (By the end of the trip we had canonized him as "Saint Charlie.") He promptly whisked us along with our twenty students away into the Salisbury Plain. My special assistant and roommate for the tour was Lisa Minchin, my charming, extrovert cousin who had come up from New Zealand. Her parents had given her this trip as a 21st-birthday present.

Determined to make every hour count, we immediately fell into our routine. Our studies would cover more than 2500 years of British history. John and I took turns lecturing over the coach microphone. (He was a wonderful team partner, doing so many of the physical tasks that I could no longer do.)

We discussed the Synod of Whitby (644 A.D.) when the Celtic traditions began to give way to those of Rome. The ultimate Romanization of the Christian church evolved while the widespread depredations of the Vikings rocked Europe.

Each student had done preparatory research and each had taken a turn reading his or her paper to the class. All together we covered a huge variety of topics: Celtic music, the Druids, the Brehon Laws, the Celtic princes and their society, The *Book of Kells* and manuscript illumination, pilgrimage, Celtic martyrdoms, spirituality, monasticism, Gaelic wisdom triads. Also the lives of Brendan the Navigator, St. Brighid of Kildare, and many others. These brought

to life the monastic ruins that cropped up all over the countryside. In sun, rain, and broken clouds we visited the old religious communities. We, indeed, saw Ireland in all weathers, in all of her "Forty Shades of Green."

John and I made everything as "location-sensitive" as possible. For instance, on the first day, before we reached Stonehenge, Penny Shell and Kit Watts began their daily

Lisa Minchin's parents gave the Celtic Tour to her as a 21st birthday gift. Dorothy appreciated her cousin's organizational abilities.

devotionals, speaking of "memorial stones." Then in Glastonbury I introduced the legends of Joseph of Arimathea and King Arthur. In Cornwall we ate a Cornish Cream Tea at Slaughter Bridge where, allegedly, King Arthur died. The little restaurant had several cheap little metal "grails" (goblets) nailed to surrounding trees.

When we returned to the coach, I asked, "So, who saw the Holy Grail?" Some had, and some hadn't. Others ran back to make sure they did. Of course, any one who really got a vision of the Grail, the Arthur legend tells us, would have been translated to heaven.

As Charlie wheeled us back onto the road, Penny stood up. "Should we take a count to see if anyone is missing?" (We were all still there.)

In Wales Penny's devotional pertained to Non, mother of St. David, patron saint of Wales. John lectured on the Welsh saints. Then we spent a long afternoon on a tortuous little road along the coast from Fishguard up to Angelsey Island and its druidic center. Green meadows and hedgerows all of the way, along with sheep, sheep, and sheep.

Anxiety ran high, however, as our coach bore down on the ferry port of Holyhead. Would we make it in time to keep our reservation? Loud cheers for Charlie as we, the very last vehicle, rolled into the gaping mouth of the catamaran. Thence to Dublin.

I knew that we were in a coach, not a bus. The latter in Britain does menial service in towns and cities. The coaches (and their drivers) reside in a measurably different class. At bedtime on our first night in Dublin Lisa pointed out, "Do you know that you said the 'B-word' (bus) three times today?" Alas!

"Remind me to apologize to Charlie in the morning," I told her.

She gave me a big hug. "Is there anything you want?" Lisa is the soul of caring, just like her mother Rosemary. Not used to such attention, I was perpetually surprised.

In due course, a stop at Blarney Woolen Mills fulfilled the desires of those who suffered a mounting need to go shopping.

Of course, at Limerick, everyone was invited to write limericks. As we became better acquainted, we used the microphone for all kinds of trivia. The first rhyme was in honor of our skillful driver, beginning: "Our Charlie he drove us through Dingle/With many small cars we did mingle ... "

At the Ardboyne Hotel in Navan we paused for a real dinner. A good experience for Americans who are too caught up in their fast-food culture, and who are too easily satisfied with bare tables, counter tops, and paper plates. There we fell back into leisurely elegance: tablecloths and serviettes, six pieces of silverware apiece, fine china, crystal goblets, fresh flower centerpieces. Our own Donna Peck sat aside in the "minstrel's corner" and played Celtic tunes on a psaltery she had made herself.

Before we left for Scotland we fitted in one more student paper on the heroic elements in the ancient Irish epic "Cuchulain."

Having ferried across from Belfast, we disembarked in Stranraer, Scotland. We then drove to Edinburgh in an endless sunset. Soft colors highlighted the islands and shore. Each little village, surrounded by cattle on green hills, seemed to call after us: "Haste ye back."

We arrived in Edinburgh at 10.00 p.m. That far north twilight lasted far into the night. A quarter moon hung over the Castle hunched up on its high rock. When we turned into lovely Princess Street, a chorus of 'ohs' and 'ahs' filled the coach. "Why didn't you tell us that Edinburgh would be like this?" several exclaimed.

"Never mind," I replied. "Edinburgh will speak for itself. And we're here for four days." Our hotel, the Jarvis Mount Royal, sat right in the middle of the old city. For me, it paid to be timely. I was glad I had "done" Edinburgh three times before. (I *knew* I could not do all the walking now.)

The island of Iona in the Inner Hebrides had to be one of our major destinations. In self-exile, Colm Cille (Columba) of Derry, the first Celtic saint after Patrick, founded a Christian community there in 563 A.D.

Our journey across the Island of Mull took an hour-and-a-half. In the uncertain sunlight the pristine landscape lit up with other-worldly color. Against the wet, gray slate rocks, and red moss, daffodils bloomed among the ferns. Foxgloves silhouetted themselves against the green hillsides where dozens of waterfalls laced the slopes before pouring into turbulent creeks and hastening off to the sea. Cunning, black-faced lambs grazed along side their shabby mothers who looked like poor old bag-ladies.

Upon arrival, I had to sit it out while everyone else explored the tiny island (three miles long and one mile wide) and its ruined abbey. The simple act of walking had, by this time, become difficult for me. So, I found a bench in front of a long row of cottages above the ferry dock. I faced the Bay of Martyrs where the Vikings slaughtered the inhabitants in 795 and 807 AD. Surrounded by gardens and warmed by the sun, however, I was content.

Presently a white terrier trotted by, followed by a red-gold cocker spaniel. Although I greeted them, they both had urgent appointments and never looked at me. Behind them hobbled an elderly lady with a cane. Arms flailing, she shouted, "Stop! I say, stop! Come back here." She halted in front of me, groaning and leaning heavily on her stick. "He's been all over town, and I just can't walk any further." She peered down the lane. "He looks back at me, and

Left. At Fionnphort, Mull, we boarded the ferry for the one-mile (ten-minute) crossing to the historic island of Iona in the Inner Hebrides of Scotland. Right. The waterfront of Iona overlooking the Bay of Martyrs. Dorothy waited here while her friends explored the tiny three-mile-long island. Non-residents may not bring cars to the island.

then just keeps on going."

"Is he still there?" I asked.

"No. But I've seen him go by here three times." The woman was perfectly rational but, by now, very angry. I got up and looked. No dogs in the lane. No people. Nothing.

I knew that the Brits take their dogs everywhere—trains, buses, and restaurants. Still, I couldn't understand why such a disobedient dog should be given the freedom of the town. "Well!" I murmured, not wishing to offend, "Wouldn't it be easier if maybe you had him on a leash?" By now the woman had turned and was stumping back toward the ferry landing.

Thirty minutes later, I went to the dock to meet my student-group. Two ferries had come and gone. The poor woman was still there, distraught, alone, and propped up on her cane. I really felt sorry for her. "Look, I love dogs too. What a heartache this undisciplined pup must be to you. Which one are you looking for? The red one or the white one?"

She stared at me. "Oh, I don't have a dog." Too upset even to realize how ludicrous our miscommunication had become, she barked. "It's my husband!

Once back in the coach retracing our way across Mull, I related the episode to our group. They howled with laughter, almost falling out the windows and rolling in the aisles. Nonetheless, I felt so sad. To be brought on an outing and then abandoned? He could have brought a wheelchair and allowed her to enjoy Iona too.

On our last night in Scotland, I spent a meditative hour at the window, just absorbing the magic of Edinburgh in the late, late twilight.

In the morning as we left, I noticed a sign at the hotel entrance. "Feel chuffed?"

"What does 'chuffed' mean?" I asked Charlie.

"To be satisfied, contented," he replied. Oddly, in my many years in and out of England, never before had I come across that distinctive (and rather boorish) British slang word. And I seldom miss a curious public notice.

The Celtic mission to the pagan Saxons, Lindesfarne subjected us to the ebb and flow of the tides around its island. Subsequently we had only a short time in Durham Cathedral. Just long enough to pay our respects to St. Cuthbert of Lindisfarne and the Venerable Bede in the lovely Galilee Chapel. Although Bede was a Saxon of Romish persuasion, but he has told us much of what we know of early British Christianity.

Celebrating our final day of the tour, en route from York to London, Penny and Kit shared Celtic poems of praise. This concluded my last—and one of the most intimate—of all of my teaching tours.

Robert Coffee pretty well summed it up in his report: "We change from

End of the Celtic Tour with John Jones and Dorothy Comm in flight back home to Southern California. They felt that they had every right to feel "chuffed."

what we were yesterday. Even from what we were an hour ago." That's what our Tour did. It changed us, in many ways. Forever. La Sierra University's first Celtic Tour appeared to be all that we dreamed it could be. Once back in London, we scattered in a dozen different directions.

To put it in the vernacular, I believe it was safe to say, "We all felt chuffed!"

CHAPTER 18

About Retirement

Some years into his retirement, Paul Eldridge (one-time president of the Far Eastern Division) told me something quite profound. "You know what is one of the most beautiful sentences in the English language?"

Here was a man who had traveled the earth, who had solved insoluble problems, who had sat in committee meetings, world without end. Knowing him also to be a skillful word-master, I was eager to hear what he would say.

"I can just say 'I am not going.'" Paul smiled, leaned back and stretched his long legs. "And I can mean it."

When you stop to think about it, that is a magnificently liberating idea. That, unquestionably, must be one of the great rewards of retirement. Even so, making that transition—as I did in January, 2000—is never a clean surgical break. A certain nostalgia shadowed me for a long time.

As late as the middle of the school year of 2006, I happened to be at a social event where I fell into conversation with two presidents of La Sierra University. I had known them both for some years. The incoming one, Randall Wisbey, exclaimed, "I just love my job. And the people I work with."

I turned to the retiring president, Larry Geraty, who had been my boss for several years. "Don't you wish sometimes that you could just peel off twenty-five years and go back to work at La Sierra University?"

"I do." Larry picked up my drift instantaneously. "I most certainly do."

We had no need to explain anything to one another. We all understood what it was like, working on that beautiful campus and in that academic climate. We were not, however, quite on one level playing field. Randy was just starting his presidency. Larry still had years of active connection with the University. I was the one in the wheelchair.

Dorothy's retirement from La Sierra University. Edna May Loveless and Mary Wilson (a former and present chairs of the English Department, respectively) hosted the dinner. They gathered up a stack of her writings for "show and tell." High enough to startle even the author.

Nonetheless, easing into retirement had given me leisure to assess the gains and losses accrued during my forty years in the classroom.

All of my life when I have been introduced to strangers, the formula has more or less been the same. "And what do you do?"

"I am a teacher." Sometimes that is enough. Sometimes not.

"And what do you teach?"

"English."

With that he or she would withdraw, as if I had a contagious disease. The hand flew to the mouth. "Oh! I. . . um. . . I can't spell." Or "I don't know any grammar." "I can't. . ." The eyes glazed over as they backed away. Another friendship lost?

It has not so much been that I was "not going." That constituted only part of it. Rather, I no longer had to be responsible. People can speak or write any way they wish. I am no longer on duty. No one (officially) has paid me any more to make corrections.

After twenty-three years at La Sierra University, I knew I wanted to stop. I had hung on as long as I could because I desperately needed the income. The on-going disintegration of my spine, however, finally forced me to face the inevitable.

Just as I was leaving, I heard the question raised in an assessment of the English Department. We had to be on the cutting edge of higher education, of course. Are doctorates more than twenty years old able to meet "the demands of current scholarship?" Fortunately, that remained an "academic

question." In reality, nothing threatened the excellent doctorate I had
earned at the University of Alberta
in 1971.

Actually I realized that the
potential friction lay within me.
Indeed, some of what I had begun to
see of contemporary research rather
worried me. People seemed to have
gone overboard investigating
"gender" and like topics. Meanwhile, I doggedly held to the view
that the world still contained a great
many other viable subjects, also
worthy of study. Probably my
"getting out of the way" would not
be untimely. After all, I had had a

rich and useful trip through the
world.

**Receiving the Charles E Weniger Award at
LSU Convocation in 2006 was a banner day
for Dorothy.**

Another "sign of the times"
came up when my class in John Milton that I had taught for twenty-two years
"went missing." I discovered that the venerable poet had been bumped off
graduate curricula in many places. Nor did he appear any more on the GRE
(Graduate Record Exam). Therefore, away with the old Puritan! Challenging
as Milton might be, I still liked him. I felt sad.

Did this also mean that I was getting obsolete? Maybe. Still, I took away
a massive amount of very satisfying memories.

Today, five plaques hang on the wall of my tiny den, and I can refer to
them whenever I wish to recall some of my high days in *academe*. The awards
all arrived unexpectedly. Indeed, they always overtook me while I was busy
doing something else. On each occasion nice things were said, and I basked,
for a while, in the approval of my peers. Not a bad thing—if it isn't over done.

The first one fell upon me from long-distance in 1991—The Don

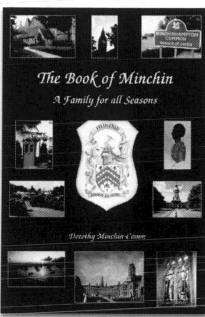

Left. The devotional book was the most important writing. **Right.** The family history had to be the most extensive—700 pages and more than 1,000 illustrations.

Neufeld Medallion of Excellence (Canadian University College). It bears the fine bronze likeness of the patient man who had tried to teach me chemistry in high school and who later became a lifelong friend.

In 1994 I received the Centennial Presidents Award from the Seventh-day Adventist Church in the Cayman Islands. In a manner of speaking, that one covered the long-standing, foreign-missions component of my life.

The Woman of the Year Lifetime Achievement Award (1998) came from the Association of Adventist Women (North American Division). I recall that it included a large dinner party, an acceptance speech from me, and three dozen red roses sent by one of my former students now "living large" in New York City.

The following year the Alumni Association of Atlantic Union College elected me Alumna of the Year (1999). They did so, I daresay, without realizing that I romped through college with a GPA (Grade Point Average) that barely

admitted me to graduate
school, even provisionally. I
felt grateful to know that I
had lived down that embarrassment!

Another one com-
memorates my twenty-two
years on the faculty of La
Sierra University. I was free
for the Winter Quarter of
2000 and then finished the
school year on half-salary.
That transition year I made
two trips to Grand Cayman.
During the first one, I

**Over the years Dorothy's sister, Eileen (Minchin-Davis)
provided illustrations for some of her books.**

helped my friend Mary Merren-Thompson write her autobiography, *Happy All
My Life*. We did nineteen chapters in just twenty-one days. That episode proved
to be a forecast of good things to come. I could keep on writing.

Other mementoes cannot hang on my wall. At a fund-raising dinner
party, La Sierra University honored me with the Dorothy Minchin Comm Dis-
tinguished Speaker Series (2005). Henceforth, the lectureship bearing my name
would bring visiting scholars and writers into the English Department. (Eileen
and Lyman even drove down from Utah to share that evening with me.) The
hosts had gathered most of my writings together for exhibition. The height of
the stack surprised even me.

Perhaps the most prized of all would be the Charles Elliott Weniger
Award for Excellence (2006). The heavy bronze medal nests in bed of red satin
and velvet in a beautifully made cherry wood box. I always admire finely
crafted works of art, and the Weniger Award is just such a piece. Something
lovely just to hold in the hands. The high quality of the medallion matches
the memory of that beloved professor who gave his name to the award almost
forty years ago.

At the very last came my appointment of "Professor Emeritus" from La

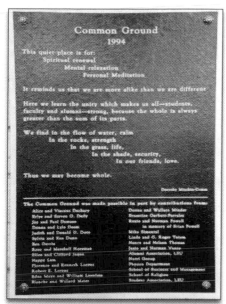

When La Sierra University dedicated a tiny prayer garden that they named "The Common Ground." Dorothy provided the words to identify the purpose of the retreat. Thus, she became memorialized (in bronze) on the campus that she loved.

Sierra University (2012).

Nonetheless, the best awards of my career have been personal, intangible. They cannot be engraved in bronze. They don't appear in public for anyone to look at. They come from the multitude of my students, numbering some thousands by now, I would think. From time to time, I get a phone-call, an email, or a knock on my door. Someone wants to tell me that I really made a difference in his/her life. Can any honors be more genuine that that?

We are fortunate, those of us who have the privilege, when we can look at our young people and realize that a bit of our lives is occasionally reflected in theirs. While they don't necessarily want to often be in the company of us Old Ones, still they float on and off our radar. In my students I glimpse traces of the better times in my own life. When I was about that age. A happy moment of recognition. Indeed, I like to think that the ultimate definition of success is the quiet work of influence. If so, than the *angst* of fame, materialism, and even obsessive self-examination doesn't matter. That makes the journey into old age much easier.

Fortunately, some parts of my work transferred quite smoothly over into retirement. The publication of my devotional book for 1999, *Glimpses of God,* prefaced what would become a major retirement occupation for me—writing. By December 1998 it had sold 70,000 copies in English. From there it went into translation: French, Korean, Tagalog (and three other Filipino dialects), and finally Chinese. Indeed, writing would move into the foreground for me. So, as I became more and more closely tied to my wheelchair, my good fortune became increasingly apparent. The computer desk became my natural habitat.

Some years ago, I was diagnosed with a vexing Essential Tremor. "What do you mean, essential?" I asked the doctor. "I don't need it. I didn't ask for it."

Alan Collins' sculpture group, "The Glory of God's Grace," became the logo for La Sierra University. The front entrance to the the campus was altered to accommodate this interpretation of the Prodigal Son (Luke 15).

I presumed it to be a generic pronouncement to cover many unknowns. At least, I didn't have Parkinsons. Actually, I realized that it was something hereditary that I got from my Dad. While the tremor comes and goes, it makes handwriting (and sometimes eating) very difficult. Therefore, I really am tied to the computer keyboard where I do all of my composition.

Over the years, I have occasionally been lured into editing and rewriting. Sometimes in the midst of my labors I have almost faded into the role of a ghostwriter. Since I have no special need to see my name in print, however, I don't care. So long as a few dollars come my way. In retirement I had to stop giving writing services *gratis*. The state of the world's economy—to say nothing of the straits in which I live personally—forced me to take that stand. Like everyone else, I keep hoping not to outlive my money.

In 2005 I contracted a very large editing assignment for Loma Linda University. Consisting of some 1,400 pages of text, the manuscript covered the entire history of the institution. Because I was paid, I was able to enjoy my last trip home to Australia and New Zealand. I managed to stay away for six weeks!

Contentment in retirement has, therefore come quite easily. Basically

The original quartet of Pomeranians that came home from the Philippines. Front L-R. Muffin and Sinta. Back L-R. Mitzi and Rusty.

I need just five things: My books and computer. Steady flow of classical music and a phone to reach out to friends and family. Plus my dog.

Having dogs has been a lifelong necessity for me. Their too-short lives have often paralleled our family's medical crises. Sometimes giving our family joy and at other times overwhelming us with grief when their illnesses coincided with some of ours. After settling in Southern California, we picked up four more Pomeranian strays: Ziggy, Tina, Patch, and Ginger.

Then when our handsome Ziggy died of cancer, he was soon replaced by Ladybird, an Australian Cattle Dog. Feeling the need of another Pomeranian, I brought Schatzi down from Canada. That six-pound little chocolate delight cohabited comfortably with the eighty-five-pound Bird. For a brief interlude, we also had a cat, Sheba. She adored Big Bird, to the great embarrassment of the latter.

Over the years our family had literally forced my mother to get over her great fear of dogs. Schatzi became her dog in a way that no other had ever

Special successors included: Left. Ladybird, and, Right. Schatzi.

been. In the last months of her life Mum even took Schatzi to church, carrying her in the basket of her walker.

The cycle of life rolled on. We lost Bird to congestive heart failure. Then Schatzi who had a heart attack and died while we were driving through the desert near Las Vegas, Nevada. The flamboyant Bugsy became the most recent of my dog family.

My choosing a retirement home did not evolve automatically.

In 1997 I lived for a year in Palm Springs in a tiny, one-bedroom condo that I co-owned with Harvey and Virginia-Gene Rittenhouse. It was a tight fit, but I spent a year there with Ladybird and Schatzi.

Since I was still teaching full time at La Sierra University, that meant a 150-mile r o u n d - t r i p commute to work. I found it well worth the effort. The Olympic-size swimming pool, with its very large accompanying jacuzzi, stood a mere twenty paces

Being at home base and being retired made taking part in family reunions at least a possibility. In 2005, 100 Minchins and their extended families spent five days at Pennyrile Forest State Park in Kentucky.

from my patio gate. Virtually every evening I crossed the palm-planted lawn to relax in the pool. Oftentimes alone, I floated in the mineral water while the clean desert air caressed my face. Usually I stayed in until the stars came out. I wanted to see every step in the glorious transition as the bright, luminous clouds formed and reformed themselves along the mountain-tops, until twilight blotted them out.

I also recall that pool in connection with the people I met there. Partic-ularly memorable was an aged Roman Catholic priest, Father Jose. Well-read

and keenly intelligent, he hardly ever missed his daily swim. I often wished that I had made notes on some of those conversations I had with the old Father. We batted ideas about like ping-pong balls across the cool, aqua-blue pool water.

Had it not been for my great glut of books and numerous filing cabinets, I might have stayed permanently in Palm Springs. Because I desperately

Between the Jacuzzi and the pool at the condo in Smoke Tree, Palm Springs, Dorothy and her co-owners, Harvey and Virginia-Gene Rittenhouse, enjoyed the pool especially at desert sunset time and savored many happy hours there.

needed more space, however, we finally sold our condo in Smoke Tree.

Meanwhile, Jack and Olivine Bohner had moved into the community of Sun Lakes at 2,500 feet elevation, invitingly situated in the pass between the mountain ranges of San Gorgonio and San Jacinto. The Bohners' tastes being unfailingly pleasant, I followed them there.

The main gateway to Sun Lakes is framed by two large, tree-shaded rock gardens with water-falls. Some 4,000 houses with red-tile roofs line the roads that wind around three golf courses. A vigorous Homeowners

Dorothy's retirement cottage. While winter strips the trees on the left and snow-topped mountains rise on the right, the palm trees prove that it is still in Southern California.

Association stands at the ready to call to task any careless householders who disturb the park-like tranquility around us. Their strict regulations provide an uncommon degree of tidiness and safety, and one could stroll the streets at 2 a.m. without fear of getting mugged.

Although Sun Lakes has several swimming pools, Bohners and I favored the large clubhouse pool surrounded by palms. We often spent a couple hours of an evening alternating between the pool and the jacuzzi. "Just think!" we'd tell each other. "Many people would save all of their lives to come here for just a week! In this perfect climate too!"

Not heeding the warnings my body was giving me, I first fell in love with a two-bedroom condo. What enticed me was the large open balcony that extended the width of the house. Up there in that "high place" I had book shelves, a long counter, two desks, and my filing cabinets. All under the light of a tall arched window.

Much as I loved my balcony retreat, however, the day came when I could no longer climb the stairs. A few blocks away I found a little house with a fenced-in back yard to contain Bird and Schatzi—and with no stair-steps. It had two master-bedrooms-with-baths, plus a tiny den in between.

In a single day I sold the condo and bought the house. Then a contingent of friends came to help me move. On my last night in the condo, I came within a hair's breadth of falling down the steps on my head. I knew I had to cut myself some slack by way of safety precautions.

So this has remained my home for more than ten years. It suits me perfectly. I have dutifully cleared out books and filing cabinets and even subjected myself to a couple of yard sales. Still I cling to my little cottage as my last link with independence. I fight against the day when I must institutionalize myself.

CHAPTER 19

Falling Among Thieves

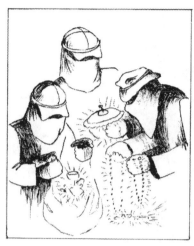

I was still some years short of retirement when, like the traveler on the Jericho road, I "fell among thieves" (Luke 10:30-35). Actually, it was not so much a sudden confrontation as a series of ambushes. Finally, they robbed me of mobility and, at times, courage.

A single moment on a Southern California afternoon became a dreadful turning point (March 9, 1994). It launched a chain of happenings that changed the course of the rest of my life. Thereafter, I would have to fight to "live above it" every day. Indeed, it has required a kind of a determination that I must renew every morning.

Although I didn't have an optimum health record, I lived about as well as the next fellow most the way through my sixties. Financial necessity dictated that I hang on to my job until I formally retired at age 72.

Nonetheless, my downward spiral started on that day more than seven years earlier. My cousin Yvonne [Minchin] Dysinger had been visiting us in California. She and I walked out into the hills behind my house above Lake Elsinore. While my lovely Ladybird chased rabbits, we had a lot of cousinly chat to catch up on. After all, we didn't see one another very often.

While walking along the slight incline of the hillside path, I suddenly skidded in the gravel. My left leg folded under me as I crashed to the ground, and I heard every bone in my ankle break.

"It's OK!" I gasped. The shock left me numb, without pain. When Yvonne helped me up, however, my left foot dangled at an odd angle. I couldn't manage even one step.

Yvonne hailed an old man on the nearby hillside. With a tractor and wagon, he was collecting rocks to decorate his garden. When he came to our aid, I climbed on to the rock pile in the wagon. Bird tried to get aboard with me, but since she couldn't, she solemnly plodded along beside me, head and tail drooping. In due course, our bizarre little procession reached home. Then the pain hit me. Larger than life.

Yvonne drove me to the nearest regional hospital Emergency Room, about five miles south of "The Farm" where I lived. By this time my pain level (on a scale of 1-to-10) had hit a 13.

Ladybird (along with Dorothy) loved roaming the hills above Lake Elsinore. After the accident Bird had to find someone else to take her exploring.

Presently the ER doctor came in with the x-rays. "Not good," he said. "The injury is too complicated for us to handle here. Where do you want to go?"

Well, Loma Linda University Medical Center, of course. They already had a substantial dossier on me there anyway. Besides, my long-time friend, Dr. Virchel Wood (orthopedic surgeon) always defended me within and/or against the bureaucratic medical system. Late as it was, he picked up his office phone.

"Now what have you done?" Woody inquired gently. As soon as I heard his voice, I burst into tears, like a suffering child falling into the arms of a protective parent. "We'll be ready for you when you get here," he promised

By now both Yvonne and I felt a little shell-shocked. She laid the envelope containing my x-rays on top of the car and then drove off on our forty-five-mile journey to Loma Linda. "Well," she eventually rationalized, "they'll want to take their own x-rays anyway." I assumed that some inquiring coyote would probably have found the xrays in the ditch and improved his mind by studying them.

Good as his word, Woody had the admitting nurse and the ER intern ready with a gurney to receive me. Both of them happened to be former students of mine, and both were pleased with the coincidence. By this time, I had gone too weird and dim-witted with painkillers to be very coherent.

The leg-and-foot specialist-surgeon, Dr. Bunnell, was waiting for me. He suggested operating the next day. Obviously delusional, I begged to go under the knife immediately.

"But why?" Everyone wanted to know. "What's your hurry?"

"Because I want to get started on healing," I moaned. I remembered that I had an appointment to meet. "I have to go to the Cayman Islands in three weeks. I need to start getting ready.

The good surgeon somehow found an empty operating room and took three hours out of his night to work on me. When he came to my room the next morning, Dr. Bunnell was positively jubilant. "Well, we got you all put together again!" That is, the screws and a long steel plate.

Still under the sludge of the anesthesia, I thought fuzzily, "Of course, he put me together. That's what he's supposed to do."

"Actually," the doctor went on, "your injury was much worse than we told you last night. Sometimes the bone is too fractured, and we can't find enough places to put the screws in."

Complete in cast and wheelchair, however, I made the trip to Cayman on time to receive (in my husband's behalf) the honors for former presidents of the Cayman Islands Mission. At old Ontario Airport my wheelchair and I were taken up into the plane like cargo. The fork lift operated in the view of the multitudes of curious passengers in the terminal. I wished that I had a paper bag to pull over my head so that I could go *incognito*. Nonetheless—and this is one of the facts of old age—you reach a point where you really don't care what people think. You just do whatever you have to do to get what you want!

A much worse disability awaited me, not far ahead. Little did I realize that I would never again be able to walk normally.

Within four months I was (for the time being) finished with the wheelchair and down to using a cane. I worked hard to maintain what was a normal life for me—teaching, writing, and travel. I again took on a full teaching load plus a contract class.

While teaching on tour with the New England Youth Ensemble in Europe and Palestine, however, I had a distinct preview of things to come. I began to find both walking and sitting almost unbearable. Still, I just advised my body to "sit down and shut up" and kept going. After all, my "bionic leg" had healed up very well.

Some months later it happened. I had just finished an afternoon seminar and was gathering up my books and papers. An incredibly sharp pain shot into my back and down my legs. I sat down again as I broke out into a cold sweat. After all of the students had left, I slowly crept down the long hallway to my office. Fortunately no one witnessed my grotesque journey. I clung to the wall, hitching myself along like a crab and gasping with pain at every step.

Once again, Woody opened up the way for me to have an MRI. In a hurry. "It's probably only muscular," he said. "Don't worry."

The next day he phoned me. "Dorothy. . ." A long silence. "It's not good." He went on to describe the deterioration in both my lumbar spine and cervical neck areas. I didn't understand much of what he was saying. I just knew that I hurt.

The next week I had an appointment with an old friend from Jamaica, Neuro-Surgeon Lloyd Dayes. He too was surprised. "I didn't expect you to turn up here." He looked at the MRI pictures and shook his head. "I have enough evidence here to place you on permanent disability." Diagnosis: Severe Spinal Stenosis.

At age sixty-seven was I going down for the count? "But I have more things that I want to do," I sighed.

"I know you," Dr. Dayes smiled. "And you will, I am sure, do them."

When I left, the date was set for a lumbar laminectomy and diskectomy on March 27. That way, I reasoned, I could finish up the quarter decently and not let my students down.

When the surgery was over, after intense negotiations with the insurance companies and all the other entities that had power over my life, I went to Desert Hot Springs Therapy Center. My daily regimen there included swimming a half-mile a day, interspersed with immersions in the hot tub every two hours. Also I received deep tissue massage, diathermy, salt baths and more.

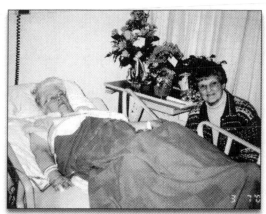

Cousin Yvonne visited Dorothy at Loma Linda Medical Center. Unfortunately, this was the beginning of a nasty habit of having back surgeries. Even amid the flowers and good wishes of friends, these "tours of duty" in the hospital were bad news.

I worked hard to derive every possible benefit, but, when the money ran out, I had to go home,

A couple of years later I again fell in a heap before the orthopedists. After two complete (and unsuccessful) rounds of epidural injections, again I met the surgeon under the big lights in the operating room. This time Dr. Shook more aggressively opened up the pathways for my tortured nerves.

Later, he showed me my x-rays. My disintegrating vertebrae were beginning to look like a ragged roll of barbed wire. "You have severe spinal degeneration," he said. Medically clueless as I was, even I could see that. And feel it too. From this point onward I had to use a cane. Well, I rationalized, a lot of people acquire that "'third leg," so I kept on going.

Another year went by. Well-meaning friends had all kinds of cures to recommend. "If you'd just take this green ... Or that natural mineral. Or these supplements." Nothing made any difference.

On one visit to Dr. Shook I complained, "I just feel that I should be better than I am at this point."

After some further discussion, the doctor said, "Actually, I believe that you were set up for this from the moment of conception."

"But," I sputtered, "no one else on either side of my family has anything like this disability."

"Both of your parents would have had the recessive gene," he replied. "The problem could go back generations."

"That's pretty tough!" I was feeling rather sorry for myself. "My parents came from opposite sides of the world. All those millions of people, and I catch it!" Not for anything, however, would I trade my family heritage, either side of it. Still, I suppose everyone should be allowed a couple times in a lifetime to ask, "Why me?"

"Look at it this way," Dr. Shook went on. "If you had been living intemperately, this would probably have hit you twenty-five years sooner." Temperate? I saw no point in telling him that I had been a workaholic all of my life. At any rate, I hadn't been drinking, drugging or smoking. Maybe that had helped a little.

By the spring of 2002 pain literally consumed me, and I began resorting to a wheelchair. Nothing, seemingly, could halt the downhill slide toward my third back surgery. This time more ruptured discs sprang up among the old

fusions. Rapidly I was becoming a nuisance to myself and everyone else.

Meanwhile, for the past three years I had been saving for another trip Down Under. I decided that if I could recover and travel some more, good. If not, I would always be glad that I made that trip. Therefore, on December 4, I locked up my house and delivered my dogs to two friends.

The first time round, Dorothy made good her intention to get to the Cayman Islands very soon after surgery. The occasion was the recognition of the mission presidents of the Cayman Islands Mission. Walt's picture is second from the left in the top row.

Then I spent a six leisurely weeks in Australia and New Zealand. By the time I got home in late January, 2003, however, my pain had pretty well immobilized me. I realized that doom awaited me. Another disk had ruptured on top of the old stuff. I had waited for it to self-correct, but it never did. My only other option, it seemed, was to live on narcotic painkillers for the rest of my life. I really wanted to keep my head, even if everything else was getting

Dr. Virchel and Esther Wood attended Dorothy's "Woman of the Year" dinner. Even more importantly long-time friend "Woody" helped her survive the vicissitudes of the medical establishment, thus contributing to her very survival.

away from me. Dr. Shook decided to do three more fusions.

Lynne Buhler kept Schatzi, and Virginia Fagal once more opened her home to Ladybird. Fortunately, by this time, Bird had worked out a living arrangement with Virginia's two cats, Smokey and Goldie. My sister Eileen had quit her job and retired to their mountain retreat in Utah. Thus, she and her husband Lyman were free to come down and see me through my third back surgery on March 5, 2003. (For variety, I had a fourth surgery the following week because an infection was feared.)

This time I had collateral damage. While the left-side pain for which I had surgery disappeared, I now had a dropped right foot and other extensive nerve damage. My ever-kindly friend, Don Roth, brought his car to transfer me out of the hospital. Medical insurance refused to pay an ambulance to take me less than a mile down the road to the nursing home to which I had been sentenced. "So," Don remarked cheerfully, "we'll just make sure to save all of those hundreds of dollars."

I spent the next six weeks there in "rehab" where surgery patients were randomly mixed with everyone else. The screams of the demented alternated with the vacant sighs of those finishing out their days as the proverbial "vegetables."

After two months of institutionalization, I finally reached home. For the first time in my life I was having panic attacks and was afraid of almost everything. Only a few of the staff even spoke English. I lost my identity, my spirit, and most of my mind. That I survived at all was because Virginia and her sister

Geneva visited me every evening. They always brought me fresh fruit, ready to eat. Most mornings, my friend Mary Alice Parker visited and brought me strawberries. Truly, they stood between me and insanity!

When I ultimately escaped—still very physically impaired— Lynne came down from Seattle to take care of me for two weeks, bringing Schatzi with her. Being at home with her and my two dogs, I thought to myself, I might even get up and walk. While that did not happen, I did improve.

A month later (using a walker and a wheelchair as accessories) I flew to Grand Cayman, this time to meet Vic and Gem Fitch (June 12-26). We spent two beach weeks in the islands.

As Eileen put it, "You have culti-

Because of her bouts with hepatitis Dorothy was not allowed to give blood to herself prior to surgery. Her sister Eileen, who shared her rather uncommon (Australian!) blood type, here made a donation.

vated friends all of your life, and now it's coming back to you." A bountiful harvest indeed to see me through perhaps what had been the lowest time of my life. Indeed, I cannot think that any medication or surgery has ever been more healing to my than the love of my friends.

Following each setback, I always weaned myself off pain medications in order to keep my head clear. In order to do this, I began spending many hours each day "in the horizontal" so that the screaming pain could abate. Reading, editing, telephoning, eating and many other chores can all be done on the bed, if need be.

A significant adjustment came the following year (2005). I traded my little Saturn in on a new Toyota Rav 4. I've always liked sleek, sporty, small cars. Trucks, vans, SUVs and great lumbering, be-chromed cars have never interested me. It became too much, however, for me to step down into the little car, descending as into a pit. Then I had to struggle to climb up out of it again. With my new car I had a hydraulic lift installed and Medicare gave me a motorized wheelchair. That event confirmed the fact that I had become a cripple. It took a while to get my mind around that idea.

In 2006 my Schatzi died suddenly. "Just wait," I told myself, "before you get another dog. Be sensible."

I lasted only six days. Then Larry helped me find Ladybug at a shelter. "What kind of a mix do you think she is?" I asked the veterinarian when I took her in for her check-up.

He shook his head. "I am not sure."

At thirteen lean pounds she looked like a Chihuahua on stilts. "Maybe a Chihuahua and whippet?" I suggested.

Virginia Fagal and Geneva Anderson gave Dorothy long and faithful nursing care. To the point that the patient declared her dear friends truly to be God's angels who just happened to be living on the earth at the time.

He eyed the lithe, tan figure with the huge brown eyes and extraordinarily long legs. "That would be about right," he agreed. She could run like a gazelle.

So Bugsy rules my house—a bundle of fanatical devotion, bright personality, and flaming intelligence. Let no one try to convince me to live without a dog. It simply cannot be done.

By the summer of 2007, I thought I had just about reached the point where I had learned to live with myself. Then three more thieves fell upon me.

First my daughter Lorna almost died from her sleep apnea and other complications. For almost ten weeks she languished in hospital, while Larry and I shared a very anxious time together.

Just as that crisis was diminishing, I was diagnosed with Type 2 diabetes. All right. So I'll now have to align myself with *that* program.

Then came one more threat to my endurance. On a July afternoon I accepted Olivine Bohner's invitation to swim in the pool in her community. Unlike the one where I live, it had the car park conveniently near the pool. My niece, LaVal Comm, who was visiting for the weekend, accompanied me. Although I could no longer swim, I did enjoy the heady feeling of walking in the water. (Walking was something I had not done since my last back surgery three years previously.)

Although I crawled up the steep steps and knelt at the edge of the pool, I could not get up on my feet. "Get my cell phone out of your car," I told Olivine. "I'll call the paramedics." Twice already I had called the medics when I'd fallen out of bed. They had heaved me back where I belonged, like a log onto the flatbed of a truck. This was part of their job. I knew they could do it.

Alas, Olivine had locked her keys in the car. While she walked home to call Roadside Assistance, I kept on struggling to get up on my feet. Forty-five minutes later the AAA man arrived. He hauled me up onto my feet.

I staggered home to a sleepless night and a very odd feeling of malaise. In the morning, taking LaVal with me, I drove myself to the Emergency Room. After a stout shot of benadryl I was sent home.

The day went badly, however, with my sister Eileen on the phone trying to direct traffic from Utah. At some point, the ambulance returned me to the hospital. I think I slept on a gurney in the ER that night.

Out of the haze the next morning, two doctors appeared in scrubs. "I think it's a heart attack," one said to the other. Then he leaned over me. "You know who I am, don't you?" I rallied enough to realize it was Dr. Gary Marais. I knew him from church. I didn't realize he was a cardiologist, but there he was in the ER to save my life that morning. I drifted away again.

I remember almost nothing of the week that followed. It included transfer to another hospital and an angiogram.

Days later, when I came to life again, the doctor was at my bedside, "I can see what happened," he said, "but how? Did you strain yourself physically? Perhaps more than you have ever done in your life before?"

Left. Bugsy has been a constant attendant in good times and bad. Right. She enjoys being wrapped in her Tiger Blanket. This time, one of the tigers stood right beside her, cheek to jowl.

Oh yes. I remembered the swimming pool. My lifelong determination to "do it for myself" had very nearly done me in. Turned out that I have a fairly good heart. I simply broke a piece of it (myocytolysis) there by the pool.

The day after I got home from the hospital, my friends Virginia and Geneva brought me lunch. Also Bugsy. (Only at the end of the ordeal did I discover where my little dog had gone.) They found me a shaking, perspiring heap of misery unable to eat. "All right," Virginia announced. "We are taking Bugsy back, and you're coming with her."

There I stayed for the next three weeks. Me and Bugsy, sleeping in Virginia's own bed and "being very quiet," as Dr. Marais had ordered. Truly, those friends of mine! They were two of God's angels who happened to live here on earth at the time. (Now they are both gone.) How lovingly they cared for us.

Messages and phone calls came in from friends far and near. Once again, it was home to my little house to recuperate. Each trip back to health, however, always fell a little short of the previous one. That is, I ended up one peg lower than I had been before.

Long ago I had had to hire gardeners to mow the lawn, trim the shrubs, and tend my few flowers. Next, I hired a succession of women to clean the house once a week.

Nonetheless, my broken heart did heal. When I sorted my medications, I just had to add one more pill each day. I looked down the road and made a conscious decision. "I am still here. I have a life. I am going to fill it up with as many good things as I can rustle up."

People frequently ask, "How are you?"

By now I had invented a stock reply: "I would be quite all right if I didn't have to drag my body around with me everywhere I go."

CHAPTER 20

A Few Lessons in Self-indulgence

In my childhood and teen years I suffered no abuse. I had all of the normal opportunities to play—though I often "wasted" them by reading books or roving through museums. Later on I had the unusual privilege of loving my work. Indeed, I maintained a rather idealistic bond between work and recreation. Perhaps something like the original plan that operated back in the Garden of Eden.

Along with that mindset, however, I sometimes felt an oppressive sense of duty. When I married, I discovered that Walt had an even fiercer work ethic than I did. Therefore, in whatever circumstances we found ourselves, we certainly never had a chance to become "party animals." In fact, the whole idea of just doing something "for fun" rarely crossed our minds.

Of course, our extensive travels inevitably provided pleasurable diversions, and we had the capacity for enjoying them. Nonetheless, everything we did had an under-lying purpose. A thread of responsibility ran through all of our plans. Any time that we took a family vacation—even a single weekend of escape—I was almost always the one who had to generate the idea.

In the main, we fulfilled public appointments, plunged into the next stage of graduate study, or made great trans-continental journeys to visit family before shipping out overseas. All the while, we had to hurry, Hurry, and HURRY! Still, for the reasons stated above, I never felt deprived or discontented with the way we lived our lives.

Probably the first time in my adult life when I went on vacation and had nothing else on my agenda occurred in June 1994. I negotiated a timeshare exchange for a holiday in Austria. Larry's enticing, almost-free air pass with Continental Airlines gave us standby status to fly to many, many destinations.

We could travel just for the
sheer pleasure of exploring
the unknown. Deliciously
self-indulgent!

Of course, I had to
work to earn such a prize.
On the appointed day, I got
up at 2 a.m. and graded
papers till dawn. Then I
invited my Graduate
Seminar in Writing down
to my home at "The Farm"
for potluck supper and the

Maria Alm, Austria. A time-share exchange in 1994 that
introduced Dorothy to the novel idea of vacationing with
no purpose other than to "do nothing." (It can be done.)

reading of student papers. Ultimately, just after midnight I set out on my 100-
mile drive into Los Angeles. As I shifted into my new mode of reckless
abandonment, a giddy thought came to mind. I was about to find out how to
pamper myself.

At the terminal, I found Larry in the waiting area, clad in suit and tie. A
great hardship for him, but this self-immolation enabled us to go First Class.
In Newark we were bumped off the Munich flight. Also the one to Frankfurt.
We considered going to London or Amsterdam, just to get across the Atlantic.
Finally we boarded a plane to Paris. Actually, we manipulated our stand-by
passes quite effectively.

After renting a car at Orly Airport, we drove into Munich. Seeing
Europe's lively mosaic of greens was a tonic. Even for us, jet-lagged out of our
minds as we were. When we arrived at our timeshare, the Alpenland
Sporthotel, our eyes glazed over with the beauty of the Tyrolean village of
Maria Alm. What a place to be stuck for a week!

Out front we saw a canary-yellow Lambourghini Diablo parked. We
meekly crept by it in our Ford Fiesta. "He's got a cracked windshield," Larry
was always the master of the commonplace. "I could fix that."

Our apartment on the fourth floor of the chalet was fronted by a black
balcony and window box in the best Austrian style. For a start, we slept, and

I rested my over-used "bionic" left leg. (I no longer had unlimited ability to walk wherever I wished.)

We feasted daily on elegant buffet breakfasts of breads, cheeses and fruits while we decided what we wanted to do next. One day I took a trip to Venice while Larry visited the Ice Caves and the fortress of Burg Hohenwefen. Another day we went together to Salzburg. On the cathedral steps we listened to a fetching young man dressed like the Pied Piper playing *tafelmusik* (for medieval banquets) on his flute. We gave one day to seeing the "Sound of Music" Lake Country. On yet another day we stayed at Maria Alm and never moved the car at all.

Exploring the high Alps, among the waterfalls and *alms* (meadows) made a full day's outing. We couldn't take our eyes off the houses in the valley below Heiligenblut. A stunning setting. Usually they were three stories with white concrete foundations and black-timber upper floors. The balcony boxes over-flowed with spring flowers. Indeed, the surrounding meadows looked like a botanical seasoning from a cosmic "Mrs. Dash." A sprinkling of white daisies, red clover, yellow buttercups and dandelions, and other unidentified *blumen* (flowers) in blue and dark pink. Widely scattered over the hillsides, the houses stood high up in the trees, the roads leading to them all carefully concealed.

Upon departure from our timeshare, we stayed well off the tourist trails. We found a little *zimmer* (room) in Linz and ate supper in the beer-garden in Gallneukirchen's town square. Although the waiter spoke no English, we got good enough food, even if it wasn't exactly what we expected.

Vienna proved to be large, confusing, and riddled with one-way streets. First we took the Danube Boat Cruise. The river begins high in Germany and flows through nine countries on its way to the Black Sea. The boat "danced" to the strains of the Blue Danube Waltz. Schmaltzy but not unpleasant. Today, however, the water is brown, not blue.

At Schoenbrunn Palace, the imperial rococo summer home of the Haps-burgs, we hired a clumsy old wheelchair. Larry propelled me through a half-mile of the forty-four palace rooms open to the public. Finally, we attended a *konzert* in a white-and-gold mirrored room. Some seventy people, recreated the intimacy of 18th-century musicales. We would like to have returned to our Haus Sanz lodging to change clothes but had no time. Feeling humble and unworthy in our travel garments, we chose seats in the back—in the fifth row of gold chairs. The Austrians, on the other hand, presented themselves very properly, some in national costume. Somehow, the eight musicians made themselves sound like a full chamber orchestra, and the singers danced right down among us. A stunning performance.

On our last day we arrived at Munich's Franz Joseph Strauss Airport shortly before noon. The terminal was startling barren. The skeletal structures had pipes, ducts, bars, steel, glass and cement—all at hard angles. (I could not be sure that Strauss would have approved.)

The Hotel Kempinski Airport Munchen displayed the same style. Swarming with seriously groomed, business people, the lobby looked like an airport hangar with a five-story wing on either side. A geometric study in The Square and Multiples of Three, the building was admirable but intimidating. Each of the lobby's thirty-six cubicles contained three flowerpots (total of 648). Each pot contained a bright bouquet of red silk geraniums. True to form, our room on the top floor featured steel fittings and black marble in the bathroom.

Fortunately we did not have to return to Paris. Instead, we relaxed in Business First Class where it took more than two hours just to work through our leisurely lunch. In due course, a magnificent view unfolded below us. The blue-and-white world of Labrador and then hundreds of miles of ices floes, locked together on an indigo sea.

Thus passed two weeks of intoxicating indolence. Although driving home across Los Angeles freeways threatened to eradicate my holiday, I managed to keep a firm grip on my nerves. Moreover, I promised myself to "do it again." As often as possible.

By the spring of 2000, I was actually tapering off toward retirement. Therefore, I could block off a piece of time to go on a winter pilgrimage to Britain with Jack and Olivine Bohner. Since they possessed a delectable assortment of timeshares, Jack, with his usual planning expertise, had carved out three very attractive weeks for us.

By then I needed a wheelchair to negotiate London's Heathrow Airport. Fitted together like a lego set, the place had become enormous. Indeed, it

On their last evening in Britain, Jack and Olivine Bohner and Dorothy concluded their three-week pilgrimage in the only appropriate way—a feed of English white fish and chips. In one dizzy hour they threw all caution to the winds. There would be time enough later to cut back on eating fat!

seemed to cover about half of southern England. The three of us, therefore, were duly grateful for the sense of direction that the wheelchair operator had. He delivered us to our flight to Dublin in the nick of time.

For our seven days in Ireland, we lodged in the former stables of Knocktopher Abbey, ten miles out of Kilkenney. (The quaint hotel had neatly assimilated the remains of a 13th-century Carmelite Friary.) In addition to the usual tourist stops we detoured to watch the glassblowers. Then we explored an old graveyard.

That night Jack shopped in a most unlikely little store and gathered up the ingredients to create our favorite Indonesian rice-and-curry supper for us. Did anyone else in Ireland that drizzly night have a dish like that? I doubt it.

We spent our second week in Sloane Gardens, London, where our penthouse apartment looked down upon the red brick row houses. The first night Jack not only produced supper but also five fresh tulips. (He knew how passionately Olivine detested fake flowers.)

We were certainly not idle in London. We saw the "Diana Shrine" at Harrods. Janet Sillitoe came from Exminster, Devon, to spend two days with us. We heard an all-Beethoven concert at St. Martins-in-the-Fields. At the Royal National Theatre on the Thames, we saw a modern interpretation of "Merchant of Venice." (Although it is hard to surpass the Brits in theatre performance, I still preferred the traditional Shakespeare version.)

I also spent two days visiting Enid Tolman in Chiswick. We went to an evening service at All Souls Church at the end of Regent Street and heard an excellent sermon by Dr. John Stott, "The Now and the Not-Yet." The dismaying thought came to me, however, that I was rapidly reaching the stage where I would not be able to climb all of those steps at the Turnham Green Underground railway station.

The third week brought us to Broome Park in Kent, a 350-year-old mansion that once belonged to Lord Kitchener. We had to climb sixty-three stairs to our

A joint birthday party for Dorothy and Virginia-Gene. Seated (L-R). Dorothy Comm, Virginia-Gene Rittenhouse, Harvey Rittenhouse. Standing. Left: Janusz and Teresa Bilinski, Right. James and Trenise Gulley and Son Devon.

apartment on the top floor. (Nothing so commonplace as an elevator could be installed in such a historic building.)

With the Chunnel now operating, Europeans dominated the scene in the town of Dover. Many of them came in on the most luxurious coaches I have ever seen. Compartments on the lower level were little lounges, complete with lamps and tables.

On our last day we had lunch in Canterbury at "Flap Jacques," a crepe house offering dishes in "the Breton style." First I had an asparagus-and-mushroom crepe followed by a lemon-sugar one for dessert. True delight at a gourmet level!

At the end of that trip I was forced to an obvious conclusion. I really could not expect to travel alone any more. Jack had borne all my burdens for me. True, I could still get myself from Point A to Point B, but I could carry virtually nothing with me. A sharp sense of loss hit me. For the first time, I think.

Happily road trips still remained with my range. At least for the time being. Soon after I got home, I packed Lorna, Ladybird, and Schatzi into my little car. Lorna had not been to Canada since childhood, so we drove up to

Alberta. While Lena's three cats did their best putting up with Bird, they paid no attention to Schatzi, our little brown fur ball. Because they couldn't be sure what she was, they left her alone.

Under the heady influence of that Continental air pass, I continued to make little forays around North America. My birthday in 2002 was a case in point. I flew to Baltimore, Maryland, for twelve days of renewal. Although Virginia-Gene Rittenhouse and I had been friends for more than fifty years, we had never celebrated our birthdays (October 15 and 17) together. When she and Harvey drove down from Massachusetts, we planned our party at the "China Chef." Suddenly, we found that the affair had been taken out of our hands. Family and friends pressed in to honor what they described as a "famous musician and a famous author." In fact, the festivities went on for days!

Among the "revelers" was my Australian cousin James Gulley (of whom I am inordinately proud with his Ph.D. and M.D.). When he met me at the airport, my wheelchair operator refused to believe that he was more than seventeen years old. A clinical research-oncologist at the National Institute of Health, he still carries his thirty-eight years almost invisibly.

James' and Trenise's two-year-old red-haired son Devon looks as if he'd stepped out of one of Gainsborough's English portraits. An enchanting little lover-boy. "Am I getting a kiss, Devon?" With blazing blue eyes and a huge grin, he clambered up onto my bed, scrambled across the bedclothes and planted a big one right on my lips. A delight to all who fall into the sphere of his sunny influence.

One additive to the trip came when I rented a car and drove up into Pennsylvania Dutch Country. (My Grandfather Bert Rhoads originated there.) I spent the weekend with my cousin Marcia Rhoads-MacKellar. She was pastoring in the Highland Presbyterian Church in Lancaster, Pennsylvania. Proudly I sat with congregation, saw her don her clerical robes, and heard her preach a fine Sunday sermon.

Although I have always been much in love with the sea, I had never been on a cruise. Basically I had known ships only as raw transportation—especially in wartime. Therefore, I set off to Alaska with two of my very dear friends, Virginia Fagal and her sister, Geneva Anderson.[1] With an aggregate age of 245

Left. Having the time (plus Larry's air pass) enabled Dorothy to get acquainted with new relatives. A case in point was a visit with Cousin Marcia Rhoads-MacKellar and her three daughters (and pets) in Lancaster, Pennsylvania. **Right.** Marcia was a pastor at Highland Presbyterian Church there.

years we three old-timers decided that we had earned the pampering that such a cruise afforded.

We drove to Vancouver, Canada, in Virginia's Buick Park Avenue. Three leisurely days later we parked it at our motel in North Vancouver and boarded the M.S. *Statendam* early on a Sunday afternoon.

At 5 p.m. we sailed out under the Lions Gate Bridge toward the Georgia Channel. Forty-five minutes later we were at table in the luxurious Rotterdam Room, being served dinner by smartly liveried stewards. The place glittered with china and tinkled with crystal. We were on the way! I looked around the elegant, balconied room and thought, "This must what self-indulgence looks like!"

We were still making merry at the dinner table when the voice of our New Zealand captain, John Scott, broke into our conversation, "We will have a slight delay." (That turned out to be the understatement of the season.)

An hour later the messages tumbled over the public address system, one after the other. "Smoke!" "Switchboard problem." "Crew members are doing what they have been trained to do." And on and on.

The word "fire" was never mentioned, but we saw men sprinting up and down the passageways. The acrid smell of "electrical smoke" filtered into our room. Wishing to avoid a panic, the officers told us as little as possible. In any case, the entire ship was defunct. Minimum lighting, no air-conditioning, and dysfunctional plumbing.

By 4 a.m. four chunky tugboats reached us. They hauled our great hulk of a flopping, helpless ship back into port. Twelve hours later our captain finally announced the cancellation of the cruise. Of the three options before us, we decided to take our money and run. That is, 125% of all of our costs, including our travel to and from Vancouver.

By the end of the day most of the 1,300 displaced passengers had disembarked. We elected to sleep on board one more night in the searing heat of the cabin, waiting until the initial rush was over. My wheelchair needed a little extra space.

Once ashore we reconnected with our luggage and reclaimed the Buick. Meanwhile, the day's newspapers described the plight of the *Statendam* as a "meltdown." We couldn't help speculating about the possibility of terrorism. How easy would it be to infiltrate the 100% Asian crew and send someone down into the bowels of the ship to disable one of the five engines? Precisely the one that destroyed all of the vessel's infrastructure.

We didn't spend much energy, however, on conspiracy theories. Instead, we struck out east into incomparably lovely British Columbia. Happily, I had friends and family all of the way into Alberta. Our stops in Creston, Lake Louise, Banff, and the Columbia Ice Fields, culminated in the weekend with Vic and Gem Fitch at Canadian Union College.

Then, having filled in our impromptu Canadian vacation days, we headed down into Washington State and resumed our original schedule of visiting friends and family. We just took time to be with each other and the people we cared about. The problem of the ship's burning actually vanished from our minds.

We made our second attempt on Alaska in August of 2004. This time we made the two-hour, direct flight into Seattle and boarded the M. S. *Amsterdam* at the Holland-America dock there. This time, because everything went according to plan, I had a chance to discover what a cruise really felt like.

After all, wealthy Dutch merchants 200 years ago were the first Westerners to experiment with the inviting concept of comfort. To a man, the ship's officers looked so tall and handsome. Quite convincingly Dutch!

My first discovery was that cruising truly is all about money and self-indulgence. Social class automatically asserts itself. We lived in stateroom 1953 at the stern on the Dolphin (lowest passenger) Deck. The "Fat Cats" (our betters) occupied balcony suites ten floors above us.

Also, we would have to live "cashless." As we submitted a credit card number, the purser urged us to "just buy and enjoy." That way lay ruin for the reckless, surely!

The first brochure read: "Welcome Aboard, the Excitement Begins." (Is that what we came for?) As it turned out, we had many options for "excitement." Indeed, at least four of the eleven decks were given over to utter self-gratification, including two swimming pools, eight bars, salons and spas, a casino and endless game rooms. The entire infrastructure pointed to but one purpose: "Indulge yourself."

Moreover, we had the opportunity every day to eat ourselves into a coma. Steaming hot food decks, displays of fresh fruit carved into works of art, every known kind of beverage, and ranges of desserts decadent enough to bring you to tears. My mind went back to our aborted voyage on the *Statendam* two years earlier. Whatever happened to all of that food intended for that trip?

Although I'd never done much by way of self-indulgence, I decided that (in a modest way) I might now learn a little. Perversely, however, I found my favorite place in the library. I even found reading lamps like the ones I had used in the British Museum Library. The hardwood desks stood at windows draped in medieval-type tapestry. So I sat there for hours, watching Alaska go by. (Finally, I had to conclude that in the area of hedonism I was, perhaps, not teachable.) The sun rose behind the backdrop of continuous blue mountain ranges. The shimmering sea in the foreground made the stage, and we passengers were the audience, waiting for the play to begin. We sailed directly to the glaciers and then worked our way back south through the Inland Passage.

Low, green hills of rich, glacial soil lined Glacier Bay. Rounded off by the receding ice, they had retreated sixty-five miles in the last 200 years. Jagged peaks, full of summer snow, baby glaciers (just calved off the big ones) swam in the milky, gray-green water, past the chiseled rock surfaces. Sadly, the ice looked much grayer and smaller than I had ever seen portrayed on a postcard.

Geneva and I both used wheelchairs to negotiate the infinitely long distances aboard. Because the chairs belonged to the ship, we could not go ashore anywhere. (The options were Juneau, Sitka, Ketchikan, and Victoria, British Columbia). Holland America Lines, I suppose, had to consider the possibility that one of us might strike off into the Alaska wilderness and never bring the chair back.

When we disembarked in Seattle, our threesome broke up again, Virginia and Geneva spending a week with their family in Portland. I divided my time between my friend Lynne Harrington in Bremerton, Washington, and my usual attractions in Alberta. As Calgary grows I constantly marvel at its vitality. While the housing developments increase, the city's limit cuts off cleanly, street by street. On one side the houses crowd in. On the other cattle graze and crops flourish.

When I arrived home soon after midnight, Lorna and the dogs didn't even wake up. The next morning my dear old Ladybird almost went over the top in her welcome-home exercises. In the middle of it all, she saw a fat gray

Left. After the fire aboard the *Statendam* and the cancellation of the Alaska cruise, Dorothy and Virginia Fagal and Geneva Anderson struck off east to create their own kind of holiday. Right. During a reststop in Cranbrook, British Columbia, Dorothy saw a fully restored Super-Six Essex of 1929. Although not a car fancier, she was thrilled with this antique. Her Dad's first car (purchased in Singapore in 1937) had been this very model, in black. Right. The three friends' second attempt to cruise to Alaska succeeded, aboard the *Amsterdam*.

cat sitting on the wall under the rose bushes. She shot outside and chased the intruder to the gate. Ten years fell off her, just like that, as she pranced about. Perhaps she should have a dose of cat every day so that she could get the exercise she so sorely needed.

Dorothy's beach hideaway at Tamerack, California, is a timeshare that she never exchanges for any other place in the world. Year after year, she and her family enjoy a winter week here. From her balcony she can feed her lifelong love affair with the ocean.

After the Alaska cruise, I made my usual autumn trip up to my sister Eileen and Lyman's mountain home, at 7000' elevation in the mountains of Utah. Whereas I used to drive the 650 miles in one day (sometimes even with the six-hour detour into Zion and Bryce National Parks) now I had to stop overnight in St. George

That was the year that I began to wonder how many more of those journeys I could make with Lorna and the dogs. Still, if people were patient with me and supplied a few of my basic needs, I did fairly well. I told myself that I had felt better before. Also, I had been a great deal worse. Now I understand my rationalizing. After my many roving years, the ability to travel had become a measurement of my "normalcy."

I had driven all kinds of vehicles on all kinds of roads, all over the world. No problem. At this point in time I had not yet faced the possibility that one day I would not be able to drive my car.

Also, I still had one excellent destination available. After two years' absence (lost to my medical setbacks) I was able to resume my annual beach-week in Carlsbad, California, in 2004. Since foreign travel was no longer the easy hop-skip-and-a-jump to which I had become accustomed, my timeshare just north of San Diego remained a huge attraction. Although very "walker dependent," I could still drive my car to get to the ocean.

I have always felt that I was born to live by the sea. Nothing fascinates me more than watching the line where land and ocean meet. No matter how cool the weather, I always leave the window open so that I can hear the surf. From my third-floor balcony, I watch flaming sunsets through the palm trees. Just below, processions of people walk the mile-long walkway above the sands. Lean young things jogging. Women pushing strollers full of babies. Dogs leading their owners along the path and pausing at their own special drinking fountain. Ground squirrels sunbathing and foraging among the rocks. Crowds of sea gulls flocking on the hard sands when the tide was out. Great brown pelicans skimming along overhead. On a clear blue day you can see all the way to Catalina Island, forty miles away.

In 2008 I fell for one more cruise. It wasn't that I had just succumbed to the temptation to spend another week eating and amusing myself board ship. No. This would begin and end in Rome's Port Citivecchio and would include Egypt, Turkey, Greece, with several islands in between.

The sponsorship by Loma Linda University insured that the tour would include at least a few of my friends and colleagues. I had been teaching Ancient World and Classical Greek and Roman literature for much of my life. Now I just wanted to see. Moreover I had been in love with Egyptian archaeology from childhood. With this justification I persuaded three of my best friends to sail with me—Vic and Gem Fitch and Annamarie Liske.

After decades of teaching Classical and World Literature, Dorothy persuaded three of her friends to go where none of them had been before, a cruise of the eastern Mediterranean. (L-R). Dorothy Comm, Annamarie Liske, Vic Fitch, Gem Fitch (2008).

Of course we partook of the usual luxuries that a cruise ship offers. (We had four days "at sea.") Still, our interests went much further than that. Vic, of course, was able to do more leg work than the rest of us.

Nonetheless, we all came
home the wiser, saturated
with culture and full of
newly created memories.

Since I had re-discov-
ered my Dad's homeland
back in 1974, I had made
several trips Down Under.
In 1993 Eileen and I
(along with her son Kevin)
took our mother to the
Sydney area for two weeks.
(At that time our standby
passes still worked in our

**Dorothy took her "strong tee-shirt" along, thereby
arousing sympathetic attention from fellow passengers.
They understood how encouraging the message could be
on mornings when one might awake a little discouraged.**

favor. Nowadays with planes regularly overbooked, "standing-by" can be a
rather bleak means of travel.) We wanted to help Mum remember what our
lives had been when we lived there back in the early 1940s. As always, the
"rellies" (relatives) enfolded us in love and hospitality. For all her eighty-six
years, Mum took the wear-and-tear of travel very well. Completely in character, she didn't want to miss anything, and we brought her home well
satisfied.

At the end of 2002 I was fully retired, and my third back surgery (fortunately) still lay in the future. Although wheelchair-dependent, I decided on
one more very comprehensive trip home to Australia. Supposing it to be my
last, I regarded it as a kind of pilgrimage. I would forego sightseeing as such
and just spend time with my cousins. Romantically I entitled my thirty-one-
page (illustrated) journal "Some Vignettes of a Fortunate Life."

It began in New Zealand with an almost 2270-mile journey in Kelvin
and Rosemary's Mitsubishi 4 x 4. A really amazing accomplishment within
two relatively small islands.

Nine Random Highlights of New Zealand (2002)

- Our little house on Walkers Road in Longburn. A lamb was in the back yard, right where Eileen's and my Peter Lamb used to be tethered.

- The two-hour ferry crossing the Cook Strait between the North and South islands, with ten-foot swells.
- Driving west from Picton and catching glimpses of coves through the giant fern trees, with spring flowers clinging to their feet.
- Cattle and sheep in clean, green pastures.
- Shopping in Hokitika. When the Maoris came to the islands in 800 A.D. they brought with them the arts of making jade weapons and ornaments.
- On Lake Wakatipu. A half-day cruise out of Queenstown on the vintage Victorian steamship *Earnslaw,* included a cheerful sing-along around the piano on board.
- At Otago University in Dunedin—a city as Scottish as a clan tartan. Lisa Minchin graduated with: BA (History), BSc. (Ecology), and the diploma in Secondary Teaching.
- Christchurch and our discovery of the grave of one of our forebears, the Reverend William Minchin of Greenhills, Ireland (d 1863).
- Wild life along the east coast of the South Island: the Royal Albatross on the Otago Peninsula, seals at Kaikoura, and the Yellow-Eyed Penguin.

A stop at Kelvin and Rosemary's property on the Tutakaka coast of the North Island of New Zealand is usually either the lovely beginning or conclusion of Australia trips. Their glass-fronted house is designed to give the best view possible of the 180-degree sweep of ocean and the Poor Knights Islands. If magnificent scenery were their only reason for travel, the Minchins would certainly never leave home.

The days in Western Australia centered, as usual, on Cousin Ellen Henley's house. We spent hours visiting home sites and lingering over our meals.

My first visit to Darwin brought me to Vic and Lyn

Minchin's new home. Within the hour I was back home in the tropics. A gratifyingly violent rain and thunder storm greeted me. I tuned in immediately with my cousins' interest in aboriginal art and music. A thirty-mile trip down the Arnhem Highway provided two amazing displays. Giant anthills and huge flights of white cockatoos. The final treat was the sight of a skittish dingo beside the road.

In New South Wales I gravitated naturally to Cooranbong and the Avondale college campus that was once home. Cousins Arthur and Joan Patrick lodged me in their lovely home surrounded by flower and vegetable gardens, plus horses and pet kookaburras. Geoff and Donna Madigan spared a weekend to take me down to Canberra, and finally all of the available "rellies" gathered for a picnic on the shores of Cabbage Tree Bay.

Only full retirement could provide me with such a leisurely progress through New Zealand and Australia. So, at the end of the seven weeks, I reached home again, truly fulfilled. While I felt alive with the joys of my journey, I wilted under the knowledge that I had to face my third back surgery.

The year after our Mediterranean cruise (2009), Vic and Gem Fitch and I designed what, it seems, became the last overseas trip for all of us. A very ambitious journey. For them it would all be new. For me? I discovered that I had one more chance to go home to Australia. I actually had someone to help me. Let's go! Vic toted all of the luggage and helped Gem pack. (Those tasks gave rise to his calling himself "The Mule.") Most of the time, he also

The next year (2009) there was yet one more journey to make, home to Australia and New Zealand. Again the same crew-members—Vic, Gem, and Dorothy. One of their first ventures was aboard the Skyrail high above Queensland's rainforest.

The publication of the comprehensive family history, *The Book of Minchin: A Family for All Seasons,* enabled hitherto unknown relatives to get acquainted. In Adelaide, South Australia, we had dinner with two cousins and their families. Chris Minchin (left) is a surveyor, son of the celebrated artist, Eric Minchin. For most of his life Nick Minchin (right) has been active in government at both the state and federal levels.

had to put on my socks and shoes before we could go out.

Only our friendship of more than fifty years gave us the confidence that we could really "pull it off." (Dreamily, we entitled our forty-page journal "One Shining Venture for Both Mind and Spirit.")

On the longer flights I was beset with the problem of getting myself to the "loo" (toilet). Sometimes Vic took me down the passageway and helped me stagger across the gaps. Other times it was one of the attendants. In any case, the aisle was always too narrow to accommodate my walker.

One time, as we passed through the First Class section, I told one smiling passenger, "Yes, I've been dancing with many strange men on this trip." One time, in fact, as I was getting off the plane, I fell into the arms of the pilot himself!

On my return to my seat, the same man waved. "May I have the next dance?"

"So sorry," I replied. "I am all booked up." Actually, everyone we met was most sympathetic with our/my logistical limitations.

We visited every state in Australia, including Tasmania. It all began in Cairns, at the Great Barrier Reef. Plus a few hours in Tjapukai Park to see aboriginal arts and dances. After Darwin, we set down in Perth the day before my 80th birthday. Needless to say, this had to be the personal highlight for the trip for me. Especially after Ellen gathered so many cousins to celebrate. Indeed, the event was so fulfilling that to this day I have no further need of

Wheelchair notwithstanding, Dorothy spent her 80th birthday in Perth, Western Australia. At an unforgettable tea, her cousins went all-out to celebrate that milestone.

birthday recognition.

We rented a car in Adelaide and drove it all the way to Sydney. Vic stuck calmly and safely to the left side of the road, and we had a wonderful ground-level look at South Australia, Victoria, and Canberra, all the way into New South Wales.

Something important had happened since my last visit. I had published *The Book of Minchin: A Family for All Seasons* (2006). With almost 700 pages, over 1,000 illustrations, and 66 Descendancy Charts, it was, arguably, a significant piece of family history. True, I put it together, but the book represents the research of more than a dozen people over a period of some 100 years.

In the process of producing the book, I had become acquainted with many relatives whom I had never seen. They, in turn, had a chance to know one another. On this last pilgrimage, then, we were hosted by heretofore unknown cousins.

In Adelaide we were guests of the Hon. Nick Minchin and Chris Minchin and their families. In Melbourne Tony and June Minchin looked

Tony and June Minchin (couple in upper left-hand corner of the photograph) discovered the unmarked grave of Dorothy's Great-Great-Grandmother Elizabeth Minchin (d 1863) in Kyneton, Victoria, Australia. On September 26, 2010, these direct descendents, young and old, came together for "Family Day" and the dedication of our pioneer ancestor's tombstone.

after us, seeing us to and from the Tasmania ferry. These were just a few of the "new" relatives I met. Like me, Tony was one of the Swan River family. He was instrumental in getting a handsome tombstone on the grave of our Great-great-Grandmother Elizabeth Minchin. He identified her unmarked grave in Kyneton Cemetery north of Melbourne. She had been lying there since 1862, waiting. Needless to say, I have been well pleased to see how tangible the influence of the Big Book has been.

We neared the end of our journey, and Vic and Gem had still not seen a live kangaroo. Fortified with a loaf of bread, Geoff Madigan took us to a site that "never fails." Sure enough, at sundown, we saw hundreds of 'roos assembled in the grounds of the Psychiatric Hospital in Morriset. Why they have, for generations, chosen that particular rendezvous point, no one can tell.

Just before our flight to New Zealand, we enjoyed two concerts in Sydney Opera House. Something special for Gem, our own concert musician.

Kelvin and Rosemary met us in Auckland and took us home with them. New Zealand is altogether lovely all round, but you can hardly do better than enjoy the view from their cliff-top home near Whangerei. I stayed with them while Vic and Gem went to the South Island. After all, they had earned a few days' freedom from care-taking me.

While one never says never, we three supposed that this was our last large, international trip. If it was, then we would have something very wonderful to remember.

All things considered, I have had a remarkable number of purely recreational journeys. While retirement provided the time for these ventures, it has been marvelous to think of how I was able to scrape together the money to go

In retrospect, I see that these travels had value far beyond the 'fun" part. I suppose the fact that I should even make this point shows that I have always been—and will always be—tied to a very strong sense of responsibility. Perhaps that rationale is one of the main reasons for my writing *Three Homes for the Heart* at all.

In summary, my experiences in self-indulgence have had four benefits. First, I have secured and enjoyed close friendships. Second, my Hall of Memories is richly furnished. Also, learning new things births new ideas— always a plus. Finally, improved self-knowledge can make one's latter years less tempestuous.

In these ways, the "fun times" have provided a wonderful and productive counterpoint to the sense of serious purpose that always dominated my life.

The philosopher Martin Buber said: "All journeys have secret destinations of which the traveler is unaware." Exactly!

---

1   Virginia Fagal was co-founder with her husband of the television program "Faith for Today."
    Geneva Anderson was still (in her 80s) a practicing nurse. Both were sisters of Harvey Ritten-
    house, so our connections went back a long way.

CHAPTER 21

The View from the Gazebo: An Essay

Life can only be understood backwards, but it must be lived forwards.
—Soren Kierkegaard
(Theologian, 1813-1855)

So, my life-circle nears completion. In human terms, I clearly have a great deal more behind me than before. I have now had ten years of retirement to review what life has been about. My findings may not be new, but at least they are mine.

Making a Difference?

Without question, foreign mission service has gaiven my life much of the color that it has acquired along the way. Almost-five years with my parents in Singapore, followed by the sixteen years that Walt and I spent in the Caribbean and the Far East.

Historically, the Christian Church has taken very seriously the injunction to "Go into all the world and preach the Gospel" (Mark 16:15). Early on, a stereotype evolved. The missionary, in white sun helmet, preached to eager natives under the palm trees.

In some places the results of missionary endeavor remain minimal—and it has not been for lack of prayerful effort. Hundreds of years of work. In the minds of non-western people, missionaries—spiritual and self-sacrificing as they might be—became inextricably entangled with colonialism. The mystique of the "White Man's Burden" was tainted with suspicion. Indeed, mixed motivations have cropped up on both sides.

The balance has tipped, in fact, with the majority of the membership of the Seventh-day Adventist Church now living outside of North America.

Today, nationals have become capable of assuming leadership and managing their own institutions

Again, beyond question, Christian missions have accomplished much good. Multitudes have been brought into the "House of Faith, Hope, and Redemption." Also, the Hindu custom of *suttee* has stopped in India. Head-hunting is no longer practiced in Borneo. Cannibalism has gone underground. Education has become a high priority. Standards of living have improved. Indeed, the Modern World has arrived!

Still, troublesome issues linger. "Just leave 'em alone," the secularists pontificate. So the Church faces the question that has always been there. Why did we go? Why are we still going? What should we be planning for the future? Some cling to the old traditions, regardless of the March of Time. Others envision the Gospel completely "contextualized" into local cultures. How long should a commitment to mission service last? Deep conflicts have arisen over missionary outreach.

Current preference runs to short terms. This arrangement is easily accomplished in the case of medical missions. Building projects and evangelistic campaigns also attract both young and old. Today's mission journeys incorporate elements of tourism into the enterprise. That, of itself, is not necessarily wrong. The world, after all, must be understood and assimilated.

While the benefits of mission service are undeniable, hundreds of new issues have arisen. I offer no solutions. Only observations. Still, I can be grateful for what I had. I worked in my own time and place. By now, I have had many years to realize that what I learned was measurably greater than anything I gave to the people among whom I lived. To say this, of course, is to voice a cliché. It happens, however, to be true. To add yet one more churchly cliché, "Only Heaven can evaluate the tasks we did."

The Falling Away

The English author, Diana Athill, has offered us a practical list of the indignities of old age.[1] She speaks first of the "falling away." Physically, in advancing years, it is all a downhill journey. We have endless instruction books about being (and staying) young. Also, there are *gurus* to help us manage our

A Philosophy of Age and Illness: A Parable

We spend most of our lives trying to learn how to be healthy. Indeed, wellness has become a billion-dollar industry, abounding with miracle drugs and health *gurus*. One way or another, most of us manage to do it reasonably well. We keep up appearances, for we are at the top of our game, and professional achievements very much matter. So far, so good. This is Person #1.

Then, sometimes in a single moment, your world turns upside down, inside out. Maybe it's a paralyzing accident. A lethal disease. Or just a debilitating decline. Your friends rally around. For a while the hospital room looks like a garden. A veritable nursery of flowers and plants. Cards pour in, urging you to "Get Well Soon."

Getting well, however, points in two different directions. The first presupposes that you are going to get back to the place where you started. Wherever you were before *it* happened. This may work (temporarily) for those who have youth on their side.

On the other hand, when old age overtakes you, the game changes. You become Person #2. You may get well, but you must now build on a different foundation. That is, you learn how to be sick. How to do it with courage and grace. As the years pass, constant pain saps your energy. You practice. You really work at it. You stifle your anger. You pray not to be envious the #1 Persons around you.

Following your friends' instructions, as Person #2, you are, indeed, "Well." Person #1 has disappeared, never to be seen again. People ask after your health. "I am well," you say truthfully. Not in the first sense. Instead, you have learned how to be ill. You are no longer the person you were before you got sick.

As Person #2 you never start the day with the question, "What do I have to accomplish today?" Instead, you ask, "What is possible for me to do today?" It may be a great project. Or it may be nothing more than loving your dog or reading a book. In either case, you are grateful for whatever it was that you did—because you have become good at it.

Eventually, you will admit that you have, in fact, become Person #2. You used to be someone else, but you got over that. You have discovered who you are now. Being old may look odd, but it isn't wrong. You just learn how to fit successfully into a different framework. *–Adapted from Athill* middle years. Few "self-helpers," however, have much to tell us about this "falling away." In the long run, cosmetics and plastic surgery become nothing but pathetic masks to shield us from the realities of Old Age. We have more important matters than these to worry about.

As our energy dwindles, we have to submit. For me, enduring chronic and incurable pain is predictable. Sometimes even boring. Some times I do get angry at my situation, but not often. Discontent consumes too much vitality. Therefore, I determine to use whatever strength I have to reach something or someone outside of myself. Hosts of people have given so much to me, and I certainly have no right to off-load misery on them. Nor can I allow anyone to suck the joy out of my own physically diminished life.

Some things just cannot be done. For example, I have always been passionately fond of classical music. My Dad very much wanted me to become a good pianist like himself. Being interested in a great many other things, however, I evaded practice. Even if I had cooperated, I know that I would never have been more than second rate. It just could not happen, and we all had to accept that fact. By the same token, when I needed another dog, I brought Bugsy home from a shelter. I was too old to start again with a puppy. That is the way it had to be, and I knew it.

Fortunately I have had the genes for being busily creative. With that came a kind of "built-in" resilience for which I am grateful. One has to subscribe to three premises: (1) No one promised us that life would be fair, (2) Bad things keep on happening to good people, and (3) Age is not just lost youth. It is a new stage with its own potential for strength and maturity. From this philosophical base, then, I have to deal with the "Falling Away."

Relationships

Oddly enough, our handicaps can make us more human. If all is well, relationships become far more important than any material property. As we age, we learn to make everything matter. The more I pay attention, the more I enjoy my situation. Some days I spend hours on the phone, just listening. If someone out there needs a listener, I can do that. I am not actually going anywhere anyway!

Moreover, I want my connections to be *real.* Being old in this technologically hyped-up world is not easy. Indeed, Facebook frightens me. I don't text, tweet, or twitter. Nor do I blog, bleep or bop. I find the telephone and email quite adequate. Hopefully, these limitations make me less vulnerable to every hacker and virus cruising around cyberspace. At least, my simple life is not spread out for the whole earth to see. Besides, I don't have to "follow" anyone. Neither do I have to worry about someone tailing me.

My view from the Gazebo is wide-open and, at the same time, private. Surprisingly, in old age it is possible to be alone and yet feel less loneliness than in the busy work years. I sit, as it were, in my gazebo and watch the world go by. If the world wants to stop and see me, they may do so. I am easy to find.

Care-giving

Inevitably there comes the often sad business of care-giving. I went through these endless motions of caring for many years. First, with my mother and my aunt and finally with my husband, Walt. Finances and transportation, appointments and entertaining, injections and diet. There it was. Although I kept up my full-time employment, I never made any plans of my own during my final years with them. Not one.

Then came my turn. It started innocuously enough with getting someone in once a week to clean the house, and someone else to tend the yard. (After all I was still working full time, and I needed help.) Still, I struggled to bury my pride as I passed from a cane to a walker and finally into a wheelchair.

Cindy DeMille had been housekeeping for me for several weeks when I made my 2009 journey home to Australia. I didn't know her very well, but we had become friends. Some instinct told me that I could trust her. So off I went, leaving her in charge of my entire house, my computer, and my dog.

We are now well into our second year with Cindy as my live-in caregiver. Groceries, banking, getting us to church, and all other domestic tasks fall into her job description. She is a good driver and manipulates my heavy, motorized wheelchair skillfully. From time to time, I tell myself that I could still drive the car if I had to. My numb legs and feet would get in the way, but I could have hand-controls installed, couldn't I? Maybe. To be honest, I have had to recognize these thoughts as rather feeble rationalization. Nothing more than my clutching at my ever-receding independence.

There used to be days when I could get into any kind of vehicle, on any road you chose, and in any country you want to name. Then I could just drive away without a second thought. In either a van or a truck. On the right or left side of the road. Or down the middle—as local custom sometimes requires.

It is painful to dwell upon those images now. Instead, I must wait in the passenger seat of my Toyota Rav 4 until Cindy brings my wheelchair around. She has to hand me my walker so I can make the transfer, a distance of no more than three feet.

The urge to keep traveling—however limited it may be—has been important to me. At least symbolically. I can feel "normal" by doing what I had done for so many years. In reality, it is all now pretty much a mirage. So one, quite literally, has to shift gears.

Learning

Before anyone starts relaxing in the gazebo, it is to be hoped that they have mastered one vital lesson. They must know that adventure—and with it happiness—is not something that happens to you from the outside. It evolves from within. An "openness to learning" is another way of phrasing the idea.

Books are but one means of the many roads to learning. A major one for me, of course. No one has ever had to tell me to read books. The greater problem has always been to stop me long enough to tend to some of life's other responsibilities. Someone said, "I have only one life to live, so I read books in order to take a holiday away from myself."

Retirement finally gave me leisure to read books that were not directly attached to my profession. I joined two book clubs where I could field new ideas with like-minded friends. Actually, I found this activity to be a pleasing little act of defiance against the shallow, nervous, and ephemeral chattering among the technologically addicted crowd flitting about in cyberspace. We read real books. Like me, however, I daresay the members of traditional book clubs are coming to see themselves as survivors of a dying species.

You need passions to keep you alive. You don't want to give up the thing that you could never get enough of through all of your work years. For me it has been the compulsion to learn and then write. Now I realize that I have been wired differently from most other people. I find having time to "go at it" without interruption to be a true gift of old age. Nowadays, the fact that the new school year is opening at the university has no effect on me. Nor does graduation. Instead, I am just feeding my addiction! The zest for life that has kept me going will linger to comfort me at the end, I am sure.

In this climate of retirement something important can happen. We have all had the experience of not knowing that we knew something until we heard ourselves saying it. Writing is a similar stimulus. Improving one's self-knowledge has to be one of the most exciting kinds of learning.

One of my first post-retirement writing projects was *The Celt and the Christ*.[2] Before it was off the press, my co-author, Dr. Hyveth Williams, and I flew to Alaska. There we presented what we considered to be a pretty good power-point program about our findings. Both of us thoroughly enjoyed the whole adventure.

Next, I took up family research in earnest. (My interest in genealogy had had to wait for retirement.) Contrary to the current distinction of being descended from Australian convicts, I had to settle for a lesser honor. Still, I found ample tribal pride in writing about my Great-Great-Grandfather with his family of five. Among the "First Five Hundred" (the equivalent of the American Mayflower families), they arrived in the Swan River Settlement of Western Australia in 1829. Free settlers but admirable pioneers, all the same. I learned much history and hooked up with my enormous extended family. My rewards have been great. Writing assignments still provide me with many busy workdays.

The Ending

Finally, comes the matter of Death itself.

We must now attend to learning our last lesson, a deeply spiritual one. That is, how to let go and embrace our faith.

Many, young and old, live in daily fear of Death. Well they might, for it comes in a thousand ways. The pessimist somehow steers a straight course through Time—hopefully with the minimum of discomfort to him/herself or others. Along the way, he has a variety of excuses for being what he is: Abusive parents, lack of education, dead-end work, rebellious kids, ill health, and/or no money. This attitude is meager preparation for the end.

The topic is not to be avoided. Indeed, it calls for careful consideration.

Every day you live past eighty is a gift. You know that. Sometimes you sense that Death is actually lurking just inside your door, waiting to pounce. Then you begin to lose a friend or two—in rapid succession. Some go suddenly. Others fight their terrible foes—fiercely, right to the end. That is when you see that Death is not, after all, the enemy. Given our mortal deterioration, it can arrive as a kindly friend.

Likely we will have some regrets? As Athill puts it, the landscape of a long life is inevitably "pockmarked with regrets." We made foolish mistakes, but we did our best to correct them. We need never stagger away bearing a crushing load of guilt.

At this point, we come to a major parting of the ways. On the one hand we have the exclusively secular people. They have carefully mapped out their path. They may be able to walk through life's last door with dignity. Maybe even with a degree of quiet satisfaction.

In contrast, the Christian believer stands and salutes his future. Quite literally he is ready to be launched into Eternity. Propelled by hope and faith, he knows that he has been personally programmed for what is to come. This is a great deal more than simple wish-fulfillment.

My university years taught me to value a place of never-ending learning and growing. Even after we attain the "terminal degree," opportunities for post-graduate experience have perpetually been set before us.

Thus we look to heaven, for now we will have passed our final exams. The grades have been computed. We are eager to meet our Heavenly School Master in Person. An endless program of "continuing education" lies ahead. This is what we have been made for.

Here, then, is my memoir. A mix of people, places, and happenings. Just now, it all appears to me to be very ego-centric. I suppose that, unfortunately, is what autobiography is bound to be. Threaded through, I hope, are useful ideas:

> *What I made, and what I did with it.*
> *What I received, and what I gave.*
> *What I taught, and what I learned.*
> *How I made mistakes, and where I fell short.*
> *What I cared for,*
> *what I dreamed of, and*
> *what I believed.*

Herewith I close the door the last of my *Three Homes for the Heart*. For us all, may sitting in the Gazebo distill some meaning out of the years that have passed.

Watching the wake of a crowded cruise ship can be a very private matter. Perfect solitude, even when you are surrounded by thousands of people. You can see to infinity, almost. A good direction to look!

1   Diana Athill, *Somewhere Towards the End: A Memoir* (New York: W. W. Norton & Co., 2009). The two other parts of her trilogy are Instead of a *Letter: A Memoir* (2010) and *After A Funeral: A Memoir* (2010).
2   Dorothy Minchin-Comm and Hyveth B. Williams, *The Celt and the Christ: Another Look at the Letter to the Galatians* (Victoria, B.C. Canada: Trafford Publishing, 2008), Illus.